THE LAST LOVE
OF
ELEANOR SANDS

A Novel

by

GARY PAUL CORCORAN

Stargazer Press
Charlestown, Rhode Island

Published by Stargazer Press
Charlestown, Rhode Island
http://garypaulcorcoran.com/

Printed in the United States of America
ISBN 978-0-9971265-2-5

Visit us and blog with the author at
http://garypaulcorcoran.com/

Praise for The Last Love of Eleanor Sands

'Charming, hilarious and heartbreaking in equal measures. A thoroughly unique romp through the sixties and early seventies, from Kennedy to Nixon's downfall, from broken dreams to the Symbionese Liberation Army and around the block gas lines. Mr. Corcoran has painted an indelible portrait of a time we sometimes long to revisit and more often would prefer to forget. And let me not neglect the star-crossed romance of a young man and an older woman at the heart of this story. I have been lying awake at night since finishing the book, unable to get their very real bliss, ultimate tragedy and timeless friendship of the heart out of my mind...'

Gretchen Schields...Artist, Jeweler, Author and illustrator for Amy Tan's children books....

Also by Gary Paul Corcoran

The Trip Into Milky Way
It's Always Christmastime In Cratchitville
The Tribe
Postmark: Paris ~ Destination: Unknown
The Twelfth Commandment
Afghan's Lipstick Warriors: First Chronicle
Afghan's Lipstick Warriors: Darkness Falls

From The Michael Devlin Series

South On Pacific Coast Highway
Love In A Dying World

With Gary Paul Corcoran

The Slow Train to Rishikesh
Purgatory: Origins

For Peggy Sue,

who forever changed the destiny of my life…

ACKNOWLEDGMENTS

Thanks to Rachel for a truly fine cover, Carole for her sterling work on the X's & O's and to everyone who endured with me that oft times exhilarating, oft times anguished and undoubtedly bizarre period of transition in our nation's history. The sixties were dead. The seventies had made that wild decade seem rather pointless and the future looked bleak ahead. From the unbounded idealism of our youth, we had passed into cynicism and are perhaps only now getting back to where we left off. So a particular thanks to all those who held onto the torch of hope these past forty years, as we groped about in the darkness, searching for what we had lost.

THE LAST LOVE

OF

ELEANOR SANDS

THE LAST LOVE OF ELEANOR SANDS

One

We stood in the driveway that brilliant spring morning, my mother, sister Rose and me, waiting for my father to back his brand new '65 Impala station wagon out of the garage. The Impala was new. Our suburban tract home was new. The whole world seemed to be brand new back in those days, with miles and miles of orange groves everywhere you turned and snowcapped mountains on the distant horizon and the sweet scent of orange blossoms wafting on the morning breeze.

Our family was off to see my brother Vincent get married up in Santa Barbara that day, all four of us starched and perfumed to varying degrees and filled with our varying degrees of expectation. Mine were not of impending romance. I had no idea I was about to fall in love, wildly so, a sweet, tender but ultimately heartbreaking love affair that would stretch over decades and completely alter the course of my life. Mere mortals never know such things in advance. When these life changing events come along, it's always as if something had fallen unannounced out of the sky.

The drive up through the oak-scrubbed rolling hills of California took roughly two hours. We exited Highway 101, followed several turns down towards the coast and ultimately arrived at the Biltmore Hotel, which in those days was nestled on a plateau of sparsely wooded rolling lawns, dotted with Spanish-revival themed private suites. Call it a dogleg par four with a view of the Pacific and you got the picture.

It was no secret that my brother Vincent had acquired a taste for the sweet life early on in his years, and hence no surprise that he had wooed this society gal named Mildred up to the altar. Her last name was 'Van something or other', her old man the filthy rich scion of a Dutch shipping dynasty.

It was also no secret that Vincent had a penchant for glamorous women, so the fact that Mildred was no beauty did give those who knew him some reason for pause. Then, the sweet life often comes with a price, which in this instance was to be marrying a woman whose face belonged in a Kansas church choir, not on the cover of a fashion magazine.

At the front desk of the Biltmore, we were directed across those rambling grounds towards a private suite. A trek followed along a series of meandering stone pathways. It happened to be one of those glorious days in Southern California when a dry wind blows out from the desert and the sky is left a brilliant china-blue in its wake. Manicured lawns rolled off into the distance. Eucalyptus trees rustled overhead. Monarch butterflies were in migration and fluttered all about in the arid breeze. Eternity seemed to be right there, a half a mile or so out to sea.

We eventually located the spacious suite and walked into a room abuzz with laughter and conversation. A wet bar stood against one wall, which did a lot to explain all the merriment.

My mother and sister went looking for Vincent. My father went in search of a drink. I stood there amidst the din of conversation and laughter, hands in my pockets, blonde hair down in my face, riveted by a beautiful woman at the far end the room. She had pale skin, a narrow waist, a pug nose and black hair that rose up like so much fluffy angora on top of her head. Having just laughed robustly herself, along with three middle aged men, the woman looked past me and returned to their ongoing conversation.

I was crestfallen. It was as if for her I did not even exist.

Moments later, my mother and sister reappeared from across the room with Vincent in tow. He had been preparing for the wedding in back and promptly gathered up the 'Van something or other' clan. Greetings and handshakes followed. The father was gray-haired and as rigid as old generals, his wife gay and warm and utterly charming, the son gunning for a younger version of the old man and Mildred's younger sister something of a mix between the two.

While our families continued chit-chatting, I kept stealing glances at the black-haired woman. Whatever was going on with her and those three men, it certainly appeared to be of a ribald nature. The woman's laugh in particular was infectious.

Eventually, the conversation with the Van something or others grew stale and the old general herded my father off to secure another drink. My mother wandered off somewhere with her counterpart. My sister Rose disappeared with Mildred's younger sister and young Mr. Van something or other went off on his own, I assumed to practice at being stuffy.

"Come," Vincent said and dragged me in the direction of the black-haired woman. "I want you to meet one of my old college professors."

I followed along, my heart in my throat over the impending encounter.

"Well, there he is!" the woman said at seeing my brother. "The man of the hour!"

They hugged with her glorious smile spilling over Vincent's shoulder at me.

"This is Eleanor Sands," Anthony said. "And her husband Dick. This is my little brother Roger."

Dick Sands smiled, winked and shook my hand firmly. With his crew cut and athletic physique, he looked like an astronaut. He winked again for good measure before returning to his conversation. Vincent ran off across the room and just like that I was all alone with Eleanor.

"So, Roger. Vincent has told me all about you."

I shrugged, mesmerized by her beauty and clueless as to what to say.

"I hear you're taking journalism," she went on when I failed to respond.

"Yeah. French too."

"Oh, that sounds like grand fun! You could live in Paris and dash off posts, just like Hemingway!"

"I guess. Something like that."

She smiled even more gloriously.

"So, would you write novels too?"

"I don't know. I hadn't gotten that far."

Eleanor laughed and asked me more questions about my life and school and listened intently to all my answers, and since no adult had ever done this before, least of all a beautiful woman, I began to think that the twenty years of age separating us hardly mattered.

We talked and talked that day and I wanted Eleanor desperately, and longed to tell her as much, but dared not blurt it out. Anyway, with word of the impending wedding ceremony spreading through the room, the crowd began to funnel towards the door. I followed along, expecting my fledgling romance with Eleanor to continue, but once outside, she started off across the lawn as if I wasn't there.

"Oh, forgive me, Roger," she said, looking back. "It's been wonderful talking with you but I'd better go find my husband. Lest he forgets I exist!"

She laughed at her feigned self-deprecation, shook my hand and strutted off in high heels.

All attention was now focused on my brother Vincent, who stood beneath a gathering of eucalyptus trees, waiting for his bride to appear. A minister of the peace stood alongside him. A classical guitarist was perched on a stool nearby, playing a sonata by Mozart.

A few minutes later, Mr. Van something or other appeared from an adjoining suite and escorted his daughter down a makeshift aisle. The melodies of Mozart filled the warm day. Monarch butterflies beat their wings and took flight. All the while, a great pain rose up in my chest, to see Eleanor opposite me in the ceremony, holding hands with her husband.

In short order, the nuptials were consummated. My brother kissed his new bride and the gathering drifted off towards a pool area surrounded by stonework and finely manicured grass. Bartenders uncorked bottles. Drinks were served. A five-piece combo struck up a tune. A feast of Mexican food had been arranged on several long tables. People commenced to eat and dance and that lawny crowd of chattering adults collectively grew smashed.

I mostly lingered at the fringes of these festivities that day, little caring about the other young people around me, and not yet privileged to my true desires.

Afternoon eventually faded to dusk. The revelers gathered to say their goodbyes before dispersing this way and that. The bartenders packed up their supplies and a crew of maids arrived to clear away the mess. Vincent and Mildred were off to Brazil the next day for a two year stint in the Peace Corp, a mysterious air lent to what was already a colorful wedding.

During our long drive back home in the gathering gloom, the memories of my encounter with Eleanor lingered in my heart, but whatever magic spell had been cast was soon lost in the daily workings of my young life. In fact, I had completely forgotten about Eleanor until the day Vincent and Mildred suddenly reappeared at my parent's door some two years later.

Two

It was a crisp, clear Saturday morning and the first day of Christmas vacation. I lay prone on the family sofa, enjoying the ersatz Greek drama of Rocky and Bullwinkle, having been grounded for borrowing the old man's Rambler station wagon late one night and wrecking it on a back-country road with three of my friends. It wasn't the first time I had been in trouble and it would not be the last.

When a knock came at my parent's front door, I jumped up to answer it, overjoyed to find Vincent and Mildred standing there under the ashen winter sky but puzzled by their startling new appearance. Vincent had let his curly, russet-colored Italian locks grow out into a giant Afro. He wore bellbottoms and an embroidered vest. Several strands of beads hung around his neck. Mildred was festooned in Quichuan muslin clothing and a peasant hat. I loved my brother greatly and expected his presence would portend a temporary reprieve from bondage for me, but even to a rebellious young kid, it seemed like these two had just arrived from another planet.

Before they came inside, we hugged around several exotic gifts gathered in their arms, among them a beaded sheepskin vest that Vincent had purchased for me in Brazil.

At this point, my mother appeared and nearly fainted. Nothing had prepared her for this moment. She was utterly clueless about the free speech movement brewing up in Berkeley. The mere utterance of the words 'love in' probably would have made her mind stall and go numb. She went about fixing Vincent and Mildred breakfast with repeated looks in their direction.

"Don't you get any ideas," she said to me.

When my father came home from a work out at the YMCA, he groused about how much money they had spent turning their son into a bum and promptly marched off to the other room with the morning paper. The Christmas holiday grew evermore bizarre after that.

Vincent did bully my father into rescinding my restriction and together with Mildred we drove down to the beach, the drive itself a journey through rapidly changing times. Where once the main drag in town had simply turned into an old dirt road and meandered off for miles and miles through orange groves, it was now paved and tract developments were popping up everywhere you looked. The old Revere House Inn was about to become little more than a passing neon sign beside a new freeway. A drive-in theater down near the coast had been closed, the empty lot around it now sprouting up weeds. The suicide lane in front of it was also a thing of the past. Some bean fields, the dirigible hangars at a World War II era airfield and a smattering of orange groves were all that remained of a quickly disappearing past.

Down at the shore, we warmed ourselves around a fire on a blustery day. A bottle of Port was passed between us. Tales of my brother's adventures in Brazil went on and on. It appeared that they had involved little more than drinking and dancing with natives in the bars of far-flung villages. I heard nothing about teaching these peasants something useful. One could assume they already knew how to drink and dance. Nonetheless, I stared out the sea, swept away by dreams of the great world beyond Orange County.

The next day, Anthony took Mildred up to the airport in LA. She was off to see her family in Hawaii. I tagged along for the ride.

On the way back, Vincent stopped to buy three of those canned Club cocktails and took his sweet time getting back to my parent's place. By the time we arrived, he was feeling no pain.

My mother, who was baking pies in the kitchen, immediately dropped her rolling pin and dragged Vincent off to a back room. As I came to understand things later on, a woman had just called from Rio, claiming to be the mother of Vincent's son. My mother wanted to know if it was true. And, if so, what Vincent planned to do about it?

Next thing I knew, Vincent was flying out the front door. I received a hurried wave to join him.

Vincent drove downtown without saying a word. All along the city streets, shoppers were rushing this way and that at dusk, bundled up against the winter cold. Christmas lights had come on. I saw a Salvation Army Santa Claus on the corner. A Currier & Ives feeling was in the air but a dark spot had appeared on America's home movie. I now looked askance at my brother and his over-sized Afro.

Once Vincent had downed a few more of those Club cocktails, and had blown off a sufficient amount of steam, he headed back to our house. With twilight enveloping the neighborhood, we spotted a Volkswagen bus parked out in front, done up in a bizarre collage of designs and colors.

"Far out," Vincent said and pulled to a stop behind it.

When he jumped out, three young men piled out of the bus to greet him, all of them with hair down to their backs and dressed even more oddly than my brother. I gleaned between the hugs and laugh filled greetings that these guys had just driven down from San Francisco. I watched one of them whisper to Vincent and suddenly all four of them were climbing into the bus.

"Go on. Go in the house," Vincent told me.

I walked up to the front door with them drive around to the alley in back.

Growing curious, I eventually wandered out to the backyard and through a gate to the alley. One of Vincent's friends was taking a puff from an odd looking cigarette and quickly hid it behind his back. Vincent waved at the air. I asked him what was going on and he ruffled my hair with a laugh.

"Nothing."

One of the guys lit up an unfiltered Camel. Someone handed Vincent a bottle in a brown paper bag. He had a good slug from it and passed it to the next guy and their animated conversation resumed. After a minute, I headed back to the house, feeling left out of their camaraderie.

That evening, Vincent's entourage was augmented by several of his fellow Peace Corp volunteers and some old high school friends. My mother and father joined in the revelry for a spell before hitting the hay.

10

Not long after they had retired, Vincent dragged me out onto the back porch and lit up another one of those funny looking cigarettes. I had seen the movie 'Reefer Madness" at school and began to suspect we were talking about marijuana. When I said as much, Vincent blew me off.

"No, this isn't marijuana. It's just bush. It's different."

No longer entirely trusting my brother, I watched him take a puff. The pungent aroma wafted up into the cold, starry night. With Vincent's encouragement, I took a puff of my own. We were out there together for several minutes, inhaling and coughing, but nothing much happened for me, besides the coughing.

Going back in from the cold, Vincent rejoined his companions and I sat off to one side, again feeling lost amongst this crowd of young adults.

Then without warning, the room grew smoky. Vincent smiled at me and there was a sudden vision of him as a swashbuckling pirate. I began to laugh and went running down the corridors of my mind, a fledgling hippie, never to look back.

I got up the following morning and found everything in my life had been turned upside down. I looked with suspicion at the toaster and cupboards. My parents now appeared to be the strangers from a strange land.

Early on, Vincent ran off with his friends in their Volkswagen bus. He returned alone late that afternoon, driving a white Porsche Speedster. It belonged to Eleanor. My father had cut Vincent off from the Rambler and Eleanor had offered up the Porsche as a solution. She had also invited us to a party down at her house in San Clemente that evening.

"You'll like Eleanor's son, Derek," Vincent told me. "He's

really hip."

I hurried off to change, not thinking about Derek at all.

With the sun having just set out over the sea, Vincent wound up into a quiet hillside community. Eventually he parked in the driveway of one of the homes. I climbed out and followed him up to the front door. Vincent rang the doorbell and Eleanor presently appeared. The living room behind her was jam packed with a raucous crowd.

I noticed that Eleanor's black hair was showing hints of salt-and-pepper. Otherwise she was as beautiful as ever. She gave Vincent a hug. I received a handshake, a few brief words of hello and a prompt introduction to her son Derek.

Given all my expectations, I was crestfallen.

That Derek and I made fast friends was some consolation. The two of us drove up into the adjacent hills in his Volkswagen bug and down through a small housing development still in the framing stage. The road came to an end at the edge of a bluff. Derek parked with the town and the sea spread out below us. Derek turned the stereo down low and pulled out a joint.

"Do you indulge?"

"Sure," I said.

I wasn't about to admit to my surprise at seeing the stuff pop up everywhere all of a sudden.

With the joint reduced to a roach and twilight settling over the town, Derek and I sat there talking of life.

Sometime later, we returned to the house and found three of Derek's friends playing pool out in the garage. Dick Sands had installed a draft beer dispenser into one side of an old refrigerator and Derek poured us two mugs from the tap. I went to use the bathroom and found the party in full swing inside. With a glance you could see that the living room was divided into separate factions; Eleanor's university colleagues over here and her husband Dick's munitions business associates over there. It was a rumpled collection of tweed coats and mustaches on one side and a sea of crew cuts and full regalia military uniforms on the other.

Dick was just then touting the relative merits of the new Cobra helicopter, and given the already fractious atmosphere, Eleanor took great umbrage at this war talk at their party. Wearing a tight black dress and high heel sandals, she pretended to grip an imaginary machine gun with both fists and let off a few rounds in Dick's general direction.

"Go get 'em, Cobra," she said to great laughter among her colleagues.

Not having heard the actual comment, but getting the general drift, that he was being taunted, Dick muttered something snarky in Eleanor's direction and herded several of his buddies out to the garage. Taunts and laughter from their quarter followed, along with the crack of billiard balls.

"Gosh," Eleanor said, "don't you just love all this sentimental Christmas slathering?"

To more laughter, Eleanor gathered empty glasses and headed towards the kitchen, taking orders for fresh drinks as she did. I followed and settled onto a bar stool behind Eleanor. She sensed the movement and glanced over her shoulder. She smiled and I smiled back.

Dick, noticing us together in the kitchen, glowered and shoved the door shut. Eleanor bit her fingers in mock fright. I smiled again, delighted to be alone with Eleanor at last.

"And what do you think of the war?" Eleanor asked over her shoulder.

She had caught me in the act of staring at her figure but went back to making her drinks without missing a beat.

"I don't understand the motivation," I said.

"And what would you do differently?"

"I liked Mailer's idea. Give the military their own island and let them blow each other to hell, if that's what they want...Then maybe we should just let women run the world," I added.

"Oh?" she said with a look of intrigue over her shoulder now.

"Yes, the treaties of men always bear the seeds of the next war," I said, paraphrasing a truism I had read in my sophomore history class.

"Gee, now who do you suppose was responsible for that particular blasphemy?"

"I can't remember."

"I can't either," Eleanor said with a finger to her lips, as if blithely ignorant. "But he ought to be shot!"

I joined her in laughter. She was a regular comedian.

"But short of this fabled island, or women ruling the world, how else would you propose to prevent wars?"

"I don't know. I think people should just try to live in peace. Though, with the establishment in power, I don't think that will ever happen."

Eleanor studied me with a smile. Then she was suddenly pensive

"It does seem that your generation has a unique opportunity to change our society, and the dreams to do it. Of course, seeing it through to practical results is another thing altogether."

"Yeah, I used to think we were totally going to change the world but now I don't know."

Eleanor smiled again and went back to concocting her drinks.

"Ah well, perhaps we should just work on peace in our little corner of the world for tonight."

She made eyes at the garage door and bit her fingernails in mock fright again. I had to laugh.

Having filled a tray with drinks, Eleanor set it on the counter between us and again offered me her glorious smile.

"So, what'll it be, old boy?"

"I don't know. I mostly drink it straight from the bottle."

"Well," she said, reaching for a glass with great flair. "Perhaps it's time to smooth over some of those rough edges. How about a Dirty White Russian?"

"Sure," I said again.

Eleanor added a bit of crushed ice to the glass, poured vodka over it, added some Kahlúa and splashed cream on top. The Kahlúa had settled to the bottom of the low-ball glass in a dark, viscous layer. I took the drink from her and tasted the mixture.

"You see, they're sweet, but with a bit of a bite."

"It's really good," I said and polished it off.

"Well," Eleanor said, laughing. "Perhaps we had better nurse them a bit. Lest your mother has me shot for debauching you."

She fussed playfully over another drink, handed it to me with a wink and started into the living room with her tray. I followed, still a bit high from the marijuana and now beginning to feel a buzz from the drink.

Eleanor went about dispensing the drinks and mingling with her friends. I found a spot against the wall and watched her. At one point she stopped to talk with my brother. Then she noticed me and came over.

"Roger, why don't you mingle?"

I shrugged.

"Come, I'll introduce you to some of my colleagues."

I followed her, shook several hands and then stood awkwardly at the edge of a group of professors while they discussed the relative merits of analytic philosophy.

Soon, I was back to my place against the wall. Eleanor found me a short time later.

"Uncomfortable amongst the academe, are we?"

"I don't know. I guess I just prefer standing back like this and watching."

"A sort of Wild Bill Hickok," she said with a wink and a quick check of her pretend poker hand.

Eleanor pressed her body against the wall next to me. I glanced down at her high-heel sandals. Her legs and feet were bare. My mind was imagining the world beneath that tight black dress.

Eleanor looked over with a smile.

"So, Roger, tell me, have you given any thought to what you want to do with your life?"

"I left off at fireman," I said.

She guffawed and then stared with her glorious smile.

"Really, my only thought is to get out on my own. I really don't care how."

"Yes, Vincent has share with me a bit about your struggles at home. In fact, he has expressed a great deal of concern about your relationship with your father."

"My father's an asshole. I run away from home every chance I get. Then the police drag me back."

With our eyes locked, I was unable to restrain myself any longer and finally blurted out what I had been dying to say since the first day I had met her.

16

"I think you're the most beautiful woman in the world, Eleanor."

She stared, still smiling.

"Well, I think you're a very handsome young man. And quite a fascinating one."

Feelings of inspiration and nobility stirred inside of me as I stared into her beautiful eyes, feelings that I longed to express but did not know how.

"Come," Eleanor said, saving me from myself. "Let's have another drink."

I followed her through the passageway and into the kitchen. The din of the party faded behind us. Eleanor made two more Dirty White Russians and we sat together at the bar. People came and went, some interrupting us with their revelry, but mostly I had Eleanor to myself. The crowd and the music and other festivities grew far away and there was only Eleanor's beauty and her smile and our conversation.

"You know," Eleanor said at one point. "I think you should pursue your original path. That of language and journalism. It will open up a whole new world of travel for you."

I spoke something in French and she smiled.

"It means, no one compares with you."

Eleanor put a hand to her cheek and pretended to blush.

"Have you looked into getting on as a foreign exchange student," she asked.

"Yeah, I wrote my pen pal about it but it's a pretty long and complicated process."

"Well, if I can be of any help to you along the way, please don't hesitate to ask…"

I knew what Eleanor meant by her offer. I knew what I was thinking.

Our conversation continued on, sometimes skirting close to the romantic dialogue I so desired, but never quite arriving there. Did she have feelings of love me, as I did for her? I longed to know the answer but never felt confident enough to ask.

When Eleanor's duties as a hostess once again swept her away, I wandered back out to the living room. Soon, it was time to leave and I stood in the driveway with Vincent and Eleanor. Vincent told me to get into the Porsche. I did and saw him kiss Eleanor. My heart sank, realizing now that they were involved as more than friends.

"See you in two days," Vincent said from the driver's seat. "And thanks again for the car."

"Just don't wreck it. Technically speaking, it is Dick's."

They laughed over their private joke and Vincent backed out into the street. Eleanor waved a final time as we headed down the block.

Driving back out the freeway, we were surrounded by darkened hills with a smattering of homes lit up among them. Vincent and I talked from time to time but my thoughts were entirely of Eleanor. Someday. As hard as it was to imagine, I felt surely one day I would hold that woman in my arms.

Two more years passed and I was finally free to leave home and follow my vagabond dreams. I traveled the world and saw faraway places. I fell in love and broke hearts. I fell in love and had my heart broken.

Somehow, in of all this, the idea of striking up a romance with Eleanor had entirely escaped my thoughts.

Oddly enough, when I returned home that following winter, I came to be living with her son Derek down in San Clemente. I did think of Eleanor from time to time but with all that had transpired over the intervening two years, the idea of a romance with her now seemed far away and absurd. In any case, I made no conscious effort to contact her.

Derek was then working at an automotive repair shop near Disneyland and I worked as a cook at a nearby restaurant, so each weekday morning we drove north up the freeway together and Derek dropped me off at my job. Since his shift ended a few hours later than mine, I usually hitchhiked down to a cottage his family owned on Balboa Island and waited to meet him there.

One day, I arrived to the cottage alone at sunset. It had rained and the streets were still wet and the streetlights had started to come on. Charcoal clouds drifted along the horizon. I smoked a joint on the back porch with the last blush of light fading to evening around me.

Inside the cottage, I kindled a fire, sat in an easy chair and kicked my feet up on the ottoman. The flames danced in the darkness.

A short while later, I heard noises out front and checked the clock. It was five-thirty, a bit too early to expect Derek. I turned my attention back to the fire, expecting it was nothing.

Then the door flew open and I turned to find Eleanor standing there, her fluffy black hair having turned even a bit more salt and pepper, but as stunning as ever. All the old feelings stirred in my heart. I wanted the woman, badly, and wondered how in the world I had forgotten that fact.

"Well, hello, Roger," she said. "What are you doing here?"

"I'm waiting for Derek."

"Oh," she said and sat on the sofa opposite me. Her legs crossed with a high-heel pointed in my direction. "I thought perhaps you were waiting for me."

She smiled blithely and it occurred to me that she had been drinking.

"It's really great to see you again," I said.

"Well, that's nice to hear."

"Where's Dick?"

"Oh, probably off with one of his floozies."

She flicked one hand in the air.

I stared, aware for the first time of how deeply imprisoned Eleanor actually felt in her marriage and wanting desperately to rescue her. And as a confident young man now, ready to do just that.

"And how about you?" Eleanor asked. "Are you in love?"

"No," I told her. "I can't seem to find what I want."

"How do you mean?"

"Oh, it seems like all the interesting women in my generation are into free love and all that and the boring ones just want to settle down and have kids."

"And what do you want?" she asked.

"I guess a woman who is both faithful and adventurous."

"We always want the impossible."

"Yeah."

"You can still go off to see the world by yourself."

"I have," I said and explained about my recent travels, and also about my approaching troubles with the draft.

"So, you came back to uncertainty."

"Worse, I guess. I just felt so terribly lonely one day. Now I wish I hadn't come back at all…Well, not now," I added.

As if unaware of me, Eleanor gazed off into the distance, her fingertips pressed together in front of her face, lost in thought.

"You see," she said, her gaze still off in the distance, "in days past, it was only the wealthy man or woman who could afford to travel. But it was in great measure how they came to be learned."

Her gaze returned to me.

"Was it fascinating for you, Roger? Living outside our culture."

"Yeah. Life was totally different in Europe. I especially remember my first few weeks traveling through France and how the highway would become a cobblestone street as it passed through each town. A café at dusk, the proprietor sitting down with us outside. A checkered tablecloth. A bottle of wine. The lights of cars moving on towards Marseilles or back towards Paris, the owner talking with us in French as night settled in. People would let us sleep in their barns. I think I had brie and bread and cabernet for breakfast every day."

I stared into the fire.

"I guess I'll always be happiest not knowing where I will be when the sun goes down.

"You are a very unusual young man," Eleanor said.

I looked up and met her gaze.

"I feel unusually lost right now. That's all I know."

"You have chosen a path outside the mainstream of society. It's a very lonely place. As you said, it would help to have a woman who understands you."

"Like you."

"Well, there," she said with a gesture and a smile.

We stared at each other with the flames from the fire dancing upon our faces. My heart beat wildly, and I was finally prepared to express my true desire in the deepening shadows, but the sound of a motor came to a halt out in front of the house.

"Ah, saved by the bell," Eleanor said.

The front door opened and Derek came in.

"Hi, Mom," he said and kissed Eleanor on the cheek.

"Ready?" he said to me without taking a seat.

I stood up.

"Where are we going?"

"Back to San Clemente. Tony's to get something to eat. Come on, let's go."

He went out to his car.

"I wish we had more time to talk, Eleanor."

"Ellie," she said.

"Ellie."

"I'll look forward to that someday, Roger."

"Come on, let's go," Derek called out from the car. I smiled a final time and closed the door.

Derek and I quickly passed down through Corona Del Mar and along the dark, empty coastline north of Laguna. We talked from time to time but I was mostly distracted by my secret thoughts.

Half an hour later, Derek and I were at Tony's, a Mexican dive on the inland side of Coast Highway. Sandstone cliffs rose up behind the restaurant, their sheer faces worn into curtain like folds by the rain. The highway passed along in front of the restaurant, paralleled beyond by railroad tracks and the adjoining shoreline.

Derek ordered dinner and racked up the billiard balls. I ordered dinner too and grabbed a pitcher of beer.

"You're Mom's really groovy," I said.

"Sometimes," Derek said as he broke the rack. "Sometimes she rides my ass."

"About what?"

"Nothing in particular."

That was all he would say.

"What's going on?" he said when I failed to take my shot.

It almost came out, that I was falling in love with his mother. A truth that was not meant to see the light of day.

Anyway, he was probably right. Best just to take the shot. My fantasies about Eleanor were nothing but personal delusions. And still the idea of her went on brooding in my heart.

Derek and I continued our journey down the coast later that night. He dropped me off at our pad and went to see his girlfriend. A young man named Jerry and I smoked joints talked together until the wee hours of the morning. Jerry had been sleeping on our sofa for several weeks so I made him a deal. You take over my room and the rent payments. I'm leaving for Hawaii. Again, I was feeling far too young and restless to be hanging around town.

Three

In timeless moments of my life, I followed the Trade Winds down through the South Pacific, slept on deserted beaches and lived beneath the stars and sun, with little more to my name than a pair of shorts and sandals and the shirt on my back.

I eventually returned to the Americas via Panama, worked my way slowly up the Pacific coast of Mexico and landed back in the place of my youth. Another two years of my young life had passed by and in my absence, much in this world had changed. In place of Dylan, Hendrix and psychedelic posters, I found Twiggy, Peter Max and polyester suits. In place of vagabond journeys, I found my old friends sitting around their darkened living rooms at night with a joint, a bottle of Boone's Farm wine and Mod Squad playing on their color TV sets. *Whatever* was the new mantra. Dreams died and you moved on.

Adrift in a changing world, I took the money I had saved from slopping hash in diners from Waikiki to Rarotonga, rented a cottage on a maple lined street of old homes and went about looking for a job. The idea of going back to college entered my thoughts and with what free time I had on those autumn days, I whiled it away writing letters and trying my hand at poetry.

Late one night, lying alone in the dark, I remembered Eleanor, along with my long dormant romantic feelings for her. Well, I *had* considered going to college, and who better to call and ask for a bit of scholastic direction? My heart beat wildly at the prospect of seeing her again.

With no small effort, I tracked down a phone number, only to have a machine answer my call. I started to hang up but went ahead with leaving a message, only to feel tremendously vulnerable over the one I had left. I had fumbled it terribly. Or so it had seemed to me once I hung up.

That was a Saturday afternoon. Five days marched by without a word from Eleanor and my feelings of vulnerability grew exponentially with each passing hour. I imagined Eleanor discerning my true motives and dismissing me out of hand.

That Thursday was Thanksgiving Day and I sat at my desk in the morning with a bottle of Harvey's sherry in front of me, making great progress with the sherry but not so much with the words of a poem. Maple trees stirred in the wind outside my windows. Children came and went. Falling leaves framed their laughter and the cold, crisp weather and holidays were a pleasant backdrop to my enterprise.

Later that day, I hiked over to my parents' home for Thanksgiving dinner. Vincent and my other older brother Frank were already seated at the dining room table when I walked in. Frank, the self-proclaimed Paisano of the family, got up and placed his arm around my neck. This was his Godfather schtick and was forever doing it in place of a hug.

"Jesus, Frank," I said and had to shove myself free of his arm.

"What's the matter?" Frank asked with mock disbelief. "Not part of the family anymore?"

"Yeah, right. I figured to be fighting with Dad, not you."

Frank made a face at Vincent, who winked knowingly at me. Frank had a reputation in the family, even if he was the last one to know it.

"Sit down and have some vino," Frank said.

I bristled at his command but did as asked. Vincent poured me a glass of cabernet and pushed it in my direction. I swiveled my sore neck and drank.

"No need to worry about Dad," Frank said, his levity unfazed. "Not since he smoked the old jointeroo with Ike."

Frank's eyes got big in the manner of a clown.

"He's the big discoverer now," Vincent elaborated dryly. "They wouldn't have found the New World without him."

"Where is he?"

"Passed out in the back room."

"Is that Donovan I hear back there?"

"Oh yeah," Frank said. "He's moving up to Haight-Ashbury next week."

My two brothers laughed. I shook my head. I knew my father for his interminable J.P. Morgan rants, not smoking dope and listening to Donovan.

"You kids, go out and get yourselves lots of money."

That's all I ever heard as a kid growing up. Go out and get yourself lots of money. Money was my father's holy grail, his one and only idea of success.

Then, as if to abuse the very core of his own diatribe, he lived like a miser. He worried over every slice of bread. He had sold the Impala and bought himself a Rambler. Some big shot.

26

A short while later, my sister Rose arrived with her husband and their newborn baby. More family members and friends appeared and two leaves were added to the dinner table. Then my father came out of the back room sporting a wide-lapel paisley shirt and mustache. You had to hand it to the guy. The times were never going to pass him by.

He took his seat at the head of the table with a big jug of Almaden wine in hand. After pouring himself a glass, the wine went on the floor beside his chair.

"So, the big world traveler," he announced sarcastically.

"At least he went somewhere," Vincent said.

My brothers laughed at this longstanding family joke. My father loved to pontificate about how he would be off to see the world at some point in the future, when everything was perfectly arranged in his life, though what those necessary arrangements might be, no one had ever been able to figure out. It was out there in the future somewhere. That was all anyone knew.

Inevitably, my brothers got around to recounting tales of their childhood days growing up in New England, and in particular all the mischief they had stirred up. With equal inevitability, towards the end of the meal, my father digressed into his tiresome retinue of quotes and sayings.

"From the tables down at Morey's to the place where Louis dwells..."

"Here we go," Rose said.

"You never mind. I'll be up in Napa-Sonoma someday, making that good wine."

"Right, Dad," Vincent said. "You'll never get out of Orange County."

"Eh, I'll have the pueblo and in the quiet shadows, all the great minds will come to discourse with me."

My father quoted Keats, something about a babbling brook, and his chin fell against his chest. He was out.

Soon, most of the family had retired to the living room. There was talk of work and raising families. A football game was playing in the background.

Feeling out of place, I decided to return to my pad. My mother wrapped up some leftovers and gave me a kiss at the front door.

The sun went down as I walked home. Back at my desk, I stared at the barren maples outside my windows, etched against the twilight sky. The phone rang shortly thereafter. It was Eleanor and my heart was back to beating wildly.

After exchanging hellos, I listened while she apologized for the belated call and related the highlights of a just completed skiing trip to Mammoth.

"Otherwise I would have returned your call sooner."

"I understand. I'm just glad you called back."

"Yeah? And so how are you doing, Roger?"

"Oh, feeling a bit lost, I guess."

"Well, one has to admire your consistency!"

I listened to her laugh in silence. And apparently sensing my bruised ego, Eleanor held out an olive branch.

"I was delighted hear from you."

My first impulse was to express my amorous feelings but I lost heart and went with the practical instead.

"I've been thinking to attend college and was wondering if I could pick your brain a bit. You know, about what kind of classes to take and that sort of stuff."

"Sure. I'd be more than willing to help."

"Thanks. That would be really groovy."

"So, tell me. What have you been doing with yourself these past few years and what kind of direction were you thinking?"

I explained about my most recent journeys, and about my ongoing interest in writing.

"Well, your journeys certainly sound fascinating. And what sort of writing have you been doing?"

"Poetry, mostly."

"I see. And were you still thinking to major in journalism?"

"I don't know. I guess I just want to write what I want to write and not go through all those other hoops."

Eleanor plunged into a dissertation on how various men of letters like Hemingway had used journalism as a springboard for their literary careers. It made perfect sense and I should go through with it.

All the while, my anxiety grew. If Eleanor solved my career dilemmas over the phone, there would be little grounds for a personal encounter.

On and on she went.

"Maybe we could meet somewhere to talk in person," I said at the first opportunity.

"Oh!" she said, "Well I'll have to look at my itinerary."

I heard rustling in the background and looked around my desk, thinking I ought to have one of those.

"Let's see, how about Saturday night?" she said.

I allowed for a short pause.

"Sure, that'll work. I have nothing on my schedule for that day."

"Well then, how did you want to arrange this? Shall we meet in a darkened bar somewhere?"

She laughed.

"How about if I just stop by your place?"

I was all butterflies in the ensuing silence.

"Sure, I guess that would be fine."

"I mean, we could meet somewhere else if you want."

"No, no, it's fine. It's just that...well...it's probably best if I explain this to you in person."

"Okay," I said, feeling tremendously vulnerable again and expecting she would put my youthful fantasies in their place soon enough.

"Shall we say six o'clock?" she said. "I'll throw some dinner together."

"That sounds great," I said, encouraged again. "I'll bring some wine."

"If you'd like, but it really won't be necessary."

"Oh, okay," I said, my hopes plummeting. "I guess I'll see you on Saturday, then."

"Yes, I'm looking forward to it, Roger."

"Me too."

We rang off after a few final words. I sat there with my fantasies unbounded.

'I'm looking forward to it, Roger'.

Oh, Eleanor. You didn't know how much.

On the assigned day I began my trek towards her house two hours early, expecting that would be ample time for me to hitchhike the fifteen miles from Lincoln Hill down to Newport Beach. It was a clear, crisp autumn day and the sea was visible in the distance, a deep blue line between the earth and the sky.

At roughly five o'clock, someone dropped me off on the road alongside the upper back bay. I was still roughly five miles from Eleanor's home. It was growing dark and a cold wind had blown up, rippling the bay. Time passed, a stream of rush hour traffic rushed by me but no one would stop to pick me up.

Growing impatient, I opened the paper bag, pulled out the two bottles of wine I had with me, chose the cabernet and placed the chardonnay back in the bag. With a key, I cleared away the wax cap, pressed the cork carefully down into the wine and took a long swig. I took another one, hid the opened bottle back in the bag and resumed hitchhiking.

Half an hour later, I was still there on the side of the road and began to walk. At a quarter past seven, I was knocking on Eleanor's door. She opened it, looking nettled.

"Well, better late than never."

Her smile only served to accent her sardonic statement.

"No one would pick me up," I said.

She took my bag and discovered the mostly empty bottle.

"Well no wonder. You're drunk!"

"I was getting cold. And restless."

She closed the door behind me.

"Well, let's see, a restless lush who doesn't know what he wants to do with his life. You did say you wanted to be a writer, didn't you?"

Neither one of us laughed.

"Well, come in, come in and let's see what we can do with cold beef stroganoff."

She shooed me into the dining room.

"I'm really sorry," I said.

"Actually, it's an improvement. I'm accustomed to being stood up all together."

I was shocked to hear that. Who in their right mind would stand up Eleanor Sands?

At her suggestion, I sat at the oak dining table and explained my trip down to her place in more detail.

"You know, I would have gladly given you a ride."

"It's not normally such a bummer."

"No. I suspect we're seeing the end of an era."

"Yeah, I was thinking the same thing."

"And the beat goes on," she said.

Her comment was a tired trope to my generation but I didn't dare say so. Anyway, I was at a loss for what else to say.

Oblivious to my thoughts, Eleanor went out to the kitchen, placed my bottle of chardonnay in the refrigerator and pulled out a bottle of zinfandel from her wine rack. The pop of a cork followed.

"I guess I should have saved the cabernet," I said.

Eleanor smiled.

"Well, amongst your other uncertainties, you couldn't have known I was making stroganoff."

She poured two crystal goblets half full, clinked her glass against mine and returned to her duties. I smiled to myself, liking Eleanor more when she was simply a sexy woman from another generation, with a different point of view.

She tossed a salad and placed it on the table a few moments later. A covered serving dish followed. A ladle protruded through a notch in the lid. Steam emanated from the dish. There were already egg noodles on our plates, upon which Eleanor ladled the stroganoff, first mine, then hers. I watched her run off again and heard music come on in the background. It was middle-era Sinatra.

"I hope you don't mind the music," she said, sitting down.

"No, I like Sinatra."

"That is an unusual state of affairs."

"What? Liking Sinatra?"

"At your age, yes."

"My parents listened to it when I was young. I think that's why. I like Big Band too."

"Well, here's to a simpler and more romantic era then."

We clinked glasses again, drank and dug into the meal.

"Hmm, it's delicious," I said.

"Thank you." She dabbed at her mouth with a cloth napkin. "You know, I was thinking. Perhaps I should give you a ride home."

"Thanks," I said. "I was rather dreading the trip."

"Yes, my goodness. We're likely to find you passed out in a gutter, given the opportunity."

This time I laughed with her.

"You know," I said, "I had the impression that people were truly afraid to pull over."

"It's not surprising when you consider this not so distant Manson affair. Sadly, events like that have truly darkened our cultural perceptions."

"Yeah, but Manson's a freak."

"The people of your parents' generation don't make that distinction. They just see the long hair and beards and lump it all together."

I acknowledged this insight with a shrug and a sip of my wine.

"You see, the American people have been trying for a generation to distance themselves from the harshness of the Depression. There was this grapes of wrath seediness about it all. So their revulsion for the free-speech movement has been something of a knee-jerk reaction, largely because of its appearances."

"I thought it was the drugs."

"That's probably true to an extent, but I feel it has been more the long hair and funky clothing. Your parents struggled a lifetime to escape that disturbing imagery."

"I suppose you're right."

"Well, have you ever heard your parents fret over a nickel?"

I nodded.

"You see? They will never be free of the depression. Not completely, and they abhor anything that reminds them of it."

I nodded again, beginning to feel inadequate in the face of Eleanor's superior education and insights.

"What have you been reading?" she asked in taking another bite of her stroganoff.

"Jack London. Bukowski. Some Phillip K. Dick. Hofstadter's *American Political Tradition*."

"That's an interesting mix," she said with a curious smile. "I've not read Bukowski."

I explained his place as an icon to the counter-culture movement.

"Personally, I like him because he's so brutally honest."

I went into a wine induced and somewhat scatter-brained diatribe about the Pentagon Papers and how our leaders were a bunch of Nazis. Eleanor listened with apparent enjoyment and then went off on her own, far more polished dissertation about the American Revolution and how it related to the current political morass.

Finished, she smiled and had a sip of her wine. I gulped down some of my own with those feelings of inadequacy creeping in again. Eleanor finished another bite of stroganoff and dabbed at her mouth.

"How about this, Roger? I'll provide you with a list of books before you leave. The same stuff my students read in preparation for a liberal arts education. Perhaps it will give you a little perspective on the history of Western thought."

"Sure," I said.

She laughed.

"What?"

"Well, obviously you're offended."

I stared at her, further annoyed that she had read my mind. Either way, we were getting far afield of my original goal.

I drained what was left in my wine glass and poured some more. Eleanor was staring at me with a smile when I looked back.

"You did say you were looking for guidance. And, of course, as the result of knowing Vincent, I've heard the various stories about your upbringing."

'As the result of knowing Vincent'. That seemed like a rather breezy way of dismissing what I believed to have involved a lot of wild screwing. I had another bite of stroganoff with the specter of their relationship now added to my other feelings of inferiority.

"By the way, how is Vincent?" she asked.

"He's living in Ohio."

"Really! Ohio?"

I nodded.

"He was out here visiting last week."

"With Mildred?"

"No, they split up about a year after their return from the Peace Corp. Did you know about Vincent getting that Brazilian lady pregnant?"

"I did not, no."

"Things weren't too great after that but I guess the final blow came in Santa Cruz, the next year. A group of people had gone off for a hike in the mountains and Vincent came up missing with this gal named Joni. For about an hour. I believe that's what finally did it."

"Alas. I know Vincent cared very deeply about Mildred but as long as our society makes sexual fidelity the sole benchmark for lasting relationships, I expect we are doomed. We grow so fraught with guilt and deceit...But listen to me."

I stared, my heart burning at the thought of her own transgressions.

"So tell me about your parents and your upbringing?" Eleanor said.

"My parents are peasants. We had no discussions at the dinner table. There wasn't a book in the house. All they did was lay down rules and fret over crap."

"Those are the calling cards of the bourgeois, Roger. Most peasants are too busy to worry and have little that anyone wants. What do they care what anyone thinks?"

"Yeah, I suppose. The peasants I saw in Europe did seem to be pretty content with their lot, if that's what you mean."

"Partly, yes."

"I'm sure we'll ruin them soon enough."

"Turn them into the new bourgeois. Get them fretting over their gross median income and such."

"Two wooden fishing boats in every driveway."

She laughed.

"What I mean to say is, peasants often have the riches of the earth at their fingertips and a tranquil setting. A bit of technology and proper medicine and the pursuit of money becomes more or less insignificant."

"Well, I'm thinking to head out to the country or something. I don't know. Anything but this. I got back here and saw all my friends had sold out for a day job they hate and TV dinners."

"Indeed," Eleanor said. She began to gather the dishes but shooed me away when I tried to help.

"Why don't you turn the album over and I'll join you in a moment."

I did as instructed and sank down into a love seat. A short instrumental interlude concluded with Sinatra's voice. It was the romance of *I've Got You under My Skin*. Eleanor's world surrounded me, warm, sensual and sophisticated. My pad was done up in cement blocks and orange crates.

As I battled my feelings of inferiority again, Eleanor reappeared, kicked off her high heels and curled up opposite me.

"So, are you seriously considering college?" she asked.

"If I can get over my aversion to classrooms, yes."

She laughed.

"And what would be your alternatives?"

"Daydreaming."

She laughed again.

"Yes. Well, there you have it. All you lack is a patron."

"I suspect there's something wrong with me. You know, that I lack all motivation and direction."

"Why don't you start college, as you were thinking? I suspect the environment will help you to sort things out."

"There's that thing about classrooms, remember?"

She laughed.

"Ah yes, that."

"My travels have made me a restless man."

In studying me, Eleanor stretched her feet and ankles. Her red toe nail polish was beckoning. It captured all that was feminine about her. I stared into Eleanor's eyes, wanting her.

"So, Roger. Tell me what you're thinking?"

Caught red handed, I considered various lies but decided to tell the truth.

"I'm wondering what it would be like to kiss you."

I waited for Eleanor to put me in my place. Instead, she quietly studied my face.

"Has this been on your mind for a while?"

"Since the first time I met you."

"At Vincent's wedding!?"

I nodded.

"Well, I'm flattered. That is a long time to wait for an answer."

"You made me feel very special that day."

"You are. To have answers, a man must first ask questions and I recognized that you were asking those questions at a very early age."

"Yeah. I just wish I could come up with some answers."

"So, go back to school. I'll help you every step of the way."

"Yeah."

She continued staring at me in the silence.

"This was all a setup, wasn't it?"

"I don't know. I just know your beauty inspires me and that I had to see you."

Eleanor stared with a wistful look now. I leaned over and very cautiously kissed her lips, but when I pulled on her body, she backed away, one hand touching my cheek.

"I really need to know where this is going," she said.

"You're asking the wrong guy, remember?"

"Okay. So did you just want to have sex? I mean, that's okay but I'd prefer to know up front?"

I blushed.

"There, there," she said. "Not used to this sort of frank discussion? Just turn out the lights and tear off our clothes?"

"I don't know."

"Well, I find it much better not to have any illusions."

"Okay, I have these noble feelings that go along with this wild impulse to make love to you and I've not thought much beyond that."

"So a romp in the hay isn't all you're after."

"Oh no. I really care about you."

"How sweet."

I kissed her again. But again, she pulled away.

"Roger, among our many unresolved issues, I have this ex-husband to contend with. And twins who still live here. I can selectively choose times to insure our total privacy. Otherwise, there's no telling who might show up."

"Are you expecting them now?"

"No, tomorrow. Their father is bringing them back from Mammoth. But you never know with him."

"I was hoping to see you tomorrow night."

"Well, normally I could. They stay with their father most weekends."

"Is that what you were going to explain on the phone?"

"More or less."

"Then you were thinking too."

"Well," she said and batted her eyelashes playfully.

"You're so beautiful to me."

She touched my face.

"I very much look forward to being alone with you."

"Not Sunday?"

"No, I want it to be in total privacy. Possibly next weekend."

"That seems so far away."

She ruffled my hair.

"Ah, the impulsiveness of youth."

I dug my fingers into her ribs, until she suffered for her humor.

"Okay, okay. Friday night."

"You're sure you don't have to check your itinerary."

"No no. Oh, please stop." I did and she fell back against the sofa smiling.

"Friday's fine," she said.

"Well, I'm glad you could squeeze me in."

With those words lingering between us, I gently pulled her lips to mine. They were as warm and gentle as a summer breeze and we were lost in those kisses until a great gust of wind rattled the door.

I jumped to my feet at the sound of it, thinking Dick had arrived back early. It was a giddy moment followed by a decision to withdraw. I followed Eleanor into the kitchen and watched as she placed our wine glasses in the dishwasher with the other dishes.

We kissed again there for some time before I followed Eleanor out to the garage and climbed into her brown Capri. The car was made in her image, sleek and wild and capricious. I was ready to sit there and kiss forever but Eleanor started the car, pressed the garage door opener, adjusted her rear-view mirror and backed out onto the street.

In a matter of minutes, we were headed on a back road up into the nearby hills. The full moon had risen above the mountains behind the hills. Eleanor let go of my hand to shift gears again. I reached over to rub her neck and shoulders.

Near the top of the hills, Eleanor turned onto Skyline Drive and followed it until the city lights came into view far below us. Eleanor parked in a pullout at the side of the road, played with the radio, found a jazz station, then opened the sunroof and invited me to tilt my seat back with hers. We held hands. A cold wind stirred in the trees above us. Stars sparkled in the black sky.

My thoughts drifted back to our first serendipitous encounter, and how we had met two years later, and two years after that, and how I had hungered for Eleanor to submit to me over all those ensuing years, and now here we were at last, with Ellie rubbing my neck affectionately. It seemed too incredible to believe. The long-awaited conquest was finally near. I looked her way, prepared to say the words I had been longing to say.

"I love you, Ellie."

"Oh, dear," she said with a humorous hand to her face.

"It's all right, laugh," I said.

Seeing I was hurt, she leaned over and reassured me with many kisses.

"I like it when you call me Ellie."

"Yeah."

"Oh come." She turned my face to her. "Okay, I love you too."

"Yeah."

"All right. I'm falling madly."

Still wounded, Ellie kissed me until all my wounds were healed. Then we both leaned back to watch the wind in the trees and the stars far, far above.

"Look," I said. "The universe dances at the sight of your beauty."

"You tell all the girls this, don't you?"

I turned my face towards hers.

"No. I've never said those words before. I've never felt this way about a woman before."

As we stared into each other's eyes, Ellie sighed and placed her head upon my shoulder, just like Ingrid Bergman in Casablanca.

"Promise you will be good to me, Roger."

"I will marry you," I said in all seriousness. "I can see our wedding on a summer day in the French countryside."

We were both lost in love then, our lips warm together in the cold night, with Ellie alongside me, like sea grass swaying in the ebb and flow of tides, following my every heartbeat, the sense of it inspiring beyond belief.

"Ellie," I said, "you do something to my heart that I really don't understand. But it is as if I have always wanted to be in this place with you. And I love the feeling of it so much."

I turned to face her.

"I love you, darling. And probably always have."

"Oh lover," she said.

"I'm here." I took her soft hair, her smell of roses and the luxurious feel of her warm lips. I found the warm flesh along her neck and lifted tenderly until her breasts spilled from beneath her bra. With her sweater pulled down over her shoulders, I kissed her soft bones, and again up to her neck and ears. A coo emanated from her parched throat.

"Oh God, Roger. I'm going to have you seduce me right here if you don't stop."

I gazed into her eyes that were like wings across the beauty of her face. I kissed her turned up nose and supple lips, again and again, adoring her with all my heart.

"We fit together so well, Ellie. Why is that?"

"I don't know, Roger."

"Perhaps it's our astrological signs."

She told me hers. I smiled.

"What?" she said and shook me gently.

"Promise you won't get jealous?"

"I promise. Sort of."

I laughed.

"It's okay. It was just one of my childhood sweethearts. She was the same sign."

"And you suppose that is significant?"

"I don't know. It might be nothing more than coincidence, but I doubt it."

"And what is yours?" she asked.

I told her and we kissed again for a long time, after which I whispered in her ear and held her very close in my arms.

"Did you want to go?" I said finally, looking at her.

"You bastard!" she said playfully. "How dare you abandon me now!"

"That was not my intent. I just thought perhaps it's best to wait until Friday. You know. To make it special."

"Yes, you're probably right. Though under the circumstances, I'm not all that thrilled about being proper."

She rearranged her clothes somewhat absently.

"I love you, Ellie."

She kissed me tenderly, started the engine and pulled onto the road with a crunch of gravel. Trees loomed above us down the empty road. Ellie's headlights followed the centerline. We held hands and looked into each other's eyes from time to time, lost in our Garden of Eden.

Half an hour later, she was pulling to a stop in front of my cottage.

"Did you want to come in?" I asked her.

"No, I suspect you were right. It's best for us to savor this moment." She reached over to touch my face. "Are you okay with that?"

"I'm not sure any more."

She waited.

"No, go," I told her. "I suppose I'll be glad about it in the end."

She pretended to be a flustered child and I laughed.

"Did you want me to pick you up on Friday?"

"No. I'll just leave earlier."

"I don't mind."

"I'll call you before then."

"Will you?" she said.

"Of course. I'll be thinking of you endlessly."

"You dear heart. Kiss me again."

I did.

"Tell me again," she said.

"I love you. I will send you words from my heart. Listen for them on your way home."

"Are there some to take with me now?"

"All the world begins with a kiss."

"What a beautiful thought."

"It's true."

"It seems to be with you."

"Goodbye, sweetheart," I said and stood up.

Briefly, our eyes were locked as Ellie pulled away. Then she was gone down the block and around the corner. I went inside and wound a fresh piece of paper into my typewriter. It was near dawn before I was able to push away from the desk and think of sleep. I read the poem one last time.

mrs. sands
please do not correctd my mistakes
exchange them for a kiss
i do not ask, I demand
as a babe, fresh from the womb,
does not politely ask for air
mrs sands,
explain all this mystery,
this espionage of the heart,
subliminal messages left
seven years hence
and now imprinted in the bells of your voice,
the sound of stars falling
into the deep, black sea
of your eyes,
aroused, yet with propriety,
the moments you left
embrace my mysterious path,
I am a changed man,
only help me, please,
my typewriter veers wildly
careening into the unknown,
is this the golden summer of love,
or only a wintry illusion?
mrs sands

bring back your enchantment,
correctd this pointless solitude,
exchange it for a kiss,
my confusion with more of your time,
the swift return of your voice
for this longing and now lonely song
from my heart.

I placed the paper down and rubbed my forehead. The words were never good enough.

In the murky light before dawn, I crawled beneath my quilt and fell into slumber.

Four

That following Monday, I arrived home at dusk, unlocked the front door to my darkened cottage and went to sit at my desk. Time passed as the shadows of evening grew darker around me. I had been out searching for work all day, without success, and a feeling of hopelessness had overtaken my life. Had it not been for my penury, I would have hit the road the next morning. Anything would be better than settling down to a workaday existence in that old town. I remained seated there with my past vagabond adventures flitting through my mind.

From years of habit, I rolled a joint and partook of the herb and it quietly had its intended effect. The feelings of longing and uncertainty and failure were miraculously lifted. Some form of peace was restored to my heart.

What would mankind do without an anesthetic, I wondered? Go mad, I presumed.

I poured a glass of sherry and watched the ink of twilight slowly envelop the neighborhood. Children played outside my windows, as usual. The maple trees grew dark and a mother called from down the block, trying to gather her errant brood.

With the darkness complete around me, I thought of Ellie and had this fantasy of us being married. That would solve all my problems. Let Ellie go off to work while I took care of the house.

Moments later, I was seized by renewed feelings of fear and apprehension. Why would she want to take care of me? I was for all intents and purposes a bum, lacking a job and all direction.

While sitting there, I noticed the black hills to the east etched from behind by a brilliant light. A contractor developing a new subdivision, I wondered? Or a baseball field of which I was previously unaware?

Then the lip of the full moon cleared the hills and I instantly understood the root of all these overpowering emotions. People had dreamed up werewolves under such circumstances.

Soon, the enormous yellow moon had cleared the hills and visions of prehistoric epochs seized my mind. Smoke issuing from distant volcanoes. Alley Oop on the loose beyond the far horizon, searching for his errant mate. Completely dedicated to Ellie for the previous three days, I was now ready to screw anything in high heels.

I should have taken her to bed, I thought. How foolish of me to deny my animal instincts. No man was a saint, least of all me. A full moon, a few excess hormones and I was headed for the abyss.

In time, the moon ascended high overhead and became an intense white orb focused brightly on my desk. An incurable restlessness followed. I washed the dishes. I vacuumed and mopped the floor. Everywhere I looked there was another chore and distraction.

In this complete state of Zen collapse, I went back to my desk and called my friend David.

"I'm seeing pterodactyls overhead."

David laughed.

"Raquel Welsh in a saber-tooth loin cloth."

David laughed again.

"If you're restless, let's meet down at The Strip. They've got a great band on Monday nights."

"All right, I'll be there in half an hour."

I changed clothes and started down the block on foot. David was already at the bar when I arrived, his tall, hulking, red-headed frame sitting atop a barstool. Strobe lights from the dance floor revealed him to me in still frame snapshots.

I slapped David easily on the back, took the seat alongside him and ordered a drink. The bar was at the opposite end of the club from the band so I swiveled on my barstool and took in the scene. There were half a dozen good looking cocktail waitresses working the tables around the club and more beautiful young women everywhere I turned. Blondes evoked carefree, summer days for me, brunettes the more passionate side. I loved women who were kittenish, ones with intelligent eyes, their ribald laughter, dark hair with pale skin. I loved most everything about the fairer sex, but I did not like being in a pinball machine, which was where the full moon had left me, prowling for sex as my one abiding principal. I was that close to clubbing some woman over the head and dragging her back to my cave.

I turned back towards David and yelled in his ear.

"Think I'll dance!"

David nodded impassively, not being one to kick up his heels.

I set my sights on a petite brunette at a table to the left of the dance floor. Her beauty was hard to ignore. She had pale skin, dark, beguiling eyes and heart shaped lips that were ornamented with red lipstick.

When our eyes met, she quickly looked away. Good, I thought. Spirited but unsure of herself. An easy target.

When I stood over her table and waved at the dance floor, she looked to her friends. The strobe lights from the dance floor made her appear and disappear. In flashes, I saw her friends encouraging her, then she was standing up, then we were dancing together, the young woman consumed with her footwork, then staring at me, then looking off in the distance, all of it revealed in still frames.

When the song ended, I introduced myself.

"Roger."

"I'm Cerise."

I held her delicate little hand.

"You're very beautiful."

She blushed and started to say something but the band started up again.

By the end of the second song, I was soaked with sweat.

"I need some fresh air," I said and excused myself

Cerise went back to her friends. David joined me outside and lit up a cigarette. The full moon was high above us.

"Beautiful lady," David said.

"Yeah."

"Did you ask her out?"

"No."

"Why not?"

I looked over into David's big deer-like brown eyes.

"I'm seeing this older woman."

David took a puff from his cigarette, his stared still locked on me.

"What's that like?"

"It's definitely different than going out with young chicks. She's really intelligent. I like talking to her. She teaches college. I've known her since I was fourteen."

"You've never said anything about her before."

I explained to David how I had crossed paths with Ellie over the years.

"Anyway, I'm going to spend the night at her place next weekend."

"So," David said. "That's next weekend."

"I don't know. I'd just feel funny about lying to her."

"So, don't tell her."

"No, you don't understand. It's like she can see through me."

I stared up at the bright moon. David finished his cigarette and ground it into the asphalt.

"Did you want to go back inside?"

"Sure," I said and opened the door for him on the way in.

I danced with Cerise again but we talked very little. Intimacy was hard to come by when you couldn't even hear your own thoughts.

Later, when Cerise was leaving with her friends, she made sure our eyes met before she went out the door. A few seconds later, a cocktail waitress came by and handed me a napkin. It had Cerise's name and phone number written on it. She had very nice script. I tucked the napkin into my back pocket and ordered another drink.

David dropped me off at my place around two in the morning. The moon had set behind my cottage somewhere but was still glowing high up in the maple trees. I sat at my desk, vacillating between Cerise and Ellie in my mind. Cerise was youth and easily pliable. Ellie offered experience and wonderfully edifying conversations. But Ellie also had a teenage son and daughter down the hallway. Completely under the sway of my animal instincts in that moment, romancing Cerise seemed like a far less complicated idea.

With both these women in mind, and for that matter, every woman on the planet, I rolled a sheet of paper into my typewriter and went to work. Five minutes later, the poem was complete. I read it over several times, surprised at how easily it had poured out of me.

The Bones of Solitude

the soft, pale flesh of your feet
below the tan line
I want to bite these,
finger to your lips,
roses in your glorious smile,
given voice
without words,
tongues and thighs,
what natural design
to be born there,
a river of pleasure
rushing through gentle cries

I had absolutely no impulse to embellish the thing, which was even stranger than the manner in which it had poured out of my sub-consciousness.

Exhausted, I crawled into bed, anticipating with dread the impending lunar collapse. It never failed. Every time the full moon waned, my emotions careened into the abyss. Despair overtook me. Self-cannibalization commenced. I would feel as if I had chugged a cup of Drano.

And like clockwork the next day, it happened.

I went in search of work, again found no success and returned home that afternoon feeling useless. I attempted to write something and that too seemed without merit. I was an insignificant little man, consumed with his insignificant little poems, fussing over a Chinese puzzle of words about which nobody really cared. I was nearly broke and would soon be typing out in the street.

Then the phone rang. It was Ellie.

"How are you doing, Roger?"

I thought to say 'fine' but her question was asked with such sincerity, I felt compelled to answer in kind.

Ellie listened to my lament for several minutes without interrupting me. At one point, I noticed Cerise's phone number staring up at me from my desk and hid the cocktail napkin under some other papers.

"You see," Ellie said once I grew silent. "That is why I wanted you to resume your education. You have enormous gifts but lack direction. A college education would provide you with that."

Turned off again by her meddling in my life, I did not speak.

"Oh Jesus. I've touched a nerve again, haven't I?"

"Maybe."

A longer silence ensued.

"All right. How about this? I'll come by, take you out to dinner and then do what a woman can do to make a man feel better."

I smiled.

"Sure. I can always use a good meal."

"You fucker," she said after a brief silence.

I laughed, a bit surprised by her candor.

"I like it when you say fucker."

"You fucker," she said in a sultrier voice.

"Aw Ellie. I've been haunted by it all weekend."

"Do you suppose you can contain yourself until Friday night?"

"It's a hell of a long time to wait."

"Well, you know," she said, feigning professorial authority. "Planning ahead is precisely what distinguishes mankind from the lower order of animals."

"Yeah? Well, screw mankind."

I smiled at the great guffaw of laughter that came through the line.

"Well, yes," Ellie said when she could gather herself. "When you articulate it like that, there's no denying our shortcomings."

"Is it all right to say it?"

"That you want it really bad?"

"Oh, I want to run my hands through your hair and watch your face when we make love."

"Oh lover. You're getting me wet again."

"I wrote you a poem about it."

"Did you?"

"I wrote two of them. One of them Friday. One of them last night."

"Let me hear that one."

I reached for the sheet of paper, aware of my lie. The second poem had been written for every woman I might want to ravish along the way, but I read it to Ellie as if it were hers alone.

"I'm going to drive over there right now," she said.

"All right. I'm waiting."

More silence.

"You bastard," she said. "You know I can't."

"I like fucker better."

"Okay, you fucker. I can't."

"You won't."

"You know I have the twins to think about."

"Yes, the twins."

"Don't do this to me, Roger."

"All right."

"I promise I'm going to make Friday night really special. Just you and me and candlelight and love making."

"All right. I'll have to wait until Friday."

"Aw. But please say something sweet to me before we get off."

"I love the way your body goes limp when I kiss you. It makes me feel like a man. It makes me want to pick you up in my arms and protect you forever and ever."

"Aw," she said again.

"It's true."

"I can hardly wait until Friday, Roger."

"Me too. I'll see you then."

We rang off but I felt little better than before. I grabbed a bottle of hand lotion and went into the bathroom.

That entire week went by as though counting seconds but at last it was Friday at dusk. Someone had dropped me along the back bay again, a few miles from Ellie's place. The salt marshes snaked off like a ribbon of glass in the fading light. Clapper rails and plovers darted in and out of the spreading darkness. I listened to their calls, enchanted.

Having lost myself in the magic, I failed to notice that an aging station wagon had pulled to the side of the road until the owner honked. I dashed up to find a cheerful old man waving me inside. He lived two streets over from Ellie and we were soon lost in conversation.

At the top of Ellie's street, he stopped and wished me good luck. I waved goodbye and watched this inquisitive old engineer drive off into the gathering gloom, grateful for his kindness and enlightenment. Given this upscale neighborhood, and the fractious times, it was the last place I had expected to find an adult interested in my generation.

I started down Ellie's street with a cool wind from the bay tickling my face. The neighborhood was dark and quiet save for the sound of my boots echoing down the block. I passed a living room window with curtains drawn. A graying executive looked up from his martini and evening newspaper. His daughter, a cheerleader, was brushing her silky hair in an upstairs bedroom, preparing for that night's football game. I imagined his wife out in the kitchen making dinner. The memories of everything I had experienced growing up in suburbia flashed through my head. And here I was, a highwayman coming home to ravish someone's mother.

Turning up Ellie's driveway, my excitement grew. I had not been with a woman for over a year. There were past images but nothing visceral.

Then I was knocking at the front door and Ellie opened it, wearing a black gown and high heels, her salt and pepper hair stunning against black. I felt her warm body against mine and tasted her kisses. The living room was darkened, save for a few candles. Jazz played softly in the background.

"Come in, Roger."

She closed the door behind me, took my coat and hung it in the hall closet. Our kisses resumed on our way out to the kitchen.

"A glass of wine?" she said.

"Sure."

"Red or white?"

"Ha," I said. "What are we having?"

"Steaks and a salad."

I pretended to be perplexed with a finger to my mouth, as she was wont to do and she laughed.

"Red it is, then," she said.

I took a seat at the kitchen bar top and waited while she uncorked a bottle and poured two goblets half full. I took mine and we toasted.

"To us," she said.

"To the loveliest woman in the world," I said in return.

Ellie placed her goblet down and nuzzled her face against my cheek. I felt her breasts against my shoulder. She was wearing nothing beneath the gown. Her face came up. Her eyes explored mine. Her fingers ran through my hair.

"Did you want to read the poems?" I said.

"Did you bring them?"

"Yes."

I pulled the folded pieces of paper from my shirt pocket and opened them. Ellie read each one carefully. I kissed her ears and neck and shoulders while she did. The lights from waterfront homes glistened along the nearby harbor. Others lights sparkled along the crescent coastline, all the way up to San Pedro.

After several moments, Ellie shuffled the papers and returned to the more recent of the two poems.

"You like that one."

"You have captured something animal here, yes."

"And the other?"

She took that sheet from the bottom and looked again.

"It takes more thought, but of course, Roger. A woman likes to be told she is beautiful, regardless of the form."

"You are beautiful. So very, very beautiful. And so very, very easy to adore."

"Well," she said and laughed at her own attempted modesty. We kissed and played.

"The salad is prepared," Ellie said, pulling back to look in my eyes. "Shall I broil the steaks now or…?"

"No," I said, then "yes" acquiescing to decorum. Ellie smiled and with a final kiss commenced to glide about the kitchen with great élan and gracefulness. In a final flurry, candles were lit. Food was placed on the table and Sinatra came to life on the stereo again. Ellie invited me to sit.

The steaks were rare but still sizzling.

"It's delicious," I said with the first bite. Ellie smiled in the glow of candlelight, reminding me of that moment three years earlier, on a rainy night in the cottage on Balboa Island. Only then I was something of a man/boy and uncertain of who I was to Ellie, whereas now I was clearly a man, with an invitation to the impending conquest. A sip of wine, a smile in the flickering shadows, words quietly spoken, all of it infused with our unspoken desires.

After the meal, while Ellie put everything in the dishwasher, I turned the album over. Then she came to dance with me in the candlelight, her body palpable through her black dress. Unable to suppress my desire any longer, I took Ellie by the hand and gently pulled her in the direction of her bedroom.

"But I thought I was the professor," she said in mock protest.

"Oh, Ellie. I've waited seven years. I can't wait another minute."

In the bedroom, she made me lie on the bed and crawled on top of me. She kissed my neck and lips and ears and methodically removed my shirt and boots and my pants, my flesh searched by Ellie's lips with the removal of every item.

When only my briefs remained, I felt the warmth of her mouth through the fabric, the briefs pulled down and my organ spring free. Liquid ecstasy rushed over me as she swallowed my cock.

I groaned and tried to sit up but Ellie gently pushed me down again.

I had considered myself somewhat knowledgeable in these matters of romance but soon realized I knew very little. Ellie revealed that fact to me vividly over the course of the evening hours. Then and on late into the night, I mostly lay there and took all that Ellie had to give, playing the role of a young, royal subject to Ellie's exotic courtesan.

Five

I knew it was morning by the sliver of light peeking through Ellie's heavy tapestry curtains. I looked for a clock, unsure of the hour, then reached for the pillow next to me and found it still warm. Images from the previous night rushed through my mind. Then I heard stirrings down the hallway and realized Ellie was out in the kitchen making breakfast. I smelled coffee and the tart scent of bacon frying.

I got up to relieve my full bladder and crawled back into bed. More memories of Ellie's sweet lovemaking came to visit my mind. Then I remembered the rent was due in a few days and that once I paid it, I would be broke.

What the hell was I going to do?

While worrying over that, I became aware of my surroundings. Ellie had the same panache for design that she had for everything else. There was purpose combined with beauty in a celebration of life's simple refinements, from the antique armoire to the dried floral arrangements to the tapestries over the windows. Conversely, my place was decorated in early orange-crate. I was a rough approximation of Gertrude Stein's observation; that a man not yet civilized at twenty-five never would be. I comforted myself with Yeats countering admonition, that young men should never worry about money. Well, I hadn't and the results were depressing. Once again, I had fantasies of being rescued by Ellie.

I had been lying there in the darkened room for another minute or so when I heard her high heels coming down the hall. The beautiful, sexy and illustrious Ellie was approaching. I lay there wondering who was I supposed to be.

She entered the room wearing a silk robe and feathered high-heeled shoes and looking as cosmopolitan and sexy as any doll in a Fred Astaire romp.

"Good morning, Roger," she said with a big smile.

Without missing a beat, she let her robe drop from her lean body and her smallish, well-formed breasts quivered ever so slightly. She crawled under the covers with me, soft and warm. We kissed and I became aroused again.

"I have breakfast almost ready."

She took hold of my swollen member.

"Though you seem to have other ideas."

She searched my face with a smile.

"Shall I start the eggs?"

"Sure, I can always use a good meal."

She pretended to be flustered and we laughed, and our laughter led to kisses. I kissed all up and around her eyes, adoring their Japanese-like quality of being turned up at the tips, and her finely chiseled pug nose, and all of her features.

Soon, she was soaring above me again, as though wanting to leave the bonds of Earth and each time she returned, I took one of her breasts in my mouth, then the other, and the other again. Then we were coming together and world was, for that brief moment, a quite unblemished place.

After lying there enveloped in each other's arms for some time, I joined Ellie in the kitchen and watched her finish cooking breakfast. I sat at the oak dining table while Ellie worked and had the breakfast delivered to me. We ate with splashes of morning sunlight on our plates. The coastline rolled off in the distance. Yellow and white and green floral wallpaper made the room seem that much more cheery.

More and more, I did not want to leave the comfort of Ellie's home. Nothing but worries awaited back at my place.

Ellie smiled at me over a bite of her bacon.

"You know, Roger. We have all weekend and you're welcome to stay."

I took her hand.

"What?"

"You must have been reading my thoughts."

"Yes? So would you like to stay?"

"Yes, very much so."

I kissed her hand and went back to my eggs. Ellie had the Entertainment section of the morning paper in front of her and turned the page.

"Oh look, here's an idea for tonight. Big Joe Turner is playing at Hungry Joes."

"What?" she said when I failed to respond enthusiastically. "You don't like Big Joe Turner?"

"He's not one of my favorites."

"Oh, well," she said with mock seriousness. "Indeed, we'll just have to call the club and have a word with them about this. I mean, how dare they try to foist off a second-tier entertainer on us. Tsk tsk tsk tsk. Hmm hmm hmm hmm."

She went on until I tickled her under the table.

"Okay okay," she begged and we laughed.

"You're right," I said. "Seeing Big Joe Turner would be really cool."

I explained my partiality for the south side Chicago blues artists, but seeing any of these old titans before they passed away was indeed a treasure.

Ellie and I talked of taking a walk but the day grew gray and cold and windy so we went back to bed. We found an old movie on TV but it played without us seeing much of it. We slept again and made love and whiled away the day with our pleasures.

In the late afternoon, I awakened with Ellie in the bathroom. I went out to the kitchen alone. A bank of dark gray clouds straddled the horizon. The sun was behind them but glowing gloriously in the firmament higher up. I sat at the oak table. Lights had begun to twinkle along the harbor. A few minutes later, the sun set in a final sliver of brilliant orange between the gray clouds and the sea.

Ellie appeared with a bottle of Spanish sherry and poured us both a snifter. We kissed, toasted to each other and drank. On her way back to shower, Ellie turned on a Grover Washington album. I thought to change it for some straight-ahead jazz but decided not to meddle. A short time later, I went in to shower

By the time Ellie was maneuvering her Capri out through the winding residential streets, twilight had settled over the neighborhood. We came to a main road and Ellie turned right down a long sloping hill towards the sea. At Coast Highway, she turned right again. To the west, the horizon was still tinted with orange. Headlights approached us from the direction of San Pedro.

We crossed the river mouth and came alongside a public beach, separated from the highway by a wood post and chain-link fence. Solitary oil pumps dotted the opposite side, each pterodactyl-like head working tirelessly in the fading light. We passed a power station, its labyrinth of pipes emitting steam into the cold night. Out ahead, the coastline was visible in a long crescent that terminated into the dark hump of Palos Verde peninsula. The lights of Long Beach and San Pedro were nestled at the base of the peninsula.

Ellie and I talked along the way and in the silences held hands and looked into each other's eyes and were very glad to be in love on a Saturday night.

A short distance past the arcade of surf and beachwear and head shops around the Huntington Beach pier, Ellie pulled into a gravel parking lot. A square, clapboard structure stood alone at the far end of the lot. The wall facing the highway was completely covered with graffiti. A billboard on the roof proclaimed **Hungry Joes'** and a sign over the door announced **Big Joe Turner Tonight**.

Ellie parked and we crossed the gravel lot hand in hand. A hostess greeted us, checked her list and led us inside. Ellie had made reservations for the eight o'clock dinner show. Joe Turner's music was playing over the PA. Delighted with things, Ellie smiled my way.

"You said you liked blues and jazz."

"Yes, thank you. It was very thoughtful of you."

When our drinks arrived, we toasted and drank. I reached one hand under the table and felt Ellie's thigh. She smiled.

"What?"

"Do you always think about it?"

"With you, yes. Until my last dying breath, I'll be thinking about it."

Ellie's hands disappeared under the table too and we were in that compromising position when our waiter arrived. He made a point of ignoring the mischief but was clearly aware of our disparate ages. I was a young man planning to take this older woman home later on and do nasty stuff to her and the waiter knew it.

Just about the time our meals arrived, a black rhythm and blues group opened for Big Joe Turner, and about the time the waiter was clearing away our dishes, this three hundred pound humpty-dumpty of a man made his appearance, his pants pulled up about his sternum, a pencil mustache painted above his upper lip and his hair gleaming with pomade. He settled his great girth precariously on a barstool, leaned on his cane and sat passively as the band eased into 'Shake, Rattle and Roll'. Then his tenor voice bellowed out and shook the darkened room.

Big Joe ended his show about nine thirty and a general exodus quickly spilled out into the parking lot. A queue had already lined up for the next show halfway out to the sidewalk. We climbed into Elli's car with headlights coming on and tires crunching against gravel and conversation and laughter echoing up into the cold night. We joined a line of cars inching towards the highway. When it was Ellie's turn to merge onto the road, dust and rock kicked up in our wake.

On our way back towards Newport, she glanced over at me.

"Did you want to go back to my place?"

I looked over at her. Lines of light and shadow crisscrossed her face.

"Yes. I'd be very happy just to be alone with you."

"And."

"And make love about a hundred times."

Ellie flashed me a beautiful smile and reached for my hand.

Back at her place, I made myself comfortable in one of the stuffed living room chairs. Ellie disappeared down the hallway and returned in the same gown and shoes she had worn the night before. Candles were lit. Music came on. When Ellie was done, she sat on my lap. We kissed.

"I wonder if you could live with me?" she said and pulled back to look at me.

When I did not answer, she bit her nails in mock fright.

"You know, the twins are going away this summer. We would be entirely alone."

She waited.

"What is it, Roger?"

"Didn't you hear yourself? '…if you could live with me…'."

"As opposed to…"

"Living together," I said to complete her sentence.

"My dear lover, it is the same thing."

"No. In the one instance, we are equals. In the other, I am your vassal, and at your mercy."

"Did you think I would…?"

"Yes," I said and fought with her hands.

"Well, at the very least, I think it would be helpful if you met the twins."

"Oh Jesus, Ellie. I'm going limp."

A truly frustrated look came over her face.

"Hey, come on," I said. "Let's put all this on the back burner for tonight, okay? It's not in the spirit of the moment."

I gently pulled Ellie's face around.

"Okay?"

She nodded like a little girl.

"Aw, did you know you're beautiful when you pout."

She buried her head on my shoulder, suddenly helpless. And aroused by her seeming frailty, I lifted Ellie up in my arms and carried her down the hall, with me Ellie's knight now and she my fair damsel. As I laid her on the bed and kissed her ankles and thighs, I very much believed in that role.

Six

A nother week passed swiftly by, during which time little to nothing moved forward in my life. I hunted for work and sought direction and was without success in either of those endeavors. Much of the week had been spent distilling my enchantment for Ellie into a single poem, an effort that by week's end appeared to be entirely worthless. Over and over I had worked on it, yet the more I did, the more I began to feel discredited as a poet.

> To the red ruby voice of your sex
> Your black hair and black eyes
> The goblets of your breasts
> Your soft, dainty digits wiggling in our bed,
> I dive beneath the shroud of sheets to find them
> In my mouth, the scent of things ripen
> All pleasures spread upon your finely woven rug
> Uplifted by the bones beneath your flesh
> I soar and crash,
> a white, frothing wave upon your willing sand.

It went on like this for several more stanzas. I read it through one last time before wadding up the sheet of paper and throwing it in the trash. I was a fraud. I certainly felt like one right then and chalked it up to the collection of poems Ellie had insisted I take home with me. I had poked through it the next day, with little accomplished by that exercise, other than to make me sound like Dylan Thomas. And I did not do him all that well.

Faced with impending eviction, I considered picking up stakes and heading back out on the road, a thought that came with a feeling of tremulous excitement. The world had always been my oyster. I had no patience for sitting around with vague hopes that some sort of miraculous intervention might materialize.

Faced with these fears of poverty again, Ellie once again arose as my beacon of salvation. How pleasant it seemed, this thought that she would take care of me.

That Friday evening, I was again standing at the side of the road at dusk with the back bay beside me and the sun going down and that 'child rushing home at dark' feeling in my heart. An evening of laughter and lovemaking loomed ahead and when I finally saw the lights of Ellie's home, all my troubles seemed to vanish.

I let myself in and called out her name and she called back from the kitchen. I found her out there wearing a skirt, a white blouse, an apron and high heels. I was enjoying her high heels and legs when she smiled over her shoulder at me. I kissed her lips then pulled the white blouse away from her neck and shoulders and kissed her there too.

"More stroganoff, darling."

"Yes, tons of it."

She smiled over her shoulder again.

"Actually, I made bouillabaisse."

"Mmm, that sounds good."

Ellie resumed chopping up her romaine.

"Roger?" she said.

"Yes?" I said between the kisses.

"I think I'm a very lucky woman."

"I think you are too."

She had a little tantrum, her palms open next to her head, all of her shaking to and fro.

"Okay, why's that?"

She turned with a serious look.

"Because I've had two lives. The one society prescribed for me and the one a woman is usually denied because of that."

"So you think they're mutually exclusive?"

"I'll never know that now. I chose a man instinctively, someone who could provide well for a family. Dick was a great provider."

"And a total loss as a lover."

"Essentially, yes."

That qualification brought my kisses to a halt.

"Please don't be offended."

"It's just hard sometimes, Ellie. I'm not much of a provider. I guess I want the other domain all to myself."

Ellie turned to face me.

"You needn't worry about that," she said. "When it comes to love making, no one compares. And I have no need for you to be a provider."

Seeing that I was only wounded more by this additional clarification, Ellie turned and pressed her body tight against mine.

"Let's make love right now," she said.

"What about the bouillabaisse?"

"Oh, of course, the damned bouillabaisse!"

She touched her nose to mine, kissed me and went to set the table. I poured myself a glass of wine and drank.

"I'm planning a trip," Ellie said as she worked.

"For the two of us?"

"Of course."

She went by on her way back to the kitchen. I turned on the barstool to follow.

"You see, I have the two-week Christmas holiday. With a weekend and a few extra days, we'll have nearly three weeks."

"To go where?"

"Tahoe. San Francisco. Perhaps take a drive up the coast to Mendocino?"

"That sounds nice."

She came around the bar from the kitchen and stroked my face. A mischievous smile came with it.

"I have an ominous feeling about what's coming next."

"Well," she said. "I did promise to spend a few days with the twins in Mammoth over Christmas. Of course, we could go on by ourselves from there."

"Of course."

She had another little tantrum.

"And please don't be concerned about money."

I nodded.

"You needn't be so abstruse, Roger."

She gestured for me to sit at the oak dining table, lit two candles, adjusted the lighting and took her own seat. We toasted.

"It's very good," I said with the first taste. "How did you learn to make it?"

"From a chef."

I buttered a piece of bread and wondered which one. All the while, Ellie studied me, to my discomfort.

"Roger, I sense something is on your mind. Would you please speak it?"

"All right. It's the twins."

"You mean, Carla and Kurt?"

"Okay, Carla and Kurt."

"Why on earth are you so uncomfortable about them?"

"Well, Jesus, Ellie. Put yourself in my shoes. They're nearly my own age. And here I am doing it to their mother."

Ellie reached out and touched my hand.

"And doing a splendid job of it, to boot."

"Funny."

"Please, Roger, we've been through this already. The twins are abundantly aware of how important you are to me. As to our difference in age? They simply shrugged. They're just glad to see me happy. I don't understand why you continue to be so burdened by it."

I nodded and continued to eat.

"You see, Roger…"

"Oh, boy, here we go."

Ellie had a big tantrum, and I could not help but chuckle at her charming impersonation of a spoiled brat. She stopped after a moment and was completely serious again.

"Roger, please accept that you can learn from other people. For instance, I know a great deal about confronting new challenges in life, an area where you appear to have few answers."

"Oh, I have answers all right. Run."

72

"Well, in any case, this brings to mind something else I've wanted to talk to you about."

"Oh boy."

"I want you to go back to school…Remember? That ostensible goal you had when you came over to screw me."

"Yes, well, now that I have."

She had another big tantrum.

"I promise I'll help you into the right classes," she said once our laughter had subsided. "With the most desirable professors."

I raised my eyebrows at her.

"There are students who wait several semesters to get into these courses."

"We can talk about it," I said.

"Please. I want you to give it some serious thought."

"I wish you didn't feel this need to control me."

She threw up her hands.

"I'm not trying to control you! I just see you as this great, unbridled talent, looking for direction, and I want to help! That's all!"

"Have you considered that maybe I don't want your help?"

At this, Ellie seemed truly stunned.

"Well, no. I hadn't considered you might feel that way."

"I'm not out to be another one of your students."

I ate with her watching me.

"Oh well, fine, don't accept my help. Though it might behoove you to consider how the other person feels in these transactions."

Her statement left no high ground or way to escape, though I searched for one. After a moment I offered a compromise.

"Okay, Ellie, let's go on vacation. And I'll consider going back to college when we return."

"You see? That didn't hurt so badly, did it?"

I shrugged, thinking probably it had. She reached across the table to touch my hand and I kissed it.

"Would you like to go out for a movie?" I asked.

"How about a matinee tomorrow?" she countered.

"All right. Then how about just going down for a drink by the waterfront?

She shook her head playfully.

"Dancing?"

This drew the same response from Ellie.

"A walk along the shore?"

Again, a shake of her head.

I tossed my cloth napkin on the table, stood up and went around to where she sat. My kisses drew her upwards. A step forward by me led to a step backwards by her. Another, and another, until we were headed down the hallway towards her bedroom.

In the darkness, clothes flew this way and that. When only Ellie's bra and panties remained, I pushed her gently onto the bed, pulled her panties off and took her into my mouth. When she could take no more of that, I drove into her softness, and with each thrust of ecstasy, her eyes closed and she bit her finger and then tugged hard at my hips and we came together and were very, very happy.

In the morning, I awakened first and lay next to Ellie, watching her as she slept. When her eyes finally opened, she smiled and pulled me close.

"Roger?"

"Yes?"

"You know what you did to me last night?"

"Hmm hmm."

"No one has ever done that to me before."

Thinking to do it again, I started down Ellie's soft, white belly with kisses but she stopped me and slid down my belly instead.

"Oh god…yes…"

A blustery, fall day stirred outside Ellie's windows as I came in her mouth.

Afterward, I lay there feeling guilty. Ellie's head was on my chest

"What are you thinking?" she said.

"I wanted to please you."

"You did."

"Not in the way I wanted."

"Please, Roger. I am very happy right now."

"Okay."

She did seem to be quite content about the whole thing so I let go.

Sometime later, Ellie went off to the kitchen and rattled about for a spell. The front door opened and closed. She returned to bed with a tray of coffee, croissants and the morning paper. We read the paper and played footsies and indulged in croissants ladled with strawberry preserves.

Thinking Ellie might enjoy it, I suggested Camelot for the matinee.

"Sure," she said with a puzzled look.

An hour later, we were seated in the darkened theater. When Richard Harris broke out into song, I looked in Ellie's direction. She met my gaze.

"I thought it was Shakespearean," I said.

"I wondered where you got the notion."

Out on the sidewalk, I stood with hands in my pockets, duly humiliated.

"Guess I should have read those books on Western Civilization you offered me."

"Well, you see," Ellie said as if waxing professorial, "the Arthurian legends were, after all..."

"Oh shut up," I said, cutting her off. "No need for a lecture."

"Very well. I suppose since we're already up here, we may as well make good use of the time."

"Doing what?"

"I noticed a porno flick playing back down the road."

I studied Ellie's face, unable to see through her dark glasses. Her white teeth were abundantly visible.

"All right, I call your bluff."

"My dear, I am completely in earnest."

Half a mile back down the road, we entered another darkened theater. Heads were scattered here and there among the seats, single men entirely, a few young ones, mostly older. Ellie and I joked about trench coats. There were none, but the atmosphere was headed decidedly in that direction.

"What, no popcorn," I joked with Ellie as we took our seats.

Every head in the theater was riveted to the screen, where a man stood behind a woman in a nurse's uniform. Her white skirt was pulled up over her back. Her stockings were pulled down around her ankles and the man was going about his business mechanically.

Eventually, he pulled his cock out and the woman knelt down to give him a blowjob. He had an enormous cock, yet the woman swallowed it readily, to the hilt. Thus, the movie's title.

"Are you taking notes?" I asked.

Ellie looked around mischievously and back at me.

"I can start practicing right now, if you'd like?"

"Well, you've certainly called *my* bluff, haven't you?"

We went back to watching the movie while secretly petting each other now.

"Look," she whispered and pointed at a man in a heavy coat. He seemed to be masturbating. When his movements stopped, he looked around guiltily.

"Busted," Ellie said with a shot of her finger.

We chuckled and returned our attention to the movie. When it ended, the lights came on and everyone looked around to see who else was degenerate enough to be in a porn theater on a Saturday afternoon.

After a brief intermission, the theater grew dark again and the second movie commenced. A woman in a seedy downtown motel was looking out her windows, lonely and filled with despair. Eventually she poured herself a drink, took it to the bathroom, submerged herself in the tub and slit her wrists.

Now dead, and having arrived to a spiritual way station in the form of an office with a desk clerk, she was offered one wish, anything she wanted. She chose to indulge in every sexual taboo she had denied herself while living. From one man to the next she went, finally having two of them at once.

Believing it was heaven, not hell; the woman ultimately found herself naked except for high heels, infused with an unbridled lust but locked in a room with a man whose only interest was a fly on the wall. The movie aspired to be philosophical. It was certainly erotic.

Out on the sidewalk, Ellie and I found the weather had deteriorated in our absence, with a cold wind blowing down from the north. Charcoal clouds raced by overhead. It looked like rain. Ellie nestled up under my arm as we walked down the sidewalk.

"So what did you think?" she said.

"I can't define eroticism but I know what it is when I see it and that second film was truly erotic. Never mind its profound thematic development."

Ellie put a finger to her lips, preparing to wax didactic.

"Careful. Class is out for the weekend."

"Oh darn," she said. "Anyway, I'd rather go do it."

Once inside the car, I stared at her.

"What?" she said.

"I like the way you said 'do it'."

"Do it," she repeated.

"Oh, I do want to do it."

"Then let's go *do* it."

On the way home, I recounted the many ways I found her erotic; the painted toe nails, the crease in her instep, made by a pair of high heels, the line of her hips and back when I mounted her from behind, the taste of her cunt, the way her lips curled gently around the knob of my cock.

Back in Ellie's bedroom, we tried desperately to extinguish our desires and made love several times but it was never enough. Once started, my lust became boundless. Lying quietly afterwards, I found my only peace was in continuing to caress her fine body. That ultimately was as rewarding to me as the sex.

I heard the rain start to fall late that afternoon, first with a pitter patter on the deck outside Ellie's French doors, then with the wind howling and rattling at her windows. We had been lounging around in bed for several hours by that point. She was propped up with pillows grading her student papers. I had a pile of books sitting on the nightstand next to me, the ones Ellie had picked out for my edification.

An hour or so later, Ellie closed her last essay with dramatic flair.

"So, what interested you?" she asked about my books.

"I enjoyed Defoe's essay on educating women."

Ellie bit her nails in mock fright.

"You see what a little knowledge will do."

"What else did you read?"

I thumbed open to Milton's Areopagitica and read.

"What's the matter, Ellie," I said after a few sentences. "You look tortured."

"You see, Roger, it's impossible to appreciate its importance without viewing the context of his discourse."

"Suppression of speech," I said.

"Suppression of liberty," Ellie amended.

"How so! And here's the word stated, couched in rhetoric though it may be. And it only took him most of a page to get it out of his mouth."

"Actually, this embellishment of language can be traced to the Elizabethan Era. Shakespeare was probably the leading culprit."

"What was it you once said about folks who ought to be shot?"

She laughed.

"I'm stunned you remembered."

"Well, I did. Anyway, it's difficult for me to see the value of this. Then perhaps I'm more sentient than intellectual. About the only thing I found worthwhile was the poetry. I opened and read from Homer.

"'So said she; they long since in Earth's soft arms were reposing, There, in their own dear land, their fatherland, Lacedaemon.' Lovely, isn't it?"

"Then that's what you should read."

"Thank you. I'm relieved."

"So am I."

I imitated one of her tantrums and she laughed.

"I have an idea," she said. "Let's have dinner at the Arches."

"The Arches. I've never been there before."

"Write it off as just another new experience, my darling."

She kissed me and headed for the kitchen with our plates.

"It sounds stuffy," I called after her but she failed to reply.

Showering, I opened a window and allowed the cool air to come in.

While Ellie showered, I dressed. Seeing her high heels at the foot of the bed, I took one in hand and smelled inside of it. The sweet, pungent scent took me back to a summer day in my youth, when a lovely woman had walked down our street and I had been possessed of this strange urge to smell inside her shoes.

"What on earth are you doing?" Ellie said, surprising me from behind.

"I don't know."

I placed the shoe down. Ellie came around and looked in my eyes.

"Do you have a fetish?"

"Maybe."

I explained about my childhood experience.

In response, she stood on one leg, slipped on a shoe, then the other. We kissed and her towel dropped to the floor. I soon had her leaning over the bed.

"Oh god, don't stop," Ellie said. "Just do it hard, lover."

Her legs were straight, her body pushing against me. The lovely curve of her waist was in hands.

Afterwards, we kissed for a long time. Then Ellie went off to the bathroom as if nothing had happened, though with the shoes still on. I was ready to start all over again.

Out in the kitchen, I poured myself a glass of sherry and got comfortable in one of Ellie's easy chairs. She had taken several photographs of me the previous weekend and had tacked them to one of her bookshelves in the living room.

"No future in Hollywood," I said when she appeared in bra and panties.

"I like that one," she said, leaning against my back. She poured herself a scotch on the rocks and disappeared with it.

"The one next to it makes me look like a politician!" I called after her. "A right-wing politician!"

"Shouting makes you sound like a right-wing politician," she said. Her face appeared around the corner of the hallway. "Anyway, it's your own fault for talking while being photographed."

I made a gesture of which she did not approve.

"And cutting your hair," she added before disappearing again.

While waiting, I found myself dreading The Arches. It was where the old money hung out. I had visions of aging women with wigs and baubles and too much make up and old men wearing cravats and captain's hats. Ellie and I walking in together was bound to turn a few heads.

Upon arriving, I found my vision of The Arches not entirely baseless. There were definitely baubles and captain's hats and cravats amidst all the gaiety and tinkling of glasses. These were people who, for the most part, never had to worry about money again.

Everything was done with a towel over the arm and a snap of the fingers. Our waiter was French. The food was impeccable.

For a bit of contrast, I dragged Ellie over to Sid's Blue Beat after the meal. It was a mix of aging surfers, blacks, lost beatniks and stoned out hippies. The music was loud. The smell of grass was in the air.

"Do you like it?" I shouted over a blues group.

"What?" Ellie shouted back.

She looked flustered at having to talk over the music so we were silent again.

"I'm ready to go," she said at the end of the first set. I finished my drink, threw some money on the table and led Ellie out by the hand. Black men, in particular, seemed interested in this fox with the fluffy hair.

"Sorry," I said once we were outside in the alley. "But now you know how it feels to be out of your element."

"Well, yes, admittedly, I've never really seen you in yours."

"Not that I'm entirely at home in that element either these days but I can see how someone would feel lost. The music, the lights…"

"The grass," she added.

I bit my nails, as if to imitate her.

"You see, Roger. Every semester I witness the shifting social currents in my classroom. Constant change, but apparently not in its raw form. I've never realized how diluted my impressions were until now."

"You know, Ellie. I think it would be a great help if you smoked a joint yourself."

"After my son Davy was imprisoned for two years over it? Surely you jest."

"It was a thought."

"Roger, surely you're not still engaged in that sort of thing, are you?"

"Sometimes, yes…You're shocked."

"Oh, not really."

"Who's clamming up now?"

"Yes, I suppose you're right. I guess I never imagined getting an education of my own in this affair."

I laughed at the perplexed look on Ellie's face.

Seven

Following coffee and croissants the next morning, Ellie and I drove down to the pier. The sky was gray, the day raw and blustery, the sea churning with white-caps all the way out to the horizon. Rain seemed imminent again.

The old dory fleet had already returned from its morning row and the fishermen were out selling to the public alongside the pier. Given the weather, I was surprised to see they had gone out at all.

The boats were scattered randomly in the sand, their hulls painted in bold blues and greens and reds with white above the bulwarks. A crisscross of wooden planks ran among the boats and a lively banter was ongoing between the fishermen and their customers.

Out of curiosity, Ellie and I strolled out among the boats and watched coarse hands deftly fillet each fish and wrap it in waxed paper. Red snapper appeared to be the predominant catch, all bug-eyed after being brought up from the depths, but we also saw some white sea bass and halibut and a bit of mackerel.

Having taken in this bit of local color, we returned to the pier and walked out to the end, bundled up against the cold and with our noses turning red. At the end, I leaned against the rail and looked north up towards San Pedro.

"You seem particularly pensive this morning," Ellie said.

I looked over at her.

"I'm having anxieties."

She chuckled.

"About what?"

"About everything."

"And would this include relationships?"

"Probably."

"And why is that?"

"Why not? She chuckled again. "I don't know. I suppose because I grew up witnessing a lousy marriage. My parents appear to have been doomed from the start. And my brothers and sister have all made a mess of theirs. I don't have much in the way of a positive example."

"And I'm afraid I'm not much help in that regard, either."

"Yeah."

"You worried about us?"

"I suppose. I just wonder. Can two people can really be happy for their entire lives? Or do they just fake it after a while?"

"I know two or three couples who appear to be happy in that way," Ellie said.

She looked back at me, brushing at the hair tangled in her dark eyes, her eyes watching mine. I leaned over the rail, my hands shoved into my coat pockets. The sea was tossing wildly, all the way out to Catalina.

"Appear to be," I said. "You spoke as if there was a catch."

"I don't go home with them," she said. "Of course, if you're looking for love to last a lifetime, how would you know until you're on your deathbed?"

"Funny."

She smiled and nuzzled close to me, her teeth like whitecaps.

I shrugged and looked back out to sea, realizing I had asked a question that was better left unsaid, especially given our circumstances.

"At least it can feel that way," I said.

"In this crazy mixed up world, that's a lot," she said.

I drew Ellie close to me, thinking she was sage and kind and wishing I wasn't hounded by my secret thoughts. A wave passed along below us and the pier stretched and groaned, the pier pilings shifting under my feet. The whole world seemed to be shifting under my feet.

"I wonder about us," I said.

"You mean, are you in a doomed relationship with a divorced, old hag?"

"Don't say that."

"I thought we were going to be honest, Roger. It's only fair to acknowledge that our love affair is going to end. That we must go our separate ways someday. It is unfortunate, but inevitable."

I pulled away from the railing and took her face in my hands. Another couple came by and stared in our direction. It was something I had noticed from the very first moment we had been out in public together. People always took notice of us, as if we were lepers.

"I am being honest," I said with a kiss. "You are the sweetest thing that has ever happened to me."

"I love you, Roger."

"I love you too, Ellie."

"Then let's pretend we're young and in love and forget about the rest of it. Whatever's meant to be will be."

We embraced and I held onto those words while the wind whispered mysterious things in my ears. Another wave pushed quietly through the pier pilings below us. I grew lost in the blustery wind and the feeling of everything moving around us.

Ellie pulled away and looked at me.

"How does the writing go, Roger?"

"Not well. I've not had much success for days."

"What have you been working on?"

"Other than a poem for you, mostly sailor's dreams."

She waited.

"Sometimes I get off on these scintillating diatribes."

"The angry prophet."

"Yes. It seems so easy to save souls on paper. But not so easily in the flesh."

"That's charming. Why don't you write that down?"

"I did. It made a nice sentence."

"Well," she said dramatically. "That's the start of a nice paragraph."

"You're wonderfully helpful."

"Aw. Come here." Ellie opened her coat and pressed the warmth of her tender body against mine. We kissed and I returned to my dreams of ancient ships and sea wrecked sailors.

"If only this day went on forever," I said. "And that we could walk the seashore from one end of this world to the other."

"Another lovely thought…"

"Ellie, let's buy a few things at the market and have a picnic down there by the point."

"Have you forgotten? I promised to meet the twins for lunch and help them pick out a gift for their father."

I nodded and looked out to sea. My effort to disguise my feelings obviously hadn't gone over too well.

"You know," Ellie said, "you don't have to come along. It's really all right. No one's forcing you."

"No, it's all right. I'm just feeling mixed up today, Ellie.

"Look, we can take the ferry back afterwards and do a bit of Christmas shopping together. What do you say?"

"All right."

"Well you don't be too enthusiastic about it."

"I'm sorry. I just wanted all your attention today."

I waved my hand at the blustery sea etched vividly beneath the raw sky.

"To remain in this enchantment with you like it was forever. Just the two of us."

"We've already had many lovely moments together, Roger. And there will be many more. But I have these other responsibilities."

"I know."

She looked at her watch.

"We still have an hour before we're supposed to meet them."

"Let's just walk," I said and started back towards the base of the pier.

Ellie fell in beside me and we went along not touching now. Other couples passed by us along the pier, holding hands and being in love.

At the base of the pier, I took off my shoes and climbed down onto the soft, damp sand. Ellie went on straight ahead to a sidewalk and turned right along the beachfront homes.

Eventually our paths converged and I stopped to wipe the sand from my feet before putting my shoes back on. Ellie waited without looking at me. I knew I was being childish but did not know how to stop it. It would have required humbling myself and I did not know how to do that, not without feeling as if I had been humiliated.

We continued on apart and with our separate thoughts. When we came to a phone booth, Ellie stopped to call the twins. I went on forward twenty or thirty paces and waited. Ripples of sand covered the sidewalk, like tiny dunes, stirring in me ephemeral memories of places long ago, like the seashore of New England and the whisper of the wind in the wild grasses.

"They're on their way," Ellie announced, coming out of the booth.

I nodded.

"Look, Roger. If this is such an inconvenience to you, just take the keys and go back to my place. I'd rather you weren't around."

I shrugged and turned away in silence. Ellie caught up with me.

"God! I can't believe how stupid this is!"

"It's all right. I can hitchhike home."

Ellie threw up her hands in exasperation.

"Seriously, Roger! I really can't believe you're doing this!"

I stared back, thinking of knives. We walked back to Ellie's car in silence.

At the bridge entrance to the island, we found the twins waiting for us. They climbed in back and introduced themselves. Then they bantered back and forth with Ellie while she searched for a parking space. I stole a glance while they did. Carla was nearly a spitting image of her father, the same straight nose, blonde hair and Scandinavian features, while Kurt looked like Ellie, right down to the nose and curly hair. He smiled satirically when our eyes met, like we both knew, 'Yeah, you're screwing my mother, but it's cool'. I looked forward again.

"I suggest we get the shopping out of the way first," Carla said once we had parked.

No one argued with her and we fell in line.

They went into one shop after another. I mostly milled around outside, hoping they would consummate the deal soon. Once that was done, a discussion ensued about where to have lunch. The twins did most of the haggling and eventually settled on a restaurant up the block. A hostess seated us, Ellie next to me and the twins across from us.

"My Mom's told me a bit about your travels," Carla said.

I elaborated on them, as she seemed interested.

"War had a lot to do with it," I said. "Escaping the war, I mean. I had thought to stay in France when I was there. I speak the language but I just got homesick one day. I guess the same when I was in the South Pacific."

"Is it true that the French hate Americans?" Carla said.

"Not if you speak French. I was never treated rudely."

"Well I hate Americans," Kurt said. "Most of them."

He snapped his menu shut and smiled sardonically.

"Kurt shares your aversion to authority," Ellie said.

"And war," Kurt said, still smiling.

"Let's hope the draft ends before you're eligible."

"Let's hope the war does."

"Or we'll have another expatriate in Paris," Carla said.

A moment of silence followed.

"So," Ellie said. "Show Roger your work."

Kurt, who was on his way to interview at an art college that afternoon, went out to the car and returned with his portfolio. Carla scooted over to allow Kurt more room to turn the pages.

"That's cool," I said about a portrait of Jimi Hendrix. His hair was on fire.

"Kurt does his graphics up in the attic," Ellie explained. "He has this remarkable workshop up there."

I nodded, thinking it odd that she had never mentioned this fact before.

Kurt had moved on to some block prints. All his work was quite well done. My own artistic efforts seem rather rudderless in comparison.

The food arrived and I ate mostly in silence. The three of them were bantering away.

"Well, we'd better get going," Carla said to Kurt when the plates were cleared away. The bill came and Ellie paid it.

Back out on the sidewalk, I said goodbye and shook hands with Kurt and Carla, but instead of them departing, a lengthy discussion broke out about Carla's early admission to college. I wandered off a bit and let them talk. The island seemed deserted. The foul weather had chased off most of the tourists.

"I'll check the mail and call you," Ellie said about an early admissions letter.

They hugged and started to say goodbye. Finally, I thought but their discussion resumed.

"Well, that wasn't so bad," Ellie said once the twins were headed down the sidewalk the other way.

"No," I admitted.

"I think Kurt has a real genius," Ellie said.

"Yeah," I agreed.

The ensuing car ride back to Ellie's condo was made in more silence. She went in and started cleaning up the kitchen. I sat alone by the windows in the living room. A man was fiddling at his work bench in the garage. His wife came out to talk to him. My thoughts were of a cheap bar I knew in the back streets of Barcelona.

Ellie went out to grab the mail, breaking me from my spell. She came back in and took the mail out to the kitchen. A minute later, she reappeared, reading from a letter out loud. Apparently, Carla's efforts to get into college a semester early had met with a snag.

"I know exactly what happened," Ellie said. "That bastard Dick forgot to send in the check with her application and now it's too late."

"You don't know that."

"Of course, Roger. Take his side."

"I'm not taking anyone's side. I'm just saying, there may have been a mistake on the university's end."

Ellie gestured in exasperation.

"So, there you have it. No one to blame."

"I'm sure no one meant for it to happen."

"Well…how convenient of you, Roger. Now that you've been an ass all morning, you're suddenly as serene as a monk."

"Ellie, I'm already feeling sad and mixed up. I don't want to fight."

"You bastard!"

At this, I stood up and started for the bedroom.

"You see, that's what's wrong with the world!" Ellie called after me. "There's no accountability anymore!"

I turned to face her.

"You know what? You're right. I was being an ass earlier. And it's the hardest goddamned thing in this world to admit, isn't it? That we all have our turn being assholes?"

Momentarily stunned, she quickly gathered herself and pointed at the door.

"Get out!"

I continued on to the bedroom and began to gather my things. A moment later, I felt Ellie's arms wrap around me from behind.

"I'm sorry, Roger."

"Yeah, so am I."

I continued packing.

"Please," she said and made me turn to face her. "Let's talk."

"Sure, now that you've got me all riled up, you're all ready to be as serene as a monk."

"Touché!" she said.

I closed my backpack and started for the front door. Ellie followed me down the hallway.

"Please, Roger. Accept my apology. Let's just sit down and talk this over."

"There's nothing to say."

"All right, then go."

I stared at her with my hand on the door.

"You've already said as much, just as I feared you would."

I opened the door and started out.

"Jesus, Roger, at least allow me to give you a ride home then."

"Thanks, Ellie, but I've bummed my way halfway around the world. I expect I can get back home from here all right."

"Suit yourself," she said and plopped down into an easy chair. "Get up on your cross if you must."

"Oh, to hell with you!" I said and slammed the door.

Halfway down the sidewalk, I decided I needed to continue the argument and barged back in through the front door but Ellie was gone. I marched down the hallway and found her lying on the bed, staring at the ceiling.

"I suppose you're real happy with yourself."

"Actually, I'm not, Roger."

"Well, you look real contented there."

While Ellie continued to stare at the ceiling, I became aware of her dainty little toes with their red toenail polish and had a sudden urge to make love. It seemed as if that might solve all our problems.

"You see, Roger," Ellie said while still staring at the ceiling. "It's rather inconvenient to muscle back into a conversation when you've just discarded it as pointless a moment ago."

Ellie looked over at me. I stared back with rage.

"You're the one who told me to get out."

She looked nonchalantly back at the ceiling.

"Well, actually, I've been thinking about what you asked of me today and I'm not so sure it's something I can't provide."

"What did I say I wanted?"

"My attention. Endlessly."

"Bullshit."

"All right, daily. What's the difference?"

I slammed my fist against the wall.

"That's not what I said, goddamn it."

"That's what I heard."

I went up close to the bed and stood over her.

"I said I wanted your undivided attention today. Just for today."

"Oh well," she said with a toss of the hand.

"Oh well?! Oh well?!"

Ellie looked over at me.

"Roger, I really think it's best if you leave."

Seeing my words construed falsely, I understood murder at that moment.

While we remained staring at each other, there was a loud knock at the front door.

"Oh Christ," Ellie said. "Stay here."

She started out of the bedroom.

"You think it's Dick?"

"By the sound of it, yes."

I heard the door open and Dick's voice in the foyer. He sounded drunk. There were words, a protest and the hustle of feet down the hallway. Dick appeared in the doorway.

"And what the hell do you think you're doing here?"

Dick came over and stood eye to eye with me, a sneer on his face.

"I guess I can't stop you from tearing off a piece but you're not going to do it while my name's still on the goddamned mortgage."

"You bastard!" Ellie said with a slap at him. "Get out!"

When I went to intervene on Ellie's behalf, Dick caught me with a good right to the jaw. I drove him into the wall but he quickly had me in a head lock.

"Get out!" Ellie kept shouting over it all. "Get out of my home!"

I finally freed myself from Dick's grasp. He stood there grinning. I licked at the blood in my mouth, my body coiled, ready for his next move.

"Please, both of you! Get out!"

Ellie stood there pointing towards the hall.

Dick did not move but I started for the front door. Along the way, I used my shirt to wipe at the blood.

"I want you out too, Dick!" I heard Ellie say.

"As long as I'm making the mortgage payment, I'll do whatever the hell I want around here."

"Dick, this is my home!"

"Like hell it is."

On my way out the front door, I heard the two of them still arguing.

It was a long walk out to the main road and a longer wait, standing there with my thumb held out, hoping for a ride. With blood on my shirt and face, no doubt I looked like trouble.

It was dark by the time I arrived back home. I had stopped for a bottle of brandy along the way and immediately filled a glass upon entering my cottage. Having downed that, I filled another one and sat there licking my wounds, literally and figuratively. My heart beat wildly each time I remembered Dick clocking me and the entire scene. Finally, I showered and crawled into bed. Always adieu, I thought, and with every adieu, another little piece of my innocence was chipped away.

Sometime later, I heard a knock on the door but ignored it. When the knocking persisted, I went to see who was there. Ellie stood on the porch with a bottle of Scotch in her hand. Her shrug at me spoke of surrender.

"Can we talk, Roger?"

I left the door open and turned away. Ellie came in and closed it. I sat in my reading chair. Ellie sat opposite me on the sofa.

I stared.

"Could I have a glass?"

I went to the kitchen and returned with one. Ellie poured the glass half full and had a good drink.

"I want to know if you can forgive me, Roger."

"For what?"

"For my failure to respect our romance."

I stared, feeling our differences were insurmountable now.

"I don't blame you for being angry with me. I betrayed you."

"Well, you just did what was natural for you."

Ellie gestured to the sky, the hurt revealed in her quivering lips. I played the part of executioner, ready to wield the axe.

"God, can we ever get it right?"

She fell back on the sofa and stared up at the ceiling.

"An hour ago, I owned all the chess pieces. Now they're on your side of the board. It's like this big fucking power game that nobody ever wins…Please say something, Roger."

I drank straight from my bottle of brandy and considered my thoughts.

"Perhaps I'm cynical, Ellie. I probably am. I demonstrated that by choosing a woman with whom I had no future."

"Jesus, you just stabbed me in the heart."

She began to cry.

"I'm sorry," I said.

Touched by her sadness, I felt pity all of sudden. I stared at her lovely face and rather loved her again. She stared back.

"Did you mean that?"

"Yes."

"What did I do?"

"I don't know. You looked so sad, it broke my heart."

She bit on a nail in thought.

"God, it's so simple, Roger. Dramatic catharsis. I invoked your pathos. The moment I became vulnerable, you were able to pity me."

"Christ, do you always have to turn life into a classroom?"

"But I had this vision, Roger." She stood up. "As though we were in a Greek play, with the sword through my heart. Then you leaned over me in sadness and we were reborn in death. Do you see what I mean?"

"I suppose. It's a bit more embellished than my version."

I watched this illustrious woman standing in the middle of the room, a bit in awe of her clarity and keenness of insight, being but a spectator while she grew enlightened before me. I did my best to be glad for her.

She came over, sat on my lap and kissed my face sweetly until I was willing again. Her body went completely limp with surrender when I gathered her up in my arms and carried her off to bed.

Eight

That following Friday was the final day of Ellie's fall semester and the beginning of her holiday vacation. The two of us were lounging around on her living room carpet that evening with brandy eggnogs and books on California history, discussing our forthcoming trip. A Christmas tree twinkled in one corner. Christmas carols played in the background. The scent of evergreen was in the air.

Early the next morning, a bit groggy from our late-night revelry and bundled up against the cold, we packed her Capri and headed east through a string of cookie-cutter towns. The snow-capped coastal mountains loomed off in the distance and kept growing closer. An hour later, we had made it over the mountain pass and into the high desert.

At a little past noon, we gassed up in Lone Pine, bought two sandwiches at a local delicatessen and continued to the outskirts of town. Ellie parked several hundred yards back from the highway, alongside a broad, shallow river. The winter sky was clear but pale. A gentle wind whispered in the pine tree above our heads. The snowy Sierras stabbed into the sky to our north. Ellie grabbed her pickle and bit into it with great panache. I laughed at her and opened one of the beers. The sunroof was open, the sunlight warm on our skin.

"Too bad things aren't always this simple," I said.

"Made for the pastoral life, are we, Roger?"

"A country boy at heart, yes."

A jay called and flew off into the brush along the river. I stared in that direction, distracted.

"You see, as a serious poet, you could live this life and people would pay you to write about it."

"I'd feel like an imposter."

"Don't sell yourself short, Roger. Just speak plainly about what you see and feel. I'm certain your innate nobility will shine through."

I soiled another napkin and tossed it into the pile between us.

"There's a bit of nobility for you."

Ellie showed her pinkie while taking a dainty bite of her own sandwich.

"I've been thinking a lot about my days in Italy. You know, the countryside dotted with ancient olive groves and ancient stone walls? It's all so beautiful and enchanting. And then you come home to power lines and gas stations on every corner."

"We could go to Italy on my sabbatical next year. Or anywhere you want."

I wadded up my sandwich wrapper and placed it in a paper bag along with our other trash.

"Think I'll practice up on being pastoral."

I went off and urinated against a towering Ponderosa pine.

"Damn a woman's anatomy anyway," Ellie said when I returned.

"Go squat behind it. No one's watching."

She did. I noticed a wet spot on her slacks upon her return

"I tried standing," she said.

I laughed as she pulled back onto the highway.

Snow soon blanketed the foothills around us, and more and more so as we drove north. Finally, the land was utterly white, save for whatever rock formations and pines and taller brush poked out of it here and there.

We gassed up in Bishop and turned up the final grade to Mammoth. The highway had been plowed a few days back and the shoulder was lined with soiled snow. Ellie drove on past downtown Mammoth and directly to the condo she owned with Dick.

"That fucker!" she said upon spotting his car parked out in front.

I waited while she went in to investigate. A few minutes later, she marched back out. Things had not gone so well by the looks of it.

"That fucker," she said again, getting back into the car. Her hands gripped the steering wheel. "I'd like to feed his head to him. He says he forgot our arrangements about the condo this week."

"So? What do we do?"

She slammed both fists against the steering wheel.

"That lying, squirming bastard." She looked at me. "He's up there screwing my best friend."

"So, let's go find another place to spend the night."

"That worthless twat lied to me, too."

I turned my head and looked out the window, expecting they weren't such good friends anymore.

"She lied to me!"

"About what?"

"That she was going to Tahoe for two days...*with* her kids."

Ellie stared until I looked at her. I shrugged.

"I suppose we'd better go look for a place then," I said.

Ellie stared for another long moment before slamming her palms on the steering wheel again.

"You see, all they had to do was tell the truth. The one thing they never considered doing."

"You're right, but all we can do now is go find some other place to crash."

"Do you realize how hard *that's* going to be in Mammoth on a Friday night? Over the Christmas holiday?"

"All we can do is try."

"That bastard. For twenty years he's been lying to me."

She beat repeatedly on the steering wheel now with both palms.

"Twenty years of my life wasted over him."

Finally, she started the car, drove out to the main road and turned in the direction of the ski lodge. A block before we reached the main incline, she turned right onto a dead-end street, parked and got out.

"What's going on?" I asked her.

"Davy lives here."

"Do we have to go see your children tonight?"

Ellie leaned over and looked at me through the open door.

"Roger, I'm going indoors where it's warm."

She closed the door and marched through heavy snow towards the cabin. After a moment, Davy answered the front door and hugged Ellie. They exchanged a few words and he waved for me to join them. I did so reluctantly but Davy warmly welcomed me inside.

Davy's hippie wife made a pot of tea while Ellie recounted every sordid little detail. Three young children scurried under and around the roughhewn dining table where we sat, oblivious to the caprices of adulthood. The fourth child was too small to participate. He simply lay there and wailed through it all.

Gratefully, Ellie declined their offer of squaw bread and garbanzo beans for supper. The two of us showered and drove back into town. Ellie passed restaurant after restaurant, unwilling to stand in one of their long lines outside.

"This is impossible," she said finally. "We're never going to find a place to eat."

"We'll just have to wait in line, Ellie. It's that or garbanzo beans and squaw bread."

I pointed hopefully at the next row of lights and she wrenched her car to the side of the road. We got out and took our place at the back of a long line. It was half an hour before we were seated with our menus. Ellie opened hers.

"Look at these prices! I detest these upstart eateries! Their only purpose is to gouge the unsuspecting traveler!"

I munched on a breadstick.

Another fifteen minutes passed before our waiter finally came around to take our orders. Ellie was ready to chew his head off by then.

"Nothing can live up to the expectations of these prices," she said without looking up.

"I'll have the soup," I said.

"Oh, for goodness sakes, don't deny yourself on my account. No one else has. Make it lobster for two. And a bottle of your best chardonnay."

She snapped her menu shut and handed it to the waiter while staring at me. The entire meal pretty much went along those lines. I considered hitchhiking back to Southern California.

Back at Davy's place, we found he had bedded us down in the loft opposite him and his wife. We were separated by about twenty paces and a tie-dye curtain, neither of which did a thing to abate the sounds.

There was moaning at first, then the pounding of their headboard against a wall. I lay with my eyes open in the dark, imagining the children downstairs. The crescendo of muffled blasphemies and screams came to a climax at last. I prayed that Davy and his wife were using some form of birth control.

In the morning, I showered early and walked around to a picnic table at the back of the cabin. It was frozen over with ice and snow. I cleared a place and sat down. A shed with Davy's pottery workshop sat opposite me. Ellie came out wearing all the appropriate snow gear. I had on Levi's and a leather jacket.

"What are you going to do?" I asked her.

"I'm going to confront Dick."

"Come on, Ellie. Give it up."

"I'm not going to let that bastard take advantage of me any longer."

"Hell, I may as well go home. I have no part in this saga."

"Yes, how foolish to expect you might defend me."

"What's the point, Ellie? Unless you just enjoy arguing."

"You act as if I was the one who instigated this."

"No, but you're probably the only one who gives a crap about it."

"You fucker." She started back towards the house.

"Find your own ride if you're leaving," she added and disappeared around the cabin.

I thought of all the gear I had stowed in the car but decided it didn't matter and started for the highway through heavy snow. I had one concern. Could I make it the four hundred miles before sundown? The day was early enough. At least I had a heavy coat.

I was down past the main village when Ellie caught up with me. She nearly took out a tree coming to a stop. Her exit from the car had the same dramatic flair about it.

"How dare you run off," she said, marching in my direction.

Fearing blows, I grabbed her wrists the minute she got close. People drove by as we struggled alongside the road.

"You bastard, you bastard. You're like all the rest of them."

There was an effort to free her arms and kick me the entire time.

"I'm like all the rest of whom?"

"Like every man I've ever known."

"No I'm not."

At this Ellie stopped and stared at me with her 'little girl' look.

"Yes you are. You abandoned me just when I needed you the most."

Seeing a tear roll down her cheek, I decided it was safe to let go of her hands. She wiped at the tears.

"You left me when I needed you most."

"You told me to leave."

"No I didn't."

"All right. It doesn't matter. I just don't want to participate in this nonsense with your husband."

"You're all I have in the world. How could you leave me?"

I had wanted to slap her. In a way, I still did, but I was touched by her sudden vulnerability and began to rub her back.

"Don't ask me why, but I love you, Ellie."

She leaned back and wiped at her tears again.

"I love you, too, Roger."

"So why are we fighting?"

She looked off as if she had seen something high up on the mountain. When she looked back, there was a change in her aura. She was chewing on her thumbnail like a little girl. She seemed to be in a state of illumination.

"You won't leave me?" she said.

"No, I won't leave you."

"Promise?"

"Promise."

"Let's go back," she said and took my hand. We walked back to the car and got in.

At Davy's cabin, Ellie pointed out Kurt's car. The twins had arrived. Presently, both of them came out the front door and crossed the snow-covered yard to greet us. Ellie greeted them and went right back to gathering Christmas presents from the opened trunk.

"I thought we were going to open them at the condo," Carla said.

"There are more," Ellie said and marched off towards the house without answering. I shrugged and joined the twins in gathering up the rest.

Soon, we were all together in the living room. The presents had been piled around the Christmas tree. Davy's children screamed and ran about the house, delighted at the sight of these newfound riches.

"Merry Christmas," Ellie said and offered everyone a hug.

"Where are you going?" Carla said as she started to leave.

Ellie stopped at the door.

"To take care of myself. Have a Merry Christmas. I love you all."

She left without another word. I shrugged. Kurt did too. Carla stared. I went out the door with the children still running around the living room and screaming.

Ellie drove back to 395 and turned north on the narrow strip of black asphalt. The land was bitter with winter all around us. A few dark crevasses remained in the high country across the valley, places where the snow could not possibly cling, and rocks and vegetation protruded from the flat terrain, but otherwise snow had completely consumed the land. I noted each ancient splintered tree that appeared along the road and pondered the many bitter winters it had endured. An hour went by like this without conversation.

"Do you mind explaining?" I said finally. We had just passed the turn off for June Mountain.

"I'm not sure, Roger. Something truly momentous. I will try to share it with you tonight when we get settled."

"Okay," I said and looked out the window.

I decided not to ask where we were going, lest it initiate another confrontation.

Ellie kept to a cautious speed on the icy roads but we made Tahoe just before nightfall. She pulled into the first available real estate office and secured a private chalet for two nights. There was a cascade of them going up the steep hill behind the real estate office, looking for all the world like part of a Bavarian village.

I finished unloading the car while Ellie showered in the loft bedroom. There was a spacious living room on the main level,

107

divided from the kitchen by a tiled countertop, and an extra room and bath down a short hallway.

With all our gear inside and reasonably organized, I started a fire. Two stuffed chairs and a down sofa surrounded the hearth, along with a rustic coffee table. Compelled by the view, I went out to the deck. Snow covered the rooftops below us. The frozen lake and casinos were off to my left.

A short time later, Ellie joined me in her robe and slippers. When she shivered, I placed my hands inside her robe and pulled her close. Her flesh was soft and warm.

"I will always remember that you didn't abandon me," she said.

"And I will always remember that I had started to walk home from Mammoth...I wish you would explain," I said after more silence.

"I will. But, please, take a shower."

I kissed her profusely around her neck and shoulders and started inside.

"Then I would like to smoke a joint with you."

I turned to face her.

"What makes you think I have some?"

"Oh, just a wild guess...And, yes, I imagine you sneaking off into the woods when I'm not looking."

"Yes Mom," I said with a deadpan look and headed off to shower.

"By the way, Roger. Where is this contraband? I'd like to try my hand at rolling a cigarette."

"It's called a joint and it's in my shaving kit."

I started upstairs, imagining the results of her endeavor as I did.

Nine

Ellie was curled up on the sofa next to me, wearing a robe and with her skin still freshly showered and pink. She had made hot rum toddies which were bracing against the cold, crisp air passing through the partly opened door. Dusk was descending swiftly over the mountains but some people were still ice skating on a pond down below us in the last light of day. A car horn honked off in the distance somewhere and echoed up from the streets. All else was quiet.

I looked askance at Ellie's pitiful effort to roll a joint. It was lying on the coffee table. She had noticed my look and spoke up.

"It's not very good, is it?"

"We all have to roll our first joint."

"Well. I feel so much better about it now."

I laughed and recounted my first attempt at sixteen while rolling a new one. The joint had amounted to more paper than marijuana and was paraded around for laughs in front of a bunch of hipsters from the Sunset Strip.

"You don't know embarrassment," I said.

We both took a few tokes before I put the joint down and let it go out. Evening gathered around us. I tended to the fire once and closed the sliding doors. Ellie snuggled up against me when I sat down.

"There's something else you've wanted to tell me," I said. "But you stop each time the moment nears."

She nodded.

"How did you know?"

"I'm not sure. I felt something below the surface and took a wild stab."

"I suspect you're clairvoyant."

I shook my head.

Hardly. It's knowing a little. Listening. Probably caring, more than anything else. Also, I have a new aura to you because you're high."

"God, I am suddenly transported. The clarity is remarkable."

"And you see me symbolically."

"Yes, yes."

There was an explorative kiss and more searching of my eyes.

"Roger, I've known you for a very, very long time."

"I thought that same thing. The very first time we met in Santa Barbara."

"Did you? Were you on drugs then, too?"

I laughed and kissed her again.

"Why is it that you care so much, Roger?"

"Who knows? Some silly notion that it might make a difference."

"Not many men are bothered," she said.

"Nor women, it seems to me."

"That's a strange perception."

"It's the one I have."

She looked out the window in thought.

"You see, I have developed a little theory."

She turned back.

"About what happened today?" I said.

"Yes."

I nodded and waited.

"It seems we all have some traumatic event early on. One that we spend the remainder of our lives attempting to escape.

"Freud," I said.

"Well, yes. But rather than seeing it as a nuisance, we should see it as the path to our spiritual enlightenment. That what happens to us in life is symbolic of our very nature. The challenge we face is intrinsic to who we are and our spiritual destiny."

I nodded.

"Do you see what I mean?"

"Yes, you've gone nuts."

She shoved me playfully.

"I suppose you have no traumatic symbolism in your life."

"Actually, I have a phobia about going pee pee in front of other people." Ellie gently touched my face and searched my eyes. "I suspect because my father beat me in the bathroom when I was a kid."

She assured me with her hands.

"You're being serious, aren't you?"

"Yes. And I don't believe I've just told you that."

Darkness had entirely consumed the room now save for light from the fire, reminding me again of that stormy evening long ago, when I had waited for Derek at the cottage on Balboa Island and Ellie had arrived instead. The flames now illuminated Ellie's face in precisely the same manner. I pulled her close, my nose touching hers.

"That was very courageous of you. To speak of your fears."

"Actually, it's a relief. You have to wonder why we dread telling people about such things."

She pulled away.

"Roger," she said. "I suddenly see this wise man emanating from your being. Like this great, suffering bodhisattva."

I shook my head and turned aside, uncertain why her words made me feel uncomfortable. The pretense probably. Maybe in the next life, if I kept learning, but I was no Bodhisattva in this one.

"So, are you going to tell me what happened? Back in Mammoth?"

She seemed to tremble, unable to confess.

"Okay, let me guess. It's some trauma involving your father. When you were young."

"Do you know what?"

She spoke now in the voice of a young girl.

"No, young lady. But I want you to tell me."

She fell back onto the sofa.

"It was daddy. When he lost his leg to diabetes, I began to despise him because he was weak now and could no longer protect me. Then one hot summer day, he asked if I would go buy him some ice-cream. I told him no and ran away. When I came back that afternoon, he was dead."

Ellie fought back tears.

"You see, he left me before I could make up for my sin, so now I must protect myself from men so they can't punish me."

In the convoluted logic of our quantum mechanical sub-conscious mine, where up was down and black was white, this made perfect sense, but in everyday life, it was like being in a house of mirrors.

"What did you do when you learned he was dead?"

"I ran off into the woods. You see, that is how I learned to have complete control of the world. To run away."

There was something she had failed to acknowledge. I waited to see if she would come to this realization herself, and when it failed to materialize, I suggested we walk down to the village for dinner. After the meal we stopped for a bottle of Courvoisier and returned home in the snow. There was slipping and laughter and the stomping of feet at the front door. Ellie opened the brandy while I shed my clothes and rekindled the fire.

"To trust," I said, joining her on the sofa.

"To trust, Roger."

We toasted.

"Do you understand now why I have never been able to completely trust in men? The difference is, you didn't abandon me."

"But, Ellie, you abandoned your father, not the other way around."

She looked at me with her little girl face.

"You're making it happen again. You're taking your trust away."

"Because I questioned you?"

"Because you don't believe me."

"I thought it was about abandonment."

"No, it's about believing in me. You see, just when I needed you to defend me in Mammoth, you walked away."

"Because I had no interest in watching you fight with your ex-husband?"

"But how can I trust you when you abandon me at my most vulnerable moments?"

I rubbed my face with my hands, feeling confused and searching for some truth in her words.

"Arguing this is pointless, Ellie. You can change and make up words all you want, but it doesn't alter the facts. You are doing to men exactly what you think your father did to you. That's what I see."

"You fucker," she said.

Again, there were tears in her eyes. I reached to console her but she pushed me away.

"You're like every other man."

"No I'm not. I'm right here. But I won't confuse this convoluted nonsense with insight."

We sat apart in silence. I felt angry with her, yet close at the same time, the way someone might feel while strangling another person.

"I'm sorry," she said finally. "I'm reacting to forces that have little or nothing to do with you."

"Pretend I'm your father for a moment."

She looked at me, biting on a finger.

"Do you forgive me, Daddy?"

"I forgive you, sweetheart."

"I wanted to get you ice-cream."

"I know, and someday we'll have ice-cream together again. On a hot, summer day."

"I'm sorry, Daddy." She put her head on my shoulder and wept. "I'm so sorry."

After Ellie had cried well and long, she went into the bathroom and returned with a wooden box that contained her jewelry. She also brought along a small knife and used it to carve a figure on the inside lid of the box. It was a crude circle intersected by two sets of double lines, a rough cross that was more or less the primitive rendering of a human being. Ellie touched it and looked at me.

"This is my covenant," she said and looked back at the figure she had drawn. "This is the circle of fear which has surrounded and held me captive."

She traced the double lines again with one finger.

"This is me and the circle no longer imprisons me. It is no longer a circle of fear. It is the circle of life."

Aware that she was having a spiritual experience, I kept my mouth shut and watched. When her gaze returned, she pulled apart my robe then removed her own and set her body against mine. If she had spoken words to express her thoughts, they would have been simple. I want you to take me, please.

The fire snapped. Flames climbed from their fuel and the flickering shadows danced across our bodies in the pine-scented room. Then we were still, and the fire receded in measure to our slow caressing.

"I am your bride, Roger."

I looked into her eyes, not knowing what to say.

She put a finger to my lips.

"Ssshh. Don't worry. I said that for me. It's how I feel."

I kissed her.

"You are the loveliest of brides, Ellie.

"Thank you, Roger."

The dying embers of our fire glowed faintly in the darkness. I saw it had started to snow outside. My thoughts leapt forward to the morning and how the mountains would be tall above us and we would ski beneath a deep blue sky.

We had climbed a mountain that night, in what had been a great struggle, and it had taken us very high, but in life, such highs were usually followed by commensurate lows.

Ten

The next morning around ten, Ellie and I started on our way up the narrow winding road to the ski lodge. Back and forth we meandered for a mile or so, up and up, until we came upon a line of traffic. She pulled to a stop behind the last car and sat there tapping pleasantly on the steering wheel.

"Some fun," I said.

"Try humming."

"Ha ha."

She did hum. I rolled down my window to the cold, morning air and groused. The line snaked up the mountain road ahead of us, as far as the eye could see, and I hated waiting.

An hour later, Ellie was strolling out to relax on the lodge terrace. I went in search of the rental counter. She had all her own gear. I had nothing.

Already in a bad mood, I waded in among a sea of down parkas and sun goggles. Here and there, I came across a Bavarian poster boy in Lederhosen. I was conspicuous in my Levi's.

By the time I got back to Ellie, I was in the mood to whack someone. Ellie had a Danish and coffee in front of her.

"Well, are we all set there?"

I sat down.

"We? Like you suffered."

"There there, dear."

"Don't there there me."

"I thought one of us ought to be in a good mood."

I looked up at the mountain looming above us.

"It would be a terrible fall, wouldn't it?"

"Here, have some of my Danish," Ellie said quickly.

I took that and her coffee.

"Now promise you won't shove me off a ridge somewhere."

"I probably won't."

"All right, then give me back my coffee and Danish."

"No."

I grappled with her hands while consuming what remained of her Danish. She groused to see it gone.

"There there," I said.

This induced a tantrum. I stood in response and pulled on her hand.

"You're very good at that, by the way."

"Aren't I, though," she said proudly.

I marveled to see the little girl from the previous night entirely gone. How did she compartmentalize things so? I would have been in my Hamlet persona for weeks.

Soon enough, our skis dangled from a lift. Snowy peaks towered above us, encircled below by Alpine forest. The sky was cloudless. The air was as cold as a freezer.

At the top, Ellie and I quickly settled on an intermediate course that turned out to be a bit more ambitious than advertised. A field of moguls shunted you onto a final steep slope leading down to the lodge. Being yet of the 'direct shot' style of skiing, I had arrived at the base with ample time to watch Ellie crisscross her way down the course. She came to a stop with a spray of snow and pulled her goggles back, smiling.

"It's just beautiful, isn't it?"

"Yes," I said.

"Well, Roger, what do you say to the crest? Then we can have lunch upon our return."

I looked up at the mountain and back at Ellie.

"If we're still alive."

"Oh dear," she said, biting her fingernails.

"You're really serious? You want to go up there?"

"Sure, why not?"

I followed Ellie over to the gondola line. My eyes were drawn continuously up to the near vertical crest.

When it was our turn, we boarded the crowded car. The valley soon fell away.

I pointed towards the Sierras to the south.

"Looks like a miniature world."

"Not at all what the Donner party would have thought."

"No, not at all what the Donner party would have thought."

As usual, Ellie's historical insight had presented a whole new perspective.

I looked back to find the vertical crest looming over us. The gondola passed over it. Ellie and I disembarked and joined another line leading to the edge. One by one, those at the front of the line disappeared over the precipitous. Beyond the edge was all sky and darkness.

"How do propose to attack the course?" I asked Ellie as we inched forward.

"On my ass."

"Great. Nothing like a jolt of confidence from your partner."

"A last kiss then?"

Our lips met in the cold air.

"You realize I have no idea how to turn."

Ellie went into a brief dissertation on the subject.

"Well, if I can dig my skis in, I'll cut across to the left. If not, I'll see you at the hospital."

"You'll be fine," she assured me.

I doubted it. She pulled her goggles down. I pulled mine down and bravely went forward first.

I was airborne for several seconds before my skis caught. Once they did, I was hurtling down the slope at forty miles an hour and quickly gaining speed. Wind whistled in my ears. The abyss was rapidly approaching.

Terrified, I swerved wildly and somehow found myself traversing the slope in the opposite direction. Ellie was above me and had not yet made her first turn. A quick glance told me she was completely concentrated on her own efforts.

With the most challenging piece of the slope behind me, I was able to relax ever so slightly. A line of shadow from the mountain passed over me. The crest was gilded with sunlight against the darkness. Powdered snow crystals swirled along the edge.

When a level spot presented itself, I slowed my momentum and stopped entirely. The swirling crystals continued to dance in the sun, high on the mountain crest. I saw Ellie approaching as a distant speck. Then I heard her skis. She pulled up twenty feet short and pushed her way over to me.

"Look at the mountain," I said. We both stared up in silence. "Wouldn't this be a lovely place to make love?"

"A kiss will have to do for now," she said.

We stood there, our noses and cheeks frozen but our lips warm and lost in passion. We pulled away as another skier went flying by us. We laughed at the sight of him flying down the hill so fast.

"How about lunch, then?" I said.

"Sure."

She pushed away down the mountain. I watched until she had become quite small and followed down towards the lodge in my own wild, hair-raising manner of skiing.

Over lunch, we reviewed a map and agreed on a more intermediate lift. That took us over to the backside of the mountain and eventually to a wooded cross-country trail. Given the great seclusion, we stopped numerous times to talk and laugh and it was getting on towards four in the afternoon by the time we slalomed down the last easy run to the lodge.

Back at our chalet, with the sun behind the mountain, we played like two children in the bathtub and were all pink and wrinkled as we finally toweled off. In the growing ink of dusk, we made love and lay a long time touching and kissing.

Then the world was back.

"I have a wonderful appetite now," I said.

"It's all the exercise and clean mountain air," Ellie said.

"I don't why, but Jack LaLanne just came to mind."

"Roger, you absolutely must put this curious acumen of yours to good use."

She got out of bed and left the room.

"How about a bit of gambling after the meal!?"

"No shouting, remember?"

Ellie peeked in at me.

"Yeah, ol' big mouth here, never to be the refined."

"Oh stop," she said and disappeared again.

I got dressed, ready to walk home again.

Over dinner Ellie could tell something was wrong but I refused to discuss it.

Later, at the blackjack table, we hit a winning streak. Then I lost my last fifty bucks. A portly middle-aged rancher and his chatty wife saluted us with their highball glasses as we left. He was busy signing for another stack of chips. The two of them had already dropped most of five grand. I was fretting over fifty dollars

When Ellie suggested a late sandwich at the hotel bar, I claimed fatigue and we drove back to the chalet in continued silence.

"What on earth is bothering you?" she asked but I still refused to discuss things.

Ellie went off to bed alone. I sat up and watched a late-night movie.

In the morning, Ellie packed and went on about things as if all was normal. She gassed up and we stopped for ham and eggs at the outskirts of town. It was getting on towards eleven before we finally started down the winding mountain road. Five miles on, we found the highway had been blocked for repairs. After a few hours of inching down the mountain and a long drive through the smog-filled Central Valley, I was ready for knives again. We reached San Francisco with a whole day of frustration piled up on top of my original resentment.

We checked into a quaint hotel downtown and took a trolley over to Fisherman's Wharf. A stiff wind had etched the bay into fine detail. Nob Hill stood out like a jigsaw puzzle against the winter sky. Ellie and I stuffed ourselves on pasta and hard crust bread. The whole time, I was still plotting in my head.

After the meal, Ellie made me huddle with her on a bench against the cold wind. People hurried by this way and that in the fading twilight.

"It's the holidays," she reminded me.

"Oh. Is that why all the lights."

"Yes, it's a thing we celebrate here in America. You know, if you set aside all the commercial claptrap, and the way we've turned it into a giant rip off, it's rather a quaint tradition."

When I had failed to laugh or speak or display any sort of affection, Ellie spoke up.

"All right, Roger. One more time. What on earth is wrong with you?"

She waited.

"Just trying to keep my big mouth shut," I said at last.

Ellie stared incredulously at me and then threw up her hands.

"I don't believe it. All this over my little comment?"

"It wasn't so little to me."

Seeing I was serious, she threw up her hands again.

"My god, I was only kidding."

I shrugged in response. Finally, Ellie pretended to be a pouting child herself. I tried not to smile but did, which made me even madder. Ellie tried sobbing next.

"I hate you," I said.

"Okay," she said. "But what do you say we head up to Mendocino tomorrow. You can burn me at the stake once we get there…Aw come on," she said when I had not responded. "Please let go of it."

"I'll still hate you.

"All right. But would a smile be too much to ask?"

I offered her a cheerless smile.

"Oh yes, that's much better."

She jousted with me playfully and I again reluctantly smiled.

"Please, I didn't mean to hurt you, Roger."

She kissed me until I relented.

"There, there," she said. "It's all right now. You see? It's disappeared in the wink of an eye."

I looked out at the bay.

"Well, not quite the wink of an eye."

Ellie chuckled and shook me playfully again.

"But it's better, right?"

"Yeah, it's better."

She pulled my face around and kissed my lips tenderly.

"I love you."

"I love you too."

We both went back to watching the sights.

"Mendocino should be fun," Ellie said sometime later. "Quite abandoned, I imagine at this time of year."

"Like, whatever, man," I said. "It's like do your own thing." I turned to Ellie." I have more unctuous sixties' platitudes if you'd like to hear them."

She smiled.

"Shall we go, then?"

"All right."

"Well, while I've got you in the habit of saying all right, please promise you'll go with me on my sabbatical next year. We'll have a grand time together in Europe."

"All right."

She kissed me.

"Believe me, Roger. I am sorry. I never meant to hurt you."

"All right."

We got up and walked.

After a number of paces, Ellie stopped and pressed her body against my mine.

"I feel we're so lucky to have found each other and to share this harmony between our two spirits. I wonder what makes it so real?"

"I don't know…"

I stared with the words caught in my throat. If only we hadn't been born twenty years apart. I would have married Ellie in a heartbeat. But as things were, we were doomed…

We strolled on with the ending I dared not speak haunting my heart. Someday, somehow, it would be over.

Back at the hotel, I disengaged from Ellie as the doorman pulled the glass door aside for us. She talked of going to Europe the next summer as we crossed the lobby. The elevator doors opened and closed with the secret still working in my mind. Ellie leaned up tightly against me.

"What are you thinking?" she said.

"Oh, nothing."

"Do you know what I'm thinking?"

"No."

"I'm picturing myself in a white dress with flowers in my hair. In Provence on a summer afternoon."

"I'm sure you will be very beautiful."

The elevator stopped at the floor before ours. The doors opened and a middle-aged couple got on. The man smiled and looked down. His wife stared.

"Going up?" I said.

"No, down," the man said.

The elevator climbed one floor and Ellie and I got off. The wife spoke before the doors had completely closed behind us.

"God, did you see that woman making a fool of herself…"

Ellie commented wryly about the old bag needing to get laid. We smiled and kissed and searched each other's eyes. So many thoughts, suddenly, that I was forced to keep to myself.

Eleven

The following morning, I awakened at dawn. Ellie still slept. I pulled on my robe and went to sit alone by the windows. The city of San Francisco lay submerged in a blanket of fog. It was the image of calm. My heart was anything but…

I glanced in Ellie's direction and considered the choice before me; honesty and purity, or continuing to hide my thoughts. It was one or the other. No matter how much I adored Ellie, no matter the indisputable magic between our two souls, our love affair would never possess the innocence I longed to experience with a woman my own age, where love felt timeless, where you did not know the ending before the beginning.

But what was I to do? Break the news to Ellie and catch a bus back home? I glanced that way again. The last thing I wanted was to hurt her. Best for all concerned if I forswore any confessions until the trip was over. We'll just limp along and do our best to enjoy things. A few Bloody Mary's for breakfast and take it from there. That was the best I had to offer.

Oblivious to my thoughts, Ellie smiled upon awakening, waved me over to the bed seductively, looked up with her kittenish face and parted my robe. I closed my eyes as she took my cock in her mouth, unable to ignore those subtle signs of aging on her face now.

When she was done pleasing me, I insisted on returning the favor. She went off to shower afterwards looking blissful. I called room service and ordered that Bloody Mary.

A bit later, the two of us were packed and back on the road. Our path north out of town led us through Haight Ashbury. I was further depressed by the state of the deteriorating Victorian buildings.

Ellie glanced over at me.

"After all the hoopla about it over the years, I didn't expect it to be so seedy looking."

"I don't remember it looking this bad. Must have been all the drugs."

Ellie laughed.

"Well, there you have it. We'll just have to light up one of those joints."

I looked back out on the decrepit neighborhood, knowing it wouldn't look all that good now, no matter how much drugs I took. How depressing, to see the magic of my youth had come to this.

A short while later, we passed over the Golden Gate Bridge, the sun came out over the green hills of Marin County and our conversation grew brighter. That lasted until we drove down to the coast and the day grew gray and dreary again. The hills disappeared into an overcast sky above us and into a sea mist below us.

Around midmorning, Ellie pulled to the side of the road and asked me to drive. It had remained a cold and cheerless day.

"I expect this will clear up farther north," she said.

"I doubt it...Not that I'm whining."

"It sounds like it to me."

"Actually, it's grousing and the two should not be confused. I'm not expecting anything to change as a result."

"You're making this up."

"Well, maybe winging it a bit. To me, grousing is an art. It's done for the sheer pleasure of it."

Ellie eyed me suspiciously and spread out a map on her lap.

"Well, then, getting back to reality."

I reached over and tickled her thighs until she begged me to stop. I did but drummed my fingers ominously on the steering wheel. Ellie went back to her map with wary glances my way.

"Promise you won't start again."

"All right, I promise. So what's on the agenda?"

"I was looking for Sea Ranch."

"Sea Ranch? What's that?"

"A development. One of my colleagues tried to interest me in a property there a few years back."

I watched her neatly refold the map.

"So?"

"It wasn't on the map."

"Perhaps there'll be a billboard along the road."

"Yes, of course. Sea Ranch Deluxe. Come escape the smog and rat race."

I darted a look at her.

"It would be nice to move up north," she went on. "Once I retire."

"And that would be…when?"

"Next week," she said and smiled at her little joke. "Actually, I have a great deal of latitude. In five years, I could live comfortably. The retirement goes up the longer I hang in there."

"Then what?"

"Why, politics, of course," she said with a laugh. "You see, Americans are always jumping from one thing to the next. Never a moment for reflection."

My mind had halted at the thought of five years in the future. Where would I be? Not with Ellie. I glanced over at her, knowing I had harbored another little secret. They were accumulating fast.

The road kept winding back and forth along the coast. The immediate shoreline had cleared but the hills to our right were still shrouded in a mist. Sometime around noon we saw a wooden sign for Sea Ranch.

"Shall I pull in?"

"Of course," Ellie said. "No doubt there's a huckster sales agent drumming his fingers right about now, just waiting for a couple of suckers to stumble in."

I turned left under the sign and quickly right onto a dirt road that paralleled the highway. A split rail fence separated the two. A plateau sloped gently down towards the sea on our left, carpeted with wild grass and dotted here and there with homes, each of them Frank Lloyd Wright looking. You could smell the money.

Arriving at another dirt road, I turned left and shortly came to a cliff. The sea was far below us.

"Which way?" I said and inched forward in the direction of the cliff.

"Not that way!" Ellie said.

I inched forward again and Ellie braced her hands against the dashboard in terror.

"All right " I said and backed up to the crossroad. "Which way now?"

"Why don't we continue on this dirt road," she said. "There must be some sort of sales office up ahead."

There wasn't. We stopped at two houses on our way back but no one answered. Fifteen minutes later we were back at the highway.

"So?" I said.

Ellie took hold of my manhood.

"Another blow job?"

"Don't tempt me."

She leaned over but became frustrated by the gearshift knob.

"You see. That's what was so wonderful about the old comfort cars."

"I can see the ads. 'The car of your dreams. Luxuriously appointed and built to provide the finest fellatio this side of Texas'."

"Gee, I don't remember ever seeing ads like that."

"They come on very late at night."

"I see."

A truck went by on the highway. Then it was quiet again.

"Why don't we go search for the sun."

"All right," Ellie said.

We passed Gualala a short time later then came across Anchor Bay. Ellie reopened her neatly folded map. The sky was starting to break through the swirling filaments above us.

"Roger, can you stop at that little market. I'm famished."

I pulled off the highway and parked.

"Are we having lunch or just nibbling?"

"I suppose a piece of beef jerky will do for now."

"And a beer."

"Sure, why not?"

I gassed up while she was in the market. Heading north, the beef jerky was soon gone but we had our beer and our bantering. And I had my secrets.

Somewhere past Point Arena the heavens cleared and the sky was at last brilliantly blue above the hills. Old farmhouses and weathered barns dotted the inland side of the highway. I braked near one of them, my bladder ready to burst.

While I relieved myself behind a clump of pine trees, a flock of sheep passed through a gate in a nearby barbed wire fence but one of the lambs got separated from its mother in the process. The two of them stood there bleating at each other with the opening a mere ten feet away. Eventually, the mother moved away with the flock, leaving the lamb to frustrate itself against the barbed wire. I looked back at Ellie. She threw up her hands. I went around and guided the lamb through before returning to the car.

"They are so stupid," Ellie said when I got in.

"I suppose that's why they have shepherds."

"Well, yes, and there you are, the swinging shepherd."

"Ha ha. Anyway, I couldn't stand to see the poor thing frustrate itself."

"No doubt."

"It's not my fault you can't piss against a tree."

"No, but you're a convenient scapegoat."

"Headline. Woman strangled in a Mendocino hotel."

"You wouldn't."

I shrugged.

"You would."

I shrugged again.

"I'll cut you off."

I chuckled. Then, in the silence that followed, I remembered my secrets. We motored on through the mostly unpopulated coastline with our separate thoughts.

Later that afternoon, we arrived to the town of Mendocino.

"Haight-Ashbury North," I said.

The town was a hodgepodge of Craftsman and Victorian structures, a great many of them dilapidated, and of those that weren't, most had been painted up in the gaudy colors. Ellie pointed at a modest looking hotel along the main street. It was painted purple."

"There," she said.

"Hitchcock on acid."

"I'm leaving a sealed note with the night clerk."

"I suspect he's on acid too."

We got out and climbed the wooden stairs to the lobby. An anemic-looking young woman in granny-glasses appeared from the back room at the sound of the bell over the door. She had bushy brown hair and a pita bread sandwich in one of her hands. She licked her fingers while offering us the guest book.

"Welcome to Mendocino. Earth capital of the world."

Ellie found the whole thing charming and struck up a conversation. I carried the bags upstairs while she paid for the room.

"Earth capital of the world," I muttered when Ellie entered the room.

"I like her," she said and started to undress.

"I would have too. Back in the sixties. On a lot of drugs."

"She was very helpful."

"And has no doubt guided us to the best pita bread and garbanzo stew joint in town."

"When on earth did you become so cynical, Roger?"

"Back in the sixties."

"Be serious."

"I am...No, it's what's happened since the sixties. What happened to the sixties. So much hope. Then they shot everybody and we ended up with Nixon. How depressing can it get?"

"Well, the bastard will probably be voted out of office next year, so not to worry."

"Are you kidding? Kennedy doesn't have the balls to run after Chappaquiddick and what's left are a bunch of has beens, party hacks and good old boys from the south."

"There's Muskie."

"Yeah. Which rhymes with musty."

Ellie laughed.

"Well, you don't elect a name."

"Come on. When have we ever elected someone with a name like that? You want a Harrison, a Madison, a Jackson. Not a Muskie."

Ellie threw up her hands.

"So we're doomed."

"Probably...Don't get me wrong. People like Muskie and McGovern are good men. And they'd probably make good presidents but they'll never get elected. Not in this day and age. It's like we're not ready to elect a Goldstein. I'll bet my right arm we're stuck with another four years of Nixon...We may as well go get that garbanzo stew."

Ellie smiled cautiously.

"Mind if I take a bath first?"

"No, go right ahead."

She was naked save for her bra and panties and stopped in the doorway for a cheesecake pose.

"Care to join me?"

Before long, I had her bent over the lion claw bathtub, savaging the bones of her sweet little cunt.

"Oh, fuck, it's so good," I said as I came.

We undulated together for a long minute before Ellie turned to face me.

"Take that, Nixon," I said as we kissed.

I got Ellie up on the vanity with my face between her legs. When she came, I had to hold my hand over her mouth to keep her from awakening the entire hotel.

When we were done, she ran the water and we took a bath together. Ellie sat with her back to my chest.

"Am I an old woman to you?" she said.

"Oh, Ellie. Let's not ruin everything because some jealous twat from Torrance made a comment?"

"You remembered what she said, though, didn't you?"

"So? That old battle ax is probably looking in a mirror right now, wishing she was you.

She turned to look at me.

"But I am old and you will leave me someday. It's inevitable, Roger."

"Ellie. We've already been through this. We have today. Isn't that what we agreed?"

I pulled her hair back and kissed her neck.

"That's why my husband left me," she said.

"What do you mean?"

"I wasn't young enough for him anymore. I stumbled across him in the parking lot of a local supermarket one day."

She looked over her shoulder again.

"In our white Porsche…Necking with a younger woman."

"Bummer…So? Did you confront him?"

"In a manner of speaking, yes."

She turned away. I waited for her to go on. Finally, she looked back again.

"I parked our Continental some distance away and waited until Dick noticed me. It gave me a pretty good running start."

"You didn't."

"I did. The Continental came to rest on top of the Porsche."

"With them in it?"

"Oh, no. They had scrambled to safety by then."

I shook my head.

"*Scrambled* somehow doesn't do it justice."

"I can't think of a better word."

I soaped Ellie's back.

"You haven't answered me," she said.

"I did. We have today. Right now. That's what we agreed."

"Why can't you just be honest?"

"Ellie! What do you want to know? How our love affair is going to end."

"So you admit it."

"Goddamn it! You're the one who told me to accept that fact, lo those many years ago."

"It was a month ago."

"Fuck! You're just being devious now."

Ellie soaped her legs in silence. When I saw her dainty toes with the red nail polish peeking through the soapy water, I started to get another erection. Ellie felt it and took me in her hand.

"Is this all there is?"

"Well, it's a large part of any romance, isn't it?"

"All right, come on. Let's do it again."

She got on her hands and knees and looked over her shoulder.

"Come on. Fuck me."

I did. I fucked her hard and good but when I went to towel her off, she fought with me. So much silliness on a blustery day in Mendocino and nothing you could do about it.

Later, lying in the bed all pink and freshly bathed, Ellie apologized.

"For what?"

"Fighting with you."

"It scares me when you lose control like that."

"It scares me too, Roger. I don't seem to have any control in those moments."

I comforted her with caresses and we were quiet. Then I sat up suddenly.

"What?" she said.

"I just had this vision."

"Tell me."

"It's that men experience their emotions as smaller than they are and women experience them as larger. To men, feelings are a nuisance, but to a woman, it's as though she's being attacked by some great beast."

Like all revelations, it sounded far less significant when expressed openly, yet Ellie seemed duly impressed.

"You are wonderfully wise and smart," she said.

I shook my head.

"No. Men who build rocket ships are smart. Men who are wise, I don't know what they do but I'm not either of those."

She waited for me to elaborate, and when I did not, she spoke.

"I forgive you for leaving me, Roger. I know you will someday. I know that you have thought about it."

"Oh Ellie. I wish we didn't have to have this conversation."

She brushed away tears and before long we were asleep in each other's arms.

At dusk, I awakened and lay there for some time with Ellie still in my arms.

"Have you been awake long?" she said when our eyes met.

"No."

She was on her knees suddenly.

"Roger, I want you to do something."

She pulled on my arm and dragged me into the bathroom.

"Now, go pee pee," she said.

"I don't do it on command."

"Please? Just try."

Reluctantly, I stood with Ellie behind me and my penis in her hand.

"It's taking a long time," she said.

"Saying that won't help."

"Okay. I don't want to hurt you, Roger."

She began to talk about her own fears and suddenly I was peeing.

"I feel the stream running through my fingers."

It stopped.

"Oh, sorry."

A moment later it started again. When I was done, she shook me gently and then came around to place her head against my chest.

"I feel so close to you now," she said.

"Maybe because we have done away with one of my secrets."

She studied my eyes for a moment, then stood on her tiptoes and kissed my lips. I went back to bed and heard the sound of the shower running through the bathroom door. Ellie returned wearing a short robe.

"Did you want to shower with me?"

"No, I'm fine. I'll go out looking like I slept on a park bench."

She smiled and disappeared. When she reappeared, she turned on a small night lamp, sat on the bed and dressed as if I wasn't there. I leaned over and kissed her back once and got up to dress.

Down in the lobby a short while later, the owner offered her opinion about local restaurants and Ellie politely thanked her. Out on the street, we were met with a near gale force wind. I half expected to see signs and clapboard siding fly down the street. I held out my arms and pretended to be swept away.

"I like this town," Ellie said when I caught up with her. "The shops and the people are so quaint."

"That's what happens to hippies when they grow old. They go off somewhere and become quaint."

Ellie poo pooed my comment on her way into a tea and boutique shop. I followed, glad to be out of the cold and gale force winds. A pot belly stove glowed with its fire in one corner. I sat down to warm my hands. The place was cheery with the scents of evergreen and holiday spices.

While Ellie poked around among all the clothing and hats, the female proprietor appeared from in back and my heart stopped. It was Ellie, twenty years earlier. I smiled when our eyes met and got back to warming my hands, not wanting to admit that I was with an older woman, or that I had been completely swept away.

The owner and Ellie were soon chatting. At one point in their conversation, Ellie smiled my way, as if to include me. I smiled back and looked away.

Yeah, okay. I am with that older woman.

I was relieved to be back out to the street.

"You know," Ellie said. "I would love to do a class together about your generation."

My mind was elsewhere. Visions of that woman kept on haunting me.

"Did you hear me?" Ellie said.

"Yeah, yeah. We'll call it, 'They came. They saw. They ran for cover'."

Ellie laughed robustly.

"But the idea of working together," she said. "That's what I'd like to do during my sabbatical."

"Sure," I said.

The remainder of the day passed by with me still haunted.

Ellie and I had a fine meal and made an early evening of it and arose early the following morning to have breakfast in a converted Victorian home. Afterwards, we walked down to the sea. The tide was low and the wide shoreline went off for miles in both directions, with driftwood gathered in great haphazard piles along the adjacent bluffs. We saw another couple a mile or so south down the shore and that was it.

Ellie and I rolled up our pants and waded through the cold surf in the other direction. Breakers crashed for miles ahead of us. Gulls came down the coast swiftly at our faces, chased by the wind. Others came up from behind us in a tacking maneuver, seemingly suspended in time above our heads.

Farther up the coast, we found a driftwood shanty made by some previous vacationers and cuddled close together in the lee of it. I closed my eyes and enjoyed the wind whispering in the driftwood. Life seemed simple when I kept to what was right in front of me but the other things in my mind would not turn off.

When the gray clouds of an approaching storm overtook the sunshine, we walked back to town. The sun never came out again that day and the other woman would not go away.

Ellie resumed her exploration of shops along the main street. Feeling restless with it all, I waited outside and made note of everyone who came and went from the tea shop. I spent all day trying to rid my mind of that woman's beauty, but failed. In the background, signs rattled in the wind.

Ellie and I had lunch, then dinner, and made love in between. Then it was to bed early again with our books.

"I really like this idea of our working together," Ellie said, putting hers down.

She was reading a biography of Thomas Paine. I was reading a Simenon.

"Hmm hmm," I said without looking up from mine.

"Are you bored, dear?"

I closed the book with a snap.

"Probably. It's not you."

"Thank you for saying that."

"I didn't think it possible, but I must be growing bored with the Irish side of me. I want the sun to come out."

"Then let's go over the mountain. Do a little wine tasting in the Sonoma valley."

"Perhaps go down to Big Sur."

"Forget the wine tasting?"

"No, no. I like your idea. We'll go over the mountain. Then stop here and there on our way south."

"Did you have a particular place in mind there?"

"As a matter of fact, yes. I know of some cabins in a state park. I've stayed there before."

"Was this alone, my errant prince?"

"Oh, Ellie."

"Relax Roger. I'm only having fun."

"Sure."

"You know it will be Christmas," she said.

"Yes. I've almost lost track."

"Today is the 23rd. Tomorrow will be Christmas Eve. Perhaps we should call ahead and reserve something."

"Okay."

"So, tell me. How did you find this place?"

"I was on my way through Big Sur with some friends one night. It was late and we stopped at the park to see about a campsite. The ranger told us he had a cabin available. It was off in the woods and nicely secluded. And came with a bundle of firewood for the pot belly stove."

"How nice."

"Yeah."

"Can we get down to the sea from there?"

"Yeah, nearby. There's a path and a little cove."

"It sounds romantic. A fire and some champagne for Christmas?"

"Just you and me and lots of champagne, kid."

She caressed my head.

"That's fine. I'm just content to be with you."

I kept thinking of Ellie's words while reading my Simenon. Champagne and two lovers and a warm cabin on Christmas Eve. It did sound lovely, only, that younger woman was there

142

in my dreams. Meanwhile, Maigret was busy catching scoundrels and thieves.

It rained that night and the sky was still gray when we started over the coastal range with two coffees the next morning. The country road meandered through the woods of elm and maple and we saw little traffic from either direction.

Near the crest I pulled over and parked under a tree. The sun had peeked out from behind the clouds and felt warm on my skin.

"It's the coffee," I said, getting out of the car.

"Well, I'm prepared to forego my modesty," Ellie said.

She joined me for a short walk into the woods. I stood next to a tree. Ellie squatted under her dress and smiled. Bright sunlight speckled the dim undergrowth.

"Rather puts you in your place, doesn't it?" I said.

"Funny," she said.

I heard the splatter beneath her and the brush glowed yellow when she stepped aside.

"What happened to your phobia?" she asked once we were on our way.

"I hadn't thought about it."

"Maybe that's the key."

I started the car and drove away.

"Yes. Funny but I just remembered Alan Watts discussing that very subject in *The Art of Zen*. The key was to be in a state of 'no thought'. Our fears were mostly engrained habit."

We entered into a deeper discussion of eastern versus western philosophy and were coasting down into the wine country before we knew it. The bare soil was dark, the sky ashen, the vineyards and countryside looking abandoned with winter.

We stopped several times to taste wines, always in warm, cheery rooms that we mostly had to ourselves. The proprietors provided us with much attention and samples, so that by the end of the day, we had a substantial collection of wines and sherry and champagne, and had lost all sense of planning and preparation along the way. It was fortunate we had called ahead for reservations.

After a pleasant lunch, we passed through the Bay area and did not stop again until we reached the fruit and vegetable stands at the northern edge of the Salinas Valley. With a bag of apples and some cheese added to our wine cellar, we crossed over to Monterey and started down Highway 1. Near dusk, we arrived to the state park and pulled to a stop at the ranger's post. He checked us in, gave us a set of keys and assured us that an abundant supply of firewood awaited in the cabin. We could also find ice in the nearby ice machine. We wished him a merry Christmas and followed the road through the woods to our lodging. I opened the door and stood back for Ellie.

"Very nice, Roger."

I brought the bags in while Ellie inspected the premises.

"How wonderful," she said from the bathroom.

She stuck her head through the open door.

"I'm going to take a bath. You don't mind, do you?"

"Of course not. I'll get things organized and put the champagne on ice."

I walked down to the ice machine and filled our cardboard box, retrieved a selection of champagne and wine from the car, pushed the bottles down into their temporary headquarters and stopped a brief moment to enjoy the end of day on the porch.

A chill came with dusk. Wind whispered high up in the pines and the forest seemed enchanted. Later, I went in to start a fire and joined Ellie in the tub.

"Ho ho ho."

"Merry Christmas," she said and splashed playfully.

"Strange somehow, not having a tree and all that."

"Screw it," she said.

"Okay. It's wonderful not having a tree and all that."

"You see. My every Christmas was spent fretting over whether or not everyone else was happy."

"Yes, yes. You've complained about it liberally."

I laughed at her sour face.

"Well, no one ever bothered to ask if I was happy."

"I'm gathering you weren't."

"Oh my, yes. This great frenzy of wrapping paper, and poof, nothing but the credit card bills to pay."

"The Scrooges on vacation."

She reached underwater to grab my thing and water was splashed in the ensuing struggle.

"Well, there. All this skirmishing has given me an appetite."

"I noticed a restaurant overlooking the cliffs a few miles back. It looked enchanting."

"Of course, we won't consider where I'd like to eat."

"In your room, if you keep it up."

Ellie played the spoiled child.

"Honestly, I'm quite happy to have dinner and come back here with you. That is the whole point of my diatribe! I don't have to perform for the world! I get to do what I want!"

"Indulge in lascivious sex."

"Lots and lots of lascivious sex."

"I'm envious, you know."

"That you can't cum repeatedly?"

"Well, not as repeatedly."

Ellie extended one leg in the air, admiring it.

"And here I fancied you were just content to get your rocks off, like all men."

"Oh yeah, that's me, Ellie. Go get 'em, Cobra."

The leg came down and her arms encircled her knees.

"Oh dear. I'm always stunned by how you remember such things."

"The point is, there are reasons to be envious either way."

"Well, your suffering aside, you don't mind me taking advantage, do you?"

"No, not at all. But let's eat first."

I finished rinsing off the soap and stood up. Ellie watched me with a finger to her lips.

"Not even a little snack?" she said.

I laughed and went to get dressed.

Over a checkered tablecloth and sparkling glasses of good wine, our playful discussion continued. The mood was festive among the refugee clientele, each reveler there in flight from some sort of holiday routine.

Ellie and I stopped in front after our meal and chatted with a local artist and his wife, mostly about the passing of a decade, an era filled with change in which this very stretch of coastline had played a major role. But all of that had long ago whispered away with the wind.

"A few less hitchhikers," the artist surmised in the end.

We said adieu but feelings of regret followed me. Momentous events had colored my early life, the many memories now darkened by a sense that we had failed somehow.

Ellie disappeared into the bathroom upon our return to the cabin. I went out to the porch and fished through the ice chest for a bottle of champagne. The smell the pines followed me back inside. I rekindled the fire and waited.

The bathroom light went out and Ellie slipped through the door wearing a pink chamois. She sat on my lap. I revealed her present from behind the seat. She carefully untied the ribbon, removed the wrapping paper and held aloft one of the strapless slippers. I fingered the fluffy ball adorning the toe.

"Where on earth did you find these?"

"I saw them in San Francisco. I called when you were in the shower and had them sent over."

She placed the pair on her feet and stood up. After a brief parade before the mirror, she returned and placed one foot on the chair. I admired the calf, the delicate ankle, the red toenails exquisitely revealed.

"I noticed the others you had were wearing out."

"Roger, you're a doll."

"And, now, to eat you alive," I said and kissed her ankle. She sat crosswise on my lap and our lips met.

"Did you want to open your present first?" she asked.

I nodded and accepted her little box. It was a watch I had admired.

"You're very thoughtful."

"Do you like it?"

"Yes, very much. Thank you."

I tried it on and we kissed some more.

"Now," she said. "Shall we retire to the bearskin rug?"

"That's a lovely image."

I uncorked a bottle and poured our glasses full.

"Cheers."

Following the ting of glasses, we drank and were quiet.

"Listen to the wind," I said.

The trees whispered and rustled against the cabin roof. Time passed.

"You know, Roger. I often wonder what it feels like to be a man."

"It's like being plugged into the universe with your pecker."

She laughed and laughed.

My hand went to where her bone was hard beneath the silk cloth.

"This makes my heart ache," I said, pressing on the bone firmly. She held my swollen organ in return.

"Only your heart?"

"No, both of them. They are connected somehow."

"I want to thank you for pleasing me," she said.

"You taught me that. Strange that a man could satisfy himself and never fulfill a woman."

"Not many men know that."

"I suspect not. Not by the ongoing battle. Then again, how many women know what you know?"

"Well, I wasn't about to be satisfied with anything less."

"Well, here's to being duly dissatisfied."

"Cheers," she said.

We had our little toast and kissed again. There remained a half empty bottle of champagne on the coffee table when I carried Ellie off to bed, her slippers still dangling from her delicate little feet. Once in the night I awakened and tended to the fire. Ellie slept peacefully without waking.

In the morning I went for a walk alone. My thoughts were of how happy and at peace I was with Ellie. So why give in to temptation? I had no answers. I only knew that I could not get that young woman's beauty out of my mind.

Ellie discovered me on the porch with a glass of champagne a short while later.

"Well, Merry Christmas," she said groggily.

"Ho ho ho."

I made her comfortable next to me. It was shady by the cabin but we could see sunlight on a ridge high across the highway.

"What would you like to do today, Roger?"

"Why don't we start down Highway 1 and see where it leads us."

"That sounds fine. We can stop wherever it strikes our fancy."

"I'd like to go fishing," I added.

"Oh?"

We laughed.

"Honestly, there's a good sport fishing fleet in Morro Bay. I expect you'd come along. How are you at cleaning fish, by the way?"

"Miserable."

"Good. That was part of the test."

"Oh."

"Well, shall we start off?" I said.

"I'd like a glass of that champagne first.

"Sure."

Blushing from a few glasses of it, we soon found ourselves back in bed.

That afternoon, as we started south, I spotted the field where my friends and I had walked down to the sea some years earlier. Ellie joined me on a trek down to the nearby cliffs. Below, the bones of old trees were scattered on the empty shore, just as I had remembered it, but the feelings were not the same. Life only went forward.

Eventually, we walked back to the car and motored along for miles in silence. Later, I found myself consumed with itching.

"I've been feeling the same thing," Ellie said.

"Perhaps there were mosquitoes last night."

"In winter?"

"No, I suppose not."

The itching grew more unbearable with each passing mile. Finally, I pulled to the side of the road, went around to Ellie's side of the car and exposed my genitals. They were inflamed with a milky rash.

"Jesus, Roger."

An image from the previous day suddenly flashed through my mind.

"Ellie."

"What Roger?"

"When you squatted down to take a leak yesterday. Coming over the mountain."

"Oh Christ. Poison oak. It's everywhere."

"Everywhere."

I scratched violently another time and pulled up my pants.

"Home," I said and hurried back into the car.

At Morro Bay we stopped for calamine lotion. Jokes followed, about sex and itching, but the humor faded with each passing mile. Finally, Ellie shrunk into herself and was silent. When it came to scratching a certain part of her anatomy, her hands were somewhat tied.

Her misery was complete by the time we had pulled into the driveway. I helped her into the house and drew a bath. The car could wait. The twins were gone for another week. At least we had privacy. Somewhere in that knowledge, four bottles of Calamine lotion, two fifths of good booze and a lot of sex, we figured to find some measure of comfort.

Twelve

The next forty-eight hours became a liturgy of laughter, tears, swear words and sex, the sex necessitated by its therapeutic value to Ellie if nothing else. Given the nature of a woman's anatomy, and the need to scratch, it was sex or a dildo and Ellie had made it quite clear early on which way that was going to go. We used calamine lotion abundantly, drank lots of eggnog and rum, ate sandwiches in bed, watched a number of good and bad movies and I got to know a great deal more about Dick Bogarde than I had ever really wanted.

On the fourth morning, I served the still suffering Ellie an omelet in bed, watched her dig into preparations for her new semester and grew depressed to think our jolly little ordeal was nearly over. The rashes had begun to scab. The jokes had grown stale. It was time for me to go look for a job.

Still lacking any direction in that regard, and reluctant to abandon our hideaway, I whipped up a fresh batch of brandy eggnogs that afternoon. Ellie, who was still in bed with her books and notepads, feigned humor at the sight of another drink but was clearly disconcerted.

"It's nearly New Year's Eve," I said by way of justifying the enterprise.

Ellie sighed heavily.

"No? You don't want it?"

"I must get some work done, Roger."

"Okay."

I started to leave.

"Come here," she said.

I went back over to the bed. She waved with her finger and gave me a kiss.

"Why don't you get the classified section out? See if there's something there in the way of employment."

"Yeah, you're right."

I left with the drinks, downed both of them in fairly rapid succession out in the kitchen and brooded a bit.

"I'm heading home," I told Ellie back in her bedroom.

"Well, you needn't go off and pout."

"Thanks. You know what, I'll just see you later."

I quickly gathered up my things and gave Ellie a perfunctory kiss on the way out the door.

The solitude of my cottage was a welcome sight upon arriving home. I opened a fresh bottle of brandy first thing, poured a glass full and sat at my desk. I was making a career out of daydreams, drinking and poverty, but so what. I looked forward to an irreverent evening of contemplation and writing. To hell with Ellie. I hated it when she acted like my Mom.

Sometime well past midnight, I fell asleep. In the wee hours before dawn, I was awakened again by a wind storm blowing out of the desert. The windows shook. The stacks on the roof rattled. I sat up, still half asleep and my heart racing.

Realizing it was only the wind, I turned over and tried to sleep again but could not and rolled a fresh piece of paper into my typewriter. My differences with Ellie haunted me. The wind seemed to be speaking of the distance between our two hearts. I sat there listening and typing and attempting to cleanse all the crap from my soul for several hours.

Wind Before Dawn

The desert wind, a hundred foot tall in the trees,
dry, cold, haunting,
a roar of hell from my dreams,
wind chimes tossing,
wires moaning and whistling,
every shingle, vent
roof stack clacking, popping, snapping,
the world ready to bend to its knees,
I get up in the blackness before dawn
to see what is astir,
remember you, pray for you,
you are in my heart this way,
crazy, dangerous stirrings,
wild in the spirit,
your warmth as distant as those lights
flickering high up on the mountain,
your love always a challenge,
a mystery,
down some lane to my soul,
I am, after all, like the trees,
bending to the gusts,

howling in the torment,
waiting for you to come
and see me still standing

I battled my weariness over eggs and toast that morning but was asleep again by ten. In the early afternoon, I awakened still feeling lost and worthless and tormented by that last scene at Ellie's place. I went out to make coffee in the kitchen but decided against it. I wandered around the house a bit and finally sat down to roll a joint at my desk. Dreams had soon taken over the day.

Still without direction, I took a shower and went for a walk. A few miles down the road, I came to an old orange grove and wandered inside. Shadow and quiet quickly surrounded me. The bustle of the modern world fell away. For that brief moment, I knew the simple enchantment I had known as a boy.

At the center of the grove, I found a meadow and sat on a tree stump. Dust and insects swirled in the sunlight. Bird melodies and old memories danced together the silences. A murder of crows invaded a break of eucalyptus trees, stirring more ancient memories. I watched the crows making havoc with each other and the world high up in the limbs.

I had been lost in this place for a spell when my financial woes returned to haunt me. My answer was to run off somewhere, but it seemed like there was no place left to run.

Feeling hopeless, I got up and headed back for the streets. The crows gave me a raucous send off.

Out past the old packing plant, I turned into a housing tract, hoping to find my old friend, Nils. Nils had been a reed of a kid back in junior high school, with pimples and a high voice, but had blossomed into an artist with rugged Norwegian good looks. Nils could discuss the relative merits of quantum physics or post-modern art with equal dexterity, then dive forty feet into the Pacific unassisted and return with a sand bass at the end of his spear. Yet he still lived with his parents. He had converted their garage into a living space back in high school and happened to be in there when I knocked, three ladies and another friend with him. Nils and his buddy were naked save for white towels and lying on separate tables, getting massages. The women working them over were also wearing nothing but white towels. The remaining woman sat alone in a corner with an astrology book. The garage was darkened and the Eagles were playing softly in the background. The place reeked of patchouli oil.

Nils looked up from his massage table and acknowledged me without emotion. The woman gave me a look too but went on massaging him as if I wasn't there.

"I thought you were in Hawaii," Nils said.

"I was. There and the South Pacific."

"So what happened?"

"Island fever. You get a little stir crazy when you're surrounded by nothing but ocean for a year."

"I'd kill to see the South Pacific," Nils' buddy said.

He smiled and closed his eyes again. I found myself staring at his pencil mustache. The towel came loose from the woman massaging Nils. She eyed me while tucking it back into place. The other woman looked up from her astrology book. No one there seemed particularly happy to see me.

"Have you been diving?" I asked Nils.

"It's winter," he reminded me.

He was right. It was winter, there was little point in diving unless you were after lobster and I did not belong in this place. We no longer had anything in common. Nil's indifference was especially off putting. We had once been the dearest of friends.

"Well," I said, getting up. "Guess I'll be going."

No one tried to dissuade me.

"Leave me your phone number," Nils said before I left.

I did, with no expectation of hearing from him.

Walking back past the packing plant, another old friend Brent happened by in his car and braked to a stop.

"Hey Roger!" he said through a rolled down window. "Far out! What are you doing in town?"

I explained briefly.

"Well hop in. I'm heading up to smoke some dope with Peter and a few of our friends."

Having nothing better to do, I joined him. Brent drove up into the hills and parked beside a small cottage. Inside, a number of people were gathered around a darkened living room. Some of them I knew. Some I didn't. A bong was being passed around the room.

One of the young men had a bandage on his right hand. The mood was grim.

"What the fuck happened?" Brent said.

The guy explained. He had lost a thumb and two fingers working at a toilet paper factory. One of his bosses had told him to clean out a machine and it had come on while his hand was in there. Everyone was commiserating. He had been scheduled to enter Buddy Rich's drum school in New York in two weeks. There went a promising career.

Brent and I left a short while later. Brent asked if I wanted to head downtown with him and I begged off. He dropped me off on another back-country road

I was headed home on foot when a car honked and this guy named Mike pulled to the side of the road up ahead. He was not really a friend of mine. The two of us had never bonded in school but we had mixed with some of the same people from time to time. I walked up and leaned my head into his open window.

"What's happening, Roger? Did you get drafted?"

This, I presumed, was in reference to my somewhat shorter haircut.

"What's going on?" I said

"I was just heading over to David and Sheila's place. We're going out for some Mexican food. Want to join us?"

"David and Sheila?"

"Yeah, you remember them?"

I made certain we were talking about the same David. We were.

"I thought Sheila was married to Leo."

"She was but she left him for David. Took the whole business with her."

"The business?"

"Yeah, man. You haven't been around."

"No, but I saw David about a month ago and he never said a word to me about Sheila. Or a business."

"It just happened a few weeks ago. The Sheila part, anyway. Hop in and I'll tell you all about it on the way over there."

Always glad to see David, and curious to find out what the hell this was all about, I climbed in.

"Hey, man. Sorry about the comment," Mike said.

"It's all right. I'm long over defining myself by the length of my hair."

"I dig it, man. Anyway, you've been like around the world and everybody's like, wow, we need to get out of this fucking town too, before we all get old and die."

"Well, after all I've been through, I'm right back here where I started so I don't know what that says about my thinking."

"Hey, you're still young. We're all still young, you know?"

"Yeah, well. Coming back here, I'm starting to feel old real fast."

Mike laughed. We were headed west through some orange groves. Then Mike came to a major avenue and turned north through all the asphalt and stucco riff raff that made the modern world so unpleasant.

"Man, you're going to love this Mexican dive," Mike said as we drove along. "The best food in the world and the tap beer's ice cold."

"Tell me more about Sheila and Leo getting divorced."

"They aren't divorced yet."

"All right, just tell me about it."

He explained in detail how the two of them had started this leather apparel business; belts, purses, key fobs, that sort of thing. David had been working in the garage as a craftsman, banging out the goods. Next thing you know, he was banging Sheila. From the sounds of it, Leo was devastated. Then, I never saw Sheila and Leo as much of a match. Sheila was far too ephemeral and earthy for him. She could sing madrigal and make a casserole, all the while dancing ballet. Leo's response would be to wipe at his spectacles and itemize the cost of the casserole. David and Sheila definitely made more sense, broken hearts aside.

"Leo and his brother agreed to cough up the leather business in the divorce settlement. Leo's going into computers."

"Computers?"

"Yeah, that's going to be the next big thing."

I nodded, trying to get my head around that one.

"So, brother, tell me about your journeys. Where were you last?"

I explained the final year in the South Pacific.

"Oh wow, man. The South Pacific. I've got to get out of this town."

"You don't think about it, you just leave."

The statement hung in the air as an indictment to my current state of apprehensions.

Before long, Mike had turned right out of a commercial district. One block farther on, he pulled to a stop in front of a towering, clapboard house. It was surrounded by a couple of acres of trees. The building appeared to have been a hotel at some point in the past. The oddest thing about the whole property was how it had been hemmed in by commercial development. It stood out like a sore thumb against the modern world around it.

"This is their place?" I said as Mike got out of the car.

"This is it."

I noticed a curtain on the second floor moving as I climbed out. Mike knocked on the door. A few moments later, a muffled voice answered from the other side.

"What do you want, man?"

"We're looking for Dave," Mike said.

"Dave doesn't live here anymore."

"Come on, man, I just left him in there an hour ago."

"Dave doesn't live here anymore."

"Well...then, we'll take his girlfriend."

There was laughter inside and the door opened to reveal a smiling Sheila. The grand old interior behind her smelled as old houses do and looked long abandoned. The worn hardwood floors were without polish and the wallpaper was peeling from the walls in places. Old couches and chairs were scattered here and there in a haphazard fashion.

"Wow, Roger!" Sheila said with a hug and a playful rub of my head. "Where did you find this guy?" she added to Mike while letting us in.

"Coming out of an orange grove."

Sheila laughed.

"Camping out again?"

"I've always been fond of nature. So where's David?"

"He doesn't live here anymore."

"Yeah, yeah. The curtain upstairs gave you away."

"Oh rats," Sheila said with feigned disappointment.

Then David appeared from upstairs and gave me a hug.

"You still going out with that older woman?"

I smirked.

"I should be the one asking questions."

David shrugged. I thumbed my nose at the stairs.

"So, you want us to come back later?"

"Neah. We can hanky-panky anytime."

"Oh, thanks," Sheila said.

David's stoic façade cracked a bit with a smile. He pushed his glasses back, seeming to enjoy the effect his statement had more than anything.

Sheila retrieved four beers from the kitchen and we settled around the living room, Mike in one of the worn chairs, David with me on one of the sofas and Sheila on a stool, leaning forward, all capricious smiles and ready for action. I furtively studied David and Sheila amidst the conversation. Together, they looked like Halloween candy. Sheila had black hair pulled back tightly into a ponytail. Mike had coarse, orange hair that had not been cut in quite a while. A gypsy and her hippie boyfriend. David was not inclined towards many words. Sheila was filled with bright chatter. David explained things tersely and Sheila flitted about within that framework, providing details. We talked about the old and new and eventually the conversation got around to their leather business.

"Yeah, yeah," Sheila said, clapping her hands together. "Come out in the garage and we'll show you."

We went out through a kitchen door to a driveway that was two, narrow ribbons of concrete with grass growing between them. The wooden garage stood apart from the house. David unlocked the side door, flicked on the florescent lights and went in. I waved Sheila and Mike to go in first and followed them. There were workbenches against the three walls and leather goods in various stages of production. The place reeked of leather and tanning products. An assortment of supplies was stacked on shelves and under the work benches.

"This is it," David stated matter-of-factly.

"Like Santa's elves," I said.

"Yes, yes," Sheila said, clapping delightedly again.

"What do you do? Set up a stand out front?"

"The swap meet," Sheila said. "However, we can make more than we sell."

David pushed his glasses back and stared at me with his amused look.

"You need a salesman."

"Hey! There's an idea," Sheila said. "Why don't you be our salesman? You even look the part."

"Thanks. You know, everybody's trying to turn me into a salesman."

"But you'd be good at it."

"Like hell I would."

"Oh, please," Sheila said. "We even have an extra car you can use."

"Forget it, Sheila. It's not what I want to do with my life."

"Oh well, it was worth a try."

She looked forlornly at David then smiled. After a brief introduction to their production methods we closed up the garage and went around the corner to the Mexican bar.

The day had gotten on towards dusk and a band was arranging their equipment at one end of the room. Half the tables had been cleared from the linoleum floor and piled into a far corner. We chose a booth in that direction and ordered a pitcher of beer when the waitress came around.

Day turned to evening and the bar had soon swelled with patrons, most of them Mexicans. A hard driving, Tex-Mex band started to play and people danced.

About the time our meals arrived, this tall Mexican kid appeared on the dance floor with an old hag. They were dancing cheek to cheek to a slow song and appeared to be sincerely in love. Then the band shifted back to a hard rocking number. More people piled onto the dance floor but the Mexican kid clung to the old lady and slow danced as though the music had not changed speeds.

"Oh look!" Sheila said.

He appeared again through the crowd and we saw a dark stain growing in the crotch area of his faded Levi's.

"He wet his pants."

"There's your salesman," I said.

"The young guy?" Sheila said.

"No, the old woman. If she can sell him, she can sell anything."

Sheila laughed and clapped her hands. I went to find the bathroom. Someone had puked in the urinal and then passed out on the floor. I stepped over him and relieved myself. When I returned, I found some freak friends of David and Sheila had arrived and were sitting in my place. We shook hands but they gave me the same looks I had received from Nils and his crowd earlier in the day. Nobody seemed to trust my haircut.

"I'm getting out of here," I told David.

"What?" Sheila shouted over the din.

"We're going back to the house," David told her and got up. He threw money on the table. I did as well and shoved my few remaining bucks back in my pocket. I was as broke as a man could be without actually being penniless. My mind was working on that fact as I went out the door with David.

It was a cold, clear night and we went along with our breath making frost.

"Think the river's already frozen over at Horseshoe?" I asked David.

He pushed his glasses back.

"I don't think so. There's only been the one good snow."

"Even if it is, I wouldn't mind getting out of town for a few days."

"Still got your tackle?"

"A bit of it. The old man threw most of it away while I was gone."

"That's all right. I've got plenty."

I took a seat on the porch while David went in to retrieve two beers.

"When could you go?" I asked when he returned.

"Not for a few weeks. Things are kind of hectic right now."

"How's this thing going?" I thumbed my nose at the garage.

"It beats working for someone else. I think we have to go wholesale. At least that's what Sheila keeps telling me."

"Big business."

"Yeah. Furry Freak, Inc."

We chuckled and sat there talking for some time. Growing cold and restless, I stood up. David stood up with me.

"Let's go fishing."

"All right. Take the spare car if you want."

Just then, Sheila came down the block alone.

"What happened to our Casanova?" I asked.

"Oh, he passed out in a corner. The old bag's got a new guy already."

"A witch's spell."

Sheila clapped. David smiled and pushed his glasses back.

"I hope you haven't taken our ribbing the wrong way," Sheila said.

I shrugged.

"It gets old."

"I understand. If doing your own thing means having to wear your hair long, it's just a new form of fascism."

"Yeah. I hadn't thought about it much until the past few days. All of a sudden, I'm working for Nixon."

Sheila laughed.

"Well, you're all right with us."

"Thanks," I said again.

"But since you already look the part, please come work for us."

"Ha," I said. "You've been buttering me up."

Now David laughed.

"I meant to say, work *with* us," Sheila amended.

"Oh yeah, much better," I said. "Well, I guess we can have another beer and talk it over."

Thirteen

I awakened the next morning with a sore heart. I wanted to hear Ellie's voice. I wanted her love and encouragement. I wanted to make things all right between us.

I glanced at the clock. It was nine. I knew she had conferences on campus that morning but called anyway, hoping she had yet to leave. The phone rang several times and went to a machine. I hung up without leaving a message.

Back at my desk with a cup of coffee, I tried to write but found my mind distracted with jealous imaginings. There was no end of shaggy haired college students, just dying to seduce Ellie. I could picture an ostensible student/professor office chat turning into some wild sex over her desk.

By three that afternoon, I was beside myself. I had called Ellie half a dozen times already, without any luck. Prepared to go defend my fiefdom, I climbed into the battered Peugeot David and Sheila had loaned me and headed for Newport.

Initially, out of embarrassment, I parked the Peugeot well down the block from Ellie's place but ultimately pulled up closer to her driveway. Worried that the twins might have come home, I knocked on the door and then let myself in when no one answered. I looked around for any sign of Ellie's schedule and whereabouts but found nothing scribbled on her calendar.

Having sat there less than patiently for a spell, I decided to make one of Ellie's famous White Russians then flipped through her copy of Thucydides. Very odd sentence structure, I thought. It seemed at times as if the man was writing backwards. I smoked a joint and he started to make a lot more sense to me.

Soon, I was back to worrying. One minute, I pictured Ellie delighted to see me. The next minute, I pictured her dashing in with some young interloper and irritated by my reappearance.

With the sun setting, I became convinced of the worst and started to leave, then decided what the hell. I'll make dinner and see how that goes. I sharpened some knives and went to work.

In that hour of dusk, with Catalina Island turning dark out on the horizon and the harbor starting to sparkle with lights and a line of cars inching along Coast Highway, I heard Ellie's car pull into the garage. A moment later, the door to the kitchen opened and Ellie came strutting across the tile floor. Miles Davis was playing in the background.

"Why, hello Roger," she said and set her portfolio down on the bar top. She smiled but I sensed her mind working hard.

I gave her a kiss.

"Such a beautiful face. I have missed you more than I can say."

"How nice to hear. I have missed you, too. Though I did wonder if you'd ever come back."

"Oh Ellie. It's just so difficult to understand my own feelings at times, let alone explain them."

"At least try. I don't do well with silence and sudden departures."

Her comment stung and my impulse was to storm off again, but I stopped myself.

"I'm sorry," I said. "Sometimes I just don't know how to deal with these feelings inside, other than to get angry. Or run off. Or do both."

"We all get angry, Roger. It's part of life but running off is a control thing. You get to have your say but I don't get to have mine."

"I know. I'm learning. That's all I can say."

"Well, that's something. I suppose that's all we can expect from each other."

"You are adorable."

It was true and we kissed, body to body and with my hands in Ellie's angora hair. When she pulled away, it was to go around and uncover the pan on the stove.

"It smells wonderful."

"Scaloppini a la Roget."

She set the lid down and turned to face me. I wrapped my arms around her waist.

"It's really nice to come home to you."

"I've been hanging around here since four or so, imagining you compromised with a number of your students."

"Oh Roger."

She touched my face and kissed me tenderly.

"Do you really not know how much I love you?"

"I guess I forget that easily."

"So? Move in with me."

"Sure. Broke and completely lacking in direction."

I shook my head. Ellie reassured me again with kisses and went to pull a bottle of Chardonnay from the refrigerator. With two glasses poured half full, we sat on the bar stools and toasted. The final blush of sunset was fading to darkness behind Ellie. Charcoal clouds marched along the sea.

"So, no job yet!?" she said dramatically.

We laughed, she more than me.

"I don't know. Maybe."

"Well, do tell."

"Well, frankly, I dread the whole thing but some friends of mine have started a leather company and they want me to be their salesman."

"I think you would be very good at sales, Roger."

I growled. She bit her nails in fright and completed the gesture with a sip of her wine.

"Would this have anything to do with that ratty hulk sitting out front?"

"Yes, I've been meaning to tell you."

"That you're getting rid of it."

"Worried about keeping up with the Joneses, are we?"

"I'm worried about being cited by the community association!"

"I had started to park it farther down the street somewhere."

"I wish you had."

She smiled.

"Perhaps you can sit there quietly for a minute while I explain myself."

She pretended to zip her mouth shut. I got on to tossing the salad.

"The alternative is returning to school."

Ellie raised her eyebrows expectantly.

"If I go to work for Mike and Sheila, I doubt that will happen any time soon. On the one hand, I could save some money and try school once I'm better settled financially. On the other hand, I don't know…"

Ellie unzipped her mouth.

"You could live with me and go to school, virtually cost free."

"And be your gigolo."

"I wish you wouldn't look at it that way."

"I'm sorry but I do."

"Why can't you accept my generosity as a gesture of the profound love I feel for you?"

"Get out!" I said dramatically.

Ellie hung her head.

"I thought we had let go of that, Roger."

"Sorry. It's rather hard to forget."

She threw up her hands.

"You know what, Roger? Let's just fuck. It's the one thing we haven't screwed up yet."

"No pun intended."

"None at all."

"And the twins?"

"They'll be in Mammoth until New Year's Day. Actually, they're coming home the day after."

"How convenient."

"How convenient."

Sensing this was a dare, I went to Ellie. She stood up and we backed into the living room step by step with the melody of *Kind of Blue* drifting around us. Ellie went from my shirt buttons to my zipper and squatted before me. After the initial rush of ecstasy, I pushed Ellie over, tore off her panties and got my face between her legs. Somehow her high heels had remained on her feet and were digging into my back. Once she was satisfied, I had my way with her and we were soon coming together.

"Oh god, I love you, Ellie."

"And I love you, Roger."

Afterward, we lay quietly on the carpet. The last strains of Miles Davis' Flamenco Sketches had come to an end. I felt enormously satisfied but my mind was working again. So many things that were unsettled. So many things I dared not speak.

"I love you," I said again in the now complete darkness

"I love you, too…But enough with this romantic blathering. I'm hungry!"

I laughed and helped Ellie to her feet. She went off to the bathroom. I slipped back into my shirt and pants and turned the flame on under the scallops. Ellie returned to the kitchen wearing a lavender gown. With everything seared a final time, she lit candles and turned out the lights.

"Mmm, it's delicious," she said.

A single strand of linguini disappeared into her mouth with dramatic flair.

I held up my glass to her.

"To the man who makes all things well," Ellie said.

"To the woman who enjoys them."

We touched glasses.

"Perhaps you should go back to being a cook," she said between bites.

"I've considered it," I said while buttering a piece of bread.

The meal was consumed with various expressions of culinary pleasure and smiles and adoring looks and conversation.

I stopped somewhere along the way and looked across the table.

"Ellie, this is so hard for me to say but I'm just so confused by life sometimes. I don't understand myself."

"Oh," she said with bemused concern.

"Yes, one minute I feel like a caged animal. The next minute I want to settle down and start a family. I don't know what is true anymore."

"Well, you see..."

"Oh boy…"

Ellie acted flustered.

"All right. Go on."

"You see," she said. "After you've lived on this planet for enough years, you begin to realize it's a matter of balance and patience more than anything else. Don't get too high, don't get too low and especially don't act on all the crap going around in your head."

"I've got a lot of crap going around in my head."

"You just have too much time on your hands. That is what I think. Once you settle on school or a job, much of your worrying will disappear."

I reached out to hold her hands.

"I really do love you, Ellie. When I forget everything but this moment, I feel such peace."

Ellie stared at me, glowing.

"What?" I said.

"I've just had this revelation. I was sitting here and had completely forgotten that I was. You see, there is this other time and place in our hearts, and we can enter that kingdom at any time we choose. It is our garden of Eden."

"And it disappears every time we talk about it."

"Oh, Roger, you are so wise."

"It's disappearing fast."

"Stop it!"

I laughed at her little brat routine and stood up to gather the plates. Ellie remained seated, watching me with a smile. I piled everything into the sink and returned to the table. Ellie's teeth and eyes stood out in the darkness.

"Come, let's go look at the Calendar section."

She blew out the candles and snuggled up with me on the sofa. I turned the pages in the dim light, waiting for her nod before going on.

"Oh, there's something I would enjoy," she said.

"Which?"

"The Cassavetes play in Westwood."

"Did you want to go tomorrow night?"

"Yes, let's do."

"I hope the twins don't come home early," I said.

"They won't. But can't you imagine being comfortable here with them?"

"No."

"Roger, I think it would seem quite normal to you with time."

"All right. Like you said. It's best if we don't talk about what's not right here in front of us."

"Like our secret garden," she said.

"You're talking."

"Okay, we'll just make eyes."

I did so, at which she laughed.

"You're not leaving much to mystery," she said.

"Ssshh," I said.

She curled up closer like a delighted child and bit her lower lip.

"You make the nicest eyes."

"Just don't get all gushy about it."

"Oh, no. I wouldn't dare get gushy with you." She smiled capriciously. "Gooshy, maybe."

She watched me laugh.

"That's okay. You go ahead and get gooshy all you want."

"I have a confession, then."

"You're...?"

She nodded.

"We'd better go have a look at this."

"Oh, good."

I put the paper down and we hurried into the bedroom.

Sometime late in the night, it began to rain. I lay awake for a long time with my eyes open and listening to it, unable to turn off my head.

It rained all through the next day so Ellie and I played around the house until it was time to head up to LA. The rain had stopped by then. The sky was clearing and there was an indefinable quality of romance to the 405 freeway on a Friday night at sunset, especially with New Year's Eve the following evening. Ellie and I had made a cocktail for the road and sipped at it on our way into the city. The lights of rush hour traffic went this way and that.

The play was all dialogue between a pair of hard-luck losers in a rundown hotel. Both men had made repeated attempts to escape their bleak existence, without success. The play was about finding peace with their failures. Back out on the sidewalk in the fresh air, I felt catharsis.

"Shall we grab something to eat?" Ellie asked me.

"Yes, something chaste."

"Like a pastrami sandwich."

"I've had them. They're very chaste."

Ellie laughed and gave me a passionate kiss, the one where a woman's leg bends at the knee.

"Come on. I know where there's a good deli a few blocks over."

"Pray tell. How do you know this?" she asked as we walked.

"It's a long story. I'll tell you when we get there."

We strolled down Wilshire Blvd. and up a side street.

"Take any seat!" a woman shouted from behind the counter. She was slicing meat for her only other customer. We took off our coats and made ourselves at home in a vinyl booth.

"So?"

"So, my cousin was here from the East Coast and needed a ride to Westwood and I had been thinking to buy a car, anyway."

"So you bought a car just to take him up to LA?!"

I imitated Ellie's spoiled brat routine.

Our world-weary proprietress walked up with a babushka over her hair and a towel in her hands.

"Spare the rod and spoil the child."

She took our orders for chaste pastrami and told us that kosher would have to do.

"Okay, so back to your story."

"So, I just happened to be buying a car that day."

"Oh."

"I saw it in the paper for two hundred bucks." I shrugged. "How can you go wrong, right? So I get there and learn this man had made the car in his own backyard."

"What?!"

"Yes. I suppose I should stop right here and confess that I've always had a terrible time with cars. Especially that part about having to take care of them?"

176

She nodded appreciatively.

"So, this guy shows me how the car was part Austin, part Triumph, part of several things. The fenders were custom made from the trunk of a Cadillac."

"Surely you jest."

"No. And it had a toaster for an engine."

She laughed.

"You are kidding."

"About the toaster."

"About the whole thing."

"No. Only about the toaster."

"Sounds like it was a good screwing, even at $200."

I shrugged.

"Did you want me to finish the story?"

"You're a fool. What else do I need to know?"

"That your sex privileges have been suspended."

Ellie had a tantrum. The waitress returned with our food and I felt obliged to tell her at least part of the story. She left shaking her head. Once she had departed, Ellie looked at me expectantly. I took a bite of my sandwich.

"Hmm. Very chaste."

Ellie bit into hers.

"So, continue."

"About halfway up here, smoke began to billow out of the engine compartment. I pulled over on the freeway and found that the plug wires had melted onto the toaster. Engine, that is."

"Oh dear."

"Oh shit is more like it…Anyway, it went downhill from there. We had to stop every few miles for the engine to cool off. We found this deli and had a sandwich before I headed back. I had left Santa Ana around noon and did not get back until close to eight. I drove straight to the man's house."

"What did he say?"

"He'd take it off my hands for $100."

Ellie made a gesture of exasperation.

"So, what happened?"

"I took the $100."

"And how many times do you suspect this con artist had sold the thing?"

"One too many."

Ellie burst out laughing. I smiled and took another bite of my sandwich.

The following afternoon, Ellie went off clothes shopping. I positioned myself in one of her easy chairs with my feet up and soon had the various sketches of a poem scattered around my lap. Time passed. The late shadows filled the room. I had but a few moments earlier begun to like my efforts. Then, just as suddenly, they became meaningless words on a piece of paper to me, the initial perceptions which had precipitated them hopelessly muddled in the act of expression.

Not knowing another writer or poet, I had no idea if this was common to all, or simply evidence of a man lacking talent. In any case, my sense of triumph in one moment was quickly followed by feelings of failure in the next and mirrored all too well the emotions of love that had induced me to write in the first place.

I scratched through a word and read the lines once more.

Younger Lovers

What is the measure of time
before us?
are we as falling stars,
brief flashes of light on a warm summer's night,
our measureless flight
from worlds unknown
here arrived to expire
in sight of our home?

Will our contribution be but a brief, brilliant flash
our legacy lost
on younger lovers arriving late
to our laughter?
remembered as something inspired?
or will they simply come as we did,
burdened by the weight of time
their dreams unraveling?

All day long, the question had haunted me. What would it be like to be in love with a younger woman, in exactly the same way I was in love with Ellie?

I was thinking again of that enchanting young woman from Mendocino when the garage door opener came to life and Ellie drove into the garage. I gathered up the evidence of my work before Ellie walked in the door. She had two large department store bags in her hands and a comical look on her face, as though things had gotten away from her a bit.

As she was setting the bags down in the foyer, the phone rang. Ellie answered it in the kitchen and talked for a few minutes before coming to sit on my lap.

"The twins," she said, if you were wondering.

"Yeah? Do we still have New Year's Eve all to ourselves?"

"Yes, and New Year's Day as well. I guess with all their school stuff being at Dick's place, they've decided to spend Sunday night there and come home after their classes on Monday."

"Oh good. I just wanted to hide away from the world with you."

I pushed my face beneath her soft, curly hair and kissed the back of her neck. We petted for a spell without talking.

"Let's take a bath," she said, standing up.

"Okay."

She drew a bath and we sat opposite each other. The bath suds rested in a sumptuous pile over her breasts.

"You know, Roger. When I go out like today, just dealing with a bunch of assholes for hours on end, it really makes me appreciate you."

"It's hard to find a more top-notch asshole."

She laughed heartily.

"I love your laughter."

I pulled one of her feet out of the water and swallowed the big toe. Ellie did the same. I moved down a toe and she did the same.

"Mmm, wonderfully sensuous, isn't it?"

"Yes," she agreed "Let's write a book on my sabbatical. A sort of *Decameron*."

"I can't imagine it, somehow."

"You mean the book or our being together?"

"No. Writing a novel. It seems so overwhelming."

"Perhaps you could just start with some stories and see where it leads."

"I would think you'd have to have the kernel of an idea."

"I like the *Decameron* one."

"Henry Miller does *A Thousand and One Nights*."

"Cucumbers and that sort of thing."

"Yes, lots of cucumbers."

Ellie pushed my legs apart and came at me with her sudsy flesh.

"Roger. You know you can do whatever you please with me."

She held me beneath the water.

"I'm seeing big cucumbers. And zucchinis."

"Okay," she said, daring me.

I stood and grabbed a towel and we were soon hurrying off to the bedroom.

Afterwards, Ellie told me to stay put and she would whip up a couple of sandwiches. I was channel surfing when I heard her call out from the kitchen.

"It's on channel 28."

"No yelling," I called back and chuckled to myself, imagining the look on her face.

I flipped back through the channels and found the public TV station. They were airing a special program about the upcoming election.

Ellie arrived with a food tray and a snooty look on her face.

"You really don't forget anything, do you?"

"Nothing. Especially not when it involves my ego."

"Well, touché."

"Yes, touché."

She made herself comfortable on the bed with the tray between us. There were turkey sandwiches along with potato chips, two beers and two pickles. I bit into one of the pickles.

"Thanks," I said.

"You're welcome." She grabbed hold of her sandwich delicately, took a bite, then put it down and wiped her hands.

"Roger, why don't come with me to the campus on Monday."

I pretended not to have heard her comment over the program, with the predictable results.

"I just want you to come see the campus and visit my class and then we'll go have dinner later on."

"Dinner sounds nice."

Again, a tantrum.

"You know, I might have to stop by, just to see you do that in front of a full classroom."

"It has been done, trust me."

"I do."

"You haven't answered my question."

"Did you know that Millard Fillmore was the thirteenth President of the United States."

"Roger."

"I'm a salesman, remember."

"Please."

"I'll need money for Europe."

"No you won't. We've already dispensed with that issue."

"All right, Ellie. I'll come by the campus on Monday. Now, can we watch the damned program?"

"I love his voice," Ellie said, referring to the narrator.

"Yes, it's comforting."

She eyed me.

"You know, those will be the finest moments of my life."

"Just don't plan too much, all right? I don't want it to be a bus tour."

"If it's Tuesday, it must be Belgium?"

"Yeah, that."

"How about being gypsies in a Volkswagen bus?"

"That sounds nice."

We finished our dinner and put the tray aside. I cracked the slider to the cool night air and we snuggled beneath the covers.

"I'd like to meet your friends," Ellie said offhand during the program.

"I'll invite them over for dinner if you'd like."

"Yes, some weekend soon."

"I'll let them know."

"Furry Freak Leather Company," she said to herself.

I tried to explain about the comics.

"The name's got to go."

"They make nice stuff."

"Who cares if the name causes mothers to hide their children?"

"That's not who we're appealing to."

"Well, you ought to. You see..."

"Oh, watch the goddamned program."

Fourteen

We made our own fireworks at midnight on New Year's Eve and spent New Year's Day doing mostly nothing. Ellie fielded a number of calls from friends and family. I watched a bit of football and we had prime rib for dinner, with scallions on our baked potatoes and Roquefort dressing on our salad, topped off with vanilla bean ice cream over a lemon cake Ellie had made. We were pleasantly gorged by sunset. I tried not to think too much about being penniless, or about my impending visit to Ellie's class on campus.

At dawn on Monday, she arose and went out to the kitchen. A short time later, she returned with a cup of black coffee and the newspaper. I lay there dreaming. The sky brightened and the world came to life outside her windows

Once Ellie had perused the paper and finished her coffee, she showered and started dressing for work. I lay in bed, further disheartened with each new article of clothing that was put in place. First her panties, then a bra and silk blouse, then a tight, green skirt. The high-heel shoes were last; no nylons. There she was, gorgeous and gloriously certain of herself, and all I could think was I wanted to screw her. She came to kiss me goodbye.

"I have this problem with a dangling preposition, Professor Sands."

I grabbed Ellie's ass but she playfully pulled away.

"Sorry, no time to go up the mountain, dear."

She blew a kiss and started for the door.

"How about just a little ways *into* the mountain!?" I called after her.

"Sorry, dearest! Meet you in the cafeteria!"

The high-heels clicked down the hallway. The door from the house to the garage opened. Her car started about the time the entry door had automatically closed. The garage door opener came to life next. I heard her back out and the garage door close. It was silent again. I got up and went to use the bathroom.

Seeing dark rings under my eyes, I took a closer look at my face in the mirror. Getting old, I thought. Or maybe it's just the booze.

I went out to the kitchen, poured a cup of coffee, sat at the bar and stared at the fog over the harbor. A few boat masts pierced the gray, lifeless cottony blanket.

I took my coffee and walked into the study. The typewriter was there. I could work on a poem instead of going to the campus. Start that novel. Then Ellie would really be pissed at me. Without much enthusiasm, I went in to take a shower.

At the campus parking lot, I was met with an unbroken sea of cars. It took quite a while to find a spot. I saw students here and there in the lot, talking, smoking, laughing, their rock & roll blaring. It was the same thing I had been doing not too terribly long ago, only in high school. The clothing and music had changed, rock opera in place of the Bay Area psychedelic sound, costumes in place of our wonderfully irreverent clothing. Glenn Miller was starting to sound more and more attractive to me.

With shades on, I walked through the glare of the sunlit lot. On campus, I picked up a class schedule. My intention was to sit in on another class before meeting with Ellie. A Lit-101 course seemed to fit the bill. It still allowed me enough time to have lunch with Ellie and follow along to her history class.

A directory led me to a bungalow at a far-flung end of the campus. I sat down next to an attractive young blonde. She smiled and said hi.

"How much do you want to bet he assigns us Moby Dick?"

She giggled.

"I've heard of Moby Grape."

I laughed.

"Yeah. I'm always getting my classics confused."

She smiled without understanding the joke. I was still having a laugh over her Moby Grape comment when the professor walked in. The clock on the wall read five minutes to ten. At ten sharp, the bell rang and the professor began to pass out a reading list. Then he wrote his name on the chalkboard and cleared his throat. It grew quiet in stages.

As I suspected, Moby Dick was on the list. I thumbed ahead quickly while he talked. It would be eight weeks before we got into anything contemporary. I sighed and stared out the door while everyone stated his or her name.

Standish stopped at me.

"I'm sorry, but I don't seem to have you down here in my class."

"I was thinking to petition you."

Of course, everyone stared.

"Yes, well, see me after class then."

The roll call continued. I escaped in a flood of students at the end of class.

Ellie was already eating when I arrived to the cafeteria. A kiss seemed to be out of the question. Even in the crowded, bustling hall, students had noticed me taking a seat opposite her.

"Hello Roger," she said.

"Hi Ellie."

"So, how is academia treating you?"

"I got here early and dropped in on a Lit class."

"Oh?"

"Yes. A chance to read Moby Dick again."

She smiled.

"You see. You're not playing the game, Roger."

"How so?"

"Well, if you've already read Moby Dick, then you simply write the paper and focus your time on some other part of your curriculum."

"Like all the crap you plan to assign me."

"Precisely. By the way, you're not eating?"

"No, I'm not really hungry."

Before Ellie could respond, one of her male students came over to ask a question related to his essay assignment. Ellie maintained decorum consistent with her position, but did so humorously. The young man left and she came back to our conversation.

"So, you were saying?"

"I wasn't. But if you were going to ask, I have this ominous sense of what my presence here portends for our relationship."

"What? Are you worried I'll blurt out in front of the class, 'here lies the golden rod that punctures the glorious bliss of my creamy twat'?"

"I suspect they'll figure it out soon enough."

I glanced around at all the students stealing glances at us.

"You don't have to come. It was a request, not a demand."

She stood up with her tray.

"So?"

"I'll be there shortly. I'd rather walk in by myself."

"All right, Roger."

On Ellie's way out, a number of students stopped to greet her. I waited until she was out of sight before following along.

Ellie's classroom was a mob. Students fought to get into her course. They were lined against the walls, in hope of one cancellation. All the desks were occupied or had books on top of them. Ellie saw me and made a gesture towards an empty seat she had saved. Heads turned. I quickly offered the seat to a young lady holding a pile of books. She thanked me and I took her place against the back wall.

Ellie took note of my gesture but she did not miss a beat. Students were crowded around where she had leaned against the front of her desk. When the bell went off, everyone who had a seat went to it. Ellie waited for the room to grow quiet.

"Does anyone not know my name?" she asked. There was a general buzz, but no one seemed ignorant of the fact.

"Very well. We will dispense with the formality of introducing ourselves, since you all know who I am and I will find out who you are soon enough. Likewise, I will refrain from passing out a reading list. There is only one thing I want you to read for the time being. The newspaper. I recommend the LA Times, though the local rag will do. Does anyone know what year it is?"

There was laughter, along with a flurry of purposefully dumb answers. Finally, someone gave the right year.

"Done with brilliance, Ted," she said.

"Now, does anyone know why that is important?"

Another barrage of silly answers followed. Ellie enjoyed it without comment. When it was quiet, she resumed her monologue.

"That's fine. You are allowed to be stupid for one day in my class. After that you will be asked to leave."

This was followed by a chorus of ooohs and aaahs. Ellie adjusted her position and her skirt came up a little higher on her thighs. I watched those beautiful legs, thinking of all the sweet, dirty things I had done to them and between them and wondered who else in the class might be sharing my thoughts.

"This is a special year," Ellie continued. "As is every fourth year in American history. It is a presidential election year and this class will, in great part, focus on that election process. Which is why you are going to read the paper. Each and every day. Is anyone confused so far?"

No one seemed to be. More fun and games ensued, and Ellie presided over it masterfully, reeling in her giddy students whenever the occasion demanded it. Our eyes met a few times. I was both awed by her and feeling second-class.

The first time she was distracted, I walked out of the room. In the nearby rest room, I found a sample of campus graffiti.

Eleanor Sands is a fox

It was scribbled in bold letters above the urinal.

I walked back to the car and sat for some time before deciding on a course of action, which was to stop at the market for a bottle of bourbon and return to Ellie's house to drink it. I was pretty well lit up by the time she came in the door. She threw her briefcase on the coffee table and came to confront me.

"Roger, I want you out of my home. And take your booze with you."

"You said we were going to dinner."

"Get out."

"Oh, that again."

I finished the drink in my glass and reached for the bottle.

"Did you hear me?"

"Yes," I said and poured my glass full, punched the lid back into the bottle and downed the drink. "I just wonder if you heard your tone right now."

"I don't have to hear myself. And how dare you walk out of my class."

"That's what it is, isn't Ellie? Your ego? There you were in all your glory, and I walked out."

"I have a former husband who treated me with that kind of disrespect. Only he paid the bills."

"Ah, punching below the belt."

"Please. Get out of my home."

I nodded and went off to gather my belongings in the back room. I added the bottle of bourbon on the way through the living room. Ellie busied herself in the kitchen as I went out the front door.

When the Peugeot failed to start, I kicked it and started down the street with my backpack. I had gotten around the corner when the Capri came barreling by and braked to a sudden halt in front of me. Ellie got out in a way that was all too familiar.

"Ellie, I swear to God. If you start up with me, I'm going to deck you."

The furious click of high-heels continued forward.

"Ellie! Jesus Christ, not here in the middle of the street!"

I fought with her arms, a struggle that quickly descended into tears while we stood there, with Ellie's lips doing a strange dance of grief.

"You bastard," she said with a wounded voice. "You degraded me in front of the whole world."

I let go of her arms.

"I doubt anyone noticed."

"You see? You're not prepared to..."

"No, I don't see! You're always saying that, as if your perceptions are self-evident to the rest of the world. But I don't see a damned thing except an otherwise intelligent woman going off half mad every other day."

Startled into silence momentarily, she quickly regained her footing.

"Well, god knows we should all listen to the wisdom of a drunken sot."

"Fine, Ellie, I'm a drunken sot."

I started down the street, having no interest in the conversation.

"And don't expect to come crawling back, Roger."

I allowed Ellie the final blow and kept walking.

A moment later, I heard her car start. Given Ellie's history, I anticipated her next move with a certain degree of apprehension but she made a U-turn and disappeared around the corner without further mischief.

I walked along the street of homes with a number of regrets. A stream of lights raced this way and that out on the nearby highway. Headed that way, I heard a car and turned to find Ellie's Capri racing down the block again. I stood back and watched her come to a halt halfway onto someone's front lawn. Lights flickered on. A number of people appeared in their windows.

Ellie marched at me with a piece of paper in her hand.

"This is a contract. I want you to sign it or I won't be able to see you again."

I took the paper and read the contents. When I got to the part about 'I shall never ask you to leave my home again' I let my hand fall to my side and rubbed my forehead, not trusting a word of it.

When I looked up, Ellie's lips were doing their strange dance of grief again. With the whole neighborhood watching now, I grabbed her arm and gently guided her back towards her car.

"Let's at least get off this guy's lawn."

She started the car and backed out onto the street.

"What did you want me to do with this," I said, referring to the contract. There was a neat column of figures on the second page.

"I don't know. I thought you should pay for your expenses."

I shook the piece of paper at her.

"This is the way you want it? Like this? Like it's a business?"

Ellie took the paper and methodically tore in half, then into quarters and so on until it more or less resembled confetti, then tossed it out the window.

"So, now what?"

"I'll sign over half my home to you if you'll come live with me."

I managed a sick laugh and tried to rub the madness from my forehead again.

"I can't do that."

"Then pay up."

She got out and tried to gather the now windblown confetti from the street.

"Oh for chrissakes, Ellie. Get in the car."

She did.

"You're not making any sense."

"Then apologize."

"Why? You're as much at fault as I am."

She bit her lower lip and stared with her 'wounded little girl' routine. It had a way of knocking me off my stride.

"What do you want from me, Roger?"

"Not to go around in circles like this. Like I've sent you out for ice-cream and croaked while you were gone."

She stared pensively ahead.

"Why don't we go get something to eat?" I said. "All this fighting has made me hungry."

"All right," she said.

We went to a Mexican joint and ordered a pitcher of margaritas. Mariachi music played in the background. When we were well drunk, I made a face like Ellie's and she laughed. We both laughed.

"Okay, Roger. Let's do this. When I get off on my little routine, you just tell me to go screw myself."

"Sure, and when the police arrive?"

"You don't trust me to be rational?"

"There is scant evidence to support that claim."

She reached across the table with a seductive lowering of her eyes.

"You see...," she started and I nearly coughed up my margarita.

"Oh Jesus," she said and threw up her hands.

"Okay, what do I see?"

The mariachi band came by our table and oppressed us with one of their songs. We listened in silence. When they were done, I tipped them. Then the waitress arrived with our food and another pitcher. I worked at getting the table organized and looked up expectantly at Ellie.

"Well, I wanted you to appreciate me today and it hurt me deeply when you ran off instead."

"I thought you were magnificent."

"Oh," she said. "Well, you hadn't told me."

"Well, you hadn't asked."

"Oh," she said again.

"You see, Ellie, this is the way I would like to see these scenes play out. You tell me you're hurt. I'll say I'm sorry and we'll go have dinner. And we'll forget all the weird stuff in between. Do you think we'd be missing anything terribly important if we did it that way?"

She pondered my question for a moment.

"Yes. The drama…"

I hung my head.

"You don't look happy, lover."

"You're going to kill me at a young age."

"Well, better that than some young tart getting her hands on you."

"Please tell me you've learned something from all of this."

"I did, Roger. I trust you more all the time."

"I guess that's something."

She reached across the table for my hands.

"Did you really appreciate me today?"

"You're so good at what you do, I was in awe…and intimidated."

"You're not coming back, are you?"

"No, Ellie. I don't know if it's because I love so much or I'm just insecure or a combination of the two but I really need to find my own way."

She smiled with a look compassion. I took her hair and head in my hands and bored my gaze into her beautiful eyes.

"I love you, Ellie."

"I'm truly glad for that. But I fear you'll waste your talents away."

"Maybe I will. I worry about that too, but my independence means more to me than anything. I realized today how utterly dependent I have become on you. Or *could* become dependent on you and it's not a healthy thing."

"I'm sorry I've brought this upon our love affair."

"There's nothing to be sorry about. It's just me, a young man, trying to find his own way. Perhaps I'm just a bit gun shy. The last time I depended on someone, it was my parents, and that did not turn out so well."

"Well, can I at least give you a ride home?" Ellie asked.

"Yes, of course. I suppose the car will have to wait until tomorrow."

"Something tells me it will still be there in the morning."

"Always the sage one, Ellie. Always the sage one."

"So let's go smoke a joint and make love."

"And unpredictable, my little hippie princess."

"Not for you, Roger. I'm utterly predictable. You have my heart."

"Aw. You are a sweetheart."

Our glasses met and we drank to our latest détente. My true thoughts were held in secret, that love always came with a catch, in this case, to be in love with a brilliant and gorgeous woman, who also happened to be half mad.

Fifteen

Having smoked a joint back at my place, Ellie and I made love and talked and talked until it was late. In the morning I felt like hell, both from the overabundance of margaritas and for having kept Ellie up into the wee hours. I called first thing to offer my love and moral support but she had already left for campus.

While seated in the kitchen and sipping a cup of coffee in my robe, the matter of retrieving the Peugeot returned to my thoughts, and that brought to mind another one of my celebrated car sagas. Vincent had given me a '49 Chevy Sedan in my sophomore year of high school and my friends and I immediately took it out for a spin on the back roads of town.

Not far from the old packing plant, amidst miles of orange groves and towering eucalyptus trees, the car came to a sudden halt. As was pointed out to me later on, a wheel cylinder had probably locked up and was easily fixed, but the idea of a dead car there in the middle of the road was just too overwhelming for me to contemplate at the time, so I made an executive decision and abandoned the thing where it sat. Key in the ignition and that was that.

Little had changed for me when it came to car problems. Faced with rescuing the Peugeot, I got out a bottle of brandy and poured some into my coffee.

Sometime around noon, with my typewriter singing away, the phone rang. It was Sheila, wondering what had happened to the car and their salesman. I assured her that I was all right but that this could not be said of the Peugeot.

Not overly concerned, Sheila suggested that we go to rescue the car the next day. We'd at least give it the old college try and I agreed.

Our expedition began with lunch in a bar. David ordered a pitcher of beer and the three of us got to reminiscing. Over our meals, the subject of leather goods hardly came up. This was encouraging. I had not entirely bought into my role in their enterprise. If I envisioned myself as a merchant of old, off on an adventure across the Seven Seas, my exotic goods in hand to show the world, things became a bit more palatable. Schlepping their belts and purses around LA was another thing.

A few hours later, we pulled onto Ellie's street. The car was still there, dead under the sun. As usual under such circumstances, it was deemed prudent to open the engine compartment. Sheila took the key and tried to start the car. David and I stared under the hood. It was akin to having aborigines monitor a rocket launch.

"What's this?" David asked, holding up a loose wire.

I pointed at a vacant connector. He put the two back together and immediately thereafter, the car fired up. Rather proud of ourselves, we went back to town and drank more beer in a bar. Little else was accomplished that day, but at least I was no longer stranded and had gained a bit more confidence in the Peugeot.

I went home, got a good night's sleep and arrived at David and Sheila's house the following day around midmorning. They and two of their friends were busily working out in the garage. One man cut the leather products. The other one edged the rough cut. Sheila replicated various designs with hand-tools. David applied stain. Purses, which required stitching, were finished by some of Sheila's friends at home. David came outside after a few minutes.

"Where did you want to go first?"

"Oh, how about the nearest beer tavern?"

David smiled and pushed back his glasses.

"I have a list of our accounts."

We went into the house and examined the information: names, locations, the volume of previous orders and possible leads. It appeared to be a lot of running around for not much money.

"People tell us about other businesses if they're not too close to compete. Usually four appointments in a day turns into six or seven."

I nodded while trying to imagine David out there on the streets. What did he do, just go in and stare at the merchant? Anyway, it sounded depressing, this idea of running around LA all day for forty bucks.

"I guess I should try to make some appointments first."

"Yeah, I'll get the sample bag together."

He went back to the garage while I made phone calls. David had the sample bag on a workbench when I returned. It was a large satchel stuffed with belts, coiled together in separate design categories. Everything was taken out.

"I've found people like to get things out and handle the leather."

"No doubt this is where you go for the kill," I said.

Sheila laughed. David coiled the belts back inside the satchel.

"I'll bet you're excited."

"I can hardly contain myself."

"Where are you headed first?" David asked.

"Hollywood."

One of the workers hummed the tune.

"So, I guess I'll see you tomorrow."

"Yeah. Good luck."

"Yeah, good luck."

Sheila blessed the enterprise with a kiss on my cheek.

I drove to West Hollywood first, where head shops and boutiques dotted the palm strewn boulevards. In the first shop, I met a woman wearing platform shoes and a mini dress. The interior was darkened. The place smelled of incense. The display window had as much paraphernalia in it as it did clothing apparel. The name on the carved wooden sign was right out of Alice in Wonderland.

Every shop I visited was this kind of shadowy place and staffed by women, who were sometimes rude, sometimes playful, frequently sexy, but no one bought a great deal of merchandise.

By two o'clock I had sold five purses and seventeen belts. That meant I had made a commission of thirteen dollars and ninety cents. I had spent that much on gas and lunch.

As David suggested, fingers were pointed and I chased about in a dozen different directions, crisscrossing avenues, fighting traffic, getting lost on frequent occasions, only to be told, come around next week, or to have someone envisioning a whole new line of wares for me. What a pain in the ass. I was enormously grateful to be headed south on the 405 at the end of the day, even though it left me stuck in rush hour traffic.

Having an idea, I pulled into a mall alongside the freeway and wandered among the shops. Everywhere I looked, swarms of people were spending their money. I had been dealing with owners, thrilled to sell two hundred dollars' worth of merchandise in a day. I saw clerks ringing up that much every few minutes.

I went home, poured a glass of bourbon straight, got out the front section of the morning paper and sat there with the last rays of sunlight filtering through the window above my desk, sipping my drink and flipping through page after page of clothing ads. Having reached the last page, I started all over again.

Clearly the fashion world was coopting the hippie scene. However watered down it had become along the way, people who might otherwise be concerned about their station in life were letting their hair down after hours and making a statement with their clothing. Yeah, I may have missed the sixties, but I'm hip with it now.

In the morning, I drove back to the shop and waved David and Sheila into the house. When I handed Sheila the sales invoices, she seemed delighted.

"Wow, did you have a gas?"

I stared at the two of them.

"You're quitting," David said.

"No."

"Then?"

"I want you to make an additional line."

I got out the ads and flipped through the pages.

"Wow, it's so commercial," Sheila said.

"Unfortunately, that's the business you're in. Go to the malls yourself if you like but this is what's selling."

David looked at Sheila and pushed his glasses back. I got up and started to leave.

"If you want me to work for you, that's what you have to do. Now, if you'll excuse me, I've got some calls to make."

I closed the door behind me.

Over the next two weeks, Sheila and David did as I asked, but I was unable to make headway with any of the department stores. I left messages but no one returned my calls. For all my efforts, I had nothing to show; not one single appointment. Worse still, the little boutiques that had been the backbone of the business weren't buying the new line. Production was nearly at a standstill and my popularity around Furry Freak Leather was on par with the plague.

Up emptying my bladder at three that morning, it suddenly hit me. I spent most of the night with my eyes wide open. Promptly at nine o'clock, when offices of all the major department stores opened, I started calling.

"Good morning, this is Happy Hobbit Leather Goods."

By noon I had three appointments, and one of those was for the following day. That damned Ellie, she had it right from the start. You couldn't have a name that scared away women and children.

I was feeling rather full of myself when I arrived to the lobby of this big corporate office the next day. Then this guy rolled in with a snappy looking cart, took a seat across from me and opened one of his sample cases. My balloon deflated. His belts were neatly displayed on black velvet, with each display removable; everything top drawer. My presentation was to throw the belts on the table.

I developed a serious case of cotton mouth while waiting, a condition seriously exacerbated by the joint I had smoked on my way up to LA.

The minutes ticked by. I was thinking to run for the exit.

Finally, this prim looking middle-age woman came out to greet me. Mrs. Stillwood. Right out of Kansas. The closest she had ever come to a hippie was flipping through an issue of Look magazine. I was led down a hallway and into her office under fluorescent lights.

"Well, let's see what you have," she said brightly.

I began pulling things out of my case and spreading them around the desk.

"By the way, I like that name. Happy Hobbit. It's so cheerful."

That just killed me. There we were, this once highwayman of the sixties and this maven of Midwest couture with a bun.

I stumbled through the presentation, my heart pounding, my cotton mouth worsening the entire time. I could not wait to get things stuffed back into the case and find a bar. All the while, Mrs. Stillwood carefully examined the samples and made a list of style numbers on her note pad.

Then abruptly, she stood up and shook my hand.

"Thank you so much for coming in."

I had my little invoice book out there, ready to write up an order.

"So you didn't want to buy anything?"

"Oh, we'll call you if we're interested. Now, if you wouldn't mind. I have another salesman to see before lunch."

I gathered up my goods, thanked her again and made for the door. It did not take me long to find a bar, one of those quiet little places that existed without sunlight. I arrived home tanked and with no heart to call David or Sheila.

My appointment the following day went more or less along the same lines. No doubt our products were quality. Buyers held each item in their hands with respect, but they weren't making orders. I was out of my league.

I got home that afternoon to find several calls on my answer machine from Sheila. I didn't answer her, then or the following day.

I finally decided to show my face at the shop on Friday. Cheers erupted when I walked in through the side door. Sheila gave me a big hug.

"Sorry about disappearing," I said. "I've been busy."

"We know. Here, sit down."

Sheila got me a stool.

"What's up?"

"Are you ready?"

I shrugged.

"Mrs. Stillwood called this morning and ordered three hundred thousand dollars' worth of stuff."

I didn't know whether to laugh or cry. When I got up and did a jig, Sheila joined me.

"Dear old Mrs. Stillwood."

"Yes, dear old Mrs. Stillwood. She said she would have ordered more but it's clearance time."

"Well, I suppose we can let her off the hook this one time."

Sheila laughed and clapped her hands and we jigged some more.

"Okay," I said, stopping. "Can I get some kind of advance?"

Sheila found her purse and gave me a hundred dollars.

"Wow, everybody. Let's go have a beer."

Everyone piled out. Ever methodical, David finished the belt he was working on before locking the garage and following us around the corner to the Mexican bar. I called Ellie very late that night, drunk and effusive and apologetic for having awakened her. Graciously, she expressed her happiness for me.

I came to the next morning, sobered by what I had wrought. The big marketing exec. My life was veering down a strange and somewhat unwelcomed destiny.

Later in the day, everyone having anything to do with Happy Hobbit Leather Goods joined together in a business meeting. As no one among us had ever participated in such a thing before, no one knew quite what to do. Sheila had possessed the foresight to bring coffee and donuts. Alan, one of the workers, brought some beer. I was far more appreciative of his contribution and cracked open a Coors. Like several other people, I lay in a prone position with my eyes shut.

David called us to order and stared until the laughter subsided. When it became quiet again, he presented a list of things to be addressed. Foremost on this list was how to facilitate making all these belts and purses. People threw in their two cents. Sheila took notes. A number of formalities were concluded, including the proper way to have a meeting. Alan was named shop manager. David sent him off to locate an industrial space and joined Sheila on a trip to the bank. Capital was needed as much as anything.

I put gas in the Peugeot, drove down to the sea and spent the day wandering from beach bar to beach bar, worried about where this new life was leading me. Once you went down a particular fork in the road, could you ever turn back?

At sunset, I drove down to Ellie's place and invited her out to dinner at a nearby Italian restaurant. It was charmingly darkened with romantic strings playing in the background.

"You will be able to do whatever you want," she assured me once we had gotten settled with a bottle of wine.

"Yeah, I'm already feeling corrupted."

"Roger, you are exasperating."

"Thank you."

"Try to look at it this way. You are young. You have many years left ahead of you. You can walk away from this at any time you like. So relax and enjoy your new freedom."

"I have my new collection coming out. Poet in a Seersucker Suit."

"That's a wonderful image."

"Isn't it though?"

Ellie reached over to hold my hands.

"Were you going to stay?"

I gave her a look. Two doors down the hallway from the twins. The headboard banging against the wall. The two of us uttering profanities.

"We don't have to make love," Ellie said, anticipating my thoughts.

"Yes we do."

"All right, Roger."

"I am thinking to rent a place down at the beach. At least we'll be closer."

Her look expressed hurt now.

"Ellie, I can't live with you there. I would feel like a perpetual guest."

Sometime later, we walked out to the parking lot, kissed goodnight and went our separate ways.

Sixteen

David and Sheila leased an industrial unit a few miles down the road from their place. It came with offices overlooking the shop floor and a storage area over the offices. I had just arrived to meet them and have my first look at the new operation. Alan and the rest of the production crew were out on the shop floor, building work benches for the production line. We were in the office, watching them through a glass partition.

We had one month to deliver the department store order and had yet to acquire the necessary raw materials to fill it, let alone the machinery. David and Sheila had gone to see about a loan earlier that morning.

"So where did you go to," I asked them.

They looked at each other sheepishly.

"Let's just say these people are known to break legs if the payments aren't made on time, " Sheila said.

My mouth opened.

"The mob? Are you kidding me?"

"Well, not exactly the mob, but close."

"If the department store pays out in three months, everything will be fine," David said.

"And if they don't?"

"We gave them your number," Sheila said with her usual mirth.

I stared at David. He pushed the glasses back from his nose.

Deciding it was best not to inquire any further, I went off to make some phone calls. Having wooed other department stores, with similar results, Sheila told me to stop taking orders. My job now was to string out these buyers until we could meet the demand, and to placate our smaller boutique owners, who were getting lost in the shuffle. The backbone of the industry, people often called them. I had agreed to hand deliver a box of belts and purses to one of these disgruntled proprietors up in Hollywood that same afternoon.

A month later, the first big delivery finally went out the door. The next day, a full-page ad appeared in the LA Times and all hell broke loose. I stood out on the shop floor with the production crew, having a good laugh. Artsy-craftsy was the defining adjective in Mrs. Stillwood's ad. That was how she had distilled the wildness of the '60s into something palatable for the masses

"Hey, you could get high wearing one of these things," someone said.

"Yeah, or busted," someone else added to more laughter.

Alan farted. Someone threw a purse at him and the gathering dispersed. Alan returned to making new designs. Sheila returned to her office work, a thing she did with both the energy of a cartoon character and the gracefulness of a ballet dancer. The phone rang and she waved at me through the glass partition. It was a call from San Francisco. That call was followed immediately by one from Ellie.

"Well, JP," she started in. "I saw the ad."

"Yeah, belt baron of the wild west."

Sheila clapped in the background.

"Sheila likes the imagery," I said regarding the commotion.

"Well, I'm so very proud of you."

Ellie launched into a dissertation on success and applauded mine at length. When she finally caught her breath, I mentioned my birthday.

"It's Friday. Though no doubt you've forgotten all about it."

"Actually, I have a very special present for you."

"Hmm, well my mother is having the family over for dinner that night."

"And dare I darken the door?"

"I had intended for you to come along, yes."

"You don't think I'll be stoned?"

"No, but that probably best describes how we should arrive."

She laughed.

"Well, jokes aside, I think it would be fascinating to see your folks again."

"I'm sure they'll be happy to see you."

I was not so sure about my mother but what the hell. Ellie was a supremely self-confident woman and I left it at that.

After a bit of love talk, I got off the phone and returned the buyer's call.

While we talked, a woman came in to interview for the new secretary position with Sheila and my heart jumped. It was Cerise, the young lady who had danced with me at the bar a few months back. I still had her phone number buried under a stack of papers on my desk back at home.

Staring at her profile through the glass partition between my office and Sheila's, I was reminded of how truly lovely Cerise was. I got up to pull the blinds but Cerise noticed the movement and our eyes met. I winked and she quickly looked away.

I left the blinds open just enough to steal glances at Cerise while she was being interviewed. There was something French about her; dark hair, fair skin, crisp white blouse and loop earrings.

At some point, I spun around in my executive chair and got lost in a business call. When I turned back, Cerise was gone. In fact, everyone had gone home.

I went into Sheila's office and sniffed at the lingering scent of perfume. I touched the chair where Cerise had been sitting. I went home and thought of her over a meal alone. She was corporeal in my mind now. Like a beautiful cancer, she was already growing in my heart.

Ellie arrived at my place about six that Friday evening. I had just showered and stood there shirtless with my hair still wet. Gray clouds mottled the twilight sky outside. My windows were open to the cool winter air. Ellie kissed my naked chest and sat on the bed while I toweled my hair dry and finished dressing.

"Did you care for a drink?" I asked her.

She declined.

"Actually, it's mandatory."

"Getting nervous, are we?"

"You have a choice. Be well inebriated, or make certain my mother is. Either will do, though both offer your best shot at surviving the ordeal intact."

"What's your poison," Ellie said, getting up from the bed.

"Scotch and soda. Make it a double."

I pulled a laundered shirt from the closet. Ellie returned as I zippered my pants.

"You look very handsome," she said.

"Thank you. You look exquisite, as always."

I took the drink and kissed her.

"Have you written anything?" she asked as we left the bedroom.

I hit the light switch and glanced at my desk out in front.

"No, it's dead."

"It's not dead."

"All right, comatose. What's the difference? I feel nothing after a long day at work. Any inspiration I might have felt in the course of the day is but a shadow by then. I'm like Thoreau's lost soul, wandering about here in my quiet desperation."

"Then write about that."

I muttered to myself, all the while knowing she was right. It was one thing for the flame to grow dim, quite another for the embers to die out entirely. Once gone, one never knew if the fire would come back.

"Here's to you," I said with a final belt from my drink.

I set the glasses in the kitchen sink and we headed out the door. My parents lived but a short distance away, over Lincoln Hill and adjacent to what remained of an orange grove.

"Hey, birthday boy," my mother said at the door.

She had spent a lifetime fussing and fretting over everything mundane, and yet a great warmth and nobility of spirit emanated from her.

"You remember Eleanor."

"Oh yes. From Vincent's wedding."

I watched her welcome of Ellie, looking for any loss of warmth or sign of trouble but there was none.

Inside the crowded living room, I was promptly confronted by my brother Frank. He was already lit up and tried to get his arm around my neck. I caught it in midair.

"How are you doing, Frank?"

"Good, good. How are you doing? Come here."

He tried again with the arm business.

"Goddamn it, Frank. Knock it off."

He laughed.

"Hi, I'm Frank," he said, introducing himself to Ellie. "I'm sure old Rog here has kept me a secret."

Ellie shook his hand.

"Actually, Roger has told me all about you."

She smiled regally.

"Oh," Frank said with big eyes. He glanced at me and back at Eleanor. "So now you know all the Dunne brothers."

"Well, at least I know they all exist."

Frank smiled and blinked.

"Well, come," he said, grabbing Ellie by the arm. "I'll introduce you to the crowd."

She went along with a look of mock fright over her shoulder. I waded through the crowd the other way, headed for the kitchen and a drink. My progress was slowed by repeated handshakes and salutations. There were nieces and nephews, husbands and girlfriends and numerous people who had simply tagged along for a good Italian meal.

I ran into my sister Rose coming out of the kitchen with her newborn son. After a hug and brief hello, I continued on and found my mother immersed in her food preparations.

"Roger, take these out to the table." She pointed at a tray of hors d'oeuvres. "And bring the extra chairs in from the garage."

She hardly noticed that I was making a drink.

"Roger, did you hear me?" she called out as I left with the tray and my bourbon.

I placed the tray down on a serving table and drank deeply. Ellie was in the corner with Frank and some other people, having a grand time of it. She waved. I offered her a snide look in return.

After retrieving one armload of chairs from the garage, I made myself another drink and started back for more chairs. Seeing this, my eldest niece, Toni, came over to lend me a hand.

"Gosh, Uncle Roger. It's your birthday and grandma's got you working."

"Yeah. The whole operation would come to a screeching halt without me."

Toni laughed and rolled up her sleeves. She was a delight, confident, cheery and already talking about her career plans at eleven years old. I could not imagine it. At her age, I was still playing with frogs.

We returned to find my mother making another sortie from the kitchen, this time holding a warming tray in her hands.

"Roger, get some pot holders. Hurry!"

I dashed into the kitchen and grabbed the first thing available.

"I told you a pot holder, Roger."

I folded the two dishtowels and got them under the tray.

"It'll do, Mom."

She was hardly satisfied but quickly moved on to the next mission.

"Let's get some paper plates out here."

"Gosh, grandma. It's his birthday. Why don't you leave the poor guy alone?"

"Never mind," my mother said and disappeared back to her domain. I shook my head at Toni.

"Aw," she said. "Aren't you glad you came?"

"Yes, and now I'm leaving."

Toni laughed.

I asked about her plans in life and she explained how she was saving up for a study/travel trip aboard a cruise ship in three years. That dovetailed into her career plans. I was humbled again. How did you know what you wanted to be at that age? At twenty-one, I still felt lost in the world.

Our conversation was disrupted when my mother barged out from the kitchen with another big tray in her hands. Rose was right behind with two side dishes.

"Chow time!" Rose called out facetiously.

"Rose, you didn't set out enough glasses."

"Uh oh," Frank said, arriving at the table. "We're going to have to fine you big time for that one."

Rose pretended to strangle my mother from behind. There was laughter all around, which only served to fluster my mother further.

Amidst all this hoopla, my father arrived at the head of the table, his entrance maximized for the greatest possible dramatic effect, gestures all around and a jug of cheap wine set down by his feet.

When Ellie joined me, my father patted her hand and encouraged her to sit beside him.

"This is where the great minds meet, eh."

Ellie feigned boastful pride at the invitation. My father poured her a glass of wine.

"To life," my father said. "Which you shouldn't take too seriously, because you'll never get out of it alive."

He drank. Ellie tasted her glass of that cheap crap and grimaced playfully at me.

"So, you are a teacher," my father said. "I remember Vincent telling me something about this."

"Actually, I'm a college professor."

My father held up his hands in mock deference. I looked to the heavens.

"To all the great minds," he said and drank.

"Wait a minute," Rose said. "Maybe we should be making a toast to my little brother before things get carried away?" Rose turned to me. "To Roger. Happy twenty-first birthday."

"Yes, and many, many more," my mother added.

All the glasses were held high, that ceremonial moment quickly swallowed by a renewed buzz of conversation.

"So, you know my son Roger, here," my father said.

I passed the plate of manicotti and eyed Ellie.

"Well, Jack, you seem to have raised three fine boys. And a lovely daughter."

"Somehow they have all managed to stay out of jail. So far, so good."

"So what do you think of Roger's recent success?"

My father's hands came up again in mock reverence. He had a real knack for variations on that theme, all of it related to his personal saga. He had risen to great heights. He had fallen from those heights and had never attempted to climb back up again, the remainder of his life lived parasitically off the successes of others. In that, I pitied him. For his sarcasm and lack of respect for my sibling's successes, and mine, I wanted to deck him.

"When I see the nice cars and million dollar homes," he said and sliced with his open hand several times. "Then we'll talk class, eh."

Ellie laughed.

"Well, Jack, you've set the bar pretty high there."

"Oh yeah, real high," Frank said. "Just high enough for him to slip under it."

Rose and Frank had a big laugh.

"You respect your father," my mother said from the far end of the table.

My father's eyes had narrowed to the size of bullets with the assault. He found Ellie's hand and patted it again.

"You never mind. I've got more class in my little finger than all of them put together."

Ellie smiled, studying my father.

"I happen to think your sons have a great deal of class, Jack."

"Well, thank you," Frank said.

"Eh," my father said, slicing away with his hand again.

He had grown up around a lot of Italians and the hand gestures had rubbed off.

"You know," Ellie said. "I remember the first time I saw Vincent walk into my classroom. There was a regal quality about him and I honestly think all of your children have that air."

"Eh. Vincent was a bum from the start. He's a bum now and he'll always be a bum."

"Stop it," my mother said from her end of the table.

"Yeah, Dad. Give us a break," Rose said.

"You never mind. I've built empires in my lifetime."

"Oh yeah," Frank said with his glass held aloft. "Here's to Diamond Jim Brady. The last of the big spenders. That's why he's got a Rambler out in the garage."

Laughter followed and the eating commenced in earnest. Bread and wine made their way around the table. Second and

216

third helpings were served. There was much conversation and laughter. My father poured himself repeated glasses of wine and ran his line of bullshit on Ellie. She glanced my way at one point, feigning a need to be rescued.

Before long, my mother's Pavlovian need to clear the table kicked in. Rose grabbed her plate.

"Mom, I'm not done yet."

"Rose, I've got to get the dessert and coffee out here."

"What is there? A schedule?"

"Oh yeah," Frank said. "Didn't you hear the whistle blow?"

Rose made the sound of a train horn.

"Next," she said.

"Okay, you too, enough."

My mother again tried to take her plate.

"Stop it!" Rose told her.

My father made one of his all-knowing gestures at Ellie.

"So, no doubt you've read Keats and Tennyson."

"Actually, I much prefer Keats," Ellie said. "Tennyson should have taken up fiction."

"Well, the Irish, you see…"

I got up to lend my mother a hand. My father was soon reciting his lines about a babbling brook.

"Relax, Rog baby," one of Frank's cronies said when I reached for his plate.

Rog, baby. I had never liked this guy much. He was a night-school attorney who specialized in keeping his friends out of jail. The mob would have loved him. I took his plate anyway.

Out in the kitchen, my mother was rinsing off dishes in the sink. I placed my stack with the others. Rose came in with more plates.

"I just love Ellie," Rose said. "She's such a doll."

"Never mind," my mother said, attacking the dishes. "A young man should have a wife. How are you going to have children with her?" she asked me without looking up.

"Maybe I won't have children, Mom."

"Maybe they're in love," Rose said. "Did you ever consider that?"

"Never mind. It's wrong. He shouldn't be fooling around with an older woman like that."

I left with a stack of pie plates. Ellie touched me when I sat down.

"So, the big businessman," my father said. "When are you going to make your first million? That's what I want to know."

"I think Roger has different aspirations," Ellie said.

"No, you stick to it, eh? Up early every day. You get out there and get them."

He made a motion with his fist and arm to punctuate his point.

I left to go look through a stack of old albums in my parent's stereo console, fed up with my father. How did you tell him? I don't envy your gods? Jesus, the hypocrisy. Quoting pastoral poets in one breath and groveling before the Morgan's and Getty's of the world in the next.

For a laugh, I put on one of Mantovani's albums. There were groans from the table.

My mother and Rose came out of the kitchen with the cake just then. The birthday candles were already lit.

"Come on, Roger," Rose called out.

I turned off the music. Everyone sang happy birthday and I blew out the candles. My only wish was to get the hell out of there.

Soon enough, all the dishes had been cleaned up and the revelers started to disperse. My father was asleep at the table. I said goodbye to all who remained and escorted Ellie to the front door. My mother joined us and stared as we climbed into Ellie's car. I waved from the front seat and she waved back before closing the door.

Alone with Ellie again, I found her presence infinitely calming. She had weathered it all so well. I kissed her face and lips.

"Roger, I love your family," she said.

"I always thought you were a bit off center."

"I'm serious. What wonderful grist for the mill."

"Yes, well, you know, I had them for just that reason."

Ellie guffawed and started up the car.

Seventeen

That following Monday, Cerise came to work as Sheila's assistant. Around midafternoon, Sheila sent her into my office with the copy of a sales order.

"Hi," I said.

"Hi," she said.

"I'm sorry. I meant to call."

I drummed my fingers. She shrugged and looked around my office.

"I'm sure you were really busy with your job."

"Yeah. That was part of it. It's a long story."

While Cerise stared, her tongue absentmindedly licked at the birthmark on her upper lip.

"Maybe we could try again?"

"Okay..."

Cerise waved the piece of paper in her hand.

"I know. Sheila sent you in here for something."

"She wanted me to check this sales order against your copy."

While searching for the file, I became aware of Cerise's hoop earrings. They swayed back and forth in hypnotic fashion. I found my copy and handed it to her.

"Better bring this back."

"I will."

She started out.

"Soon."

She looked over her shoulder.

"Dinner some night?"

She stopped with her hand on the door.

"Okay."

I smiled with corruption and excitement doing a tango in my heart.

With Cerise gone, I looked again at the check on my desk. It was the commission for that Stillwood order. It was enough to make a down payment on a house. I had a sudden idea and snapped my fingers.

"Got to run," I told Sheila on my way out the door. "By the way, Bullocks is still on my case about that order."

Sheila looked out at the bustling production floor in thought.

"We can start filling it next week. I think."

"I'll tell them."

"Let me talk to David before you do."

"Where is he, by the way?"

"Paying off the mob."

I smiled and shook my head.

"Where are you off to?"

I waved the check.

"Off to deposit this and figure out some wild way to spend the money."

"Don't be stupid."

"Well, you know me."

I smiled a final time for Cerise on my way out the door.

The following morning, I pulled up to the shop in my snazzy new Alfa Romeo convertible and parked it in front of Sheila's office window, assuming that certain parties would be watching from the other side of the reflective glass. For a bit of extra flair, I jumped over the door rather than opening it. All I needed was a scarf and a martini.

Inside, Sheila wasted no time in giving me the razz about the sports car. I gave her a high five and looked for Cerise, who wasn't in the office. Then I noticed her out on shop floor, talking to Alan. I was beginning to hate that guy. I looked back at Sheila.

"And don't you dare tell Cerise about Ellie," I whispered.

"Sorry. I already did."

"Fuck!" I said under my breath.

"Roger. No way am I going to let you play with that young lady's heart."

"Oh goddamn it, Sheila. I'm not married...Christ. You know, I felt myself really falling in love with her the other day."

She shrugged. I was about to continue my rant but Cerise returned, her look at me aloof now. She was a million miles away. I looked out at my snazzy new Alfa Romeo. Ten grand, and for what?

I grabbed a few things from my office and headed up to LA.

Within the week, Cerise was dating Alan, and they did little to keep it a secret. Every day at some point, I would notice them sharing little lover's kindnesses around the shop. I was inconsolable. It seemed that something truly dear had slipped through my hands.

With my literary aspirations abandoned, I had begun to feel like Mastroianni in *La Dolce Vita*, that last scene, where his abandoned muse calls to him from across the bay. Hey, remember me? Come back, come back! But Mastroianni waves her off and turns down the shoreline with his dissolute friends, his corruption complete. That was how I felt. Everything dear and meaningful had died and was drifting away.

Adding salt to my wounds, it no longer seemed that I was one with my peers. Like David and Sheila, I was management now. I had turned a hippie garage business into multi-million dollar operation, only to find myself apart from my own generation. When I walked out onto the production floor, everything went silent. When I left, the fun and games resumed in my absence.

A denizen now of freeways, malls, hotels and airport bars, I hardly knew the man I saw in the mirror. On the one hand, I had the world by the tail. On the other, I felt as hollow as the smoke from my constant cigarettes. There were days on my way up to LA when I'd think, let's just keep going. Take the coast road up through Big Sur to Monterey and Santa Cruz. Drive until you forget what you have become. And then it was back to another week of business.

I was working late in the office one Friday afternoon and happened to notice Cerise and Alan playing lover's games out on the shop floor. When our eyes met, I reached up and closed the blinds to my office window.

I had dinner plans with Ellie that evening and was soon headed down the freeway to my consolation prize. If only Ellie were my age, I thought. It would have made all the difference.

At our candlelight soiree, Ellie suggested we get away for her mid-term break.

"Sure," I said.

"I was thinking of Catalina," Ellie said.

"Sure," I said, that image of Alan and Cerise playing together stuck in my head.

Anyway, I dreaded the idea of three days on Catalina. It was just the sort of trip to make my skin crawl. The hours would be dripping with ennui and suntan lotion. And I would be thinking of Cerise and Alan the entire time.

"You see," Ellie was saying. "I only have three days, so it's a perfect escape. Twenty minutes on a plane and we're there. No travel time, no hassle."

"If you can get a hotel reservation."

"I already have something lined up. The Zane Grey. Just in case you wanted to go. It's a lovely place. Cascading down a hillside above the harbor. You could drag along your typewriter."

"Oh yeah. And stare at the fucker for three days."

"You don't know. You might feel inspired."

"After a month of complete isolation, I might."

"Roger, I've never known a more difficult man."

"Thank you."

I stared off into the darkness around our candlelit table.

"What are you thinking?" she said.

"Oh, the big white ship just came to mind. Did you ever take it over to Catalina?"

"Yes, many years ago."

"Yeah. I went with my parents when I was a kid. The Mills Brothers were playing. Everyone had a cocktail. It seemed so elegant and fun."

"Sorry," she said. "I think it's moored up in mothballs these days."

"Yeah, I know. Just thinking. What kind of plane is it?"

"A World War I biplane."

224

My eyes snapped around.

"Just seeing if you're paying attention."

That night, when I made love to Ellie, I found myself thinking of Cerise. What a nightmare.

The day of our departure, we drove up to Long Beach Airport. The plane turned out to be a refurbished P-38. It was waiting for us out on the tarmac, its polished aluminum pocked by a thousand rivets.

"A biplane might have been safer."

Ellie pooh pooed my concerns on our way out from the terminal.

A stewardess greeted us at the door and told us to take any seat. Once the plane had filled with passengers, the pilot came back and asked if someone would come up front and act as ballast. Ellie encouraged me to go forward, so I did.

Lifting off, it felt as if we were a kite in the wind. I looked back in Ellie's direction with real fright. A commercial jet did not prepare you for this feeling, not even in bad weather.

The pilot hugged the sea at five hundred feet. White caps rippled below us. The surging sea made it feel as if we were changing elevations, though we were not.

Fifteen minutes later, the pilot swooped up and around to the back side of the island, then dove down to the runway above Avalon. The runway was situated on a long, sloping plateau of grass that ended at a cliff. I thought we were going over. Thankfully the pilot stopped just in time.

Ellie and I caught the shuttle into town and she pulled out her imaginary 'to do' list along the way.

"First off, I have a hike planned for after lunch. I knew you'd be dying to see the wild buffalo. And then there's the little tour of the Wrigley mansion."

She pretended to check things off on her list.

"Of course, we'll do the glass-bottom boat ride. Can't leave that out. That should leave just enough time before dinner for that lecture at the casino on Hollywood's role in developing the island."

She put the imaginary pencil to her tongue and prepared to cross out another item on the itinerary.

"Let's see, have I left anything out?"

I pretended to strangle her and her tongue came out with her hands flailing about.

"Actually, I plan to do very little this weekend and to enjoy the hell out of it. Decadence is my motto. What do you say?"

"I'm all in for that."

"Well, there you have it."

She tossed her pretend list out the window.

"Decadence it is."

As Ellie settled against my shoulder, the shuttle rounded a fold in the hills and the harbor came into view, all cheery blue and dotted with sailboats. On the northern point, the cake-shaped casino sat with its red clay roof. Ellie pointed to several structures cascading down a craggy hillside above the casino.

"That's the Zane Grey."

"Looks lovely."

"A little orange juice, croissants and jam, the morning paper and a carafe of French coffee."

Ellie delighted in her picture.

"And then the bus tour guide honks his horn."

She panicked.

"You're funny."

"So are you. Maybe you'll write something this week."

"Please, no pressure."

"Well, you see..."

I gave her the evil eyes and she settled back against my chest with a smile.

After checking into the hotel and unpacking, Ellie and I walked down to have lunch at a fish joint along the quay. What had appeared to be cobalt blue seas from high above was now translucent green water, lapping lazily below our window. Everything smelled of brine. There were schools of sardine darting about and the usual drifts of kelp. Out in the harbor, the sea still looked cheery blue among the yachts and sailboats.

Later, Ellie and I walked out to the casino and wandered among the rooms. There were framed photographs mounted on the walls, reliving the golden age of Hollywood. We saw an announcement for a ballroom dance that Sunday evening but that was our day to head back.

Upon returning to the hotel, I found decadence already settling in. I wanted to write but as always found it impossible to start in the middle of the day. My conscious mind was awash in static and meaningless drivel. Nothing I had to say seemed important so I drank instead.

"Maybe we'd better consider that tour," I said to Ellie.

She lay next to me in the afternoon sun.

"I know, let's go snorkeling," she said.

"Did you know that the waters around Catalina are populated with moray eels?"

"Then let's not."

I winked at her. She wiggled her toes for me. Her legs were now half in shade. The sun was disappearing behind the hills. A warm day was growing cool.

"Actually, snorkeling sounds like a nice idea. Let's do that tomorrow."

Ellie got out her imaginary list again.

"Okay, so that leaves this afternoon and this evening."

"Is there anything on there about screwing?"

"Gosh, no, not a thing. But there is something here about l'aaahmourrr."

"They're the same thing."

I laughed as her usual routine played out.

We took a shower later and crawled into bed. Curtains partly darkened the room. The outside world appeared in flashes as they swayed in the breeze. Ellie took hold of me and our passions began. Ecstasy led to a weightless moment, a flash of bright white light and then we had tumbled back into the lazy afternoon.

"No wonder people kill over it," Ellie said in the silence.

"Yes," I said.

"Won't it be fun to live like this on my sabbatical?"

"Yes."

"Perhaps we'll never come back."

"Perhaps not."

"You seem awfully distracted," she said.

"It's my work. Or the lack thereof."

"Don't worry. It will come."

I nodded, my mind with another woman.

The vacation continued along these lines for three days. We drank, screwed, ate and wandered around a bit. And I did my best not to feel corrupted. I was relieved when our brief sojourn came to an end. I had written nothing.

Within a month of our return, I had grown completely bored with the business and began to devise various excuses to explain my lengthy absences—a meeting here, a conference there—when in fact I was surf fishing down at Scotchman's Cove, or sitting at home with a blank sheet of paper in my typewriter. It was blank at the start of the day. It was blank at the end. I had started a screenplay about the sixties but never got past the opening scene. It was a great opening scene. A man on acid, swallowed by a swarm of bodies at a rock festival. I was very talented at starting things. Bringing them home was where I got bogged down.

I walked into Ellie's place one Friday evening and found her immersed in a flurry of gourmet food preparations. The evidence was scattered all over the kitchen.

"You look surprised," she said.

I held up my hands.

"I'm sorry. Did I forget something?"

"That wine and cheese party for my colleagues tomorrow afternoon?"

"Oh Christ."

"Yes. *That* wine and cheese party."

"Sorry. I've been busy ditching work."

"Oh dear."

I grabbed a kiss, a deviled egg and went to terminate Al Green's moment on Ellie's turntable. Billy Paul was next. We got a thing going on. Christ. I exchanged it for the latest Steely Dan album and made for the shower.

Ellie had a glass of cabernet sauvignon waiting for me when I returned.

"Think I'll go surf fishing tomorrow."

"You bastard."

"Sorry."

"Why are you so deathly afraid of my colleagues?"

"I don't know. The peasant, remember?"

She put her knife down and came around to face me. Dissatisfied with the logistics, she took my glass, placed it on the counter and forced her way between my legs.

"What on earth is bothering you?"

"Hell, everything. Where do you want me to start?"

She kissed me passionately on the neck and face and placed her hand on my crotch.

"How about here?"

"My pressure valve."

She rubbed me firmly.

"Just the goddamned, fucking, crappy pain in the ass world getting your head in a knot."

"Yeah."

"Come."

She led me into the living room and pulled my zipper down.

"Oh Ellie."

"So full of frustration. Come on. Come on."

"Oh god."

She deftly pulled her nylons and panties off and bent over the coffee table.

"Oh lover, just give me that sweet cream," she said as I pounded her without restraint. "Oh, I love it when you're hard in me."

"Oh, I love being hard in you, you sweet doll."

"Oh yes, yes, yes."

The music had stopped by the time I was done but we remained there moving in slow undulations together for some time, the shadows of a Friday evening rushing through our lives.

Ellie pulled away finally.

"Lover, you should never let it build up that long."

She caressed my cock again, kissed me sweetly and returned to her culinary duties.

"Crackers and brie," she said when I came in. "Mmm mmm mmm mmm mm."

Later, Ellie grilled two New York steaks rare and tossed a salad. We ate at the counter and talked about the upcoming election. Nixon was so far ahead in the polls, it seemed hopeless. In the back of my mind I was thinking about Ellie's party. Indeed, why did I dread being around her colleagues so much?

Ellie fell asleep early. I returned to bed late after reading and lay awake watching the wind move through the ornamental maple tree outside her window. How would it end? That question dogged my thoughts.

In the morning, I went to play racquetball at a local club. I returned to find one of Ellie's friends already there, helping with the preparations. By the time I got out of the shower, several more guests had arrived. I dressed and went out to play the role of a young gigolo.

Ellie had left a selection of wines opened on the coffee table. Classical music played quietly in the background. The guests were sampling brie and crackers and critiquing them. Ellie introduced me around.

"So, Ellie tells us you've become something of a tycoon," her colleague Mike said.

Mike was a shaggy headed, Gallic looking, wry pain in the ass. Otherwise, I liked him. I looked around the room. Mike's comment hung in the air. I decided not to touch it.

"Actually, I love the idea of business," he went on. "It is the mutual screwing of individuals for their common benefit."

Everyone laughed.

"Perhaps we could orchestrate the entire process to madrigal song."

"Oh yes. In tights and all," a lady said, delighted with herself.

There were more comments along these lines and the associated laughter. It was the mutual screwing of my dignity for everyone's benefit.

The doorbell rang and a man of Pakistani origin was ushered in. Ellie and everyone in the living room made a great fuss over him.

"This is Saji," she said, introducing me to him. "Our resident prodigy on campus. He swears it's only because his parents are rich."

She rubbed Saji's back and went off for a fresh tray of brie and crackers. I ditched Saji and made myself inconspicuous in a corner.

A minute later, this frumpy looking woman in wire rim glasses was introducing herself to me.

"Hi, I'm Marge. Ellie has told me a bit about your colorful past."

Colorful past. Her laugh was like fingernails on a chalkboard.

I gave Marge a brief version of my travels and learned a bit of her past. She had gone from early marriage to a recent divorce with a few trips to Europe in between.

We discussed points of interest the both of us had seen.

"Oh, I just loved this place." "Oh, I just loved that one."

She was very nice. I couldn't wait to escape.

I looked over to find Ellie engaged in animated conversation with Saji and several of her colleagues. The entire room was filled with laughter and conversation.

"So, JP, old boy," Mike said over a bite of brie and cracker. "Tell us more about this wonderful scheme of yours. You know, I'm thoroughly intrigued by the notion of making a quick buck."

"Roger's actually a very fine poet," Ellie said.

She went on to explain the seminal event that led to my success in business. I stared on, the subject of her documentary.

"Oh, I'd love to see your goods," Marge said. "I simply must acquire a little Haight-Ashbury outfit for my bohemian moments."

Everyone was staring at me. I was ready to scream.

"Well, what do you say, Roger old boy?" Mike enthused. "How about showing us some of your samples?"

"I don't have them here."

Groans spread through the room. I stared on silently.

"Roger only likes showing them to these old biddies who buy for the department stores," Ellie said.

She smiled at me with a wink. The chatter drifted on to other topics.

The minute everyone was distracted again, I disappeared into the bathroom. After a long look in the mirror, I slipped into Ellie's room, packed some heavy clothing and exited out the side door without being noticed. I had hoped to do the same backing my Alfa-Romeo out of the garage but Ellie heard the noise and appeared in the driveway.

"What on earth are you doing?"

"Going fishing."

"Roger, I take this as an insult, not only to me but to my friends as well."

"Ellie, you don't need me around for this."

I waved my hand in the general direction of her party.

"Well don't think you're going to use my home as the staging area for your various conquests."

"Please don't start a scene, Ellie."

"*Me* start a scene? Roger, you disparage me and the culture I have tried to bring into your life at every turn."

I repeated Mike's disparaging comments for her.

"Roger. He was just having a bit of fun."

"Some fun."

Ellie threw up her hands.

"I can't believe you're doing this."

"Sorry. I guess I can't change what I am."

"No, I suppose you will always be a peasant at heart."

" So the question becomes, Ellie. Is that good enough for you?"

"I don't know." She started back in through the open garage door. "I will have to give that some serious thought."

I backed out into the street. Ellie hit the garage door button. The two of us were staring at each other as the door came down.

I sped north on the Newport Freeway, hoping the scene at Ellie's place would fade with each passing mile, but it did not.

To hell with her, I thought. I was headed up to fish in the Sequoias. Hopefully David would join me. The idea of us fishing together up in the pine country brought calm to my heart. David might ask to borrow a lure, and if he lost it, I wouldn't care. He might screw up the morning eggs and neither of us would think twice about it. There was just too damn much at stake in a romance.

Pulling into the driveway at David and Sheila's place, I found Sheila sitting on the front porch. She smiled, looking very pregnant. Someone was playing an acoustic guitar in one of the upstairs bedrooms. The music drifted out of the window. It sounded like David. I climbed out of the car and walked over to say hello. Sheila pulled back the loose strands of her hair, still smiling.

"Well, I'm sure you didn't drive all the way up here to see me deliver."

"I came to steal your husband away."

"Oh, good."

The music had stopped upstairs and David appeared through the front door a moment later.

"Let's go fishing," I said.

"Yes, yes," Sheila said.

David pushed his glasses back.

"What about the shop?"

"We'll manage without you. Please. Go fishing with Roger."

David stared at her, unmoving.

"Go ahead. You need a break. We *both* need a break."

"Okay."

She clapped her hands together with a laugh. David and I went inside.

"Let's take your car," I said.

"Sure. How much should we take?"

"As little as possible. I want to leave plenty of room for booze."

He laughed.

"I'll go pack my stuff."

I went out the back door and got all my gear arranged in his Volkswagen square-back. David came out with a light backpack.

"Should we take my tent?"

"No," I said. "I've got mine if it rains."

"All right. I'm ready."

Sheila came out and I threw her the keys.

"Don't roll it," I said.

"Oh good. I'll take Cerise out on the town."

"Something I'd like to do."

"Uh oh. I smell trouble."

I stared at her and pretended to push my glasses back, just like David. That got a big laugh.

"See you in a week," I said as David was starting his car.

"Will you be gone that long?"

"I don't know. If I see leather belts in David's eyes, I'll know it's time to come back."

She laughed and clapped her hands.

"That's good, Roger."

She went around to kiss David.

"Put in the good word for me," I said as David backed out of the driveway.

Sheila pretended to scold me. David pulled down the street and I immediately felt foolish for having made the comment. I knew how these things went. It was going to grind on me for the entire trip now.

No, to hell with it, I thought. I would get my waders into a good stream and not worry about a goddamned thing.

Eighteen

On our way up through LA, I found myself grousing over the episode at Ellie's place, unable to let it go. When I finally shut up, I felt even worse for having aired my dirty laundry in public. It was the matter of decency. You didn't lynch someone without a fair trial. There was also the inscrutable nature of women, which no amount of complaining would ever resolve. I had known some really dumb ass men, who, when faced with their own war of the roses, had displayed a great deal more grace and aplomb than I did.

In the end, I washed away what remained of my wounds with a pint of Wild Turkey, so that by the time David and I had started our ascent into the high country on state route 178, I was feeling halfway repaired.

Scrub pines began to dot the hillsides. I rolled down my window to the cool mountain air and let my thoughts drift ahead to the Roads End Lodge, where we hoped to stay that night. Men would be there by the fire, talking of fish and game over glasses of bourbon and David and I would join them around the hearth, and then in the morning drive the thirty miles out to Horse Feather Camp, park there and hike even further up into the mountains, until there was nothing but a clear stream and wind whispering in the pines and two of us wading in with our poles.

David and I had stopped for supplies at Lake Isabella and were prepared to drive straight through if the lodge had no rooms, but they did—one, with two twin beds—so we paid for it, showered and walked up the remaining bit of gravel road as night settled in among the Ponderosas.

"Think it's because of your age differences?" David said matter-of-factly about my struggles with Ellie.

"Come on, David. People fight no matter what ages they are. Don't you ever fight with Sheila?"

"No. She fights. I listen and then go do something else."

"I don't know whether to admire or pity you."

"I don't see the point."

"Yeah, well, you'd have to be Irish and Italian."

David laughed. I glanced over at him. It was not that he lacked passions. Only that nature had endowed him with enough gray matter to allow a disinterested view of his own emotions. I imagined David looking down on the illusory world of feelings, weighing the pros and cons of a particular response, and deciding it was best to do nothing.

We walked along beneath the dark trees in silence. Occasionally, we heard the sound of a bird calling and its sudden flight through the forest. There were other sounds of movement in the twilight, no doubt nocturnal creatures coming out for the night, but mostly it was silent.

"Well, for the record, David. I'm tired of the fighting too. I just don't know how you stop it. I have every intention of staying calm when she starts up. Then everything spins out of control again."

238

"I guess life would be kind of boring without the dramatics."

"And on that score, I can assure you, Ellie is in complete agreement."

"Maybe you should have tried Cerise instead."

"Thanks, David."

He looked my way without expression.

"Look, I admit it. There's no getting around the age thing. But there's no getting around the fact that I love her, either."

"Yeah," was all he said.

The road came along the river and we stopped to watch it from a stone wall. The snow pack had been heavy that year and the river was ready to top its banks. The roar of it filled the canyon. I had a sidelong glance at David. Something was on his mind that I did not particularly care to hear. After a spell, we turned back towards the lodge. Our footsteps crunched in the gravel. Complete darkness now surrounded us.

"It's being gutless and afraid that I hate the most," I admitted along the way. "I think of getting back out on the road these days and the prospect of all that solitude just overwhelms me."

David looked over.

"It always seemed hopeless to me. Not because of her age, but because she can't have kids."

"So that's what's been on your mind."

He shrugged.

"Well who says I want kids?"

"Someday you will."

"I don't know. Children terrify me."

"Without them, all you have is life growing old."

"Well aren't you fucking sage tonight."

"I worked all this out in my head just a minute ago."

"By the looks of Sheila, it was a bit earlier than that."

David smiled.

We walked back into the glow of the lodge, ordered venison and a bottle of zinfandel, heard tales by the fire of how the Kern was running too strong to fish and did not say another word that night about women.

Early in the morning, David and I had a hearty breakfast and were turning up Thirty Mile Road well before the sun peeked over the snowcapped mountains. At a little past noon, we pulled into the U.S. Forestry camp and parked. As usual, the camp was mostly empty. I counted three cars. We picked a spot at the end, gathered our gear and slipped unseen into the woods.

At the top of the ridge, we turned north. The camp was well below and to our left now. We heard the report of a man chopping wood and saw him down through the trees. Each time the axe came down, a report echoed off a few seconds later.

"Fucking Davy Crockett," I said.

David laughed. The sound of the axe kept breaking the silence but slowly faded as we rounded a knoll and hiked steadily north. Soon we heard the whisper of the wind in the pines and our footsteps and little else.

A mile on, we crossed another ridge and saw a stream slicing through a canyon far below us. We worked our way down to it through the trees, then continued upstream a few hundred yards. There, the stream ran deep and dark in several pools but it would be good fishing down below the falls too, where the stream was shallower. Either way, we no longer had anyone around to bother us. There were the trees tall against the blue sky and the sun and the stream and nature quietly going about its business.

We made camp in a spot secluded by a vault of granite walls, got our gear out, hiked back down a bit closer to the falls and waded into the dark waters. The loops of our lines glistened in the sun. I tried to think only of the rhythm of my casting but Ellie was there, and the other woman too.

Before darkness set in, David had three trout. I had two. We went back to camp and David cleaned the fish while I gathered wood for a fire.

"No potato salad?" I said when he handed me the pan. The pan smelled of butter and trout.

"Shoot, I guess we'll have to hike back to town."

"We? You fucked up. You go get it."

He smiled. I shook some salt on my fish. A can of beans sat warming next to the fire.

"How about corn on the cob?"

"Forgot that too."

"You're worthless. I hope you didn't forget the bourbon."

"Got that, all right."

"You're a good man, David."

He cracked an ice cold beer from the stream and handed it to me.

"Oh god, that tastes good."

I belched. We had one case to last us all week, if we stayed that long.

"The fish is good," I said.

"The stream's got them nice and firm."

"Yeah, nice and firm."

I dumped half the beans on my plate and took another drink of beer. A coyote howled somewhere up the canyon.

"He's smelling the fish," David said.

241

"He can have this," I said and threw the bones of one down by the river.

Once I finished my beans, I leaned back against my roll and picked at one of the trout with my hands. The flesh tasted of the mountains, just the way an oyster tastes of the sea.

The pines whispered. The night was clear and full of stars.

"I'll clean up tonight," I told David when he finished.

"All right, camper number one."

"All right, camper number two."

He leaned back to where only his orange hair and glasses glowed in the flames of the fire.

"Think I'll buy some land," I said.

"Where?"

"Maybe up here."

"Sheila wants to buy some land in Mendocino."

"I like it up high. Too much undergrowth down below. I equate undergrowth with human trash."

"Sheila wants to grow stuff. Raise some animals."

"Wow. Then you can really practice ignoring shit." He laughed. "They'll find you wandering deliriously below Ft. Bragg somewhere."

"I don't want my life to be like my dad's. Living in a stucco box surrounded by concrete and a patch of grass."

"Mankind strove millenniums to achieve that state of affairs, David."

"Yeah."

"And here you come along, screwing it all up."

"Yeah," he said with more enthusiasm.

"Hell, don't ask me. I don't pretend to have any answers. You get away from society. Then you want to go back."

"We're all making it up as we go along, as best I can tell."

242

"Yeah. And sometimes not very well, at that."

We sat in silence for a spell. Then I took the plates and pans down to the stream to clean up.

"Where's the bourbon?" I said when I got back.

"I'll get it," David said.

I was up first the next morning and started the coffee. The sky was growing pink in the east and the air was freezer cold. The memory of Ellie smoldered like the ashes of our campfire. I felt angry and bitter inside each time I thought of her. I felt hope each time I thought of Cerise.

Rather than cook, David and I split a can of peaches for breakfast and headed down below the falls. I let David wade into the stream before me. He looked like a big orange-haired grizzly bear. His rod and reel looked small in his hands. I worked my way above him and closer to shore.

Later, when the sun came over the mountain, we both crossed the stream and sat in a clearing. David had the best trout of the day so far, a big brown. When the sun grew hot, we worked our way back up into the shade of the falls, trying different flies and different pools. In the afternoon we sat in the sun again and ate peanut butter and jelly sandwiches. We drank one beer a piece. We were good and hungry when we got back to camp that evening.

"How long do you want to stay?" I asked once David had cleaned up the plates. I worked on my teeth with a fish bone. He settled in next to me. We both had our shoes off and the fire crackled pleasantly near our socks.

"From what Sheila said, I'd better stick it out most of the week," he said. "Friday at the latest?"

"I might try to screw you by then." He laughed.

"Maybe a day sooner, huh?"

"Do you think Cerise wants to have kids," I asked him.

"Sure, she tells Sheila everything."

"And Sheila tells you."

"Not everything."

"Well, what part are you going to tell me?"

"What do you want to know?"

"Do you think she's in love with Alan?"

"Sheila's never said anything about it."

"What do you think?" I said.

"I don't think Cerise knows."

"What about Alan?"

"You mean does he love her?"

"Yeah."

"I don't think it matters much to him. He's more interested in his rock band."

We watched the fire for a spell in silence.

"I kick myself for not calling her now."

"You still have a chance."

"How so?"

"Hand me the bourbon and I'll tell you," he said.

We fished each day and it felt good to have the stream pushing against our bodies, to be moving in the wheel of life, to lay in the sun and dream and have fish to eat. Sometimes our dreams led to conversation and always we concluded that the world was too complicated and looked forward to a time when we could live our days in a simple way; not something soft or easy, just a way of life that lent itself to peace and quiet contemplation. That was the life we imagined having.

At some point during the sixth day of fishing, I pulled two beers from the cold water of the stream. There were only two more left. I walked up to the clearing with David and we finished our trout from the day before and the beer. I had been thinking of Ellie all morning. It seemed I was ready to take off the gloves. Or put them back on. I wasn't sure which. Anyway, it was Friday and the twins would be gone with the end of day.

The sun grew hot, and David and I moved into the shade.

"Should we spend the night or head back?" I asked David.

"How do you feel?"

"Hungry for answers."

"It's been nice," he said.

"Let's head back. There are some things I've got to know."

"Yeah. We've got the bourbon for the road."

"I hope we get back to the river again soon," I said walking with David back to camp.

"Towards the end of summer, maybe. Things slow down for a while then."

"Yeah," I said. "Us big businessmen have to think of such things."

"We're only children in the sun," David said.

I liked it when he said simple things like that. I wanted to be a child at heart but was in fact all hung up—about love, about being in business and especially about my failure as an author.

We buried all traces of our presence there in the mountains, finished the last two beers and struck out for the campground. I had mostly forgotten the world but it all came back when I heard a stereo playing in somebody's car. I was ready to turn around and head back to our hideaway.

Darkness came somewhere below Lake Isabella and the remainder of our drive home was a drone of engine noise and drifting conversation, awash in bourbon. I cracked the front door of Ellie's house in the gray hour before dawn and slipped down the hallway, not knowing what to expect. Ellie lay on her side with her back to me. The line of her hips and waist was molded in the comforter. I placed my hands close to her shoulder and kissed her cheek. She jumped and sighed upon seeing me. We stared at each other in the dim light.

"Hello Roger, I thought you were never coming back."

"I'm back."

"I'm sorry," she said. I continued to stare. "Do you forgive me?"

"Sure," I said.

"Please yell at me. I'd feel better."

"No. I'm going to take a shower."

"All right. Hurry back."

I ran the water very hot and anticipated making love to Ellie while I bathed. The many moments we had shared passed through my mind; like the day we sat on the beach at Mendocino with only the sea and the wind in our ears. All the memories seemed close and yet distant now, as if they were on the other side of time. Then I was freshly scrubbed and in bed and warm her against skin.

"What was it like?" she asked.

"Quiet. Peaceful."

I kissed her face, then her shoulders and breasts. She made me look at her.

"Tell me you forgive me."

"I forgive you."

"Have you gone away from me in your heart?"

"I don't know."

"You have."

The room had grown gradually lighter and I felt weariness overtaking me. Business matters were also invading my thoughts and I just wanted to sleep.

"I'm afraid we'll always be patching up the same mess," I said.

She turned away.

"You have."

"Can we talk about it tonight?"

I rolled over and pulled the quilt up to my neck. We lay there in silence.

"I can't sleep," she said.

"Oh, for god's sake, come here."

Nineteen

Ellie had made breakfast and came in to awaken me. I rolled over groggily. She leaned down to kiss me with the food tray in her hands.

"Thanks," I said and sat up.

It was bacon and eggs, with rye toast, coffee and orange juice.

"Tell me more about your trip," she said as I ate.

I recounted most of what had happened.

"We need to talk," she said once I had stopped.

"Please, not now."

I looked out the windows. Something was lost between us. I had felt it upon my arrival but did not entirely understand my own coldness in the matter. It was as if another man had loved Ellie and I had taken over his body. The vestiges of his emotions remained but they were vaporous, the splendor no longer attached. I had adored Ellie at one time but no longer felt that way. The only emotions I felt were sympathy and grief and I wanted to escape them.

"God, I can't believe this is happening," she said.

"What do you mean?"

"I'm hanging off a cliff, and for what? Jesus, Roger, if not for l'aaahmourrr, mankind would never feel this helpless."

"I know."

She stared.

"How do you do it, fucker?"

I shook my head.

"I told you earlier. I feel like we're going around and around in circles. That we're not learning from our mistakes."

"So you grow cold."

"Maybe I'm just one step ahead of you, Ellie."

She threw up her hands in frustration.

"All right. You don't want to talk. Did you want a quick screw? I have a conference on campus today."

Embarrassed, I placed my fork down.

"Oh well, I guess I can't even give *that* away."

She went off with the tray.

"Let's talk over dinner tonight," I suggested when she returned to use the bathroom.

"All right, Roger."

The door closed. I heard the shower running but was soon fast asleep again. When I reawakened, Ellie was gone.

It was Saturday and the sky was blue. I had nothing to do and went to grab a beer from the refrigerator. Looking out over the Pacific, I thought of Scotchman's Cove and decided to drive down for a swim. Heading out the door a short while later, I grabbed another beer for my backpack.

The shore was cold and blustery and mostly empty. I saw a young woman sunbathing without a top nearby and a man farther down the coast playing fetch with his Doberman. The man kept throwing his stick in the direction of the woman. She looked at me once and went back to sunbathing.

Both of us looked up at the shrill squeal of a squirrel. The Doberman had crippled it along the cliffs and was now playing with the animal for sport. I went over and chewed out the owner. Initially he argued with me but finally called off his dog. I saw the squirrel's bones disjointed and quickly crushed its head. There was a brief squeal but the suffering was over. I buried it and went for a swim. The water was very cold. A line of dolphins passed through the surf heading north. The young woman came out and swam near me.

"Thank you for doing that," she said.

I looked down at her breasts and back at her face. She was young and fair and beautiful.

"Hell, if the dog had just killed and eaten the damned thing, I wouldn't have minded so much."

"That's cruel," she said, not liking me so much anymore.

"That's life," I answered.

A passing wave pushed her body into mine and I held her up until the white water passed. Once back on her feet again, she pushed the hair from her face.

"Anyway, thank you," she said. "It was making me sick."

"Likewise. And I'm sorry. My comment wasn't meant to be cruel."

"Kathleen." She held out her hand.

"Roger. I'm going to catch a few waves."

I dove beneath the water and swam along the bottom until I was outside the turbulence of the breakers. The dolphins were near me when I surfaced, dark silhouettes no more than fifteen feet away. I watched with both excitement and fear until they had all passed to the north. Then I caught the next wave. Kathleen stood in the white water, watching me. I swam back out and rode another swell. The next time I looked up, she had returned to shore.

Back at my towel and drying off, I noticed the Doberman digging furiously for the buried squirrel. I went to chase it off and got into another row with owner. Finally, he leashed his Doberman and went south down the beach. Kathleen sat up as I walked by. I stopped at her towel. A lifeguard drove by in a Jeep and offered a thumbs-up smile, neither of which was intended for me. Then I was alone with Kathleen. We looked out to sea.

"You certainly don't mind having your way, do you?" she said.

"Most people consider it a pain in the ass."

"A man should know what he wants."

"Hmm. I wish it were that simple."

"It's simple enough for me."

I looked again at her face and breasts and back out to sea.

"Where do you go to school?" I asked

"What makes you think I'm in school?"

"Okay, what kind of work do you do?"

"I don't work. I go to school."

She smiled when I looked at her.

"I won't ask you any more questions."

"Like why I don't wear a top?"

Without taking her eyes off me, she lay on her back. Her slender waist fell softly away from the line of her ribs. There was not much hidden by the remaining portion of her swimsuit.

"Why aren't you in school?" she asked.

"Because I have a job."

The corners of her mouth turned up. Her dark eyes never wavered.

"We can meet here Monday. Unless you have to call in sick."

"I don't have to call in sick."

"Why?"

"Because I'm the boss."

She rolled over and faced me with her hand holding her head. The other hand touched my shoulder.

"I like to go dancing," she said.

"Where do you go?"

"There's a ballroom in Anaheim."

"Is that where you live?"

"No, I live in Fullerton."

I nodded.

"What?"

"That's where I work."

"I could get into a bar if I went with you."

"Maybe we'll do that."

"Here." She made room on her towel. "Come lie down."

I did so and she rolled on her side towards me so that her breasts touched against my flesh.

"We can go dancing tonight if you want."

"I can't."

"Why not?"

"Because I have other plans."

"Next week?"

"Sure."

I got up.

"I'm going for another swim. Do you want to come in?"

She shook her head.

I dove into the surf, turned off by Kathleen's coquettishness. When I looked back to shore a few minutes later, she was gone. Back at my towel, I found Kathleen had left a card with her phone number on it. I searched up and down the shore and along the sandstone cliffs but she was nowhere in sight.

By early afternoon, I was wet and cold and hungry and ready to go. I packed up my things and tucked Kathleen's number safely out of sight in my glove box.

The dark beach sand gathered around my feet as I showered at Ellie's place. I dried myself, put on some fresh clothes and poured myself a glass of wine. I watched the traffic down on Coast Highway and waited for the looming conversation with Ellie. I did not want to talk about things. I did not know how to be honest with her.

Ellie came in about six. She looked very mature and sexy in a dress and high-heels and wasted no time in pressing between my legs.

"Can we just skip the stupid conversation, Roger?"

"I've considered that."

She kissed my neck and ears.

"Well, there," she said with a laugh. "It's all better. Now let's go have dinner."

I nodded and watched her face.

"Roger, each time we fight there's a little less left to lose."

She took my glass from me, toasted and drank.

"So, screw my little wine tasting parties and my notions of etiquette. Apology accepted?"

"Sure," I said, relieved and maybe even a little hopeful again about our love affair. I did care for her, more than age and time could ever eclipse.

If only I had no secrets. I followed Ellie out the door with a tempest of them brewing in my heart.

The following Monday morning, Cerise came into my office for something and I watched with my secret thoughts. When she left, Kathleen popped into my head. I retrieved the card from my wallet and dialed Kathleen's number. The phone rang and rang. Then Kathleen's mother answered the phone, telling me Kathleen was not at home but she would take my number.

It was late in the day when Kathleen returned my call. I kicked my feet up on my desk and watched Cerise at work with a perverse feeling of satisfaction.

"I wondered if you would call," Kathleen said. "Can you pick me up?"

"When?"

"Come by at six."

"And your mother."

"You mean about your age?"

"Yes."

"She knows I go out with older men."

"Okay, give me the address."

I jotted down the directions and rang off. The day passed by filled with fantasies, guilt and regrets. Each time I saw Cerise, I felt regrets. Each time I thought of Ellie, I felt guilt. Each time I thought of Kathleen, I had fantasies.

At six, I was knocking at her door. She greeted me with a kiss and shouted goodbye to her mother.

"Where to?" I said out in the Alfa Romeo.

"Go this way," she said, pointing to the left. "I'll show you this secret place up in the hills."

After negotiating the backstreets of her neighborhood, Kathleen guided me out a country road. It wound up and up into the dry hills. We passed stands of oak and pepper trees. The asphalt road came to an abrupt end at a gate. Beyond it was the dirt access road of an oil company. Kathleen opened the gate and I drove through. There were oil pumps working up among the pepper trees and an old, worn company sign. The sun had gone down and the pepper trees grew dark with dusk. I kept glancing at Kathleen. She was like a young gypsy with her skirt and blouse and hoop earrings and sandals.

Finally, she had me park on a knoll above an elementary school. The lights of homes dotted the hills below us. The flat plain of civilization sparkled beyond it. I put on a Steely Dan tape and the first song echoed off into the twilight.

Go back, Jack, do it again, wheel turning round and round.

Kathleen got out and walked up among the trees and tall grass. I followed.

"Come, lie down," she said.

She took off her long skirt to use as a blanket.

She quickly had my boots and pants off and crawled on top of me. That got her aroused and off came her panties. I groaned as her silky cunt slid down my cock. I reached up and undid her blouse and touched her breasts. They were small and pubescent. Sweat had beaded along her back and hairline. Her animal scent was on the warm wind. I saw her eyes in the shadows as she gyrated against me. When she was pleased, I took her hips and lifted her up and down until I was satisfied.

We lay there for some time with the full moon rising over the hills. Then Kathleen jumped up suddenly, pulling on my hand.

"Come, let's go dance in the moonlight."

"Where?"

"In the school yard."

I turned up the stereo and followed Kathleen down the hill. She was fifty yards ahead of me, already leaping and pirouetting across the football field. When I caught up with her, she was squatting down to urinate in the grass.

"Come," she said, standing up again. "Let your inhibitions go."

When I did not respond, she leapt off and danced her way around the entire field. I stood and watched until she came back.

"I want to go," she said.

"Where?"

"Home."

"Why?"

"Because you won't dance with me."

"Let's go to a bar," I said.

"No, I need to go see my boyfriend."

She was already dancing her way back to my car.

"You have a boyfriend?" I said, getting in.

"Yes."

Fuck. What a nymph. We drove back to her house in silence.

The minute I had braked to a stop in front, she jumped out.

"You need to get over your hang ups."

With that, she ran inside. I drove home, eviscerated by her comment. My self-image was that of a daring and unbridled young poet. That sprite had left me feeling bourgeois.

I limped back to Ellie's place the following weekend. What the hell. She was adorable. The sex was great, the conversations unparalleled. Enough libations and I could forget all the rest— my lies, my defeats, the loss of my dreams.

I was lounging around that Sunday afternoon, feeling thoroughly decadent when a knock came at the door. Before I could get up from my chair in the living room, Ellie came out of the kitchen and answered the door. It was Derek, along with his latest girlfriend and her three children. I stood up to shake Derek's hand.

"Long time," he said. "What's happening?"

"Not much. How are you doing?"

"Cool, man. Cool."

I said hello to his girlfriend Cynthia and cursed myself for not having left sooner.

Cynthia's three children were introduced, after which they immediately rushed off to play in the backyard.

Derek smiled at me with the unspoken dangling between us. So, you've been hanging around banging my Mom all weekend. How's that going?

"We were just passing through," he said and went to grab a beer from the kitchen. Not knowing quite what to say to him, I stayed behind with the girl chatter.

"So, what's happening?" Derek said again when he reappeared from the kitchen.

"Oh, nothing," I said. "Just work."

"Far out. Tell me about it."

Derek took the chair I had been warming. I sat on the sofa and explained about Happy Hobbit Leather Company.

"Hey, I'm really stoked for you. I really like it when my friends make it at something."

Cynthia and Ellie had disappeared into the kitchen. They quickly reappeared with drinks in their hands. Now we were two couples hanging around the living room together.

"Yeah, maybe you could sell for me," Cynthia said. "I have a line of bathing suits I'm trying to get off the ground."

"Actually, I'm trying to get out of sales."

"Oh, bummer."

She looked around at everyone with a laugh.

"Yeah, there are plenty of other salesmen."

"Yeah, but not like freaks, you know. I don't know if I could deal with some straight character selling my stuff."

She laughed again and pulled her hair back from her face. She was not a particularly attractive woman, owlish looking in fact, with thick spectacles, but she was endowed with enormous breasts and I suspected that was what had attracted Derek to her. He had a thing for huge breasts.

The children rushed into the living room, going the other way now. The one boy, the oldest of three children, spoke for the others.

"Mom, can we go down to the park? Can we? Just for a little while?"

"Okay, but keep an eye on your two sisters."

They rushed out the front door in a state of great excitement. Ellie resumed her conversation with Cynthia. Derek got out a bag of grass and started to roll a joint. I glanced at Ellie.

"Oh, I guess I've confessed to my little secret somewhere along the way."

She feigned embarrassment. Derek lit the joint and passed it around the room. The commensurate laughter set in, our conversation drifting between the silly and philosophical. We seemed to be a happy little fraternity all of a sudden. The day wore on with many drinks being poured.

Ellie and I ended up alone in the kitchen at one point. She suggested I offer up a joint of our own. There remained that unspoken tribal aspect with grass.

I went off to retrieve our stash box from the bedroom, noticed Derek and Cynthia missing and discovered them engaged in coitus on Ellie's bed. Cynthia was on top, her overly large breasts flopping around this way and that. Derek looked over at me with a smile.

"Ooops," I said and quickly closed the door, the image of Cynthia and her huge breasts now seared into my mind.

"They're doing it on your bed," I told Ellie.

"Oh dear," she said without seeming to be overly concerned about it.

I poured myself a stiff bourbon and soda and stared out at Newport Harbor. So this was Derek's pay back, marking his scent on our bed.

The children came back about the time Derek and Cynthia emerged from the bedroom. Cynthia looked a bit sheepish but Derek displayed no sign of embarrassment at all. He cracked open another beer and resumed the conversation as if nothing had happened. All the while, the children ran about the house screaming.

Ellie offered everyone dinner and gratefully they declined. In what was for me a rather prolonged and torturous departure, the children and everybody slowly drifted towards the front door. Then Ellie and I were waving from the driveway, like the old folks saying goodbye to their kids on a Sunday afternoon.

Twenty

At the start of that summer vacation, Kurt and Carla flew off to a dude ranch in Wyoming. I drove down that Friday to spend the weekend with Ellie. All those months had flown by but I had never fulfilled my promise to rent an apartment down at the beach, closer to her place.

We engaged in our usual routine of fine cuisine and love making over Friday night and Saturday, then awakened on Sunday morning to find the Watergate scandal splashed all over the news. Ellie and I hung around the house all day, glued to the television set like it was World War II unfolding.

"That fucker is so busted," she kept saying.

That was the buzz on the streets but the Nixon administration quickly went into damage control mode and within two weeks, the impending Democratic National Convention had completely taken over the news cycle.

With the summer days growing hot, the neighborhood was ripe with the scents of backyard barbecues and suntan lotion. Cars came and went, piled high with beach crap and screaming children. Everywhere you looked, people were out mowing lawns and washing their cars. Elton John was singing *Crocodile*

Rock. For many people, this was the sixties. For those of us who had been there, the seventies were but a nauseous time of people and dreams growing lost.

In July, Sheila gave birth to a baby girl and she and David bought the old clapboard house where they had been living. With three stories and twenty rooms, it became a haven for all their friends and fellow workers. I heard tales of wild parties but had yet to attend one. I had enough troubles without their Bacchanalian adventures. Being devoted to Ellie had become impossible for me, but leaving her too painful, so I began secretly having affairs. When a man frequented boutiques and shopping malls as part of his business, he was confronted on a daily basis with scores of gorgeous young tarts.

When Ellie announced that she was going down to a teacher's conference in San Diego one weekend, I declined an invitation to join her for dinner on Saturday night. There was a lovely little blonde vixen named Laura I planned to seduce.

Ellie went off believing that I would be tied up on business all weekend.

I invited Laura to a costume party at David and Sheila's place and found her dressed as Galadriel when I stopped by to pick her up. Her red-haired friend Megan came dressed as a nymph. I was the Mad Hatter. A bowl of psychedelic punch sat waiting for all to partake in as they passed through the front door.

The sprawling, labyrinthine home swarmed with people in togas, masks and assorted costumes. One man appeared to have a midget sitting on his head. Round and round he went, tipping and swaying. Another man came as a chair and waited in the living room for the unsuspecting to sit on his lap. He would groan and one more person would leap up like a Jack-in-the-box. Laura wandered from room to room with her magic wand. I followed along, babbling about tea parties and hat prices.

At some point we came upon Laura's friend Megan in the kitchen. All three of us were peaking on the acid by then. David appeared, having extracted himself from the maze of rooms and hallways upstairs. Apparently, it had been a long journey.

"Wow," he said, looking down at his feet. "They're a hundred feet away."

I nodded.

"Space as we know it has ceased to exist."

Laura and Megan stepped across the kitchen floor in a surreal rendition of a chorus line. They went out one door in the kitchen and came back through another. On their way through the second time they grabbed David. I watched, immobilized but laughing. The very act of walking had become monumental.

Then Laura and Megan were dragging me upstairs and down a crowded hallway. The next thing I knew, we were in a converted attic together. They disrobed down to their bras and panties and crawled into bed. Laura waved a seductive finger my way. I stripped down to my briefs and crawled in with them.

With the two of them having disappeared under the sheets, there was a knock on the door. The women giggled. The knock came again and their heads reappeared.

"Go away," I said.

"It's Sheila."

"I'm busy."

"I know, but I thought I'd better tell you something."

Perturbed by the interruption, I got up and cracked the door.

"Ellie's downstairs," Sheila whispered.

"Oh wow," I said.

That knowledge came with a jolt of adrenalin and brought me right back down to earth.

"All right. Keep her occupied. I'll be down in a minute."

"Ooookaaay," Sheila said.

I closed the door and found my shirt and pants.

"Where are you going?" Laura asked. I looked over at the two faces now propped up with pillows against the wall.

"A friend of mine came by to see me."

"It's his old lady girlfriend," she said to Megan.

"You're going to leave us for her?" Megan asked.

I went out the door without answering.

Having forced my way downstairs and through a throng of people, I found Sheila standing protectively next to Ellie at the edge of the crowd. Ellie was wearing a business suit.

"Here he is!" Sheila announced.

"Sorry, I was talking with some friends."

"Interesting business conference you're attending," Ellie said.

"It was nice meeting you," Sheila said and quickly disappeared.

"Let's go outside," I said to Ellie over the hubbub.

Once outside, Ellie lay on the grass in her suit. She was prone on her back, staring up at the sky in silence. It was a warm night with the wind blowing out of the desert. The universe was alive with stars.

"Nothing matters, does it Roger?"

I sat down next to her.

"I thought you were going down to San Diego for a conference."

"I did. It was a drag and I missed you. And, by the way, don't change the subject." She looked over. "Your canard about being distracted by business."

"This party just happened spontaneously, Ellie."

"Yes. It certainly looks like it."

She turned her attention back to the stars. I sat there in silence, wondering about a number of things, like how Ellie had found this place and how were the two young women upstairs going to take my abandoning them.

"You were up there ready to fuck someone, weren't you?" Ellie said.

"Well, sort of."

"Sort of. How do sort of fuck somebody?"

"Well, there were two of them. I wasn't sure what to expect under the circumstances."

"Oh, well, that makes it much easier to take."

"I abandoned them for you, if it matters."

Ellie was still staring up at the stars.

"We're all going to die and fade away someday," she said. "And the stars will be staring down at the next person. And they will all have the same foolish ideas of what is important, so they will fight and battle everything in life until they die. Then the next person will come along, and the whole, damned stupid drama will start all over again."

"I'm sorry, Ellie."

She looked over at me.

"It's all right. I understand."

"No, I really am sorry."

She touched my face.

"What is it that holds us together, Roger?"

I looked away.

"A lot of things."

"Roger?"

I looked back.

"I offer you what no young woman can. Freedom to explore love without demands. And still it isn't enough."

She was very serene and beautiful and I kissed her lips. The wind rustled her fine fleecy hair. I ran my hand through it.

"I don't want you to go away," she said. "I had nearly forgotten you must."

She looked back at the stars.

"I only want stolen apples," she said.

In that moment, she pierced my heart and I lay next to her. I thought of all the things that had gone through my head over the past few months, all the scheming and cheating and planning and machinations, and suddenly none of it mattered. Ellie was more important to me than anything in the world.

"I love your conversation," I said.

She looked at me and held my hand and we looked back up at the stars together. A long time passed with the two of us talking in the desert wind. Sometime later, I got into my car and followed Ellie back to her place, my surrender complete; we two wild animals caged once again, our stolen apples exchanged for something that I had no heart to express.

Twenty One

The following week, still chastened by my debauchery, and determined to avoid any further grounds for moral self-immolation, I told Cerise to say I wasn't in each time Laura called at the office for me. I longed for a clean conscience. That seemed like an impossible goal, but a man had to try.

That Friday afternoon, I wrapped up things early at work and arrived down to Ellie's place around two. She was making herself a sandwich in the kitchen.

"Did you want one?" she asked with a kiss over her shoulder.

"Sure."

I changed clothes and returned to find Ellie setting our sandwich plates down on the patio table.

"Something to drink?" she said on her way back to the kitchen.

"Sure, a beer if you have one."

I took a seat outside and stared off at the sea in the distance. Ellie brought two beers and we toasted. I dug into the sandwich.

"Good?" she said.

I started to speak through my full mouth but nodded instead. It was cold meatloaf on sourdough, with Swiss cheese and red onions. I drank of the beer.

"You really know how to make a sandwich."

She let on with a smile that she considered it quite a talent.

"I've been thinking about us," she said.

I bowed my head. Ellie had a tantrum. No doubt she thought I had been screwing around behind her back all week.

"It's so hard when you know it must end," she said.

"Ellie, please."

"No, I want to get it out in the open and face it." She looked out towards the sea. "I feel like a man who is to be executed at dawn. There is so much beauty we ignore because of our little plans." She turned back to face me. "Especially when they no longer mean anything..."

I sighed and worked on the sandwich.

"Good meatloaf."

"You're not going to allow me my little drama, are you?"

I shrugged.

"What I mean to say is this. Let's dispense with our illusions, acknowledge the end and just enjoy each other as long as we can."

"And forget all the drama in between? I know. I believe I had said that very same thing to you at some point in the past."

She sighed dramatically. I smiled and looked back out at the sea, suddenly aware that nearly the entire summer had rushed by without once dipping my feet into the surf.

"Let's go to the beach," I said.

"All right," she said with a big, white smile. "That sounds lovely."

While still finishing my sandwich, Ellie went off with her plate and came back wearing a black, one-piece bathing suit with a pair of high heel sandals. She looked stunning. She always did in black. She took my plate out to the kitchen. I stared after her. Her tight little ass and painted toe nails had me going.

I really love you, Ellie, I thought with a tear in my heart.

We drove down to Crystal Cove, parked on the highway and hiked down the bluff to the shore. For a summer day, that stretch of open coastline was delightfully abandoned. A row of old cottages lined the bluff above and behind our heads. The piers at Balboa, Newport and Huntington were visible up the coast. Lines of surf broke that way as far as the eye could see.

We took a quick swim and returned to our towels. The color of the sea looked wonderfully dark blue with our sunglasses on.

When the sun grew hot, we took our chairs down to the edge of the surf and sat there with the sea washing over our feet. Later, we lay on our towels with our bodies entangled. The afternoon had grown late. I had the taste of seawater in my mouth and looked for another beer. We were out.

"Let's go to the Crab Cooker," I said.

"Tonight?"

"No, right now."

"But I'm all wet."

"I know, and we'll look like tourists but let's go."

I pulled Ellie to her feet.

We shook out our towels, packed our belongings and started up the trail. Our sandals lifted dust as we went. The hills beyond the highway were dry and brown from summer but the sea was blue and cheery behind us.

Twenty minutes later we were walking into the Crab Cooker. The architectural theme was the seashore in New England, the restaurant painted white with red trim around the windows.

"It reminds me of my youth," I said to Ellie.

"You mean in New England?"

"That too but more just going to the beach on a summer day and stopping someplace to eat on the way home with the sand still on your feet. I look back at those days and think, I didn't have a care in the world. At least that's the way it seems."

"Then let's pretend we don't have a care in the world."

"Okay, let's do."

We sat there staring at each other.

"It's not working," I said.

Ellie pretended to have a tantrum.

"It was a nice try."

"A nice try."

The waitress arrived and took our order for the crab feast and two beers. A short while later, we pushed back from a mound of empty crab shells and soiled napkins.

We got into bed that night with our books and brandy and spent Saturday lounging around the house with grog and good food and other indulgences. Ellie had disconnected the phone so as not to be bothered.

Late Saturday afternoon, we were stretched out in the living room, having just smoked a joint, when there was a grand commotion outside the front door and it flew open. Kurt and Carla were standing there, along with a family friend whose daughter had also been at the dude ranch. Ellie got up to greet everyone.

"Gee. I didn't expect you back for another week."

"The weather turned bad," Kurt said.

I had quickly lit up a cigarette to hide the other scent and waved from the background. The commotion continued with them getting all the luggage in through the door.

"Why on earth didn't you call in advance?" Ellie said.

"We were lucky to get on a plane," Carla said. "And you weren't around this morning when we called from Reno so we called Carol instead."

"Sorry," Carol said, smiling first at me then at Ellie. "We didn't mean to interrupt you."

"Well, of course I'm just glad you made it home all right," Ellie said.

After more chit-chatting in the foyer, Ellie hugged Carol and Carol made her exit. The twins went off to put their luggage away. I shared a look with Ellie. She went off to query the twins further. I was considering how to make my own exit.

When the three of them reappeared, it was to make sandwiches in the kitchen. I sat around hearing tales of their summer's adventures. When it got on towards dark, I offered up an excuse about needing to attend to some business.

"You don't have to cut out on account of us," Kurt said.

"No, really. I was leaving anyway."

"Yeah right," Carla said.

The two of them exchanged sardonic looks. Kurt started off for the shower.

"Just keep the tortured screams to a minimum."

Carla sat with a knowing look.

So that was it. The ice had been broken and as much as it was convenient for me to sleep over with Ellie, we were one big happy family.

Summer passed into fall and the three of them went back to school. I continued on in my ostensible role as the head of marketing for Happy Hobbit Leather Company but my heart was no longer in it. I did enough to keep the spigot flowing and otherwise spent my days hanging around my cottage in a bathrobe, trying to rediscover that muse.

At least my conscience was clean. It had been over three months since my last sexual escapade. The lust for things I could not have went on, but a clean heart beat the hell out of where I had been.

If anywhere near Ellie's neighborhood at the end of the day, I usually headed over to her place and walked in one evening to find Kurt and Carla with Ellie at the dining table, discussing Watergate. I made myself a drink and joined them. News of Mitchell's secret slush fund had just broken. It was becoming more obvious with each passing day that the Watergate break-in was just the tip of the iceberg.

"CREEP," Kurt said in reference to Nixon's re-election committee acronym. "Only the Republicans could revel in something that creepy."

"What do you think?" Ellie said as I sat down.

"Oh, Nixon will find a way to weasel out of it."

"No way," Kurt said. "That bastard is so busted. They're all busted."

"I heard Mitchell's going to be indicted in the next couple of days," Carla said.

Ellie threw up her hands.

"If we had a Democrat in the White House, they'd have already tarred and feathered him and ridden him out of town! How do these bastards get away with it?"

I shrugged.

"You have to have a serious pair of Rebozos."

It took a split second for the three of them to get the joke but soon we were all falling out of our chairs.

"A pair of rebozos," Kurt said once he was able to catch his breath. "Good one, Roger."

"Yeah, it just kind of popped into my head there all of a sudden."

After a moment of calm, we were all in stitches again.

"Okay, okay," I said, gathering myself. "I still say the bastard will find a way to weasel out of it."

"Why do you think that?" Kurt said, waxing serious again.

"Because. Everyone around Nixon is willing to fall on his sword for him, including Mitchell. They're as disciplined as the Third Reich."

"They are the Third Reich!" Kurt said.

"Yeah, and what do we got? Eagleton for a running mate. Who just got out of a nuthouse."

"Give the guy a break," Carla said. "He just had some shock treatments."

"Just some shock treatments. Great...Look, I don't care if the guy was doing life without parole in San Quentin. It just looks bad on the face of it. McGovern picks him and fires him two weeks later? Americans hate nothing, if not weakness."

"So you really think Nixon will be reelected?" Ellie said.

"Hey, when you've got a pair of Rebozos."

There were smirks.

"Well, on that note," Ellie said. "I'd better go grade some papers."

"I won't be voting for him, if that brings you any solace."

Ellie threw up her hands in departing.

"I'm just the impartial historian."

272

"I'm not," Kurt said. "If Nixon gets reelected, I'm buying a gun."

"Well, we were about due for another assassination anyway."

Carla smiled. She and Kurt looked at each other and leaned in closer to me.

"You know it's our Mom's birthday in a couple of days," Carla whispered.

"I've heard something about it."

"Ha ha," Kurt said. "So what were you planning to get her?"

"Something from Frederick's of Hollywood, of course."

Kurt smiled.

"Okay, we were going to get her a new business suit, but we're kind of broke."

"So we thought we'd hit you up," Carla said.

"Well, more like rob you at gunpoint," Kurt said.

He smiled again in his charming way.

"Fair enough. We'll go in together and get something nice. Did you want to hit the mall?"

"Sure," Carla said. "But what do we tell Ellie?"

"Tell her we're going to score some drugs."

"Ha ha," Kurt said. "By the way, did I ever thank you for turning her on?"

"Not formally."

"Well, thanks."

"The floor recognizes our distinguished colleague from Newport Harbor High."

"Wow, cool southern accent."

"Can we get back on point?" Carla said.

"I thought scoring drugs was on point," Kurt said.

Carla threw up her hands and went off to get ready. I went and told Ellie that we were off on a secret mission. She hardly looked up from her papers.

"Oh boy," Kurt said as we headed out the door. "Off to engage in a bit of degenerate American consumerism."

We took his Volkswagen bug. The mall was packed so that we had to park way out at the far end of the lot. Weaving our way between cars, we suddenly had a bundle of twenty dollar bills blowing across our path. Kurt and Carla chased them down. Once counted, there was over three hundred dollars.

"I guess we should turn it in," I said.

"I think we should go ahead with that drug deal," Kurt said.

"Haven't you already toasted your brain cells enough?" Carla said.

"Yeah. Otherwise, I'd be just like you."

"Shut up, jerk."

"All right, all right. Let's get back to the money."

"We could use it to buy mom's present," Kurt said.

"Yeah, that's great. 'We found this money, Ellie so we got you a really neat present'."

"Hey, karma works both ways," Kurt said.

"I don't know. Maybe Roger's right," Carla said.

We started off across the parking lot, the money having taken on great philosophical significance.

"How about if we give part of it to a bum or something," Kurt said.

"We already have," Carla said, making a face at Kurt.

"All right," I said when we got to the store. "You two keep the money if you want. I don't want any part of it."

"Let's turn it in," Carla agreed.

274

"Let's just tell the cops we have it. Then if someone claims it, we can make sure it was theirs."

"Right, what if the cops lie about it?"

"Okay, okay. Maybe it would be easier just to throw the money back into the parking lot."

"Hey, I had some pretty good bush planned for that dough."

"Look," Carla said, "I'll keep the money and we'll think about it."

"Fine, now let's get the present."

"It's not fine with me," Kurt said. "How come she gets to keep the money?"

I went into the mall with the two of them still arguing.

We found a blue blazer suit for Ellie and added two scarves. I bought her some Chanel #5 independently and we headed home.

"That was far out," Kurt said over his shoulder. "It's like the whole meaning of the universe was tied up in that money."

"Is," I reminded him.

"Yeah," he agreed.

"You guys are making too much of it," Carla said.

"It gets to the question of whether or not someone is watching," I said.

Kurt bit his nails in fright.

"I just don't understand you kids these days," I said.

He laughed.

"That's far out, though, Roger. I never thought of you as worrying about karma and everything."

"Are you kidding? I'm from the sixties, man."

Kurt laughed again.

"Yeah, far out. I kind of forgot that."

Back at the house, Carla went to study. Kurt crawled up into his attic hideout. I went off to buy a couple of swordfish steaks at the local fish market.

With the blustery fall day, I threw some logs in the fireplace. The four of us had dinner and eventually drifted our separate ways, Carla to her studies, Kurt to his attic hideout. Ellie was in the back grading papers again. I had just poured another glass of wine when the doorbell rang. I went to answer it and found my brother Vincent standing on the front porch. He looked as if he had not seen a shower in a few days. From the smell of him, he had seen the inside of plenty of bars along the way.

Perplexed by his arrival, I gave him a hug.

"What's going on, Vincent?"

"I just drove through from Ohio."

"Wow."

He thumbed proudly at an older Ford F-150 out on the street. It had four-wheel drive and was jacked up high enough to require a step ladder. That or you'd need a running start to get in.

Inside, Vincent quickly requested a drink. While I poured it for him, Ellie came out to investigate the voices.

"Well! Vincent! Hello!" she said. "What on earth are you doing here?"

They hugged. I handed Vincent his drink and we sat down in the living room. Vincent drank heavily and did what he could to dress up his recent exploits. Reading between the lines, he was bombed, homeless, broke and in need of a place crash. His first drink disappeared quickly so he asked for another. His condition quickly deteriorated but Ellie insisted on indulging him, as if she were seeing the magnificent man my brother had been ten years earlier.

"So, I guess he's the big master of the house around here," Vincent said to Ellie, as if I wasn't there.

She shrugged at me with a smile. I glared at Vincent.

"I don't think you get it, Vincent. Ellie and I love each other very dearly."

"Yeah? Well I had her first."

"Vincent, really," Ellie said. "That's not necessary."

"Yeah, maybe it's best if you just get out of here," I told him.

With that, Vincent stood up and came at me. Assuming his intentions were violent, I stood up to meet him.

"Now, Roger, please don't start anything," Ellie said.

"Me start something?"

While looking her way, Vincent sucker punched me. I warded off a second swing and wrestled him to the carpet. Kurt came flying down from his hideout.

"Hey, you two! Cut it out!"

Before he could separate us, a lamp fell over and broke. Then we were apart and glaring at each other. I wiped at my bloody mouth. There was blood on my clothes and on the carpet.

"So, had enough, punk?" Vincent said.

"Fuck you, Vincent."

"Goddamn it!" Kurt shouted. "If you're going to fight, get out of this house!"

"Please, Roger, let's not make this any worse," Ellie said to me.

I felt my swollen lip and looked at her.

"You think I started this?"

"Well, in fairness, your mannerism was threatening."

I flushed with anger.

"Yeah, you're right. I should have allowed him to take a cheap shot while I was sitting down."

277

Vincent came at me.

"Now wait a minute, Vincent."

Ellie turned to me.

"I doubt he would have hit you if you had remained sitting."

"I don't fucking believe this."

"Look, let's just sit back down and try to sort this out peacefully."

"I have a better idea, Ellie. You two sort it out. I'm leaving."

His territorial drive satiated, Vincent sat down with the bottle of Scotch. Ellie followed me into the back room. I stuffed everything I could get into one suitcase and grabbed one of my suits from the closet. Ellie tried to stop me.

"Get the hell out of my way," I said, going out the door

"I thought we weren't going to run away any more, Roger."

The clip clop of Ellie's heels followed me down the hallway.

"Let the li'l' fucker go," Vincent said as we passed through the living room. Ellie ignored him and followed me out to the street.

"Roger, don't leave."

I threw my belongings into my car and climbed in. Ellie held the door open. I looked up at her.

"And to think of all that little girl shit you gave me. Then you pull this."

"Roger, you stood up like you were ready to fight."

"No, Ellie. I had no intention of doing anything, other than to defend myself."

"I'm only trying to be impartial."

"Then you make a lousy judge."

"Damn it, Roger. This is the last time. Are you going to stay and work this out or not?"

"No. And you're right, Ellie. This is the last time. I don't ever want to see you again. I'll come by for the rest of my shit tomorrow while you're at school and leave the key."

I started the engine and pulled the door closed. Ellie went around and stood in front of the car.

"Get out of my way or I'll run you over."

Instead, she lay down on her back in front of my wheels. Fed up with her theatrics, I shoved the transmission into reverse and maneuvered around her. As I turned right out of the cul-de-sac, I looked in my rearview mirror. Ellie was still lying flat on her back.

I got on the freeway and headed north, feeling as if a horse had kicked me. Needing someone to commiserate with me, I drove to David and Sheila's place. Parked in front, I sat there with my head against the steering wheel, hoping I was in the right place. It was several minutes before I headed up to the door.

Sheila answered, started to say 'hi' then gasped and reached out with her hand when she saw the blood and my swollen mouth.

"Oh my god, Roger. What on earth happened?"

"Is this the home for down and out boxers?" I said.

"Of course, of course. Come in."

With the door closed, she had a closer look at my mouth.

"What on earth happened?" she said again

"A sucker punch."

"Who?"

"My older brother. I'll explain it all for a drink."

"Sure, sure." She put her arm through mine. "You know you're always welcome in our home."

"Look what I have here," she called out. David appeared through the opening to the kitchen, wiping his hands on a towel.

"Don't ask," I said.

"Want a drink?"

"Please. Make it bourbon, straight."

"Oh good," Sheila said, clapping. "We'll have a little party."

We went into the kitchen. David opened the cupboard over the refrigerator and handed me the bottle. I sat with Sheila at the kitchen table.

"What about Ashley?" I said.

"Oh, she can make do with a bottle for a couple of days. And you might want to behave yourself."

"Why?"

I unscrewed the cap, drank from the bottle and winced. David brought over some Ginger Ale.

"Why?" I repeated.

"Cerise is on her way over."

"Yeah? With Alan?"

"No. Alone."

"Yeah? So what?"

Sheila stuck her tongue out at me. I took another stiff drink from the bottle and felt my lip.

"I'm going to take a shower," Sheila said and left with her drink. I took another belt of bourbon and explained to David what had happened.

"Did you deck him?"

"No, hell, by the time we got done with wrestling around the living room and breaking things, I was already pretty unpopular in that neck of the woods."

"I don't get why she defended him," David said.

"I don't either and I don't care. I'm done with her."

"Yeah. You may as well get married and have kids."

"You have a one track mind, David."

I took another drink and winced. He was right, though. I might as well have something to show for my struggles, besides regrets.

A short while later, Sheila returned with wet hair and a bottle of Merthiolate tincture in hand. She made me a proper drink and went to work on my lip.

"Oww."

Sheila dabbed at the wound one last time and put the lid on the bottle. I drank and winced again.

"Here's to my cut man," I said and held up my glass.

Sheila got a kick out of that. David came over and set the pan of fish on the table.

"Last of our trout," he said.

"Are we going to eat it like barbarians, David?"

He pushed his glasses back and stared at Sheila. She went to make a salad.

"Have a drink," I told David.

I made him one that was not quite translucent.

"Thanks," he said and held up his glass. There was a ting and we drank.

"Thanks for what?"

"We owe everything to your efforts."

"That's a hell of a nice thing to say, David. True or not."

I hung my head. The adrenalin was beginning to wear off and the grief was cutting into me.

"Oh, it is true," Sheila said. "I think we were ready to give up before you arrived."

"Well, here's to the two damned finest people I've ever known."

"Damned finest," Sheila laughed.

"That's cowboy talk."

"Cowboy talk," she repeated.

"Sure, home on the range. Been a long time, partner."

"Oh give me a home, where the buffalo roam."

David and I finished the song together while Sheila tossed the salad and put some plates on the table. I cut and buttered thick slices of fresh-baked wheat bread. The three of us sat down and ate under a dim light in the old-fashioned kitchen.

"Do you remember how my mother made everything so bland?" Sheila said. "You had to chew it for an hour to get any taste."

"It lent itself to conversation. I'll give you that."

"It was healthy for you, too," Sheila added.

"Give me pepper or give me death."

David laughed and drank from his amber colored drink.

Over the course of the meal, Sheila explained what had transpired between Alan and Cerise. Apparently Alan, the wild rock and roll guitarist by night, had treated Cerise more or less like another one of his groupies, and upon discovering this, Cerise promptly abandoned him.

"At least you're in the same boat," Sheila said.

"Sure, we can cry on each other's shoulders."

"I don't think that's what she has in mind."

Sheila offered me a knowing smile. I said nothing, not wanting to confess to my secret longings.

"Anyway, I have something I want to show you before she arrives."

"Is this the educational documentary?"

282

"Yes, this is the documentary," she said and took me by the arm. "I'm sure David will clean up the dishes."

He sat at the table with no expression. It was the picture of cold lake water along a shoreline.

Sheila led me upstairs to Ashley's room. She opened the door carefully and we slipped into the nursery. The room had been nicely finished with knotty pine. A butterfly mobile hung motionless over the crib. Ashley was asleep with one thumb in her mouth. A sparkle of city lights and the eastern hills were visible out the windows.

"Don't you want to have one of these someday?" Sheila whispered.

"I don't know. They terrify me."

"Come on. Look at her."

"Like I said, they terrify me."

"Well, okay," Sheila said, "that concludes the educational film." I followed her out of the room and waited as she quietly closed the door.

"Be nice to Cerise," she said as we descended the staircase.

"I've wanted to be nice to her for a long time, Sheila."

"Okay, be dependable."

"I thought I was."

Sheila smiled and squeezed my arm.

"You have been. While all our friends have been out goofing around, you've been as steady as a rock."

I smirked. Viewed from the inside, I had been anything but steady, or a rock.

"Thanks for the kind words, Sheila. And now if you'll forgive me, I think I'll get steadily drunk."

"Maybe you want to slow down a bit? At least until Cerise gets here."

"All right. Until she gets here, and then all bets are off."

David was still doing the dishes when we returned. We helped him finish up, made a fresh round of drinks when we were done and went to sit at the piano. David played and we sang.

Some minutes later, the doorbell rang. My already wounded heart fluttered. Sheila rushed off to answer it and soon returned with Cerise, the two of them whispering together as they came towards to the piano. Cerise had her dark hair pinned up and red lipstick on her heart shaped lips. She looked stunning.

David glanced that way but continued playing. I smiled as best I could under the circumstances.

"Ouch," she Cerise, seeing my lip.

"Yeah, long story…Care for a drink?"

She saw our nearly opaque cocktails and smiled at Sheila

"What are we drinking?"

"Bourbon and whatever you want," I said. "Come on," I added and grabbled Cerise's hand.

Out in the kitchen, she watched as I checked the refrigerator.

"I guess we've got ginger ale," I said and held it up to her.

"That sounds fine," she said.

I mixed two drinks and handed her one.

"Cheers."

Our glasses met.

"I've been waiting for this moment for a long, long time."

She stared intently at me, her tongue to the birthmark on her upper lip, her dark eyes searching mine.

"You're not just saying that."

"No, I'm not just saying that."

I reached out my hand but she stepped back, her dark eyes still searching mine.

"Look," I said. "I made a choice back then and it was probably the wrong one, but that's all over with now. Okay?"

"Is it?"

"Is it with you, Cerise?"

She stared. I touched her face gently with the back of my hand.

"We're kind of in the same boat, yeah?" After a moment, she nodded. "So? All I can say is, I'm so very very glad that you're here."

Every so slightly, she nuzzled her cheek against my hand. I smiled and stepped forward and gave her a cautious hug. David was churning up a bluesy melody out in the other room.

"Come on. Let's join the party."

We touched glasses and walked back to the piano.

Late into the night, the four of us sang and drank and laughed together and when I walked Cerise out to her car, we talked for a long time beneath the stars.

I waited while she climbed in and rolled down her window.

"When can I see you again?" I said.

She found her purse and wrote down her phone number.

"Call me."

"I will. Tomorrow."

I leaned in and gently kissed her.

"Ow," I said.

Cerise reached out and touched where my mouth was split open. Our eyes remained locked for a long moment before she drove off.

David was in the kitchen when I walked back inside. I made a fresh drink.

"Last call," I said and drank down half of it.

Seeing red lipstick on the glass, I reached for a napkin.

I was half drunk when I crawled up to sleep in the attic. Several times in the night, I awakened, haunted by the memories of that scene at Ellie's place. Cerise was there, too, a little nugget of joy at the prospect of love beginning anew, but all through that long, lonely night, Vincent's sucker punch and Ellie's betrayal continued to grind away at my heart.

Twenty Two

Sometime late the next morning, I was awakened by the wail of a siren. I sat up with my heart racing. Terror was afoot. Someone had been mauled by the wild beasts of a modern world.

While sitting there, trying to collect my thoughts, the siren raced by, then another one came and went, and quickly another one, their Doppler shift disappearing down the street. Finally, I was left with my hangover and uncertainties.

Remembering Cerise, I got up and stared out the windows facing east. The autumn sky was clear but ashen, the attic awash in pale sunlight.

From my vantage point, a flat terrain of homes and commerce marched off towards the nearby hills, those hills cut through by a recently completed freeway, its ribbon of concrete sprinkled with only a handful of automobiles on that Saturday morning. Someday soon, it would be bumper to bumper, day in and day out, but on that morning, it was as if mankind had just arrived here to utilize it.

I felt my lip and the events of the previous evening flashed through my head again. One love affair was over. Another one had yet to begin. I started to dress, wanting Cerise right then.

Downstairs, I found a note from Sheila. She and David had gone off to visit relatives with the baby. I phoned Cerise but she failed to answer. Feeling worse for that, I headed home to my place. I wrote and drank, not necessarily in that order, and the day slowly faded into evening. I had called Cerise several more times without an answer.

Sunday passed by with increasing uncertainties. Cerise still had yet to return my calls.

Call me, she had said...Oh sure.

I struggled over a poem for her and finally gave up. It was a lousy poem anyway, written more with the hope of getting laid than anything else. When darkness settled around me that night, terror came with it. I was alone, morally bankrupt, a junkie, addictively trying to replace to one woman with another.

Monday morning, I went into the office with the same hollow feeling in my gut, but with a chip on my shoulder too. Cerise was there working on invoices. She smiled and winked at seeing me. I nodded and went to my desk.

She came in a short while later.

"I'm sorry," she whispered. "My girlfriends dragged me out of town for the weekend. I would have called back otherwise."

I nodded.

"You're mad."

"I'm not mad."

She shook me playfully

"I really had a good time Friday."

I nodded.

"Come on. Let's go out to dinner tonight and I'll make it up to you."

"All right."

"You're sure."

"Yeah, sure."

"Okay. What time did you want to pick me up?"

I looked at the watch Ellie had given me.

"I have to run out on a sales call in a bit. Say six o'clock? I should be free by then."

"Okay."

She jotted down her address.

"Don't lose it," she added with a wink and left.

Yeah, yeah. I got the irony.

With Cerise gone, I turned in my chair and called Ellie, prepared to hang up if she answered the phone. When her machine picked up, I grabbed my briefcase and dashed out the door.

I had no guarantee the twins would be in school and circled the block twice before finally getting up the nerve to knock on the door. When no one answered I let myself in and called out their names. I went from room to room. Seeing the coast was clear, I quickly gathered my belongings, my heart racing with every passing car outside.

Back at my cottage, I walked in the door with the phone ringing. I let the machine pick up. It was Ellie, offering me the same tired entreaty. I turned down the sound and went about unpacking. The phone rang four more times while I put things away. I erased all the messages without listening to them and called the office to check in. Cerise answered.

"Your girlfriend's called here several times."

"Goddamn it...All right, I call her. And it's *old* girlfriend."

I hung up, downed a glass of sherry and dialed Ellie's number on campus.

"I'll always love you," she said at hearing my voice.

"I've moved my stuff out."

There was silence.

"I'm sorry that I've ruined everything, Roger."

"It's fine. Just stop calling me, please."

"Will it help to say I was wrong?"

"No."

"Roger, I'm taking my sabbatical this summer and I want you to think about going to Europe with me. Please. I believe it can be a renewal for us. A new springtime for our romance."

"There isn't any romance," I said flatly.

"Roger, please have dinner with me."

"No," I said.

I got up and paced. My heart beat wildly.

"Is there someone else, Roger?"

"Yes, there's someone else."

A long silence followed.

"How long, Roger?"

"It doesn't matter."

"It matters to me," she said.

"I've got to go. And please stop calling the shop."

"Roger," I heard faintly as I dropped the receiver into the cradle.

I had been sitting there, feeling like hell for several minutes when the phone rang again. I let it go to the answering machine, figuring it was Ellie. Then I heard Cerise's voice and rushed to pick it up.

"Hi."

"Hi," she said. "Are you all right?"

"Yeah, I'm all right."

There was a long pause.

"Roger, do you think you need some time to sort things out?"

"No."

"Well, it sounds like you're still seeing her."

"No, I'm not."

Reluctantly, I explained what was going on.

"I drove down and grabbed all my things from her house a little while ago. I didn't want to bother you with the sordid details."

"Are you sure you don't need some more time?"

"No. It's over, Cerise...Please don't push me away. I need you now more than I need any break."

"All right. Then are we still going out tonight?

"Of course. I'll see you later on."

"Okay. I'll be waiting."

"I'll be there as planned."

The rest of the day went by tediously. Then it was dusk and Cerise was opening her apartment door for me, dressed in a fawn-colored suede skirt and dark-green blouse, with her dark hair pulled back on one side, revealing a silver loop earring. I stole a glance at her dancer's legs and fine-boned ankles. She was gorgeous and utterly enchanting.

"Did you want to come in?"

"Yes...No...I don't know. We'd better go."

She laughed and closed the door.

I headed for the coast, wanting that additional enchantment, and settled on a restaurant at the backside of Newport Harbor. The road crossed a bridge from Lido Isle and out past some rough and tumble docks along the waterfront. The restaurant was nestled in a cove nearby, with wooden steps leading from the parking lot up the front door. The atmosphere was dusky inside. A hostess led us down past the milieu of laughter and voices and ting of glasses to a window table. We had a view of some trawlers and the harbor mouth. A waitress soon came and took our orders for lobster and a bottle of Sauvignon Blanc.

With the waitress gone, I reached for Cerise's hands. It was young love at last, that dismal sense of there being a knowable end out there in the future nowhere in sight.

"What a lovely smile," I said.

"Oh, aren't you the dazzler?"

"No, it's just. I'm so sorry about everything but so very glad that we're here now. Please don't ever go."

Cerise smiled and squeezed my hands. The waitress came with the wine and we disengaged while she filled our goblets. Once she was gone, our hands met again and we stared in that dream of first love.

"Let's go someplace far away."

Cerise smiled.

"I've never been anywhere."

"Never?"

She shook her head.

"Where would you like to go?"

"I would love to see Europe."

"Paris then. We'll kiss on a boulevard at twilight."

"Oh you."

"Oh you," I repeated.

Cerise smiled and tickled me playfully under the table.

It was late in the evening when I finally paid the tab and we pushed away from the table. We had talked of many things, such as our families and how we had arrived where we were.

Back at Cerise's apartment, she invited me in. We had a glass of wine and sat on her divan and kissed and soon found ourselves wrestling on the floor. In the end, though, she withdrew. I sat up across from her and drew an imaginary line on the carpet.

"This is a cliff. If you jump, I will catch you."

"How do I know that?"

"You don't. You must jump to find out."

Her dark eyes searched mine. I saw passion there, but also concern.

"I'm not ready to jump tonight."

I reached across the space and kissed her. It grew passionate again but again she pulled away.

"I'm not ready tonight."

We went on battling playfully for some time before I finally got up to leave. Our kissing continued at the door. I knew she wanted me to stay. Her look said as much but I went home alone with my desires unfulfilled.

At least the world was young at heart again. My only regrets were for Ellie, lying there abandoned and growing old all by herself.

Twenty Three

The next morning, I made coffee first thing and toddled about the house in my bathrobe, fielding client calls in one moment and toying with the words of a poem in the next. Each time I thought of Cerise, I felt grand. Each time I thought of Ellie, I grew depressed.

Around noon, I showered and drove over to the office. No one was around when I walked in. Curious, I went out to check out on the shop floor. It hummed with machinery. Happy Hobbit Leather Company had long ago traded the clang of hand tools for hydraulic presses. The one enduring creative process was drafting new designs for the toolmaker, which Alan did.

Being the only person not completely preoccupied, I asked him if he knew what had happened to David, Sheila and Cerise.

He listened impassively over the drone of machinery and rock and roll.

"David and Sheila had an appointment at the bank. Cerise is in the head."

Satisfied, I went back to my office. When Cerise appeared, I popped my head into her office.

"Hi."

"Hi."

I saw Alan had his back to us and gave Cerise a kiss.

"Like to have lunch with me?"

"I'm a bit swamped from all these orders you brought in last week."

She made a funny face. I smiled.

"How about dinner then?"

"Tonight?"

"Yeah."

"I'm sorry. I can't. I already made plans with some friends. Maybe tomorrow night?"

"Sure."

I was thinking to give Cerise another kiss but Alan looked our way. I went back to my desk, made a few phone calls and dashed across the boulevard to a beer and sandwich joint tucked away in the opposite industrial complex. It was a haven for blue collar workers. I hung out inside the darkened interior for over an hour, bored with my life, frustrated that my seduction had been further delayed and otherwise dreaming of faraway places.

When I arrived back to the office, Cerise was still at work on the other side of the glass partition. Our eyes met from time to time with an exchange of smiles.

As I was about to leave at five, the phone rang. Someone wanted to know about an order. I told the client I would check on it and call right back.

Out in the warehouse, I fell into conversation with some of the shop people. We were standing just outside the back door. The sun had gone down. The parking lot was now in shadows.

With all of us paused after a joke, the sound of high-heels broke the silence. Everyone turned to stare. It was Ellie strutting across the concrete floor in a tight red dress. I could tell from the smile on her face that she had been drinking...more than a bit.

Following a terse introduction and some deft diplomacy, I quickly herded Ellie outside. I did not have to look back to know that Cerise had been watching this entire scene unfold.

"Come on. I'll walk you back to your car," I told Ellie.

Catcalls followed us around the building. Out in front, Ellie leaned seductively against her car with a big smile.

"I've got your friends going," she said.

"Ellie, you can't do this."

From supremely confident, she was suddenly maudlin, in the way only people who have been drinking can do. She reached towards my swollen lip but I pushed her hand away. Her eyes teared up.

"I'm sorry, Roger. I am so sorry, but I can't give up hope. I won't."

"You should."

"But you love me. I know you do."

"It no longer matters that I do."

I glanced past her at the glass front of our office, unable to see Cerise on the other side but quite certain that she was watching.

"Is that your new girlfriend?"

I nodded, pained to think that I was hurting her, but my heart was as hard as stone.

"She's very beautiful. I'm sure she will give you everything you need. Everything I couldn't."

Again, I just nodded. The idea of hashing things out only made me feel sadder. It was fruitless. Our love affair was over and walking away from it with dignity was all that remained.

"Please, Roger," Ellie said. "Let us have our moment in the sun before you go. Take my sabbatical with me. I need that special moment to remember."

I found myself unable to look at her. The pleading tortured my soul.

"I do love you, Ellie, and I'm so grateful that you came into my life, but it's over now. It's over and there's no going back."

"It's the years, isn't it?"

"I can't lie to you. It's part of it, yes, but it wouldn't have mattered. You've betrayed me now twice in front of other men and my heart can no longer forgive you."

She licked at a tear that had slowly rolled down to her mouth.

"I'm sorry, Roger. Please try to forgive me."

I nodded and turned to leave.

"Roger?"

I looked back with my hand on the door of the office.

"You are my last love," she said. "I will never love again."

With great sadness, I opened the door and went inside, hoping to find Cerise and explain things, but she was gone and all the offices were now darkened except for mine. I called the customer back about his order and left too, locking the front door behind myself.

The next day, I called in and told Sheila I would be out in the field all day. It was an excuse. I did not want to see Cerise or be grilled about yesterday's episode. I especially did not want to face the fact that I had initiated a new love affair out of desperation. My real emotions were all about Ellie, this terrifying tsunami about to engulf my life. I wasn't sure what to call Cerise in this metaphor but it was much like what remained after the tsunami had gone back out to sea.

Moved by the pain I had visited upon Ellie's heart, I wrote at my desk until the afternoon grew late, filled with sorrow but resigned to the path I had chosen. I poured another glass of sherry to numb the feelings and read the poem again.

So Long, My Friend

My heart shouts out to let go,
Even as I scramble to escape this dull mass,
this avalanche of remorse that swallows me whole,
It was foolish and impulsive of me, perhaps,
to have walked away,
yet your indifference to my bloodied hands
cuts more than knifes
and leaves me riddled with revenge.
And still the finality of my choice
leaves no peace,
my blood runs hot
into emptiness so profound
I cannot direct these thoughts,
my lungs hunger for smoke,
my heart for a drink,
god help me,
someone, somewhere help me,
I hate,
then love,
wander desperately in circles
exhausted and entangled by own words,
words that fail to express what is now
the end of this dear love affair,

the dearest and sweetest thing
I have ever known.

Just then a knock came at the door. I opened it to find Cerise standing there in her gray business skirt, a white blouse and high heels. She kissed me passionately. I was taken aback by the kiss but invited her in.

"What's going on?"

"Sheila let me off early. I made up an excuse. I wanted to see you."

She glanced at my desk.

"Is it all right?"

"Sure."

"You don't sound very happy to see me."

She eyed me with a coy smile.

"I'm sorry. I've been writing all day. My mind is elsewhere."

"Did you work on my poem?"

"Yes," I lied. "It's not done but I can read what I have."

I uncovered the poem from a pile of papers on my desk. I had started it with great enthusiasm. I had left off with my words in a heap of disingenuous emotions. I sat in my desk chair with Cerise leaning against my shoulder as I read.

In The Wind At The Sea With You

You unfolded from time,
seashells and sand,
the fathomless oceans calling at your feet.
These footsteps of a grieving fool

staggered into your sensuous hold
and swallowed soon
by a long forgotten femininity,
as though by the sea.

The present had looked behind,
the hours then reversed
and turned forward by your gypsy child.
There is only the dark pool of your eyes now,
and what gift can I offer
to the wings of your beauty,
but to soar here in my paper lines?

With this pale reflection in hand,
and the magic of our moments to sustain me,
I met the shadowed lanes of dusk with a sigh.
From uncertainty and emptiness
your beauty rose to reclaim me,
so I rush again to your shores,
these words but a pale reflection of the sublime.

"That is so beautiful," Cerise said. She leaned down to kiss my lips and ears passionately. "No one has ever written a poem for me before."

I stared up at her gypsy beauty with loop earrings, her dark eyes flashing, glad the poem had touched her but thinking it was the most pathetic thing I had ever written.

"I'm ready to jump," she whispered and pulled away to look at me, her tongue pressed against the inside of her upper teeth.

I stood up to meet her body and we kissed a long time.

"Let's have dinner first," I said, pulling my head back.

Cerise laughed and playfully rustled my hair.

"Come on," I said. "I'm famished and I just want to savor your beauty right now."

"Okay. Where do you want to go?"

"How about The Mining Company?"

"Oh, I love that place! I love to sit at the bar and watch the city lights sparkle."

"Okay, let me change then."

It was a short drive from my place up into the hills and the restaurant. We took our seats with the sea of city lights twinkling at twilight for miles and miles far below us. Almost at eye level, a commercial jet banked into view and began its descent down towards the airport by the coast.

Cerise and I held hands.

"So, tell me more about your travels."

I painted a picture of the day I had left Paris for Bordeaux and ultimately Spain. I could still smell the diesel and see the traffic heading south. I had been standing there on the highway on the outskirts of the city, at almost the exact same time of day.

"God, I can't believe I've never been anywhere," Cerise said.

"We can go if you want."

"Oh, I'd love it. My parents would probably freak out."

"Who cares?"

She laughed and tickled me under the table.

We talked of life and the things we wanted to do and after the meal drove back to my place. Cerise used the bathroom. I placed an album on the turntable. When she reappeared, we danced in the darkened living room.

Knowing what Cerise wanted, I carried her to my bed and kissed her, from her delicate ankles up her legs and into her

301

thighs. Her scent came through her panties. I soon had them off and burrowed my lips into her womb.

When she cried out tenderly, I thought of Ellie. She had taught me so much and now it was my turn to be the mentor.

Somewhere around the fifth or sixth orgasm, Cerise pulled on me. I crawled up and looked into her eyes. She held my face and kissed me.

"Oh god, I see your women never stray."

Her dark eyes studied me for a long moment before she rolled me over and went down to return the favor. When I could no longer restrain myself, I got on top of Cerise and penetrated her sweet, young virginal bone and savaged that tender beauty. And all the while memories of Ellie swirled around me like newspapers in the wind.

Cerise and lay there afterwards, caressing and kissing. Ellie remained my thoughts. She had offered me things that perhaps Cerise never could, but Cerise offered me things that Ellie never would. Well, I had made my choice and was mostly glad with it.

Within the week, Cerise had moved into my place. Within days of that, I found myself torn by the decision. I loved seeing Cerise about the house in high heels, and the sex and sheer joy of two young lovers first out in the world, but I hated the loss of my precious solitude.

When cautioned to watch my drinking, I drank more. When threatened in my authority, I struck back with biting sarcasm.

By the end of the first week, the two of us had fought and made love in equal proportions. When I learned that she had voted for Nixon, I was especially furious. The bastard had been reelected in a landslide, just as I had feared. From Kennedy and all our young hopes and dreams to this. It was like the Nazis had won the war instead.

"Nixon?!" I said to Cerise. "How the fuck could you have voted for that bastard?!"

She had no explanation. Her father was a Republican so she had gone with the party line. I was unable to speak to her for the rest of the day and thereafter embarked on an indoctrination program. It was as if Cerise had gone through the sixties cultural revolution in a state of suspended animation. I wasn't sure she had learned anything from my diatribes but doubted she would ever vote Republican again.

That Sunday, David and Sheila invited us over for brunch and a jam session at their place. The house was overflowing with friends, many of them musicians. Beers and Bloody Mary's were being consumed in equal proportions. Cerise and Sheila and some of the other women were out in the kitchen cooking.

I sat on the outskirts of the session, watching. David called over to me during a break.

"Didn't you say you played a blues harp?"

"Yeah, when I was bumming around the world. It kept me entertained while I was waiting for the next car to come by."

Someone produced a harmonica and David moved a microphone stand in front of me.

"We've been trying to do this old blues song and it wants a blues harp." David tapped the microphone. "Go ahead and give it try. It's live."

I blew a few notes tentatively. With the Fender blues amp, the harp sounded like a saxophone.

"Hey, how about that."

"Yeah," David said. "Let's give it a run."

They broke into a Muddy Waters' tune and I layered in some harmonies. Cerise and some of the other women came out from the kitchen to watch. I looked over at Cerise and winked. This was a whole new game. I could see turning my poetry into lyrics. I'd take Hollywood by storm.

At some point, the ladies set up a buffet on the dining room table with omelets, English muffins and jam. I took a break and flipped through David's collection of old blues records while I was eating.

Sheila came by.

"Did you know we were planning to move the business up to Santa Cruz?"

"Well, as your head of marketing, I'd be the last one to know."

She laughed and clapped her hands.

"David and I were just talking about it between ourselves until we were sure. We're tired of LA. You're welcome to join us, of course."

"I don't know, Sheila. I don't know what I'm doing anymore."

"You're tired of it, aren't you?"

"Yeah." I waved at the scene around us. "I just want to do something creative like this."

"So sell us your shares. You'll have enough money to start a studio or something."

"Yeah. Something."

David had started up another blues tune and waved me over.

"Excuse me but Blind Boy Dunne is wanted."

Sheila laughed and clapped. I stepped into the tune, more confident in my skills with every bar.

That night at home, Cerise and I got into a fight over money and our plans for the future. I just wanted out, to make a clean break, to say, here, this is now a new creative time for me, but Cerise thought I should wait to sell. The company was really growing and my shares would be worth a lot more in a couple of years.

Ellie and I had never fought over such things because, one, she didn't need my money and, two, somewhere deep down inside, I guess I had always known that we had no future. It struck me while sitting there in my fury towards Cerise that lovers mostly fought over money, that and their plans for the future.

"I don't have a couple of years," I told Cerise in the end.

Monday morning, I decided to stay home and conduct business in my bathrobe. In the past I had done this with great relish. Now, with Cerise knowing my secrets, it was not nearly as much fun.

"Sheila was looking for you today," Cerise said when she came home from work.

I looked up from my desk, my emotions still bruised from last night's battle.

"She knows where to find me."

I went back to the lyric I was writing. Cerise came to look over my shoulder. That infuriated me even more.

"Pterodactyl Blues," she said.

I hid the lyrics and glared up at her.

"Okay," she said. "I just thought you should know. I overheard her and David talking about hiring another salesman. I don't think they think you can handle the growing business."

"They're probably right."

"Don't you care? I mean, it's your future."

I slammed my hand down on my desk.

"My future isn't in that fucking business, all right! When I'm ready, I'll sell out. If they don't offer me enough, I'll wait. Now can I please get back to my work?"

Cerise walked away. I sat there unable to concentrate now. Just what the hell *were* Sheila and David up to? There was a thought to go apologize to Cerise but I didn't.

I looked back at my lyric.

Volcanoes smoking on the far horizon,
strange creatures flying overhead,
I came home to an empty cave last night,
Must be those Pterodactyl blues again.

I started in on the second verse and slammed the pencil down. Goddamn it. I went to find Cerise and dealt with both our frustrations by taking her to bed.

By the end of that month, the plans to relocate Happy Hobbit Leather Inc. up to Santa Cruz had become a reality. David and Sheila were already up there organizing the new shop. The plan was to transfer up all the machinery over that weekend. I watched Alan and some of the other shop workers break down the equipment and load it up on trucks.

Cerise had been on my case for days.

"What am I going to do? Sheila wants me to come up and keep working. You haven't even told me what you have planned."

Finally, I had to take her face in my hands.

"I...will...take...care...of...you...All right? Now chill out."

She cried. I poured a drink.

"Look, you said your brother was coming into town and you were going up there to visit at your parent's place this weekend, right?"

She nodded.

"All right. We both need a break. I'm going down to visit with an old friend of mine in North County San Diego."

"So who's that?"

"Just an old friend. Now forget about the leather business. It's done. I don't know. Maybe we'll go rent a place down at the beach or something. Just go see your family and we'll talk on Sunday. I'll make sure to be back here for dinner."

It took Cerise two hours to pack but she finally left for her folk's place. I waited half an hour to make sure she was gone and pointed my Alfa Romeo north. It was almost three years since I had been to Santa Cruz. I had to go find out for myself. Motoring past Aptos and Soquel and the stands of redwoods along the road, it all came back to me. So many wild adventures we had shared in our high school days.

I went downtown and wandered around a bit and then went up to visit some old friend on the north end of town. Jacob's older brother Michael came out first and gave me a hug.

"Far out, man. What are you doing?"

I explained, most of it.

"Well far out. Come on in."

Jacob came out of the kitchen.

"Far out. I thought you had died or something."

"Yeah, I probably did a bit."

There was laughter. A half dozen young people were gathered around the living room. They had Nixon hung in effigy in one corner of the room.

"Fuck, can you believe it?" I said in reference to the election.

"We'll nail his ass yet," Michael said with a smile.

"I don't know. I think he'd start a civil war before letting go."

Someone threw a dart at the effigy and there were cheers. I sat down and took my turn at a hash pipe going around the room.

"Fuck it," Jacob said and started into a spontaneous, poetic rant. He was like a wild Irish lord.

In our youth, we had shared this oral tradition, out in the shack Jacob and Michael had built on their father's farm east of town. Michael had gotten into making guitars. Jacob did iron sculptor, and of course his wild rambling verse. This one was about politics and corruption. I sat there in the candlelight, embarrassed to call myself a poet.

Michael appeared from his workshop in back later on, playing a guitar, and everyone followed him down to the cliffs along the sea, laughing and joking and singing songs. It was a clear night and we remained there under the stars until it was very late.

In the morning, I decided to drive up the open coastline north of Santa Cruz. A light rain was falling and puddles had gathered on the road. Suddenly my Alfa Romeo was hydroplaning towards the sheer cliffs on the opposite side of the highway. A million things flashed through my mind in that instant, one of them being the advice we had received in our high school driving class—always turn into the slide. That was followed by another instantaneous recognition. Doing so would cause me to miss the adjacent guard rail, and lead to certain death.

Faced with a three hundred foot plunge into the sea, I allowed the car to skid into the metal barrier. That violent collision was followed by a slow motion spin back across the highway. I dropped the Alfa into gear and tried to grab the road, without any luck. Headed for a concrete channel on the opposite side of the highway, I slid way down in the seat. When I finally came to rest, I was upside down.

I struggled free from my seat belt and squeezed out from under the car. The wheels were still spinning. The rain had started coming down harder. I wandered along the side of the highway in shock from the blow to my head.

Two men in a Corvette came along and braked to a stop.

"Hey, are you all right?" one of them said, getting out.

They both came near and examined the cut on my head.

"It's not too bad. Are you sick to your stomach?"

I nodded.

"We'd better get you to a hospital."

I looked over at my car. The wheels had come to a stop and I saw that one of the tires had a bald spot.

"Help me to change the tire," I told them.

"Hey, buddy, you're not thinking straight. You need a doctor, not a tire change."

"No. That tire is probably what caused me to slide and the cop will cite me."

I started for the trunk. They shrugged at each other and came along. In short order, we had the tire changed. A patrolman showed up not long after we were done.

"You're lucky," he said while writing up his report. "We just put up that guard rail last year."

"You mean like random?"

"No, the highway crews always put up a new one where someone goes over."

The patrolman continued on with his report. I absorbed this news with a flurry of emotions. In meeting his death, a man had saved my life. Why him and not me? You had to wonder. Life must still have plans for me, I thought.

The two guys in the Corvette wished me well and motored off. A tow truck arrived soon after and the driver gave me a lift back into town. The Alfa Romeo was totaled and I needed stitches.

I arrived back to Michael and Jacob's place with dusk settling over the world and their tribe of friends gathered around the living room, getting high. I added a quart of Myer's Rum to the festivities, quickly explained my wild adventure and went off to use the phone, hoping to book a flight back home that evening. None were available. The first available flight was the following morning. I got back to the festivities and my quart of Myer's rum

I tossed and turned on the sofa all that night, thinking of Cerise. Suddenly, I loved her very much again.

Back in Orange County the following afternoon, I grabbed a cab at the airport and directed him to the nearest dealership. Half an hour later, I was driving away in a brand new Bronco.

Naturally, Cerise wanted to know what had happened to my Alfa Romeo when I arrived back home. I had to admit to the accident, given the cuts on my face, and told her I had totaled it down in San Diego. Cerise consoled me with kisses and welcomed my newfound devotion, oblivious to what had actually transpired.

"Let's go rent that place down by the beach," I said. "Just you and me, sweetheart."

"Why don't we buy a house, Roger? We need to start planning for our future."

I did my best to smile. A house. Kids. A mortgage. Oh god.

Cerise tickled me

"What's the matter? Are you getting nervous again?"

"Okay, okay. Let's not go overboard. Let's just rent a place and then we'll start poking around for something more permanent. Okay?"

"All right."

"Just you and me, sweetheart."

Cerise smiled and led me off to the bedroom and made sweet love to me and we had a fine dinner later on and I went to sleep that night, certain that I would love her dearly for the rest of my life.

Twenty Four

Cerise and I poked around a local beach town for most of a week and finally settled on what was the last clapboard cottage on a street that ended at the chain link fence of an elementary school playground, two blocks up from the sea. A narrow, gravel driveway led past the cottage to a one car garage in back and the property as a whole was towered over by two great trees, a maple in front and a pine tree in back. A large bay window overlooked our front lawn and with it being autumn, and with school back in session, maple leaves blew all about our yard and the voices of children at play echoed in through our open windows.

Soon after we had gotten settled, I sold my interest in Happy Hobbit Leather and Cerise quit her job. As a result of the musicians I had met through David's Sunday jam sessions, a prominent rock group bought the lyrics to Pterodactyl Blues and our home soon became a creative hub for all manner of musicians, artists and bohemians. Cerise cooked and made our many visitors feel welcome and the good times went on late into the night.

When Cerise told me she wanted to take some fine arts classes, I encouraged her. When I learned that she had applied to the college where Ellie taught, I grew secretly apprehensive. When the two of them ran into each other, I was hardly surprised.

"I saw Eleanor today," Cerise told me one afternoon, upon arriving home.

"Yeah?"

"She was really nice."

"Good."

"She offered to help me around campus in any way she could."

"That's nice."

"She invited us over for dinner some evening."

"No. That is not going to happen."

"Well, I just thought I should tell you. She was really very nice."

"I'm glad but you can forget about the dinner."

Cerise said nothing more about Ellie and the issue of their camaraderie mostly slipped from my mind.

With the holidays upon us, Cerise and I bought a tree and decorated the house. I strung Christmas lights on the maple tree out front. Cerise made popcorn garlands and we hung them around the bay window.

It rained the following night. A fire burned in our fireplace. A rhythm and blues holiday album we had discovered at a local record store played in the background. We had rum toddies and our hearts were full of cheer. I did not think I could be more happily in love.

The following day, I sat at the kitchen table with the checkered tablecloth, eating one of Cerise's turkey sandwiches. I had a pickle and chips and a beer to chase it all down.

Hearing the mailman come down our dead-end street, Cerise went out to retrieve the mail. A minute later she returned bearing assorted envelopes, including a fresh batch of Christmas cards.

"It's raining again," she said sitting down at the table. That was our signal. What better thing to do than make love to the pitter patter?

I looked out the back door and saw the wood on the porch steps growing dark. The wind blew hard and rustled in the pine.

I continue eating my sandwich while Cerise sorted through the pile of mail. It was quiet except for the moaning of the wind and the rain on the roof and the sound of the mail being opened.

Cerise dropped the mail all of a sudden.

"We have such a happy life, Roger."

"Yeah."

"One day we'll have children and a cozy little home of our own, just like this one."

"Yeah."

"And a white picket fence."

"Yeah."

She laughed and shook me playfully.

"You always say 'yeah' but I wonder what you're really thinking."

She didn't want to know. When I thought of children, I thought of diapers and screaming. It terrified me.

"What's this?" Cerise said about an envelope in her hands.

She held it up. I read the return address.

"It's something from the musician's union."

"It looks like a check."

I finished my mouth full.

"Probably."

"Don't you want to open it?"

"I will when I'm done."

"Let me open it."

I was inclined to say no but knew that would only pique her interest. I gestured to go ahead and watched her open the envelope.

"Wow! It's for over five thousand dollars!"

"Hmm."

"So what's it for, Roger?"

"It must be for one of my songs that were recorded."

"Wow. It must have been a pretty good song. Who recorded it?"

"I don't know."

She kicked me playfully under the table.

"I'm sure. You must know what it's for."

"I write a lot of lyrics. I don't always know what happens to them."

"What's this mean?" she said, examining the check further. "First run royalties for *I'm Late*."

"I guess that's the name of the song."

"You guess."

Cerise dropped the check on the table.

"It's about you and Eleanor, isn't it, Roger?"

I stared at her, busted and not much liking it. The song was in fact about the timeless love a young man had for an older woman, their only curse being to have arrived on this planet at different times.

I'll have to keep a better eye on the mail, I thought to myself.

"You're still in love with her, aren't you?"

"No, Cerise."

"Yes you are. I know it."

I put the sandwich down.

"It was a good story to tell, that's all."

"You're still in love with her," she said knowingly.

"When I tell you something, please don't argue with me. I know my own heart. I don't need you telling me what I'm thinking and feeling."

"I just know you're in love with her. A woman can tell these things."

"I'm not!"

"You don't have to yell."

"Well, fuck! There you were, trying to arrange dinner for the three of us just last week. All one big chummy family. Now you're freaking out because I wrote a lyric about her. It's over. I said it's over so don't shove words down my throat!"

Cerise sulked off to the bedroom and came out a few minutes later.

"I'm going over to see Lisa."

It was a friend of hers from school. I didn't say anything or bother to look up.

Day turned to evening as I sat there alone with the house growing dark around me. I battled with my heart but eventually gave in and reached for the phone. A recording came on; telling me the number had been changed. I jotted down the new one and dialed again.

Having butterflies, I got up to pace.

"Hello," the voice said.

"Hello, Ellie. It's Roger."

"Well, Roger. Do tell? Has something gone awry with your little romance?"

"No. Not really."

"Oh, drat."

"I hope you don't mind me calling."

"No, Roger. I've rather expected it. You see..." Laughter came through the phone. "Oh dear. It seems I just can't help myself."

"It's all right. Go on."

"Well, I was going to say that most young women are governed by their instincts. They have little capacity to muse about their lives."

"So you figure I'm bored."

"Well, yes. I'd probably wager quite a bit in Vegas on that one."

"How about you?"

"Oh well. Life goes on. You know I moved?"

"Yes, I gathered that from the prefix. Huntington, isn't it?"

"Yes. Where are you?"

"Apparently right across town."

There was silence. I carried the phone to the sofa and kicked up my feet. The house was now completely dark. Maple leaves sparkled in the rain outside the bay window.

"So, have you sent the little misses off somewhere for the evening."

I explained to her about the lyric.

"And she ran off in a huff."

"Yes."

"You know, Roger, this is beginning to have a certain French ring to it."

"So, what are you doing?"

317

"Nothing. Would you care to stop by and discuss your problems over a glass of brandy?"

"Okay."

I wrote down the directions to her house and drove straight over. Ellie met me at the door in high heels, silk pants and silk blouse. The color was lime-green and when I hugged her, it felt as if she were slipping about inside the silk.

"Here. I've put the bottle out," she said, pointing to the coffee table.

I sat down and poured two glasses half full.

"Here you go, Ellie."

"To l'aaahmourrr," she said.

"Yeah, l'aaahmourrr, indeed."

She winked and pretended to shoot me. We both drank.

"So, tell me about all your troubles, dear."

"Tell you about it…Hell, sometimes I'm happy and sometimes I don't think the damned thing has a snowball's chance in hell."

"Dare I say, Roger, perhaps your expectations were too high."

"So what else is new?"

Ellie laughed. I drank.

"All right, go on."

"Well, I suspect you had visions of easily duplicating our romance, but it is my experience that such love affairs are very, very rare. Perhaps we are lucky to have one in a lifetime. Two of them back to back? I think you were asking a lot."

"I don't know. We share magic and then we fight. It doesn't seem like there's a whole lot of difference between the two love affairs to me."

I smiled, watching her laugh.

"It's your intellect, Ellie. That more than anything. Take that song. They're only words but Cerise totally freaked out. How can I ever tell her what I'm thinking?"

"I can see how a woman would feel threatened."

"Yeah well, whose side are you on, anyway?"

Ellie laughed again. I topped off my glass and held the bottle out to her. She declined.

"Have you tried discussing your feelings with Cerise?"

"I think about it…And then I turn back."

"Well, under those circumstances, it hardly seems fair to blame her for the lack of communication."

"Yeah? Well I do."

I downed my glass and poured another.

"She told me about running into you on campus. And about inviting us over for dinner."

Ellie bit her nails in mock fright.

"Yeah, well. That wouldn't be such a great idea."

"I was just trying to show you that I was over it, Roger."

I stared at her, feeling the sorrow all over again.

"I'm sorry, Ellie. I never meant to hurt you."

"It did a great deal, Roger."

"I know."

"Well, the point is, I have learned there are no guarantees. There is only the feeling that something is valid at any one moment. And I will not hesitate to enjoy such a moment with you if it should happen to arise again."

I leaned over and placed my head on her shoulder.

"Of course," she said. "What you do with your little tart is your business."

"Hmm. So much for your magnanimous geniality."

"Oh well," Ellie said, pretending to be blithely ignorant.

I laughed.

"I came over to talk with you." I kissed her once and touched the silk over her breast. "And now everything else is stirred up."

"What did you expect?"

"I don't know."

I kissed her again.

"Sometimes I miss you terribly."

"Look," she said, opening the wooden box on her coffee table. Her fingers touched the cross she had made that night in Tahoe. "There is nothing to fear. I am everything which touches me."

I stared at her.

"I don't understand you."

"I don't know that there is anything to understand, Roger. If everything can be taken from us, then what is there?"

"This moment."

She nodded in agreement. I reached up and held her face between my hands.

"It's this, Ellie. It's your mind that seduces me."

"That's fine. We can just talk if you like."

"You fucker."

"I love it when you say fucker," she said.

I smiled at the memory of our first encounter and pressed my head against her breasts. Her hand reached down and gently stroked my hair.

In the silence that followed, I reached over and pulled the cord under the lamp shade. Her eyes sparkled in the darkness. Then our lips came together as two things wanting to be devoured. I unbuttoned the silk of her blouse and her breasts spilled out. I pressed my lips under the weight of them and slowly ascended, first along one then the other, until the nipples were both hard. We went from the sofa to the carpet to the bedroom, struggling with our clothes along the way, and for those few, passionate moments, I could not remember for the life of me why I had ever left her. Only later in the night, while Ellie slept in the darkness, did the punchline come back to me.

It is knowing the end before the beginning.

Shortly before dawn, I pulled into the gravel driveway, killed the motor and glided to a halt alongside the cottage. The roof was still wet from the rain. The sky was growing pale on the eastern horizon. I sat for a moment, contemplating my speech, then quietly opened the back door. Feeling hollow inside on several accounts, I poured myself a glassful of beer and downed it. Cerise had not awakened from my rustling about, so I took a shower and joined her in bed. Finally, she awakened and turned to face me.

"Where have you been?" she asked.

"I went down to visit an old friend in Laguna."

She searched my eyes.

"I didn't know you had a friend in Laguna."

"Yeah. A guy named Steve. I went to school with him. I hadn't seen him in years. I just drove down there, feeling restless and remembered he lived in town."

I stared through my lie with such sincerity; her suspicions had nowhere to pry.

"I wish you had called."

"We got drunk and the next thing I knew, it was three in the morning."

"I wish you wouldn't drink so much."

"All right, Cerise."

"Okay. I'll leave you alone."

I started to turn away but her arm reached out for me.

"I'm sorry about last night. I should have trusted you."

"It's all right, sweetheart. I wouldn't do a thing to hurt you."

"I love you," she said.

"I know. I love you, too."

She pulled me into the sweet tenderness of her warm embrace and I hung all my guilt there. Sometime later, it began to rain again and we slept.

When I awakened, Cerise was not there. I found her out in the kitchen making a cake.

"I'd like to go down to the Port Theater for the matinee," she said. "I saw a foreign film playing there."

She pointed to the newspaper on the table. I looked. The film was *La Dolce Vita*. I shook my head. It did seem as if life was beginning to imitate art, and that all storylines were converging together.

"Have you seen it?" she said with a look over her shoulder.

"Yeah, a long time ago."

"Do you mind seeing it again?"

"No. I could watch Fellini forever."

"So," she said, pressing her body against mine. "What would you like first? A bite to eat, or me?"

"I think you first. Then lunch after the movie."

"Well then, big boy, come and get it."

Slowly, methodically, and with her eyes trained on me, she backed me into the bedroom.

At the theater later on, we went outside for the intermission and saw that it had begun to rain again. By the end of the film, the brief storm had broken and charcoal clouds moved swiftly against a blue sky. The sidewalks were wet and the cars swished going by.

The wind was calm directly in front of the theater but the minute we walked past the façade, we were hit with great gusts blowing in from the sea. Cerise's hat blew off and we had to chase it down the sidewalk.

Eventually, we came to a narrow bridge and crossed onto Balboa Island. I had not intended it but we passed by Ellie's old cottage, jogging my thoughts back to that day long ago, when we had crossed paths as a storm was breaking, just like this one. I remembered the intrigue I had felt for Ellie as a young man and relived that moment of excitement again.

With it being winter, only one of the ferries was running and it was just then churning off towards the opposite side of the gray harbor as Cerise and I walked up. Two cars were already parked, waiting for the ferry to return. We sat on a nearby bench and watched the gulls dart in and out of the wind.

The ferry eventually returned and we waited while the steward got the two cars parked onboard. Then he waved the pedestrians on and locked the gate and the pilot backed away from the dock. On the way across the harbor, the steward came around and collected our fares.

On the other side, Cerise and I walked past the fun zone and out onto the end of the pier. Huddled there in the wind, we eventually grew cold and walked back to a cafe along the boardwalk. We had a late lunch with a view of the sea and lingered after the meal, drinking Irish coffees.

"What do you think the girl represented at the end?" Cerise asked me. "You know, waving from across the bay?"

I explained my previous observations.

"Fellini often uses the sea at the end of his movies. I suspect because it was symbolic of something pure to him."

Cerise cupped her Irish coffee without answering.

"Anyway, I liked the woman in the bar at the beginning."

"Which one?"

I imitated her hand gesture.

"Oh yeah."

Cerise made the gesture too.

"All you need is the hat."

"It's such wonderful imagery. What do you think he meant by that?"

"I think that whole opening montage was just was to show us the decadence of the rich. To show us a class of people who never have to worry."

"Wouldn't that be nice?"

"My sense is that Fellini was disgusted by it. That goes back to the last scene. It was like he could see himself being swept away by his own success but couldn't seem to stop it."

The waitress came and I paid the check.

"A great movie though."

Cerise did the little hand routine again on our way out of the restaurant.

"I don't know why but I find that so sexy."

We hugged and went walking down the sidewalk in the brisk wind.

"Let's rent a TV for the holidays," Cerise said.

"Sure, we can watch all the cheesy Christmas specials."

She laughed.

"You make it sound like watching television is decadent."

"It is, but let's do it anyway."

We crossed the sand towards an empty lifeguard tower and climbed up to the lee side of it. Cerise sat between my legs. Clouds marched along the horizon. The sea was churning gray and white under the blue sky. Cerise smiled and kissed me over her shoulder.

We had been sitting there for quite a while when a man on a pair of skis suddenly sped past with a parachute out in from of him. We laughed.

"Wow, look at how fast he's going."

We watched him race swiftly down the beach and out of sight.

Later, we retraced our steps to the car and started home on Coast Highway. Along the way, we found a hole in the wall TV sales and repair place and rented an old Zenith. It was late that afternoon when we got back to the house. I hooked up the TV for Cerise and went to take a nap. My duplicity haunted me as I drifted off to sleep. I heard Cerise rustling about in the kitchen and the television playing low and swore I would never cheat on her again.

Two days later, I found myself back at Ellie's place. There was no pretense this time. We made love without restraint then got out a bottle of champagne. Ellie was in her robe. I wore my briefs.

"I've opened Pandora's box," I said.

She poured the champagne and held up her glass to me.

"To, well, whatever."

"You're not listening to me."

"Of course. You can't get the lid closed."

I stared at her over my glass.

"So what am I going to do?"

I drank and she refilled my glass.

"You know, Roger. You've got everyone worrying about you. Who are you worrying about?"

"Thanks," I said.

"There, there. I'm only reminding you that there is more than one person involved in this drama."

"Well." I stood up. "Am I to blame that every time I come over here, you slit me open like a clam?"

"Where were you thinking to go, Roger?"

I looked down at my briefs. She patted the sofa next to her. I returned to my seat and champagne.

"I suppose this is a lousy time to be bringing this up," she continued.

"If you have to say that, it probably is."

"Well, I doubt there will be a good time."

"Then don't bring it up."

She pretended to throw one of her tantrums.

"All right, what is it?"

She came closer and rubbed my chest.

"Roger, I want to know you'll spend some time with me over Christmas."

"Shall I print up a schedule and post it on a wall at home?"

"Roger. I have not made any great demands on you."

I acknowledged this with a caress of her neck.

"No, you're right. I'll find time."

"Thank you."

"I'd best be going."

"One for the road?"

She held out the bottle.

"Sure, one more for the road."

A few nights before Christmas, I was mixing up two rum and Egg Nog's out in the kitchen. As an afterthought, I had hung lights in the pine tree too and saw them swaying in the wind through the window. A fire glowed in the fireplace. Charles Brown sang *Merry Christmas, Baby* on the stereo. I splashed a little extra rum on my drink and sprinkled nutmeg over both glasses. The phone rang.

"Would you get it, Roger," Cerise called out from the living room. I set her drink down on my way to the phone.

"It's Ellie, Roger. You know, that other tart you keep across town."

"Oh, hi," I said cheerfully. Cerise looked once and went back to wrapping presents. I turned away and cupped the phone.

"Ellie, I asked you never to call me here."

"I want some attention, Roger."

"I'll try and call you later," I whispered.

"No, I think the three of us had better sit down and talk this over right now."

"Oh sure, sure," I said with a smile and a wink at Cerise.

She looked away again. I headed for the kitchen.

"Goddamn it, Ellie. You're drunk."

"Yes, and I'm suing for equal time."

I heard the last chord of the song and the turntable arm lifting off the album.

"Ellie, I promise I'll call you tomorrow," I whispered and pressed down the receiver.

"Yes, yes, that will be fine," I said out loud. "We'll talk about it after the holidays."

I placed the phone down and went to turn the album over.

"Who was that, honey?"

"Oh, someone with a record company. He wants me to write some lyrics for one of his new bands."

"How exciting."

We exchanged smiles and I changed the album. Cerise reached for her Eggnog and held it up to me.

"Merry Christmas, baby."

I kissed her and took my drink over to the bay window. The TV was on without sound. It was Clarence and George and the angels. Cerise went on cheerily with her enterprise. After a moment, she looked up at me with a smile.

"What are you doing?"

"Just enjoying the wind in the trees."

I sipped my drink and maintained my vigil. Cerise chit chatted with me about this and that while I did.

It took about fifteen minutes for the headlights to turn down the block. I immediately headed for the back door via the kitchen.

"I'm going out to the garage for some more firewood," I called over my shoulder.

Once outside, I raced down the driveway and caught Ellie at the curb. She was loaded.

"Well, hello there, Roger. Now, let's see if we can get this little mess of ours all straightened out."

I grabbed her arm and pulled her back around to the Capri.

"Ellie, you've got to leave."

I opened her car door.

"Oh no," Ellie said, trying to pull away. "Not until we've had ourselves a nice little chat."

I looked back and saw Cerise's head in the picture window. She was still busy with wrapping her Christmas presents. I prayed to god she wouldn't look up.

When Ellie attempted to pull away from me again, I pinned her against the car.

"Do you know what you're doing?"

"Yes, I'm screwing up your lovely little romance."

"You're screwing up our romance."

"I can't see how it could possibly get any more screwed up."

"All right, this is it. I can never see you again."

"Is that your choice?"

I nodded.

"Allowing your dick to think for you, dear?"

She reached for my crotch but I intercepted her.

"I want you to go," I said.

"Fine. That's all I wanted to know."

She kissed me and fell into her seat. I squatted next to the car and Ellie rolled down her window.

"I'm sorry, Ellie."

"It's only Pandora's box." She wiped a tear from her cheek and smiled. "I wish I could get the damn lid back on."

She touched my cheek sweetly and drove off.

I called Ellie the next morning and drove over to her house. It was Christmas Eve. She poured us both brandies. I held her close and drank until the words came.

"I want something to last."

"Nothing does, Roger."

"I don't know that."

"Ah well, you'll find out soon enough."

"Don't you see, Ellie? I have to find out."

"Yes, you have to find out."

"Remember? You said I was only thinking of myself."

"Yes, I did say that, didn't I?"

"I can't do it any longer. I have to think of someone else."

"And you had to hurt one of us."

"Yes, it's only instincts, Ellie."

"She's really very beautiful."

"She said the same of you."

"Did she?"

"Yes."

"Go to her, Roger. If it matters, I forgive you."

"Thank you, sweetheart. I'll always love you."

She held up her glass again.

"Our timing was just a little bit off, that's all."

I held Ellie in my arms until her sorrow was mostly spent and then left.

Twenty Five

Later that afternoon, Cerise and I bundled up against the cold, gathered our presents and drove down the coast to my family's Christmas Eve gathering. It was being held that year at my brother Frank's condo in Corona del Mar and as usual his crowded street was lined from end to end with parked cars. I finally found a spot way up at the top of the block.

Cerise and I grabbed everything out of the trunk and started down the sidewalk with eucalyptus trees rustling in the cold wind above our heads and a glimpse of the sea visible far off beyond a collage of rooftops. Several members of my family were on a wooden deck extending out towards the sidewalk from Frank's condo and they erupted in boisterous calls at seeing our approach. Cerise looked at me anxiously.

"Don't worry. They're mostly harmless."

When my mother answered the door, she delighted in Cerise.

"Hello, I'm grandma."

Cerise received a big hug.

"Come in, come in," my mother said and opened the door wider.

"Hello, baby," she said to me with her face scrunched up for a kiss.

"Hey, Rog," Frank said. "And who is this?"

Frank made a gesture at Cerise and she laughed. While I got our presents arranged under the Christmas tree, he dragged her off for more introductions. Out of the corner of my eye, I noticed my sister Rose and Cerise becoming fast friends. When Cerise was introduced to my father, he put on his usual show.

I headed off to make a drink in the kitchen and passed my mother on the way. She made the same hand gesture Frank had made.

"She's a beauty."

"Thanks. Where's Vincent?"

My mother shook her head sadly. Off in the world somewhere getting drunk, it was assumed.

Frank came out to the kitchen and started mashing the potatoes.

"That's the best piece of ass I've seen you with in a long time."

Frank had to be coarse. 'Hey, beautiful lady' wouldn't do.

"What's the matter, Rog? Get your feelings hurt?"

"No, Frank."

Knowing he wouldn't understand, I didn't bother to explain. I took my bourbon and went out to the living room.

When a Count Basie Christmas tune came on the stereo, my mother started to dance, her eyes closed, her shoulders coming up with each beat.

"Come on, Roger. Dance with me."

I took her hand and we jitterbugged around the living room carpet. Cerise came out to watch with a big smile. When the song was over, I hugged my mother and went to sit with Frank's son Barry on the sofa.

"Hey, how are you doing?" Barry said.

He really didn't care so I didn't answer him. There was a pro football game on TV and he had a bet on it. That was the most important aspect of Barry's life, making calls to his bookie.

When Dallas got a first down, Barry groaned.

"I've got twenty dollars on the spread," he told me.

When Dallas scored a touchdown on the next play, he laughed cynically at his fortunes. There went his spread.

Frank joined us on the sofa.

"What's the score?"

Barry told him and the two of them became glued to the game. The acorn never fell far from the tree. Barry was Frank without the cockiness.

Frank's much younger fiancé Cyril came out of the kitchen, looking for him. She was a Bavarian doll, with lustrous blonde hair and an A-type personality.

"Frank, we need more chairs…Frank!"

He glanced up from the game with a look of dismay.

"Are you listening to me?"

"How could I not be listening to you, Cyril?"

"We need more chairs."

"What do you want me to do? Make them?"

"Frank!" she said very loudly and disappeared.

Frank looked at me. I smiled. It's your turn, buddy. Frank had found himself a beautiful, vivacious young gal, with a neurotic need to control the universe, my brother included.

Before dinner, Frank took me out on the deck to cut my hair. Frank had once owned a chain of beauty shops and was the family barber by default. I sat on a bar stool with a towel around my shoulders. Frank clipped away, so enjoying his drink and

333

the view of the sea, he absentmindedly clipped off a part of my earlobe.

"Jesus, Frank!"

I stood up and accidentally kicked the piece of ear down between the wooden deck planks.

"Oh shit," Frank said. "Here, let me have a look at you."

He pulled the towel away from my ear. The blood was pouring out.

Cerise appeared.

"Oh my god, what happened, honey!?"

I explained. The blood had dripped all over my clothes and the deck by then.

"Where's the piece?"

She got down on her knees to look. Frank laughed.

"I think it's mulch now."

"We have to find it," Cerise said.

I shook my head.

"Forget it, sweetheart. The deck's six inches off the ground. Anyway, what are we going to do if we find it? Have them reattach it at the hospital?"

She stood up and worried over my wound again.

"Honestly, it's okay," I told her. "Maybe you could find some mercurochrome"

She went off to look. I held the towel to my ear and Frank finished the haircut. Cerise returned with the bottle. Everyone had come out to investigate. There was more talk of taking me to the hospital, mostly instigated by my mother. I waved them off and prepared for Cerise to apply the mercurochrome.

"Oowww!" I said when she touched the lotion to the ear.

"Okay, buddy. You're all done," Frank said.

He swept up and I went off to make another drink.

Having accomplished that task, I joined Barry on the sofa. The football game droned on. Barry spoke to me but rarely took his eyes off the TV set. A catatonic quality overtook everyone who got near the television set. Hating this, I turned on some Christmas music and Frank told me to turn it off.

I made myself comfortable in a chair by the fireplace and fell sway to this contented vision of my life—the weary veteran having just come home from war. It was a bright, winter day. The house was filled with the wonderful scent of a bird roasting in the oven. After much grief, all was now good and happy in the world. My family's predictable insanity aside, it was a pleasant Christmas gathering. There were lots of hugs and laughter and presents and good cheer. I worked on becoming inebriated while Cerise doted on my war wounds.

On Christmas Day, Cerise and I went to visit her family, an event that could not have been more polar opposite than the previous day. For one thing, her mother and father were strict Catholics, indignant that I was living with their daughter out of wedlock. And two, the old man was a staunch Republican and Nixon supporter. I had been dreading this encounter from the moment Cerise had told me about these people, and for good reason.

Their home was a big Spanish style, cookie-cutter place up in the foothills. I could see the old man had a hard on for me the minute we walked in the door. He was Dutch and French, short and stocky with black hair and a bulldog nature. Probably figured I ought to marry his daughter, buy her a big cookie-cutter Spanish style home up in the foothills and start having kids.

A simmering tension brewed beneath the not so polite atmosphere. References were made about hippies and what shit they were. By the time the old man got around to cutting the bird at the table, talking of God and how great Nixon was for the country, I had had enough and pushed my chair back.

"You'll excuse me," I said and headed for the front door. The old man caught up with me in the foyer, his sleeves rolled up.

"You son of a bitch," he said with his Dutch accent. "I'm going to kick your ass."

I walked out and started down the driveway. Cerise's mother had restrained him on the front porch. The last I saw, Cerise and her mother were trying to drag him back into the house.

Thinking of Cerise, I returned and threw the keys onto the seat of my car before continuing on. With every step, I expected to hear her racing up to my rescue but she never did. The walk down to the nearest main boulevard was almost a mile. A long journey hitchhiking home followed. It was dusk by the time I arrived. First thing in the door, I put some serious punch into an Eggnog and brandy cocktail and downed it. Then I made another one and went to stew in the darkened living room. I had a good buzz going by the time Cerise finally pulled in.

"You didn't have to leave," she said.

"No, you're right. We could have marked off a ring and gone three rounds. Then settled in for a nice turkey dinner."

"You don't have to be so sarcastic."

"No, you're right about that, too. We'll just call it good."

"What do you mean by that?"

In answer, I just nodded. To hell with her. The relationship was finished, as far as I was concerned. You did not abandon the people you loved. As soon as the holidays were over, I was on the road.

Sadly, we had everything there to cook Christmas dinner. The Christmas tree lights were twinkling away. The house was filled with holiday scents. We had each other but were miserable on that cold, wintry night.

Seeing I had no desire to talk with her, Cerise went off for a walk alone. I immediately used this opportunity to call Ellie. She sounded a bit disconcerted by my call. The phone was cupped for a moment and she came back.

"So how is everything going, Roger?"

I explained about the scene at Cerise's parent's house. The phone was cupped several times as I did. I heard rustling and the sound of laughter in the background.

"Well, I'm very sorry to hear that," Ellie said when I was done.

"Yeah."

Again, the phone was cupped. Then Ellie was back on the line.

"Well, listen, Roger, I really can't talk right now. Perhaps another time?"

"Sure, sure," I said.

"Well, Merry Christmas to you."

"Yeah, the same to you."

I hung up and sat there stewing. So, Ellie had company, and it was not her children. Touché. My dealings with these two women had been duplicitous at best, and now I had been delivered my just dessert.

Feeling cuckolded, I made another drink. When Cerise's gutless abandonment of me earlier in the day came back to mind, I made another drink. Allegiance to your mate was always first and foremost in this world. Anything less went against the grain of nature.

Something had died inside of me with all that. I knew my feelings for Cerise would never be the same. In the days that followed, there was hardness to my every thought and deed. Even when Cerise and I made love, I found myself plotting.

Right after the holidays, I organized a blues group to play at local pubs but purposely kept Cerise in the dark about the whole thing. She, meanwhile, was excelling in her art classes and had become something of a darling on campus. One of Cerise's professors placed her work in a local gallery. I wanted to think it was on the basis of her beauty. The guy just wanted to get in her panties, but there was no denying Cerise's talent, or her growing independence. The role I had once played in her life was vanishing, and my feelings of superiority with it.

One day, I came home to find her alone with my guitarist, Zen. Ostensibly, he had come by to see me, but given his dandy appearance, I knew he had other designs. Whether or not he was having an affair with Cerise, the idea was on his mind. No doubt about that. I said nothing to him, but the minute he left, I made it clear to Cerise. He was not to come around the house in my absence ever again.

The following day, I received more unsettling news from Cerise. Ellie had invited us over for dinner and Cerise had accepted the invitation. I smelled a rat and my portents were proven right. Saji, the Brahmin prodigy from India, answered the door when we knocked.

While he charmed Cerise out in the living room, I went out to pour myself a drink in the kitchen. Ellie was there at the stove preparing the dinner. I poured myself a bourbon straight, downed it and poured another.

"What's the matter, Roger?" Ellie asked nonchalantly. "Looks like you swallowed the parakeet."

"Screw you, Ellie," I whispered.

"There there, dear," Ellie whispered back. "Let's be civilized. Just because I've found my little Hindu lingam to take your place."

"Screw you," I said again.

"Well, ironically enough, I had wanted just that. And, well, here we are."

"You shouldn't have done this," I whispered vehemently.

She gestured blithely as one who is ignorant and went back to her dinner preparations. I turned to find Saji and Cerise standing at my back. Red-faced and furious, I took a seat at the dining table and attempted to assess how much of our conversation they had heard. Gauging from the pleasant smile on Cerise's face, not much. I drank from my bourbon, wishing I was anywhere else in the world.

"Well, I must say," Ellie chimed in with a big smile over her shoulder. "Cerise has become something of a celebrity in the art community around campus. You must be very proud of her."

"Mm hmm," I said.

Ellie's smile grew measurably wider. Clearly she was loving every minute of this not so subtle torture.

"Yes," Saji added with enthusiasm. "I am very much liking that transformation series she does on fast food. Where that round head with the pointed nose turns into a toilet. What is the name of that food place again?"

I spoke it out loud for him.

"Ah, yes. Thank you. It is a wonderful concept she does there."

"Yes," I said. "It weds the sinking moral compass of contemporary culture to the very junk they serve us. We are what we eat, so to speak."

Ellie offered another smile over her shoulder. I found myself drumming my fingers. Saji was sitting across the table from me with a smile. Cerise joined Ellie and watched as each leaf of romaine was toweled dried before being chopped. They talked of cooking.

"Well, everything's ready," Ellie said with a large salad bowl in hand.

Saji and Cerise sat down, cheerily chirping away together. Ellie went off to retrieve a piping hot fish casserole from the oven. She disappeared again, this time into the living room, and returned with Frank Sinatra's voice at her heels. It was an all too familiar love song. Ellie was glowing. I wanted to smack her.

"Has Saji told you about his proposed doctoral thesis?" Ellie asked me.

I shook my head. Doctoral thesis? The little prick was just finishing up his first year of undergraduate work. How in hell had he moved on to his PhD?

"Yes, thank you very much," Saji chimed in without me asking. "It will be on the disposition of computer sciences to integrate Third World countries into the capitalist marketplace."

"Fascinating," I said. "Don't forget to address the commensurate population explosion and the natural resource disasters we can expect as the result of your plans."

That did not go over very well and the conversation quickly spun off in another direction without me.

After the meal, we sat as two couples in the living room. Ellie snuggled up to Saji. Cerise and I sat on the love seat with a cold distance between us. The three of them moved on to discussing all things academic. On and on they went. I was contemplating crucifixions along the Appian Way.

Back at the house later that evening, I went to my desk. Cerise was rattling around the kitchen. At some point, she announced she was going to bed. I nodded.

Up late, my every thought was how to escape. I longed to be out on the road again. Our bed was a war zone now, mined with bitterness and resentment and to be avoided at all cost.

Twenty Six

The day after Ellie's dinner, a devious notion took root in my head. I drove down to the bank and withdrew a considerable sum of cash. All the while, various far flung destinations were calling to me. The Caribbean came to mind, the Orient. Maybe I would just go back to Europe. I still had an active passport.

My ideas were all over the map, but in the end, I simply decided to hitchhike up north. All I really wanted was a day where I didn't know at dawn where I was going to be when the sun went down.

I waited until Cerise had gone off to school the following morning and walked out to the nearest boulevard. I hadn't said a word to her about my plans.

With it still being winter, I wore boots and a sweater and a leather coat for warmth. To the passing world, I was a bum and I did nothing to dispel that notion, or to announce that I had a pile of money in my pocket.

The journey up through LA turned out to be the usual bummer. Abandoned at one godforsaken off ramp after another, I began to question the wisdom of my ways. I was stuck downtown for most of an hour, surrounded by decrepit apartment buildings, old factories and graffiti. A stream of cars rushed by me without stopping.

At last, some guy pulled over and got me up to Ventura. By early afternoon, I had reached Santa Barbara. Ten or fifteen hitchhikers were already staggered along the road in front of me but I finally felt good inside. Santa Barbara had always been the demarcation point between LA and the road going north.

I had been standing there for several minutes when a car dropped off the next hitchhiker in line, a young man with rust-colored hair and a floppy hat. I waved him over. What the hell. That was the whole point of it. Let life flow where it will. Don't strangle your soul with preconceived notions.

"Roger," I said as he pulled up with his backpack.

"Billy. Where are you headed?"

"I don't know."

He laughed.

"And you?"

"I guess the same."

Billy pulled a bottle of Port out of his backpack and we shared a few pops. Within half an hour, we were the first hitchhikers in line. Five minutes later, we caught a ride from the two guys driving up to Frisco. They had picked up a beautiful young lady in Oxnard and she was sitting in back, rolling up a joint from some terrific grass. Soon the five of us were having a gas.

Amidst the joints and laughter and storytelling, it was decided to divert our course over to Highway One. In Cayucos, we stopped for a meal and continued on our merry journey up through Big Sur with several bottles of wine. In time, the empty bottles were rattling around on the floorboard of the old Chevy

343

station wagon. We stopped occasionally to relieve ourselves and howl at the moon and were soon pulling into Santa Cruz. Billy and the beautiful lady decided to continue on to San Francisco. I decided to stop at David and Sheila's place for the night and bid my compatriots goodbye.

It was getting on towards nine o'clock by the time I knocked on their door. Sheila's reception was less than ebullient. I assumed that news of my disappearance had preceded me. I was right.

"Cerise called a little while ago, in tears. She said she had called everywhere trying to find you."

"I was headed down to the hardware store and got lost."

Sheila shook her head. David appeared and we sat down in the living room with a bottle of bourbon. I explained myself and my journey, as best I could.

"It's never going to be right again," I said, "and I just wanted to be like one of those guys you read about in the paper. They walk out the door one morning and never return."

"Yeah!" David said with a big smile.

Sheila slapped at him.

"It's not very fair to the other person," she said to me.

"Nothing in life is fair, as far as I can see. Just look at Nixon. And I'd be keeping a close eye on your husband over there, by the way."

David laughed. Sheila slapped at him again.

"Maybe you should come up and live with us," she suggested. "Perhaps Cerise just needs a new place to blossom."

"And we're starting a new band," David said. "So you can be the rhythm guitar player."

"Yeah. I'll just learn how to play overnight."

"I can show you the chords. It's easy. You'd be good at it."

"And," Sheila added, "we have an attic you can use for a spell."

"I've not had much luck with attics," I reminded her. Sheila chewed on a thumb nail, studying me. "You're supposed to laugh and clap."

She did a mechanical version of it.

"Well, I've been thinking about getting out of LA every day, but you know, Cerise is in school, and I just don't know about the two of us being together anymore."

"So, stay on your own for a while," Sheila said. "Sounds like you two could use some space. Maybe by the time school lets out, you'll be ready to fall in love again."

"Ha."

"Well, at least call her and let her know you're all right."

"You call her. I just can't talk to the woman right now."

"All right."

Sheila seemed intent on playing the matchmaker, a motive I did not entirely trust. Unless a woman was trying to steal somebody's boyfriend, she always sided with other women. It was the way of the world and you could never change it.

I went to sleep in the attic with the rain coming down. Thunder rumbled and rattled through the walls. I battled with my maelstrom of emotions. One moment, I pictured being happily in love with Cerise. The next moment, I could not be far enough away from her.

In the morning, I walked far down the fields above the coast. The sky was clear and fresh after the rain. I collected wild flowers and upon my return pressed them into the pages of a book. I thought of Cerise and called her. She cried and apologized for that scene with her parents.

"Please, Roger. Let's move up north together and make a new start."

In that moment I set aside my every reservation and said all right.

Back home a few days later, I learned that Cerise wanted to finish her spring semester. I couldn't wait to join David's band and headed north with one suitcase and all my musical equipment in tow. Cerise was to sell off all our belongings as best she could, either before or after school let out.

Over the next two months, Cerise and I wrote endless love letters, mine with wild flowers pressed between the pages, hers signed with a kiss from her lipstick. When we talked, the Watergate hearings frequently came up. They were being televised each day and Cerise seemed to be catching on.

"Everyone on campus thinks he's going to be impeached."

"Yeah and I've been saying for the last year that he'll weasel out of it somehow, but maybe not. Maybe they'll really nail him this time."

"If anyone can do it, I think that Ervin can. He's like a bloodhound. Slow, methodical but unrelenting."

"Yeah?"

"Yeah, that's the picture I get of him."

I smiled to myself and got off, feeling hope for both Cerise's political acumen and our relationship.

Having made a pact never to fight again, I boarded a plane for LA in June with great hopes and expectations. There had not been a bit of trouble between us for that entire two months. Within twenty-four hours, we were at each other's throats again.

We spent a day saying adieu to family and old friends before locking up the house a final time and turning the keys in to the landlord. On our way over to pick up Cerise's last paycheck from the campus book store, her old Volkswagen broke down. I cursed and got out.

Having fiddled inside the engine compartment for a few minutes, I walked back around and leaned my head in Cerise's door. She had remained sitting in the car the whole time.

"Guess I'll have to go look for help."

"Okay, honey."

"Aren't you coming with me?"

"No. I'm wearing high heels."

Disgusted with her, I started down the busy boulevard alone. High heels, I thought. She had a pair of tennis shoes in back.

By the time I got the car towed to a mechanic, it was dark. There was nothing to do but rent a motel room for the night. After a long shower, I called a cab and directed him down to the harbor. I was in the mood for steak and lobster. Cerise came along with that great yawning gulf of silence between us again.

Soon we were dining by the water's edge. The sun was setting beyond all the million dollar homes and boat masts. We had steak and lobster and wine before us.

Somehow in all this, Cerise decided to raise the topic of marriage and children.

"Why don't we just try to enjoy today, Cerise? When people do, they tend to come back for more.

"That's like saying you can't get everything you want from the same person."

I stared at her with a piece of steak in my mouth, wondering how her response had any relevance to my comment. Against all caution and sound reasoning to the contrary, I went ahead and suggested as much.

"Cerise, I don't know what the hell that had to do with what I just said, but since you brought it up, no one can expect to be everything to another person."

She seemed stunned by my comment.

"Well, see, you just want to get away from it. I mean, it takes a lot of burden and a lot of respect but people can spend their whole lives together."

"I didn't say they couldn't."

She wiped her mouth delicately and regrouped.

"Well, I mean, you have to take the balance. You have to stimulate beyond the intellect. I don't know. Maybe I'm not very good at explaining myself, but I know if you don't take the balances the result is pretty neel."

She stared at me seriously and I struggled mightily to contain my sarcasm.

"Nil," I said.

"What?"

"The word is *nil*."

"Well, okay," she said embarrassed. "You know what I mean."

"No," I told her. "I haven't the foggiest idea what you just said."

"You fucker."

She threw her napkin down and hurried to the ladies room. I went on eating, thinking that expletive sounded a lot sexier when Ellie said it.

It was several minutes before Cerise returned. She had been crying.

We finished our meal in further silence and went back to the motel. Sometime late in the night, we made love, but without really making up.

Not surprisingly, the fight started all over again the next morning. This time, Cerise got into me about having a beer for breakfast.

"How are you going to be a father like that?"

"I'm not going to be a father," I told her. "That's how."

"You fucker," she said. "You're a liar and I never want to see you again."

She left all her belongings and started out the door. I sat there without the slightest desire to stop her. Eventually I showered, paid for another night at the motel and went out for breakfast. Back at the hotel, I felt too depressed to bother with the mechanic about Cerise's car. Instead, I drank and watched an old movie. At some point I would catch a flight up north. I didn't know when or have any plans beyond that.

The phone rang about noon. It was Cerise. I turned down the TV so I could hear her. There was the sound of traffic in the background.

"What are you doing?"

"I picked up the car."

"So, where are you?"

"Fifty miles north of San Luis Obispo."

"And just where the hell do you think you're going, Cerise?"

"I'm going to Santa Cruz."

"Goddamn it," I yelled, standing up now. "Stay the hell out of my backyard."

"I hate you and never want to see you again."

She hung up. I mixed another drink. The phone rang a few hours later. Cerise was crying, again with traffic in the background.

"Where are you now?"

"Fifty miles south of San Luis Obispo."

This time it got to me. The poor woman was driving around helplessly in circles. Bastard that I was, I could not help but caring.

"Go to Santa Cruz," I told her. "And I'll see you there in a couple of days. Are you sure you're going to be all right?"

"I don't know. The Volkswagen's been making weird noises."

"All right." I gave her Derek's shop number. "Call him if you have any problems. And call me as soon as you get there."

"I love you," she said.

"I love you, too."

"Will you pick up my check before you head north?"

"Yes, I'll stop by the campus tomorrow."

I rented a car in the morning, left everything in the motel room for another night and drove over to the campus. What the hell, I decided. I longed to see Ellie and found her in her office, but not alone. A big, strapping black student sat opposite her desk. Their conversation stopped when I came in. Ellie introduced us. He got up from his chair, said it was nice meeting me and kissed Ellie on the cheek before going out the door. I hung my head.

"Gee, Roger," Ellie said with playful irony. "You're not looking well."

"I never expected things to turn out this way."

"Oh dear, what on earth has happened now?"

"Don't change the subject," I said, looking up at her.

"Oh, you mean about Terrell?"

"Yes, about Terrell."

"Well, a woman has her needs," she said with mock satisfaction.

"And where does that leave us?"

"I will always remember our love affair as the loveliest moment in my life, but…"

"As raunchy sex goes…"

"Something like that," she said.

I hung my head.

"Oh, Roger, you know I will always love you…"

"I know. And I will always love you."

"So, tell me, what has gone awry with your little love affair this time?"

I explained about the ups and downs, and about Cerise calling from the road a few hours earlier.

"Where are you now? Fifty miles north of San Luis Obispo."

"And where are you now?" Ellie added, playing along.

"Fifty miles south of San Luis Obispo."

We laughed. Then I was serious.

"I begin to feel it's all my fault. I'm never satisfied with what I have."

"Well, Roger, who knows? Cerise does have some innate perspicacity. She may well become the woman you want her to be, if you're willing to wait."

"I know. There's always a catch."

"With me you were waiting for another lifetime. Now you're only waiting five or ten years."

"Yeah, I guess we're headed in the right direction."

As I sat there staring at Ellie's big smile, I remembered Cerise's call again.

"Fifty miles south of San Luis Obispo."

We laughed and talked about Watergate.

"They're going to nail that fucker," she said.

"Until he's gone, I'm not ruling out tanks in the streets."

"You never know with that bastard, do you?"

"No."

We sat there staring. I wanted to seduce Ellie, if only because she understood me right down to my soul. But seeing a tryst was not in the works that day, I said goodbye and walked across campus to the book store.

Back in the motel room, I waited to hear from Cerise. She finally called around five, saying she had made it okay. She asked me about the check and what I had been doing all day. I lied and got off the phone, tired of my own deceit. Had my heart ever been pure? The only time I could remember such a state of affairs was in the very first moment I saw Ellie. I remembered feeling like there wasn't another woman in the whole world. How sweet. Where had it all gone wrong?

Rather than hassle with a flight, I drove the rented car north and arrived to David and Sheila's place late the following afternoon. Cerise was out on the back porch with everyone else who lived on the farm when I walked up. Two women from the shop had made a home for themselves on the upper floor of the barn. Another couple had converted a long abandoned chicken coop into their living space. Dale, the bass player in our band, was living in the basement. Someone handed me a joint. The coast north of Santa Cruz was visible off in the distance. Amidst the salutations and coughing, I wondered what had been said behind my back.

As the sun went down, Cerise and I went upstairs to explore the attic. We kissed and looked into each other's eyes.

"I'm sorry," she said.

"Me too."

We kissed some more.

I sat on the bed and leaned against the wall. Cerise joined me. The big attic room was empty except for the bed, a shelf with books and my musical equipment. A tapestry hung beside the stairwell for privacy. The roof came down low around the entire perimeter of the room and windows lined those short exterior walls. Some windows looked out to the sea, others up towards the forested hills across the highway. In one direction, a horse grazed in an open meadow. The meadow was surrounded by trees. Cerise and I watched the horse graze while we talked. The wood floors of the room gave off a dull glow in the last light of day. People had begun to cook dinner in the kitchen below us.

"Are you hungry?" Cerise asked.

"Yeah but let's go have dinner on the town."

"All right." She crawled on top of me in her seductive way. "But let's not fight anymore."

I looked at the stairwell.

"Did you want to make love before we go?"

Cerise kissed me in answer to my question and we both began to tear off our clothes. She was above me, wet and descending onto my bone, her red lips kissing me, the sweetness indescribable, the enchantment complete. The thought flashed through my mind. Have we learned anything from our silly battles? But it did not matter. We were two young people in love, living and dying by our unchained desires.

Afterwards, Cerise and I smoked a joint, drove downtown, then sat in the car and talked for an hour before going in to dinner. After the meal, we walked down to the Catalyst and ordered two beers. The Catalyst was dimly lit, the smoke-filled air abuzz with conversation, as it had always been. A thousand old memories passed through my head.

"Was it always like this?" Cerise asked me.

"More or less. It used to be across the street. I remember the first time I walked in and ordered a beer. I was sixteen, peach fuzz on my face. No one bothered to ID me. People were playing music at their tables. Flutes and guitars. Everybody singing along. It was a trip. I guess because everybody was tripping."

She laughed and looked around.

"I'm so glad to be out of the rat race. I can't believe I put up with it so long."

"All three years of it."

"You turkey. It seemed like a long time."

"I know. It's good to be here."

"I'm excited about the band. Aren't you?"

"Sure. I think David has different notions about it. That is the problem with bands. It's like getting married to five different people at once."

"And we know how you feel about marriage."

"All right, let's not get started."

We drank until we were drunk and went home. Cerise immediately went upstairs. I talked with David a few minutes before I followed. There was a rustle behind the tapestry and Cerise came out naked except for a gold chain around her waist and a pair of strapless high-heels on her delicate feet.

"Is this what you had in mind, sweetheart?"

"Oh, you doll, you." I picked her up in my arms and carried her off to bed and took her from behind and she was before me like a tawny gazelle galloping ahead in my dreams.

That night, very late, I heard coyotes near the house and heard Sheila's ducks quacking away. The ducks had been brought home to combat the giant slugs devouring her vegetables. In the morning we found blood and feathers everywhere. Sheila immediately erected a better fence and went off to buy more ducks. David went off to the shop.

Cerise and I followed a path bordered on either side by thick blackberry hedges. The berries were young and still green on the vines. The scent of wet farmland mixed with the salt air from the nearby sea.

At the bottom of the cliff, we came to the highway. Tiger Beach was below it. We walked down to the beach and I told Cerise about a day back in the sixties. A tribe of us had gone down to build a bonfire and party. One of our friends had caught a leopard shark and we broiled it in an open pit and everyone danced in front of the fire as the sun went down. Cerise listened to these memories as one who so badly wanted to go back and live what she had missed.

And why not marry her, I thought in that moment. She was so damned beautiful and filled with spunk. She would learn, I kept telling myself. She would learn, and we would grow together for a lifetime. Whenever I thought in that way, I was very, very contented in my heart.

Twenty Seven

I awakened the next morning with Cerise gone from the bed. The sun in the eastern windows had left oblique rectangles of light on the wooden floors. It looked to be late morning.

Wondering what had happened to Cerise, I pulled on my Levi's and went downstairs. She was seated at the farmhouse kitchen table in her robe, gazing out the window in thought, her dark hair pulled to one side and draped over her shoulder. A big mug of coffee was cupped in her hands. No one else appeared to be in the house.

Respectful of Cerise's space, I touched her shoulder on my way by without saying a word. She reached for my hand in return. Her eyes had remained focused on the garden out back.

"How do you feel?" I asked when I had my own cup of coffee and was seated beside her.

"Like a whole new life has started," she said.

Her eyes met mine and looked back out the window. The sun was bright in the yard but we sat in the cool shade. White clouds drifted by in the blue sky. I sipped my coffee and watched the ducks waddle and quack in Sheila's garden. The corn grew tall around them. Squash and melon vines had already begun to climb her new fence.

Cerise turned to look at me.

"I love you," she said.

I kissed her lips, knowing her as another woman now, perhaps as the woman I had always wanted her to be. In any case, all the terrible fighting seemed to be in the past.

Later that morning, we walked back to where the berry hedges had grown thick above the sea and saw that some of the berries had already ripened and picked those we could reach. By the time we headed back, Cerise had several handfuls of them in the fold of her blouse. We made love in the afternoon and spent the remainder of the day reading and talking quietly together.

That night, the band's usual practice session took place in the basement of the house. Cerise sat among us and added the occasional tambourine. Dale, who took care of all the business, had secured a dance gig at the local Legion Hall and wanted to introduce a new tune for the occasion, one that started with a harmonica solo.

"Do you think you can play it?" he asked me.

"Sure."

While the band worked on another tune, I went outside and experimented. I returned a few minutes later and played the opening solo.

"Far out," Dale said.

We ran through that tune several times and then moved on to a Dead song he wanted to play. Dale's musical tastes tended in that direction. The piano player dug jazz and country swing. David and I were into blues and any kind of rockin' music. The drummer had his own eclectic tastes and when all these disparate styles blended spontaneously, something clicked.

That week at the Legion Hall, a small following began to develop. The students asked us to do another gig and others followed. In the ensuing months, we played clubs all around the county. Dale did the footwork, lined up the gigs and set up the PA—all the mundane stuff that no one else wanted to do. If not for him, the whole thing probably would have fallen apart. Certainly David was of no use in that regard. As the prodigy among us, he played music for the love of it. The idea of becoming the next great rock group was absurd to him.

"The Vanilla Creampuffs," he said when Dale was trying to come up with a new name for the band.

I was of a similar bent. I loved the sheer joy of playing music but making it big in the industry seemed like such vanity to me, and went against the grain being a private person at heart. I preferred staying in the background. If there had been some way to achieve success in the recording studio without spending the next five years as a road band, I'd be into that. Otherwise, I was happy writing lyrics.

As summer turned to fall, I filled notebooks with poetry and lyrics and spent most afternoons hiking with Cerise in the fields and woods, especially after a good rain, when the forest was refreshed and the woodcocks called in the growing dusk, the end of those days becoming timeless when we shed our muddy clothes and slipped into the old antique tub, candles lit while we soaked together in the steaming water.

Then, often times, we would hurry into town for a meal and always it seemed that we had smoked a joint on the way and become entranced in one discussion or another, parked there under some trees, the restaurant across the street, the two of us with our backs to the doors and facing each other, eyes and teeth gleaming in the gathering darkness; strange moments as dusk turned to darkness and Cerise cautiously gained a foothold in the world of ideas.

Then, without warning, the band fell apart when Dale's obsessive need to control shit came up hard against David's unwillingness to have other people control him. Perhaps it was just the difficulty of getting five people to be happily married. In any case, faced with Dale's endless practices, David took to bolting off on his own esoteric riffs in the middle of a take and when everyone else stopped to stare, he would push the glasses back on his nose and stare back, like, 'what's the problem'. Or he would show up at practice high on magic mushrooms and lie there staring up at the ceiling, unwilling or unable to play at all.

The final straw came one night while we played a gig at a local bar. David, again high on magic mushrooms, spun off into one of his psychedelic riffs during a song. He and Dale glared at each other, Dale trying to take the band in one direction, David in the other. It was as if two different bands were playing on stage that night, each one trying to drone out the other.

"Why don't you guys go get yourselves a couple of Marshall stacks," someone in the audience shouted as the song concluded.

David smiled, pulled the plug on his guitar and went to drink at the bar. Stunned and without any answers, the other members played one more set then left in disgust. The bar owner refused to pay Dale.

"Thanks a lot," Dale said to David as he shuttled his band gear out the door. David just stared back in silence.

I ordered another beer and sat next to David. Sheila sat somberly at his side. I expected she would miss the fun, but she had her hooks in David in other ways. She was shrewd. She knew the leather business was their gravy train. With every spare cent she could take from the business, she had been buying up local land, certain the two of them would never have to worry again.

To Cerise, on the other hand, that night represented the end of the world. She had never imagined the band breaking up.

"It'll work out," she assured David as if he cared. "You guys just need to mellow out a bit."

He stared at her.

"Well, don't you want to make it work, David?"

"It's pointless trying to be the next Rolling Stones."

Around ten o'clock the following morning, Dale appeared in the kitchen and made an official announcement. The band was breaking up. It was all very serious. David shrugged and went off to the shop. The day was gray and dreary.

Later that afternoon, I found my brain working. How would I survive in the years to come? How would I support Cerise and a family? For all David's intransigence, he had his feet firmly on the ground. I had discarded the security of the leather business as someone might consider hunger insignificant after a grand meal.

I weighed the expenses, calculated them out for a year and saw at some discernible point in the future where Cerise and I would be broke. I had enough verse to make a collection of poetry, and there was always that novel taking shape on the fringes of my mind, but neither of those two things held the prospect of financial gain any time soon. My only immediate hope was to sell more song lyrics down in LA.

I glanced over at Cerise as she drew in her sketchbook. How would she take to the idea of us heading back down to LA? Not very well, I expected.

The next morning, recalling my earliest dreams and Ellie's frequent encouragement, about using journalism as a springboard for my career as a writer, I drove down to see the editor of a local paper in Salinas. It was another gray and dreary day. The workers in the artichoke fields around Castroville were bundled up in a half dozen coats and scarves and hats and a thousand different colors.

The jazz station out of Monterey was featuring Miles Davis that day. Something cool and urban from his middle period came on and my mind took off. I was back in LA, cruising down the coast on a hot summer day, palm trees lining the boulevards, everything sunny and hip and happening.

I went through with the interview process but my mind was already gone. To hell with Northern California. I was moving back down south. I hardly noticed the promise expressed by the editor in my talents.

Back home with my decision, I was not entirely surprised by Cerise's reaction.

"I can't even believe you'd want to go back there," she said.

"Look, you want me to take care of you? The only way I can do it is to go down and establish myself as a lyricist in LA. Once I've done that successfully, we can go anywhere."

She sat on the bed and looked out the window.

"Don't you remember how horrible it was when we left? The smog and traffic? Everyone running around like mad? How much we wanted to have nature around us?"

I paced from window to window in the room, frustrated by her resistance, but determined.

"Look, Cerise. You want kids and a white picket fence? And now you're going to give me shit for trying to give it to you?"

Cerise came from the bed to where I stood at the window and placed her arms around me. She rubbed my arms and shoulders quietly, then my neck.

"Please, Roger. Let's not make any rushed decisions. That's all I'm asking."

I turned to face her. She smiled feebly.

"I love you," she said.

"I'm going south. If you want to come with me, fine. And if not, that's fine too."

"So I don't have a say in this."

"I just told you. This is about financial security. You want to start a family and buy a house? How the hell are we going to do that slopping gruel at the Happy Hobbit Organic Café?"

"If you hadn't sold your interest in the leather company so soon, we wouldn't be in this position."

I slammed my palm against the wall.

"Goddamn it! I'm just trying to follow my dreams!"

"But you have to be practical too."

"That's what I'm doing! I'm going down south where the money is! And now you're going to beat my balls for making that decision!"

Cerise sat there silently and looking away.

"Fine. You know what? Just forget the whole fucking thing. The marriage. The kids. Everything. Okay?"

Stung by my outburst, Cerise gathered her sketchbook and went downstairs. I heard Marley come on the turntable. *No Woman, No Cry*. It had to be Dale meddling. I went down, took a beer from the refrigerator and left for town. By the time I returned that night, I had the whole thing worked out in my head.

"I'm going down south to see my family and poke around," I told Cerise after crawling into bed. She didn't say a word.

I said goodbye in the morning and drove off in the rain. I pulled into LA with a desert wind blowing. Gasoline was being rationed and tempers were short. I got into a line at a gas station that snaked around several blocks. Half the drivers were standing with their car doors open, looking for trouble. The Arabs had us on our knees. We had been turned into a third world country. People were ready to lynch somebody.

I finally got down to the beach with no idea what to do with myself. I called Ellie and she invited me over for a drink. Even before I had my cocktail in hand, our discussion had turned to Watergate. It was a few days after the Saturday Night Massacre.

"What did I tell you?" Ellie said. "That fucker is so busted."

"Yeah? And I still say, he'll have tanks rolling down Beach Boulevard before he gives in."

"He wouldn't."

"He would. Shit, look at the mess this country's in. The Arabs have us by the balls. I just got out of a line for gas that went around the corner and down six blocks. He could call a state of national emergency and say he's doing it to protect the country."

Ellie threw up her hands.

"God, we're living history, Roger. This country hasn't seen this level of turmoil since the Great Depression."

"I know. It's a real trip...So before the tanks get here, can we talk about something personal?"

"What's the matter, baby?"

"I'm dying inside."

"Oh no. Not again."

It was my turn to throw up my hands.

"You know, Roger. It's just l'aaahmourrr. It's bedeviled mankind since the beginning of time. Things are always changing but we want them to stay the same."

"Can't you tell me something I want to hear?"

"Well, you probably don't want to hear this, but I have a new beau."

"You're right, goddamn it. That's the last thing I wanted to hear. I needed your comfort right now."

"Oh, there, there."

I drank, besieged by a great pain.

"I tried knitting and waiting, Roger, but it just wasn't in me."

"I guess not. Aw, goddamn it."

I finished the drink and poured another one.

"Who is it this time?"

"A former student. He dropped out and got into sales."

"Sales?"

She raised her eyebrows at me.

"Well, yes."

I was so steeped in my creativity now, I had forgotten my own origins.

"So, how old is he?"

"A few years older than you."

"I don't suppose you'll ever find men your own age attractive."

"Why should I bother?"

"God, Ellie. I feel so fucking sad and jealous right now."

"Because you love me, Roger. The same as I love you."

I sat closer to her.

"Can't we still make love now and again?"

"We'd better not," she said and pretended to shoot me with her finger.

I jumped at hearing the garage door opener kick into gear.

"Well, that brings back memories."

"It's Dick!" she said with mock fright.

I shook my head and moved away from her.

"Oh, here's Ray now."

Ellie got up to greet him at the door. They kissed.

"Roger, I want you to meet Ray."

I stood up and shook his hand. He was wearing a wide lapel, polyester suit, had a mustache and hair down just over his collar.

"Ellie's told me all about you," he said.

"Yeah, far out."

He sat down next to her.

"So, what brings you to town, Roger? Business or pleasure?"

"Business."

"Really? What kind?"

"Oh, I'm looking into a number of things."

"Well, if you're interested, I've got a terrific opportunity in a mutual fund investment. It's great for pensions and individuals. It's set up to be very responsive in today's market."

"Yeah. That sounds great, Ray, but I'll have to get back to you. I've got a date with an old friend."

I stood up, and they stood up with me. Ray shook my hand.

"Nice meeting you, Roger."

"Same here."

Ellie walked me to the door.

"Take care, Roger."

"I will. You too."

I drove around for several more days, digging up old friends and trying to reestablish connections in the music industry but everywhere I turned, it was a dead end. Most of the people I once knew had moved from the area or had move on to jobs in the straight world. Making it big in LA was going to take a lot more footwork than I had imagined.

I checked in on my family but that only did more to depress me. My parents had moved out to the desert somewhere, which sounded just like my old man. Nobody around for fifteen miles. Vincent was out there in the desert, too, bouncing around from rehab joint to rehab joint. Distraught, my mother told me that the last she had heard from him, he was at one in Indio. I had no reason to see Frank and Rose failed to answer my calls.

Arriving back to Santa Cruz, depressed and with nothing to show for efforts, I found Cerise up in the attic, painting a long, ribbon mural along the ceiling line. She had on a tie-dye shirt with no bra. Her nipples were clearly visible through the jersey fabric. She had permed her hair too.

I was disconcerted. Cerise kept changing. She was not the same woman I had left behind a few days earlier.

"What's all this?" I asked her.

"What do you mean?"

She hadn't bothered to look over at me. Finally, she did.

"The hair, the blouse."

I waved my hand.

"You don't like the tie-dye?"

"I mean without the bra."

"Other women do it."

"Well, you're not other women. You're my old lady."

She shook her head, dabbed her brush and resumed painting.

"I'm *not* your old lady. I'm not *anyone's* old lady."

I sat down at my desk with my head in my hands.

"What is going on, Cerise?"

She dabbed her brush again and glanced once before continuing her work.

"Nothing. I took a trip on mushrooms the day after you left and realized how submissive I have been to you. How I did everything on the basis of whether or not it would please you."

"Well?"

"Well, none of it ever did. So I'm going to do what I want from now on."

"Oh really. On whose checkbook."

"I figured you say that."

"Well? Do you propose to embark on this great path of liberation while I sit around calmly bankrolling it?"

"I figured you'd say that too, Roger. So I got a part time job to supplement my work with the band."

"Your what?"

"Oh, sorry. You wouldn't know. The band has regrouped and I'm singing with them."

"Oh, so I suppose that's who you took the trip with?

"Would it have mattered?"

"Yeah, goddamn it. Did you think I wanted you whoring around with the band while I was gone?"

"You're an asshole, Roger."

"I'm an asshole? No, I'm a fool, Cerise. A fool to keep trying."

"I've changed, Roger. That's all. It doesn't mean that I don't love you anymore. But I can't help it if I've changed."

At the kindness of her words I went to sit by her side, but when I tried to kiss her, she turned her face away from me.

"Hey, I love you."

She nodded skeptically.

"Come on, honey. I thought you wanted to get married and start a family."

She pulled away from me and tried to resume her artistic efforts.

"Let go of me."

I watched disconsolately as she began to paint again. It was very nicely done. I rather hated her for being so good.

"Roger, I don't know how to tell you this. It's just that, well you didn't want the things I wanted." She looked at me. "So why should I trouble myself over them?"

"Well? Maybe *I* want them now."

She shook her head sadly.

"Roger, you don't know what you want from day to day."

"Fuck it, Cerise. I can't talk to you."

I left, hoping she would beg me not to go, but she didn't say a word. I went down to the wharf and had a beer, then went from bar to bar. Cerise was asleep when I crawled into bed. Graciously, she made love to me, but there was no real passion in it.

The next morning, I found Dale standing naked in the kitchen making breakfast. Cerise came down and conducted herself as though it was utterly normal. I fixed myself a bowl of granola and sat on the back porch alone, feeling cuckholded again. I had become addicted to a role with Cerise, from which she was now liberated. To make matters worse, I was beginning to feel like an outcast among my own peers again. The sixties lived on with this tribe of people and I had become like someone's father.

Standing there, a dangerous idea took root in my head. I had long been riddled with guilt from all my deceit over the previous two years and wanted to be rid of it. It was time to confess. It was time to come clean.

I took Cerise for a walk down to the sea. We sat together on a rock. I looked out to sea.

"I had an affair with Ellie. I'm sorry. I just needed to tell you."

Cerise stared at me.

"What do you mean? When you were down south?"

"No, Cerise. All along. For a long time."

I explained in detail about my transgressions and felt much better for having gotten it off my chest. I hadn't thought how Cerise might feel in hearing it. I somehow expected her to forgive me instantly. Instead, she stood up and wandered down the beach alone. When I caught up with her, she was crying. I tried to comfort her but she pushed my hands away.

"You fucker," she said. "I trusted in you all this time and you were fucking another woman."

No matter how I tried to comfort her, she pushed me away and finally walked back to the house alone.

"I'm leaving," I told her when I found her back in the attic.

"You don't have to go. I'll leave."

"No, I don't fit in here any longer."

"Where will you go?"

"I don't know."

I packed my bags, hoping with every item tucked away that Cerise would rush in to stop me, but she never did.

I left before dark and in my madness headed north instead of south. I spent the night in Half Moon Bay and drank myself to sleep in a motel room. The next day I thought of turning back the other way but kept going north. Somewhere much father up the coast, I pulled into gas station and learned I was in Pt. Arena.

I found a local realtor and rented a furnished cabin. It had a bed and a dresser, a stove and refrigerator and red-checkered curtains. A small grove of redwoods shrouded the point to my north and the sea was visible from there down to where the highway made a sharp turn at the outskirts of Pt. Arena.

My landlord Walter and his wife Clair ran a small general store there and my cover with them and everyone around town was that of being a novelist.

"I'm up here to write a book."

Walter was duly impressed.

"You hear that, Clair? We've got a famous writer up here writing a novel."

I grimaced at hearing those words but did nothing to discourage the idea. Writers drank. Writers bought a lot of booze. That provided me some measure of cover. I did my best to scatter my purchases around town and otherwise stayed hidden away in my cabin. It was a place where a man could drink without being bothered, and I did just that, a piece of paper always in the typewriter, snippets of lyrics and poems growing across the blank pages, maudlin rants aimed at old lovers, bellicose diatribes offered up to the president and all his men, a novel that never came to fruition. I had the answers and all the great minds would beat a path to my doorstep. I had become my father.

The holidays came and went that year with hardly a notice. I had my memories. But a year earlier, Cerise and I were happily in love and filled with Christmas cheer. I tried not to dwell too much on whom she was now loving instead of me.

It took most of three months before it finally sank in. No one gave a crap if I sat there with the curtains drawn and drank myself to death. And seeing this, I grew determined to change. I wanted Cerise back into my life and packed a few things one day, headed south for Santa Cruz.

Cerise was up in the attic with Dale when I arrived, the two of them kicked back together on what once had been our bed. At the sight of me, Cerise visibly shrank into Dale's arms. It took a bit of diplomacy on my part but I finally persuaded her to join me out on the back porch.

"When did this start?"

"It doesn't matter, Roger."

"All right. I came to see if you would give our love another chance."

"I'm sorry, Roger, but I can't go back to it. Too much has changed."

"What has changed? You still love me and I know it."

She buried her head in her hands.

"What?"

She was crying softly.

"What?"

"I had an abortion, all right?"

"Aw, Jesus, honey." I put my arm around her. "We could have had the baby. Why didn't you tell me? Why did you go and do that?"

"Because I didn't know whose it was, Roger."

There was a pause before I flushed with anger. My mind raced through the times and dates and possibilities.

"What are you talking about? When did this happen?"

"It doesn't matter."

"It does to me. When were you fucking some other guy?"

"About the same time you were fucking some other woman."

"When? Just answer the question."

"The last time you went down south. You went down to see Ellie, Roger. I know you did."

"No, I didn't, Cerise."

"Oh, what? So she already had a new boyfriend?"

I stared at her.

"You really must think I'm stupid, Roger. Really stupid."

A succession of things raced through my head, about what to say and what to do. Her side of the street wasn't any cleaner than mine, but what did it matter now, who the other father might be? All that remained was to bow out gracefully.

"It's okay, Cerise. You're fine. We just couldn't seem to get our timing together."

She looked up through her tears and held my hand sweetly.

I kissed her on the forehead, rubbed her back once and left for Pt. Arena.

Twenty Eight

It was a little past three in the morning when I arrived home. I stopped outside the door to my cabin and sniffed at the cold wind. Wisps of dark clouds raced in from the sea. A storm was stirring. Nature was on the move and rain imminent. That knowledge brought a measure of peace to my heart as I unlocked the door and went inside.

While emptying my bladder in the bathroom, I became aware of my image in the mirror. Who was the man in the black, fathomless spaces within my eyes? And what had he done to my life?

Back in the living room, Cerise's many kindnesses revisited me, the warmth of her lips, the tender feel of her embrace, her smile, the way she had whispered playful things in my ears, kindnesses she had shared with me on stormy nights just like this one. I recalled each and every moment as if she were still there, when in fact she was gone from my life forever now.

It was as if the sun had died, or the color red had been stricken from existence, and there was no one to blame but me. I had not properly cherished a woman's love and was left to face the consequences. I wanted that love back but the hour was too late now.

A sudden gust of wind rattled the windows and disturbed me from my thoughts. I became aware again of the storm blowing in from the north. Flecks of rain had started to dot the glass.

Come take me, I thought, and went to pour myself a glass of brandy. It was fine brandy and my only comfort on a cold, winter's night.

The wind moaned and the memories jabbed again and again at my heart. Something good and decent had been laid at my feet and I had thrown it all away.

So I was lonely. That was nothing new in this world. I may as well have begun a tale by saying that fish swam in the sea, that rocks were ancient, that birds sometimes fell from the sky. We all knew the feelings. What good would it do for me to convey my own version of them?

As I sat there drinking, it occurred to me that this was all Ellie's fault. She was the one who had led me to believe that lovers could be all and everything to each other, a vision not even she could discharge. Lovers came and went, even if it took death to part them. Romance arose from the most serendipitous convergence of circumstances, and life was forever after trying to tear that love apart.

Another gust of wind buffeted the cabin and the rain began in earnest. I was glad. The patter of raindrops was a comfort to my soul. We were compatriots, the rain and I, in our uniformity of natures.

A memory came to me with sudden clarity and I went to retrieve a notebook and pencil. The words appeared without effort. I changed a few of them, but mostly my thoughts had arrived fully formed.

When finished, I poured a fresh glass of brandy and read the poem again. Perhaps someday, Cerise would hold a book of verse in her hands, rendered to tears by this memory of our passing love.

Summer Berries, Autumn Leaves

I peered inside the darkened lobby
waiting for a Saturday matinee to begin,
pushed on the locked door several times
on that late autumn afternoon,
impatient for the theater to open,
impatient with the hours of my life,
the distant snowy peaks, reflected through glass,
unmoved by falling leaves, passing clouds
or the memory of you.

Growing empty and cold with the approaching dusk,
I was glad to see the lights finally flicker on inside the lobby,
the kid came and unlocked the door,
I paused there with the scent of popcorn wafting out,
distracted by the dry maple leaves,
their prickly voices
fleeing under parked cars
and into the growing shadows.

On the mountains, a mist had nestled among the pines,

a ridge once brilliant with harvest colors
now dull ocher,
reflections of one summer's sun,
fading slowly on the smoky, northern wind.

I stood alone in twilight's hour, a dying warmth
before winter, a distant memory of you
and your smile again in my heart,
your blouse filled with summer berries.

I fell asleep in the storm and that winter consumed me. I learned to drink with new vigor. I filled pages with my words — what always seemed to me so profound in the night but so maudlin and pathetic in the morning light. I regularly passed out on the sofa in the afternoons, a bottle nearby, my heart recoiling a bit each time that darkness drew near.

The birds and fowl of the air had long ago headed south down the coast, fleeing to the warmth of the sun, but what could a man do? I was left to migrate in circles around my cabin, a ghost on gray and dreary days, unable to find the equator of my own heart.

Occasionally a smile greeted me during my trips to the market, the fleeting kindness of welcome eyes in the produce section, that electricity of being desired that I took home with the bag of groceries under my arm, a coward in my own eyes each time I failed to let something new be planted in the desert of my heart.

Just as well, I would tell myself as the curse deepened, for I was a man better off alone in this world.

Sometime in the spring, the spell was finally broken and I began to nurse my way out of the gloom. Blue skies and cheery days encouraged new dreams. Of course I wanted to share my heart with another human being. Someone would come along. Someone always did. All I asked for was a beginning, where you did not already know the ending.

Then one day, I remembered the lovely lady with her tea shop up in Mendocino. Perhaps she was still there. Perhaps she would be glad to see me.

I headed north along the sea, past all the hopeless little rickety cottages that looked as if they might soon be swallowed by blackberry vines or blown away by a good wind. Thoughts of Ellie passed through my heart and the journey we had made along this same stretch of coastline, the sometimes pain of it, but the mostly loving moments of laughter and friendship, the timelessness of our camaraderie and how I would always adore Ellie in my heart. I winced to recall how my irrepressible young instincts, combined with my equally naïve assumptions had led me to believe I could easily replicate that romance with someone my own age. With the age of the universe as a backdrop, the two of us had missed our mark by only twenty years. How sad. I went along my drive up the coast, these memories conjured from the past and talking to myself as a man will do when he has been too long without conversation.

In Mendocino, I easily found the little gingerbread tea shop, the speech I had been working on still taking shape as I parked.

My health hasn't been so great of late. Thought I'd look into some herbs and other remedies.

I hoped like hell the woman wouldn't remember me from that day with Ellie. I ascended the wooden steps outside with my mind working on another line of bullshit, in case that came up.

Inside, I was met with the scents of incense and old wood. The woman was there, doing paperwork behind the counter. My heart raced at the sight of her. She glanced up with a quick review of me.

"Welcome. Please help yourself."

"Thanks."

She went back to her paperwork. I started in among the aisles and apothecary jars, stealing secretive glances at her as I could.

"Dandelion would be good."

It was a tinkle-bell voice. I turned to face the woman. She searched my eyes without emotion but the gentle melody of her voice lingered in my heart.

"Dandelion and red clover," she said. "Invigorate and flush out the poisons."

"Yes. I've been thinking to cut down on the coffee."

The corners of her eyes and mouth crinkled up a bit.

"Okay, the booze. I could stand to cut down on the booze a bit too."

"You will be going around in circles, then."

"I'm very good at that."

She started back to her work.

"Please, don't give up on me yet. Perhaps I need the tea of enchantment."

"The enchantment is always there."

She looked up.

"It's simply a matter of being aware of it."

She went back to her paperwork. I resumed my now perfunctory search among the jars, a bit aggravated by her all-knowing attitude.

Still, I went about stealing glances at her beauty. She had pale skin and a shock of glistening dark hair and her face seemed to be alive and shifting, as a brisk wind will make distant objects appear to move on a clear day. Perhaps it was the youth of Cerise and the sagacity of Ellie, with a bit of the mystic throw in.

I went up to the counter empty handed, my heart racing again, not knowing what to say. The woman looked up from her paperwork.

"Do you own the shop?"

"Yes."

She offered me the requisite smile and went back to her book.

"It's a nice place to be on a spring day."

She offered me another mechanical smile, along with a raise of her eyebrows, and went back to work. I started to walk away but turned back, knowing I would be overcome with feelings of self-loathing if I failed to act.

"Please have lunch with me," I said.

She looked up.

"Why?"

"I want to talk with you."

"About what?"

I heard the ticking of a clock in the background. A car passed down the street. Dust drifted in the still air between us.

"Hell, I don't know. I just need someone's conversation."

"But why me?"

"Did you need me to explain the nature of men and women?"

I took her smile as an invitation and started to explain all that was good and noble in my heart.

She interrupted me.

"It's all right. I recognize your interests aren't that narrow."

"So, will you have lunch with me?"

"That isn't what you're thinking."

"No, you're right. But you're reasonably safe as long as I'm eating."

I stared at her. She looked at the clock on the wall.

"Please."

"Oh well. Why own a tea shop in Mendocino if you can't close for a serendipitous lunch date?"

"I was thinking very nearly the same thing."

"Very nearly."

"Well, it had tea in it."

She smiled beautifully then and closed the register. A straw hat and purse appeared.

"What's your name?" she asked over her shoulder.

"I assumed you would know."

She came from behind the counter.

"I'm not a mind reader."

"Oh, okay…The name's Roger."

"Diana."

She welcomed me outside and locked the door behind us.

"You're disappointed."

"I was thinking Galadriel somehow."

She put on her straw hat in the bright sun. I put on my sunglasses. She pointed at a cafe down the street as a possibility.

"As long as it's not too terribly organic."

"Sprouts and gluten bread and the likes."

I let out a mortal groan. She gave me a reproving smile and we started that way.

"It's not that bad. They even serve wine."

"Oh, thank god."

We went into the cozy cafe. She ordered herbal tea and soup. I looked at the menu and settled on the avocado and sprouts sandwich. My glass of wine arrived with her tea.

"As you no doubt have gathered, I intend to work at this new regimen slowly."

"Or not at all."

"No, I'm very serious about it. It just may take a bit of time to ramp up."

I watched her pour tea.

"So I take it you're a mystic."

"It's a term people use."

"Then what are the boundaries?"

"I hear other people's thoughts at times. Not to be confused with other forms of clairvoyance."

I sipped my wine and watched her, fearing she could see through me. I tried different thoughts to see how she would respond. She smiled and shook her head at one.

"You're making it too easy," she said.

"Sorry."

More tea was poured and stirred with lemon and honey.

"Mostly I have a vision of someone's life. Where they are going, what their choices are, what the dangers will be."

"And no doubt I'm in danger?"

"Any quack could tell you that...In fact, I see danger in almost every direction your turn."

"Yes, yes. More danger than I had ever wanted."

Our soup and sandwich came. I bit in. She sipped.

"Perhaps I could do your chart. See what forces are working on you."

"I don't do very well when bared to the world."

"All right, then I would encourage you to find your own oracle. The I Ching works for many people. Tarot cards."

"Perhaps it would be easier if you did my chart."

She studied me carefully and had another spoonful of her soup.

"Does that mean yes?"

She smiled over the soup.

"Can you get a room in town for the night? I'd like to talk quietly for an evening, get in touch with your spirit and I'll do the chart tomorrow."

"I'm not very good with unfamiliar rooms, either. Particularly empty rooms."

She set down her spoon abruptly.

"Guess I'll get back to the tea shop."

I reached across the table and touched her hand.

"Please understand. It's the safety of my little cave. The bottle, too. I'm rather lost without them right now. Terrified without them, really, but I'm trying."

"Roger, don't forget. Once you scratch deep enough, we're all the same. Just give me the exact minute of your birth and the location. I'll do your chart tonight. We can talk later this evening, or anytime."

I jotted the information down on a napkin, along with my phone number and pushed it over to her side of the table. She stared at the napkin, then at me.

"Like I said, I have this bottle of bourbon that will miss me."

"Strictly a medical opinion?"

"I know, I know, but please. No moralizing."

"All right. I'll duly note that on your chart."

After our meal, I paid the check and we walked outside together. The day was now stirring wildly in the afternoon wind. The sea was white-capped beyond the cliffs. Diana held her hat in place, lest it blow away.

"If I don't hear from you tonight, I'll call you tomorrow."

"You don't mind if I call you late?" she said.

"No. I wander in circles until all hours."

"Hopefully you'll be sober."

"I'll consider that a subjective term."

I watched her walk back to the tea shop, angered with myself that I had been so flippant. I was in my Bronco and halfway down the coast before it dawned on me that I had failed to buy a damned thing for my health.

Diana called a little before midnight."

"Did I wake you?"

"No. Is it bad news?"

A silence followed.

"Can you meet me tomorrow at Salmon Point?"

"Where exactly?"

"On the south side of the bridge."

"What time?"

"At one?"

"That's fine."

"I'll see you then," she said and hung up. I held the phone in my hand for a long moment, both anticipating and dreading the encounter.

We met at the bridge as agreed. Diana wore a long dress with delicate leather shoes and had a net bag over her shoulder.

After a cautious hug, she started up along the river ahead of me, lost in her own world. I followed behind, growing distant. Unless a woman was swept off her feet by me, I had no idea what to make of her.

We had continued on for most of a mile, with no signs of mankind, when Diana suddenly crouched down at the base of a cottonwood.

"These are good."

She pried the mushrooms from the soft soil, placed them in her bag and continued upstream. I lagged behind, still feeling distant but enjoying her graceful movements. She appeared to walk among things unseen.

When we passed from beneath the trees into a meadow, Diana placed her bag down and pulled her dress over her head, revealing black tights.

"Come, lie down with me," she said and spread the dress on the ground. I lay on my side with my head in my hand. Diana pulled a folder from her bag and opened it. Inside was a piece of paper with many lines drawn in colored pencil. She held the paper so both of us could see it.

"Do they all look like this?" I asked, noting the equilateral triangle in the center of the chart.

"No," she said. "They very rarely look like that. In fact, I have never seen one, other than in books."

"Oh."

We both stared at the chart.

"Do you see this second, red triangle? Just off center from the other one?"

"Hmm hmm."

"That's the danger."

"As in?"

"Well, I would venture that you've been in love with at least one Scorpio woman."

"Two. Right in a row. Actually, there was another one. When I was much younger. Is that the danger?"

"Not necessarily, but it is one form it could take."

"No. I think we could go with a definite there."

She studied me before looking back at the chart.

"This triangle? It's your moon sign Taurus and points to the sun. It is at the very heart of the universe. The other triangle is Scorpio, your rising sign and leads to Mars and possible destructiveness. With the zenith of both nearly touching, it's as if a single pebble in a pond could disturb you from your destiny."

"A great one or a drunken one."

She nodded and looked again at the chart.

"It is not necessarily true that a Scorpio woman will lead you into danger. You see, both legs are solidly positioned, but with Mars here at the top, it could go either way."

I rolled over on my back and enjoyed the pleasantness of the meadow. The sound of the wind in the leaves, the butterflies darting among the tall grass, all together they transported me.

"Why is it a danger?" I asked, thinking again of her words.

"Scorpio is very demanding. It tends to be threatened by the other power. The vision I have is of a man dying with a broken heart, realizing that he has forsaken the great calling of his life for a little bit of tenderness."

"Perhaps a home and family is all I want."

"You have gone to the edge of that precipice and turned back. How did it feel?

"You're sure you don't read minds?"

"I know enough to sense what you really need."

"And you, what do you need?"

"I can never be what that lonely little boy needs."

"To be waiting for me always." She shook her head. "Yeah, I don't know. I don't know what the hell these feelings of uncertainty are anymore or what the hell I'm turning back from."

"Do you want my opinion?"

"Sure."

"You need to build a better ship. And be more patient. What you want takes time."

I turned to look at Diana.

"And what if I wished to share with you while I build that ship."

"Take me as a friend."

"Take you?"

"Of course. You're a man. You know how to follow your own instincts."

Gently, I placed a hand around her hips and pressed her willowy body against mine. Her lips tasted sweet in the wind and I nearly cried from the tenderness of it, from the smell of a woman and to feel the hardness falling away. We became a part of the meadow around us, of the leaves turning and the clouds coming in from the sea and the blue sky above us.

When we were still, I tried to hear her thoughts and wondered if she knew mine.

"Love is for a season," she said and touched my body.

"But seasons return."

"Yes, but we nomads of the heart, we are rarely in the same field when spring comes again."

"I would search many fields to find you."

She smiled and kissed me.

Diana came to visit the following week. I cleaned and made my cottage presentable, modest as it was, but she immediately suggested we drive down to Santa Cruz for a few days.

Reluctant, I paused at the door to my cabin.

"What is it, Roger?"

"The proximity of Scorpio? Remember? "

"Come, I'll be with you. I want you to meet an old friend. Someone immersed in raising a family. I find it cures me of the impulse."

I remained reluctant.

"Roger. Whatever it is, they still make it, including bourbon."

"Okay, but let's stop at the local market down here so I can grab a beer for the road."

Late that afternoon, we arrived in Aptos and found Diana's friend in her wooded backyard with five children. She welcomed us to sit while she hung laundry on the line. The children scurried here and there about her feet.

We had tea when she was done and attempted to conduct an intelligent conversation amidst the commotion. I was glad when we had done our duty and said goodbye.

"I'm cured for a lifetime," I told Diana.

"I find it requires a yearly dose," she said. "It is sobering, isn't it?"

"You needn't have so many of them."

"No, one or two is all the planet really needs."

"I'm still hearing voices."

Diana laughed. We crossed under the freeway and turned along the access road, heading north towards downtown.

"Where are we headed?" she asked.

"I wanted to stop at the pier."

"And the fun zone?"

"Sure, but the pier first."

"Something tells me that libations are involved."

"Spirits, my dear. Wonderfully quixotic spirits. Something you should understand and appreciate."

She became distracted in thought while I searched for a parking spot. The entire shore area was packed with tourists. It took several passes around the block before we stumbled upon a family just then leaving near the foot of the pier.

Setting out on foot, we heard screams from the roller coaster. Halfway up the pier, I stopped at Pagnacio's and reached into the tin barrel for two beers. Upon clearing away the ice from the cans, I called out to a man standing nearby in waders.

"What's with the pop tops?"

"What am I gonna do. They send them, I gotta put them out."

He came over with a can opener.

"You dig a little deeper. There's some of the old style in there."

He reached in and found two Coors with the older tops. There was a frothy crack as the can opener plunged into the metal, along with a burst of dry carbonation. The fisherman made two triangular holes in the other can and handed it to Diana.

"Here, drink. It'll make you even more beautiful."

He took my five and walked back behind the fish counter.

"Give me two of the herring with that."

He came back with the change and the two smoked herring wrapped in waxed paper. I handed one of the herring to Diana and she placed the end in her mouth.

"No no," the fisherman said. "What do you think, it's a popsicle?"

He pretended to tear off a piece of an imaginary herring with his mouth.

"Like that."

Diana mimicked him.

"That's good. That's good, there, beautiful."

"How many kids do you think he has?" she said when he left.

"I don't know. That's your department but if they all come out like him, the world will be a better place."

I stuffed the bills in my top pocket and held up my can to hers.

"To a day at the beach."

We strolled together out on the pier and leaned against the rail. The squeals of children ebbed and flowed in the salty air.

"Good herring," I said.

"It goes good with the beer."

I finished mine.

"Shall we get two more?"

"Just the beer for me."

I walked back and returned with two more.

"It's the herring that makes the beer taste dry," I said, handing her a can.

I bit into another piece of the fish. People came and went behind us.

A few minutes later I saw two figures far down the pier and felt a shock of recognition. It was Cerise, coming down the pier with Dale. I turned away but Cerise recognized me as they approached and came over.

"Hello, Roger. How are you?"

I nodded.

"I'm fine Cerise."

Reluctantly, I went through the introductions, relieved when she had left but devastated to have seen her so happily in love with someone else. My relationship with Diana was at arm's length in comparison.

"You long to be in love that way, don't you, Roger?"

"I suppose."

I looked over at her.

"And us? Do you think that would ever be possible?"

"I don't know. Maybe we're too wise for such things."

I scoffed and looked out to sea.

"Or cynical. Christ. I mean, does falling in love always have to get so screwed up? So hung up and pathetically attached?"

I turned back to face her.

"I don't want to feel that it's wrong to love you in that way."

"You shouldn't. But for me, it would be better to say goodbye."

"Why?"

She brushed the loose strands of hair from her face.

"I'm sorry, Roger."

"So what? We can't just stick to enjoying each other's company the way we have?"

"Oh Roger."

She touched my face sweetly.

"I think it's best if we head back."

"Goddamn it," I said and pushed away from the railing. "Please don't do this. Please."

"Roger, you want something from a woman that's not healthy for me."

"All right, fine. Let's go."

She reached out sweetly again and held me back.

"I know something awaits you, and I would only be getting in the way."

I nodded. There was nothing to say. We walked quietly back to the Bronco. It was dark when I pulled to a stop in front of my cabin. I got out and waited while Diana climbed into her car.

"Roger. Remember your work. It will always be there. It is what you really need in this world."

"All right. Thanks for all your loving kindness. You were better than all the herbs and teas in Mendocino."

She smiled and drove away. I went inside, poured a glass of bourbon, sat at my typewriter, rolled in a fresh sheet of sheet of paper and quickly typed four lines.

Then someone comes along,
you find you're singing a song,
and you forget the blues,
forget the blues…

It was a fine chorus for a song. Now all I had to do was recount all the heartbreaks I had ever known in three verses.

I poured another glass of bourbon and stared at the words, hating myself for having chased Diana away. Why hadn't I just flowed along with things the way they were? But no. When it came to love, I had to take prisoners. I knew it. She knew it and there was no denying the fact.

Perhaps the woman was right. Truth and disaster were too closely bound in my life. Ellie had said it, too, lo those many years ago. I longed for the impossible in a woman, a wild and free spirit like Diana, who would always be there, taking off my boots and making me dinner as the years passed by.

I fell asleep with the bottle half gone and those same four lines staring at me from the typewriter.

Twenty Nine

In the morning, still wretched over the loss of Diana, I did the usual and poured a glass of bourbon over the feelings. The bottle was my friend. The one thing I could count on through thick or thin, until death do us part.

The hours passed. The sea murmured down the coast. The pain of her departure burned in my heart, but beneath it was an even deeper wound, that image of Cerise being happily in love with another man. So. For whom did the bells toll now? There were no answers, and neither of these two wounds would go away. I faced life alone in my cabin on the barren coast of Northern California. That was the only truth I knew.

After a week of this, my innate restlessness began to take hold. The enchantment of that god forsaken spit of land had grown lost on me. Longing for any form of change, I decided to head south and impulsively packed everything into the back of the Bronco. The vision of a sunny little beach town with rustling palm trees had seduced my heart.

On my way out of Pt. Arena, I stopped by to drop off the keys with Walter at the market. Walter smiled broadly when I went in.

"Hey, there's our resident writer," he said.

"Hello, Walter."

I handed him the keys and his smile partly went away.

"Sorry, I've decided to go to Europe for a spell."

In keeping with the façade I had cultivated so far, I decided to lie again about my next destination. Who knew why? It just seemed better for all concerned.

"You can keep the cleaning deposit," I added. "I know it's short notice.

"No, that's all right. Don't you worry."

"No, it's okay Walter but I wondered if you would mind checking the mail for me, just in case something slips through the forwarding card."

"Oh sure. In fact, I'll have Clair head up there tomorrow afternoon. She likes to make sure everything is turned off."

"Sure. I left the place clean."

He finished packing the grocery bag in front of him and took a twenty dollar bill from his lady customer.

"Did you hear that? Roger here's going off to Europe. He might never come back."

The woman smiled in my direction.

"It sounds exciting," she said. "Are you going over there to write your next book?"

"I hope so."

She laughed. It was wonderful, these deceptions. So much so, I had begun to believe them myself. The lady went out the door with her bags.

"I want to thank you again for everything, Walter."

"Sure, you bet." Walter settled back and wiped his hands on his apron. "Say, how can I get in touch with you if we do get some mail?"

I jotted down the address of Derek's auto repair shop in San Clemente.

"Here, just send it to this address. It will get forwarded to me somehow."

He studied the address for a moment.

"Say, what happened to that beautiful lady you had around one day? What was her name?"

"Diana."

"That's the one. Wouldn't it be nice to have her along?"

"I thought so. Maybe I'll meet another one along the way."

"So she's gone, eh?"

I nodded

"That's too bad."

"Yes, they're all gone, Walter."

"Eh, you'll meet another soon."

"I hope so. I guess."

He laughed.

"Just stop chasing them away."

"I do my best not to, Walter. I really do."

"Aw, don't you worry young man." He leaned forward as if Clair might be listening. "There's plenty of fish in the sea."

"Thanks again," I said, shaking his hand.

"Hey, don't forget to send us a postcard," he said as I went out the door.

That day, driving south on Highway 101, I played Miles Davis' Flamenco Sketches over and over on my eight-track stereo and the piano notes fell like icicles through my heart. I was back to asking the age-old questions. Who was I and what had I done? And was the love left behind me more than the love waiting up ahead? Or would I always be alone and longing for someone to appear in my life, prepared to give all my tomorrows for that one bit of kindness?

I thought yes and that I had not learned very much after all.

I stumbled into San Clemente two days later and spent a few nights in a cheap motel before locating an office for lease in an old building downtown. The rent was $100 a month. There was a bathroom with a toilet and sink across from my flat and a shower down the hall. One of the tenants offered me a bit of history on the building. It had once housed the town's whorehouse, which purportedly explained the shower.

My office had four French windows overlooking a cascade of red-tiled roofs that sloped down towards the blue sea and left the impression that the sea was tilted in reverse and about to spill back up into my room. And at night, the fog drifted in through the opened windows and bounced off my back wall. It could not have been more enchanting.

For over a month I sat there writing song lyrics by day and doing seminars and conferences up in LA at night and on weekends. I contacted A&R people with all the record labels and schlepped my wares at every opportunity but without success. Easy listening was now in vogue, funk and heavy metal.

"Can you write me one like this?" an agent would ask of the latest hit on the airwaves and I would try, but creativity died for me whenever I chased the money.

Always the rebellious one, I once again found myself a dinosaur in a changing world, with what I had to sell having gone out of fashion.

As penury set in, it struck me how few employable skills I actually possessed. I had my experience as a cook to fall back on. Otherwise, I was without prospects. If not for my cheap rent, I would have been out on the street.

One of my few pleasures was following the news and watching Nixon start to squirm in the White House. They had yet to corner him entirely, but it was getting easier to imagine that they would. A few transcripts of the tapes had been released and even members of his own party were starting to hold their noses. With the issue of releasing the rest of the tapes before the Supreme Court, the world was left to wonder. What would come first, the tanks in the streets, or the final shoe dropping?

There was a bar across the street from my office, one of those nicely darkened places, and the bartender always had the congressional hearings playing on the TV up behind the bar. Like Vietnam a few years earlier, the saga had wormed its way into America's collective consciousness.

"Can you believe I voted for that son of a bitch?" Barney, the bartender was always saying.

Yeah, I could believe it. The political lines, so bitterly drawn by the war in Vietnam, had begun to soften with Nixon's fall. Suddenly, guys in white shirts weren't so trustworthy, and someone with long hair wasn't necessarily a bum.

And to think that son of a bitch had taped his own downfall. The Greeks would have viewed the story with admiration.

At some point during those days, I ran into Derek, and with both of us being single, we got together for a wild night on the town. I awakened the next morning with hundred dollar bills spilling out of my coat pockets and a bag of coke in my pants. Derek called around noon from his auto repair shop.

"Do you remember anything?"

"Vaguely," I said.

"See you tonight?"

"Yeah. I'll see you after work."

Night after night, we paraded through the living rooms of our friends and seduced the women who inhabited those places. And in the desolation of each dawn, I awakened, knowing little about who was next to me and even less about what had happened the previous night.

There was nothing to do but splash a little coke on the mirror for breakfast and start all over again.

When a heat wave hit Southern California that July, I had thoughts of moving back up to Pt. Arena. I suffered in the heat and was dogged by visions of my old windswept cabin. If not for bullshitting Walter about that trip to Europe, I might have done it. I just hated having to go back and face my lies, more than I hated to heat.

The heat wave dragged on for weeks and merchants took to sitting out in front of their shops with umbrellas and tin buckets filled with ice and beer. I had a view of this daily ritual from my second story windows and could pretty much anticipate the ideal time to head downstairs for a free beer.

One very late morning, feeling particularly ragged from the previous night's adventures, I decided to hit the bar for breakfast and a Bloody Mary. I showered, went downstairs, dashed across the street beneath the blazing sun, climbed the concrete steps to the old adobe structure and entered the cool, darkened interior. The door snapped closed behind me and the brightness of the world disappeared.

Barnie already had the Cubs game on. They were playing the Giants, and losing. I ordered that Bloody Mary, along with ham and eggs and turned my attention to the top of the fifth inning.

All of a sudden, a news bulletin came on.

"We interrupt this program to make a major announcement. President Nixon has agreed to resign from office and will be addressing the nation this evening."

"Son of a bitch!" Barney shouted. "They finally nailed the bastard!"

He came over and turned up the TV. There were five of us in the bar with every one of us glued to the screen. I thought of Ellie and all our discussions and wondered what she was thinking right then. I wanted to call her.

After my third Bloody Mary, I went back upstairs to my office and called Derek.

"Finally got him," I said upon hearing his voice.

"Yeah. We finally got him. Sounds like a party tonight."

"Absolutely. I'll see you later."

There had never been so much Bacchanalian mischief visited upon someone's political grave. The guy throwing the party had hung a poster of Nixon on his backyard fence and every man there took his turn pissing on it. Even some women gave it a shot.

When the sad, sorry bastard came on, there were hoots and catcalls. At the start of his speech, we somehow got everyone quieted down, but that did not last long.

"The fucker's drunk!" someone shouted the minute he started speaking.

"I am not a crook," someone said in character.

"Yes you are," someone shouted back.

When it was over, I almost felt sorry for him. He was human, after all, as hard as it had been to think of him in that way over the past five years.

"Democracy fucking works," someone shouted out to great cheers and the downing of libations.

"Hey," Derek said. "Did anyone think of this? That son of a bitch is going to be moving in right down the block from us."

That brought on more jeers.

"Fuck, let's make a giant banner saying 'I Am A Crook' and parade down the beach in front of his place!"

"We can all wear Nixon masks!"

I sat down in a corner, watching the crowd.

"Why don't we just invite him over for a drink instead?" I said.

"What?"

Things grew silent. Everyone looked my way.

"Why not? It's part of history now. Let's see what the fucker has to say."

There was a moment of silence, then laughter broke out.

"Sure. That's a helluva an idea."

"Yeah, let's throw a party for him down at Olamendi's. His photos are all over the walls."

The crowd was suddenly running with the idea and I was left to my thoughts. Our generation had won a battle. Far out. On a more personal note, I had been secretly dodging the draft for the past five years and it was as if, with Nixon gone, that horror show was finally over.

The next morning, I woke up, both physically and culturally hungover but not about to miss that son of a bitch leaving office. I quickly showered and dressed and dashed over to the bar. As usual, it was pleasantly dark inside and Barney had the TV on to the news. The cameras were focused on the South Lawn. Nixon was expected out any minute. I ordered another Bloody Mary.

An hour went by with Cronkite chronicling every face and footstep. I ordered steak and eggs and another Bloody Mary.

About the time I was pushing away from my meal, a silence fell over the White House press corps and Nixon appeared. The Fords were with him, his wife Pat and daughter Julie and David Eisenhower. I sat there on my barstool, transfixed. The king was about to meet the sword.

Two hours later, I walked back out into the bright sunlight, half drunk and in a strange state of catharsis. The world was old. The world was new. There was some kind of miracle in having survived the sixties, and to witness Nixon getting the boot.

The next morning, I got up and counted what money I had left. Enough to pay the rent and get by for another month. After that and I would be out on the street. It was a sobering assessment.

Down on the sidewalk, several of the local vendors were out with their metal tubs and iced beer. Feeling rummy, I walked down to grab one.

"And how's our resident bohemian?" Betty said as I walked up.

Stepping inside the shady alcove in front of her antique shop, I nodded from behind my dark glasses, took a beer and sat in one of her lawn chairs. Betty was tough and sweet all at once, one of those middle-aged women who had grown so completely into her extra weight, it would never come off. She was dressed in oversized slacks and blouse and perpetually seemed to be wearing a wig, even though she wasn't. Despite all that, I liked her and let on that I was fine.

"How about you?"

"Well I'm glad as hell to see that son of a bitch out of the White House." I chuckled. "Now if somebody would just turn off this heat. Burt here says he's going to close up shop if things get any slower."

I drank from the beer without comment. I had learned to conjure the same I-don't-give-a-damn attitude that worked so well for me up in Pt. Arena. No one had the slightest idea I was broke, and I was not about to tell them. For all they knew, I had a few hundred grand in the bank.

"Maybe I'll break down and buy that roll top desk today."

"Hell, it's a beauty," Burt reminded me. "Give you a deal on it."

I nodded.

"Neah, Burt, I'm just bored as hell. Next thing you know I'll be looking for a job. Just to keep me from going stir crazy."

"Honey, now don't you get carried away with the heat," Betty said. "Not even the flies want to be busy today."

"No, you're right. No sense in taking a job that's going to bore me to death."

Betty patted my knee and wiped at her sweat simultaneously. She had one eye on a stray couple coming down the sidewalk. As they turned into the shop, she smiled and looked away. Burt got up with a grunt and followed them in. Betty tried to wave him off but he kept going. Burt was never one to let folks browse.

I heard his voice and the couple came out a moment later. They headed down the street in the blinding sun. Burt returned to his seat with another grunt.

"Another couple of lookie loos," he said.

"Hell, you don't give them a chance, Burt. You'd run the pope out of St. Peters Square with that tongue of yours."

Burt didn't take kindly to Betty's words but kept his mouth shut. Betty turned her attention to me.

"Actually, I have one hell of an idea for you, young man."

I showed my interest with a raised eyebrow and another drink of my beer.

"I'm dead serious," Betty went on. She looked at Burt now. "You know that Fred over at the local paper?" Burt nodded with a sour look. "Well, don't die admitting it," Betty said. She looked back at me. "Well that Fred was over here just yesterday saying they needed an extra hand. Someone to do a human interest column. You know, something simple about local people and events. And believe me, honey, you'd be perfect for the job. Why don't you give him a call?"

I nodded as though disinterested when in fact I was inclined to run back to my place that instant and give Fred a call.

"Well? What do you think, honey?"

"I might just do that, Betty."

"You're doing my story first thing, mind you."

"Of course, who else?"

She smiled and patted me on the knee again.

I engaged in idle conversation for another few minutes then crushed my empty beer can, excused myself and walked casually up the street. Once inside the big wooden door, I raced up the stairs and down the long hallway. I tried reaching Fred by phone but his secretary said he was out of the office until the morning. With nothing better to do than dissipate for another evening, I did. My hopes and expectations would have to wait another day.

Thirty

That Friday afternoon, Fred's secretary escorted me into his office. He was wearing a plaid shirt, the collar unbuttoned in the blistering heat. Sweat had beaded up on his forehead. His disheveled hair was in need of a trim. The office was equally disheveled around him.

Fred leaned forward to shake my hand as though it was an inconvenience. He did not appear to care in the least what I did with my spare time. When it came to my snazzy, cream-colored linen suit and silk tie, he seemed to be anything but impressed. He waved at a seat.

From the looks of him, Fred had enjoyed his own share of libations over the years and was far too concerned with the mythical deadline to be worrying about my potential for personal disaster. He quickly dispensed with the small talk and made clear that, all a man had to do was smell a story and form a decent paragraph. If you screwed that up you belonged in another business.

I understood. Know how to make a big deal out of nothing and keep it down to a column or two. That wasn't too much to ask of a young man with a depraved imagination and a penchant for bourbon.

Fred hired me on the spot and my life quickly assumed this southern parish quality, a listless drifting from watering hole to watering hole as I chased stories that maintained my affinity for such places, drinking just enough to feel breezy but not enough to screw up the gig, which was writing script for a two section rag that catered to retired Marines, old goats who fancied themselves country club heroes and old biddies in search of the next bingo match. I had never been so happy.

I kept a bottle of bourbon under the front seat, a camera over my shoulder and was banging every woman who got in my path, the old ideas of falling in love forever and ever now relegated to the trash heap of my childhood innocence. I was twenty-three years old and had serious doubts that I would make it to thirty.

Not much of note happened that summer or fall. A hillside collapsed, taking a few houses down the hill with it. A soils report revealed that the builder had performed inadequate soil compaction. The city went looking for him, only to learn he had skipped town long ago. That got various city officials to pointing fingers at each other. A guy threw himself under a train so Southern Pacific filed plans to put a fence up alongside the railroad tracks. That got the local surf community into an uproar. The state, Southern Pacific and city officials were still trying to sort things out.

Probably the strangest event of all happened one night when I was heading out my door, chasing after another local news story and that first cocktail in a neighborhood bar. I found this seedy looking bum standing at my doorstep, his jacket soiled, straw in his hair. I had no idea who the hell it was for several seconds. Then it hit me. It was Vincent.

Repulsed by the sight of him, and far from having forgiven Vincent for that sucker punch he had thrown, I told him to get lost and hurried down the stairs. Five minutes later, at a bar across town and with that first drink in front of me, I stared at myself in the mirror, pictured my brother's despair and thought, fuck. The poor son of a bitch might actually kill himself.

Faced with the specter of my own cruelty, I bummed two dimes from the bartender and went to call a lady I knew from the pay phone in back. She had four cats, two dogs and a tragic streak. I explained the situation to her.

"Please. Go by and give him twenty bucks. I don't know what the hell he wants but see if you can make him comfortable somehow."

I learned from her later on that Vincent had taken a shower at her place, had used to $20 to buy some booze and had sat on her back porch drinking for two days before disappearing. Chastened by the experience, I went about my personal indulgences with a new degree of caution. God help me if I ever ended up like that.

Towards the end of the summer, I was assigned to cover a big wedding in town. The local fire chief was giving his daughter away. His father had been the fire chief before him, and so on, back three generations. Even the mayor came around to send this gal off.

I knew her vaguely through Derek. They had dated once. She was a gloriously beautiful and buxom redhead with white skin and ample breasts. Just the way Derek liked them. You couldn't blame him for still being infatuated.

Stepping into the church that Saturday, I played the part of a big fish in a small pond. Everybody in town knew me, the beat writer with a camera in tow, a man on the move, perpetually disguised behind dark glasses. Finally, after all the twists and turns of my brief life, I had come to play the part of Mastroianni.

Searching for a place to set up, I immediately spotted the head of silver hair in the middle pews, went to sit behind her and spoke in Nixon's voice.

"Well, is this the um, uh big wedding here?"

Ellie spun around, curious, then shouted out "Roger!"

"Hello Ellie. How nice to see you again."

We kissed each other on the cheek.

"Oh, it's so good to see you, Roger. The man on the beat, I hear."

"Yes, I hope you're happy with your goddamned prophecy."

She laughed and attempted to look innocent.

"Well, you see, many an important writer has…"

I pretended to strangle her and we laughed together.

"And are you alone again?"

"Yes, Ellie, and you?"

"Alas."

"Let's get together after the reception."

"Of course. We'll go find a cheap bar somewhere."

"I know just the one. Listen, I need to get a few shots before they start throwing rice. If I don't talk to you before, I'll see you at the clubhouse."

We kissed again, rubbed noses and I slipped down the aisle towards the altar. It was about as close as I was ever going to get to one, or so it seemed.

I arrived to the reception late and found Ellie dancing with one of Derek's friends. I hit the bar and made myself comfortable against a wall. Ellie spotted me between songs and came over.

"I'm surprised you haven't called," she said.

"Oh, I imagined you being happily in love with Ray the investment counselor. Whatever happened to him?"

"Alas, he turned out to be just a sleazy salesman after all."

"I'm looking pretty saintly in comparison."

"Well..."

We laughed at ourselves.

The disc-jockey got back to work and 'Mack the Knife' came over the sound system. Ellie grabbed my free hand and pulled me towards the dance floor. I set the drink down and we spun across the room. Derek held up his drink and smiled as we went by, finally all right with the whole mess, it seemed.

Later, Ellie and I were seated at a corner table alone. The day was growing late. Our conversation went on and on. I noticed the bride and groom preparing to leave. Derek was still trying to bang her.

"Please stay," I said to Ellie. She pretended to thumb through her calendar.

"Well, let's see here. Mm mm, mm mm mm mm. So many prior commitments. I don't know."

I pretended to strangle her again.

"You don't forget a thing, do you?"

She smiled.

"Not a thing."

"Let's get out of here," I said.

"Right now?"

"Right now."

"What did you have in mind?"

"That seedy little bar, of course."

We drove out to an Italian restaurant on the north end of town. It had a quiet bar and a handful of red booths. We grabbed one of the booths. There was the sound of conversation and laughter trickling in from around the restaurant. Ellie ordered a Gibson. I ordered a Myer's and pineapple juice. I stirred the drink and dispensed with the straw.

"To my one and only true love."

Our glasses met with a clink.

"I'm being buttered up here for something."

"You know I mean it, Ellie."

"Yes. You're right, Roger. Nothing has worked out the way we had planned, has it?" She held up her glass. "To the best love I've ever known."

She sipped her drink, set it down and held my hands.

"You know, Roger. There is something I've wanted to confess all these years. I am truly sorry about that scene with Vincent. Looking back, I don't understand my actions. I suppose I saw myself as maintaining peace somehow. I'm not sure."

I related that I had seen him earlier in the summer. She was saddened to hear the story. We were both saddened. It did not seem there would be a happy ending.

"Anyway, it's all right," I told her. "It was worth the price of you lying down in front of my car."

"Oh dear...I'd nearly forgotten about that part. I was rather devastated when you simply backed up and went around me."

"Yes, I should have run you over when I had the chance."

We both had a good long laugh.

"All right, all right. I am truly sorry. Now, will you please get rid of that long face?"

"All right."

We sat staring at each other.

"So, Nixon."

"God, can you believe what's going on in this country, Roger?"

"Curiouser and curiouser. You couldn't make this stuff up."

"No, indeed. I mean, Patty Hearst! With a machine gun!"

Ellie pretended to brandish a rifle.

"Go get 'em, Cobra," I said.

We both laughed again for a good long time.

"Oh god, Roger. We do have such a love affair of the heart. I suppose we'll never understand it."

"We weren't off by much."

Ellie threw up her hands.

"Maybe it just has to be that way in this world. Bittersweet. We couldn't take it being all one way or the other."

"Yeah. I wouldn't mind trying though."

"Aw, Roger. Always the romantic."

Ellie reached across to hold my hands again.

"Please stay over with me, Ellie. I'm so alone right now."

Ellie pulled one hand free and placed an index finger to her lips, feigning the innocence of a child. We laughed again.

"Ah Ellie, you are so dear to me."

"What is it?" she asked, seeing me grow silent.

"Hell, I don't know. How did this happen? I never imagined there being so much loneliness."

"What ever happened with this other lady? You know, the mystic you had mentioned?"

"I expected too much of her." Ellie threw up her hands. "Yes, touché. And you? No one since Ray got the boot."

"You mean my last love?"

"Yes, and that was supposed to be me, by the way."

She smiled.

"Well, there was a brief tryst, in which we agreed to keep it a good screw and dinner on the town, in varying order. Neither one of us entertained the slightest illusions about our intentions."

"And how was that?"

"Terribly boring in the end."

"We're probably better off with our illusions. Though, I'm not sure I'll ever have them again."

"You're still young, Roger. You will fall in love again."

"I do dream of it, though nothing can live up to this Garden of Eden you conjured up for me. You know, you really did screw up my life pretty good."

"Alas, it's the same with me," she said.

"Yes, destiny cast us up together on this shore, only to abandon us with our fatal flaw."

Ellie squeezed my hands.

"I think all great romances are fatally flawed, Roger."

"Darn."

"Yes."

"So? Shall we order another drink?"

"Are there other options?"

"A bottle and my place?"

"I like that one," she said brightly.

Ellie followed me over to my place from the restaurant.

"God, nothing has changed with this town," she said as I pushed open the big wooden door for her.

At the top of the stairs, we turned right down the hall.

"Eisenhower's nephew is writing a book down at the other end."

"Do tell. In his pajamas?"

"No, but he often sees me in mine."

I opened the door to my flat.

"How quaint," Ellie said, walking in. "I love the windows. Gosh, you can even hear the sea."

"The fog piles in through the windows late at night."

"What a wonderful place to write a book," she said.

"Yes, if I only had one to write…Don't start," I said in response to her look.

"Drat."

I made two drinks and handed one to Ellie. We toasted, drank from them and stared at each other. I took a step at her, then another. She began to back up playfully until her knees buckled on my bed. The drink was set upon the night stand and she pulled at my belt buckle.

"You're such a delightful lover," Ellie said afterward.

She lay naked, with her legs and arms poking out from under the sheet. Only her womb was hidden. She was growing old in various ways, but now it did not matter to me. I saw her spirit and loved her and pulled away the sheet to kiss her down to the fluff of hair. I nuzzled my nose in the curly fibers and replaced the sheet. Ellie lay there all the while, looking at the ceiling with a smile. I started to speak, but she stopped me with a finger to my lips.

"Roger, you know why this is so beautiful? Because neither of us is pressured by any expectations. So, please, don't screw it up."

"Afraid you'll get hooked on my poetic adoration?"

"Oh, probably."

"You are the fairest and sweetest of them all, my dear."

"God, Roger. Please do something with your talent."

"I'm trying. I'm trying."

"We are so lucky to have transcended ourselves and the crap society has placed upon us. What poetry there is in that."

"So, did you care for dinner?"

"Sure."

Ellie went off to the bathroom. She reappeared a few moments later with a look of fright on her face.

"What on earth are you growing in that toilet? An experimental mold?"

"Guess I'm not much a homemaker."

I poured the remainder of her drink into mine and downed the glass. Ellie came over and shook my shoulders more than playfully.

"Roger, I'm worried about you."

"Because there's mold in my toilet?"

"No. Because of this," she said, pointing at the nearly empty bottle. "Don't let yourself end up like Vincent."

"I won't. I promise."

We went out and had a lovely steak and lobster dinner at the golf course restaurant on the south end of town.

By midnight, we were back in bed. Tendrils of fog had begun to drift in through the open windows. They met the back wall and rebounded. More piled in and met the same fate.

"That is absolutely enchanting," Ellie said. She played with my naked chest in thought. I reached for my drink.

"Roger?"

"Oh boy, here we go."

"No, I just worry that a part of you is dying."

I pretended to expire. She pretended to have a tantrum, but it was a very little one.

I stared at her.

"Please. Just tell me. Where are you? Have you given up?"

"No, it's just hard to believe that anyone is interested in hearing my crap."

She was silent for a spell.

"Do you remember that one poem you wrote? It must have been, gosh, that night after we first kissed. God, it was so powerful. A river of ecstasy running through gentle cries. I'll never forget those words."

"I was horny."

"You bastard. Don't you write at all now?"

"Sometimes late at night. When I drink. Nothing I would want to show to anyone."

I got up suddenly, possessed of some maudlin need and dug through a stack of papers on my desk. I found what I was looking for and brought it back to Ellie. She read it while I sat on the edge of the bed.

You are the one
who has lasted through the ages,
who has passed through all the stages
of my life.

And like the sun
now shining on these pages,
through all the seasons, you remain
my enduring love.

As she read it out loud, I broke down and wept. Ellie held me with the poem still in her hand.

"I'll never love again," I said when my emotions had been spent.

We both laughed.

"You remember when I said that to you."

"Of course."

"Silly, wasn't it?"

"But not so much now."

"Oh Roger. What a pair we are."

"I know. Jesus. All this crying has made me thirsty." I went off to my makeshift kitchen. "You want one?"

Ellie shook her head and watched. I came back with another Myer's and pineapple juice.

"You see, they're sweet but with a little bite."

"Jesus, you never forget anything, either."

"No, I remember every little thing we've done." I drank. "Because I love you."

Ellie held my face.

"Roger, don't give up. Believe in your talents."

I sighed.

"Jesus. Am I pressuring you too much?"

"No, it's just...I'm not even twenty-four but I feel so old at times."

"Roger. You're still young. You've got a long way to go yet."

"I know."

"You'll figure out how to tell the stories in your heart."

"I guess."

"You will," she said. "I know you will."

Ellie arose very early in the morning and dressed. I watched. There was barely any light in the room. My windows faced to the west. Probably the sky was gray above the foothills, but it remained nicely dark in my room.

When done, Ellie came to sit on the bed.

"No need to walk me down."

"I want to."

I got up while she was in the bathroom.

"Survived the green menace again," she said triumphantly on her way out.

"I'll clean it today. In your honor."

I finished putting on my rumpled linen suit from the day before but dispensed with the tie. Down on the street, Ellie climbed into her car and rolled down the window.

"I will always love you, Ellie."

She kissed me.

"We are the dearest of friends, aren't we, Roger?"

"Yes, so very, very dear."

"Write," she said one last time and drove away.

I walked around the corner and up to the doughnut shop for a cup of coffee. The sky had grown pink in the east by the time I came out. I saw my reflection in the glass door as it closed, the rumpled suit, the disheveled hair.

A bum sitting on the sidewalk against the building hit me up for some change. I had none and handed him a five dollar bill.

"Thanks," he said, looking at the money, but not me.

Feeling as if I had atoned for my sins somehow, I started down the street of shops towards the sea. The town was quiet at that hour. No cars or people were moving yet in the pale light.

Down at the shore, I rolled up my pant legs and walked along the foamy surf barefoot. There was warmth in the dry wind already. It would be another hot summer day. It grew lighter around me. Probably Nixon was down the coast a mile, praying for redemption, or revenge. Foolishly, I prayed to fall in love again. Completely, devotedly, the way I had once felt towards Ellie in my heart. There had to be some magic left in this crazy, mixed up world.

A short while later, as I was crossing back to the street, a convertible Mustang pulled up to the curb a hundred feet ahead of me and a stunning young woman with a mane of thick blonde hair started to get out. I saw her foot with the Barbie Doll shoe and red-painted toe nails first, then the sleek ankle, then the legs and a summer dress. Flamenco guitars and castanets were playing wildly in my chest.

Aw, Jesus, what a god awful wonderful feeling it was to be alive. I could have spent all eternity, capturing how that one brief moment felt.

She had gone to open the little boutique adjacent to her car. I walked up and held out my hand. She took it without emotion.

"Roger." I said.

She studied me.

"Yes, you work for the paper. I've seen you around town."

I nodded.

"Oh, I'm sorry. Violet."

I reached for one of my cards.

"I have to know."

She frowned, shaking her head.

"Know what?"

"Why this feeling."

She had gotten the door unlocked and paused before going in.

"Please, Violet. I want to see you again."

"Well, I guess you could come by and do a story on my shop."

"I'll do it this afternoon."

"Okay."

"Okay. What time is good for you?"

Violet considered it.

"Four, I guess."

"Four it is, then. I'll be here with my camera and dinner arrangements."

I looked her up and down, from the dainty little toes to the shock of luxurious blonde hair. She had a look at my rumpled suit.

"And with fresh clothing."

"Okay," Violet said, inching her way into the shop. "I'd better get to work."

"This afternoon," I reminded her and turned to leave.

Heading up the street, I turned back once to look but Violet had gone inside.

Would she be there at four? Would she keep our date?

Oh, hell. It didn't matter. My day was filled with excitement now and I had a story to tell and I liked myself for having been courageous enough to stop.

Continuing up the street, I saw that image of Violet's dainty foot and high heel stepping out of the car once again and felt the fires of eternity burning in my heart.

About The Author

The product of an Irish/Italian family, Mr. Corcoran was transplanted from the clapboard New England of his youth to the cookie cutter, stucco subdivisions that increasingly littered the old ranches and disappearing orange groves south of Los Angeles in the 1960s. Ever rebellious, and true to the folk music/coffee house idealism that helped shape my early worldview, he chose to resist the Vietnam War, was a man without a country for several years and can count incarceration in a Mexican prison as one of his many colorful experiences from that era.

Having pursued a love of reading and writing in various forms all his life, Mr. Corcoran finally took that passion seriously around the turn of the millennium and has dedicated the remainder of his days to authorship. In completing the circle of destiny, he has returned to the New England of his youth and presently resides along the Rhode Island shore.

www.ingramcontent.com/pod-product-compliance
Lightning Source LLC
Chambersburg PA
CBHW021843010726
47493CB00005B/1534